More

P9-CQL-507

ALSO BY LAURA JOH ROWLAND

Black Lotus

The Samurai's Wife

The Concubine's Tattoo

The Way of the Traitor

Bundori

Shinjū

The Pillow Book of
Lady Wisteria

Laura Joh Rowland

St. Martin's Paperbacks

THE PILLOW BOOK OF LADY WISTERIA

Copyright © 2002 by Laura Joh Rowland.
Excerpt from *The Dragon King's Palace* copyright © 2003 by Laura Joh Rowland.

Library of Congress Catalog Card Number: 2001058864

ISBN: 0-312-98378-6

Printed in the United States of America

St. Martin's Press hardcover edition / April 2002
St. Martin's Paperbacks edition / April 2003

St. Martin's Paperbacks are published by St. Martin's Press, 175 Fifth Avenue, New York, NY 10010.

10 9 8 7 6 5 4 3 2 1

To my editor, Hope Dellon,
for her keen perception and wise advice.
My heartfelt thanks to her and
everyone else at St. Martin's Press.

Japan

Genroku Period,
Year 6, Month 11

(December 1693)

Prologue

"Virtuous men have said, both in poetry and classic works, that houses of debauch, for women of pleasure and for street-walkers, are the worm-eaten spots of cities and towns. But these are necessary evils, and if they be forcibly abolished, men of unrighteous principles will become like raveled thread."

— FROM THE SEVENTY-THIRD
SECTION OF THE LEGACY OF
THE FIRST TOKUGAWA SHOGUN

Northwest of the great capital of Edo, isolated among marshes and rice paddies, the Yoshiwara pleasure quarter adorned the winter night like a flashy jewel. Its lights formed a bright, smoky halo above the high walls; the moon's reflection shimmered silver on the encircling moat. Inside the quarter, colored lanterns blazed along the eaves of the teahouses and brothels that lined the streets. Courtesans dressed in gaudy kimonos sat in the barred windows of the brothels and called invitations to men who strolled in search of entertainment. Roving vendors sold tea and dumplings, and a hawker beckoned customers into a shop that sold paintings of the most beautiful prostitutes, but the late hour and chill weather had driven most of the trade indoors. Teahouse maids poured sake; drunken customers raised their voices in bawdy song. Musicians played for guests at banquets in elegant parlors, while amorous couples embraced behind windows.

The man in an upstairs guest chamber on Ageyachō Street lay oblivious to the revelry. A drunken stupor immobilized him on the bed, which seemed to rock and sway beneath him. Singing, samisen music, and laughter from the parlor downstairs echoed up to him in waves of discordant sound. Through his half-open eyes he saw red lights glide and spin, like reflections in a whirlpool. A painted landscape of gardens slid along the periphery of his vision. Dizzy and nauseated, he moaned. He tried to recall where he was and how he'd gotten here.

He had a faint memory of a ride through winter fields, and cups of heated sake. A woman's beautiful face glowed in lamplight, eyes demurely downcast. More sake accompanied flirtatious conversation. Next came the hot, urgent intertwining of bodies, then ecstatic pleasure, followed by much more drink. Because he possessed a hearty tolerance for liquor, he couldn't understand how the usual amount had so thoroughly inebriated him. A peculiar lethargy spread through his veins. He felt strangely disconnected from his body, which seemed heavy as stone, yet afloat on air. A pang of fear chimed in his groggy consciousness, but the stupor dulled emotion. While he tried to fathom what had happened to him, he sensed that he wasn't alone in the room.

Someone's rapid footsteps trod the tatami around the bed. The moving hems of multicolored robes swished air currents across his face. Whispers, distorted into eerie, droning gibberish, pervaded the distant music. Now he saw, bending over him, a human figure—a dark, indistinct shape outlined by the revolving red light. The whispers quickened and rose to a keening pitch. He sensed danger that shot alarm through his stupor. But his body resisted his effort to move. The lethargy paralyzed his limbs. His mouth formed a soundless plea.

The figure leaned closer. Its fist clenched what looked to be a long, thin shaft that wavered in his blurry vision. Then the figure struck at him with sudden violence. Pain seared deep into his left eye, rousing him to alertness. A squeal of agony burst from him. Music, laughter, and screaming rose to a cacophonous din. Turbulent shadows rocked the chamber. He saw a brilliant white lightning bolt blaze through his brain, heard his heart thunder in his ears. The impact heaved up his arms and legs, which flailed as his body convulsed in involuntary spasms. But the terrible pain in his eye pinned him to the bed. Blood stained his vision scarlet, obliterated the person whose grip on the shaft held him captive. His head pounded with torment. Gradually, his struggles weakened; his heartbeat slowed. Sounds and sensations ebbed, until black unconsciousness quenched the lightning and death ended his agony.

1

The summons came at dawn.

Edo Castle, reigning upon its hilltop above the city, raised its watchtowers and peaked roofs toward a sky like steel coated with ice. Inside the castle, two of the shogun's attendants and their soldiers sped on horseback between barracks surrounding the mansions where the high officials of the court resided. A chill, gusty wind flapped the soldiers' banners and tore the smoke from their lanterns. The party halted outside the gate of Sano Ichirō, the shogun's *sōsakan-sama*—Most Honorable Investigator of Events, Situations, and People.

Within his estate, Sano slept beneath mounded quilts. He dreamed he was at the Black Lotus Temple, scene of a crime he'd investigated three months ago. Deranged monks and nuns fought him and his troops; explosions boomed and fire raged. Yet even as Sano wielded his sword against phantoms of memory, his senses remained attuned to the real world and perceived the approach of an actual threat. He bolted awake in darkness, flung off the quilts, and sat up in the frigid air of his bedchamber.

Beside him, his wife, Reiko, stirred. "What is it?" she asked sleepily.

Then they heard, outside their door, the voice of Sano's chief retainer, Hirata: "*Sōsakan-sama*, I'm sorry to disturb you, but the shogun's envoys are here on urgent business. They wish to see you at once."

Moments later, after hastily dressing, Sano was seated in the reception hall with the two envoys. A maid served bowls of tea. The senior envoy, a dignified samurai named Ota, said, "We bring news of a serious incident that requires your personal attention. His Excellency the Shogun's cousin, the Honorable Lord Matsudaira Mitsuyoshi, has died. As you are undoubtedly aware, he was not just kin to the shogun, but his probable successor."

The shogun had no sons as yet; therefore, a relative must be designated heir to his position as Japan's supreme dictator in case he died without issue. Sano had known that Mitsuyoshi—twenty-five years old and a favorite of the shogun—was a likely candidate.

Ota continued, "Mitsuyoshi-*san* spent yesterday evening in Yoshiwara." This was Edo's pleasure quarter, the only place in the city where prostitution was legal. Men from all classes of society went there to drink, revel, and enjoy the favors of the courtesans—women sold into prostitution by impoverished families, or sentenced to work in Yoshiwara as punishment for crimes. The quarter was located some distance from Edo, to safeguard public morals and respect propriety. "There he was stabbed to death."

Consternation struck Sano: This was serious indeed, for any attack on a member of the ruling Tokugawa clan constituted an attack on the regime, which was high treason. And the murder of someone so close to the shogun represented a crime of the most sensitive nature.

"May I ask what were the circumstances of the stabbing?" Sano said.

"The details are not known to us," said the younger envoy, a brawny captain of the shogun's bodyguards. "It is your responsibility to discover them. The shogun orders you to investigate the murder and apprehend the killer."

"I'll begin immediately." As Sano bowed to the envoys, duty settled upon his shoulders like a weight that he wasn't sure he could bear. Though detective work was his vocation and his spirit required the challenge of delivering killers to justice, he wasn't ready for another big case. The Black Lotus investigation had depleted him physically and mentally. He felt like an injured warrior heading into battle again before his wounds had healed. And he knew that this case had as serious a potential for disaster as had the Black Lotus.

A long, cold ride brought Sano, Hirata, and five men from Sano's detective corps to the pleasure quarter by midmorning. Snowflakes drifted onto the tiled rooftops of Yoshiwara; its surrounding moat reflected the overcast sky. The cawing of crows above the fallow fields sounded shrilly metallic. Sano and his men dismounted outside the quarter's high wall, which kept the revelry contained and the courtesans from escaping. Their breath puffed out in white clouds into the icy wind. They left the horses with a stable boy and strode across the bridge to the gate, which was painted bright red and barred shut. A noisy commotion greeted them.

"Let us out!" Inside the quarter, men had climbed the gate and thrust their heads between the thick wooden bars below the roof. "We want to go home!"

Outside the gate stood four Yoshiwara guards. One of them told the prisoners, "Nobody leaves. Police orders."

Loud protests arose; a furious pounding shook the gate's heavy wooden planks.

"So the police have beat us to the scene," Hirata said to Sano. An expression of concern crossed his youthful face.

Sano's heart plunged, for in spite of his high rank and position close to the shogun, he could expect hindrance, rather than cooperation, from Edo's police. "At least they've contained the people who were in Yoshiwara last night. That will save us the trouble of tracking down witnesses."

He approached the guards, who hastily bowed to him and his men. After introducing himself and announcing his purpose, Sano asked, "Where did Lord Mitsuyoshi die?"

"In the Owariya *ageya*," came the answer.

Yoshiwara was a world unto itself, Sano knew, with a unique protocol. Some five hundred courtesans ranked in a hierarchy of beauty, elegance, and price. The top-ranking women were known as *tayu*. A popular epithet for them was *keisei*—castle topplers—because their influence could ruin men and destroy kingdoms. Though all the prostitutes lived in brothels and most received clients there, the *tayu* entertained men in *ageya*, houses of assignation, used for that purpose but not as homes for the women. The Owariya was a prestigious *ageya*, reserved for the wealthiest, most prominent men.

"Open the gate and let us in," Sano ordered the guards.

They complied. Sano and his men entered the pleasure quarter, while the guards held back the pushing, shouting crowd inside. As Sano led his party down Nakanochō, the main avenue that bisected Yoshiwara, the wind buffeted unlit lanterns hanging from the eaves of the wooden buildings and stirred up an odor of urine. Teahouses were filled with sullen, disheveled men. Women peeked out through window bars, their painted faces avid. Nervous murmurs arose as Sano and his men passed, while Tokugawa troops patrolled Nakanochō and the six streets perpendicular to it.

The murder of the shogun's heir had put a temporary halt to the festivities that ordinarily never ended.

Sano turned onto Ageyachō, a street lined with the houses of assignation. These were attached buildings, their façades and balconies screened with wooden lattices. Servants loitered in the recessed doorways. Smoke from charcoal braziers swirled in the wind, mingling with the snowflakes. A group of samurai stood guard outside the Owariya, smoking tobacco pipes. Some wore the Tokugawa triple-hollyhock-leaf crest on their cloaks; others wore leggings and short kimonos and carried *jitte*—steel parrying wands, the weapon of the police force. They all fixed level gazes upon Sano.

"Guess who brought them here," Hirata murmured to Sano in a voice replete with ire.

As they reached the Owariya, the door slid open, and out stepped a tall, broad-shouldered samurai dressed in a sumptuous cloak of padded black silk. He was in his thirties, his bearing arrogant, his angular face strikingly handsome. When he saw Sano, his full, sensual mouth curved in a humorless smile.

"Greetings, *Sōsakan-sama*," he said.

"Greetings, Honorable Chief Police Commissioner Hoshina," Sano said. As they exchanged bows, the air vibrated with their antagonism.

They'd first met in Miyako, the imperial capital, where Sano had gone to investigate the death of a court noble. Hoshina had been head of the local police, and pretended to assist Sano on the case—while conspiring against him with Chamberlain Yanagisawa, the shogun's powerful second-in-command. Yanagisawa and Hoshina had become lovers, and Yanagisawa had appointed Hoshina as Edo's Chief Police Commissioner.

"What brings you here?" Hoshina's tone implied that Sano was a trespasser in his territory.

"The shogun's orders," Sano said, accustomed to Hoshina's hostility. During their clash in Miyako, Sano had defeated Hoshina, who had never forgotten. "I've come to investigate the murder. Unless you've already found the killer?"

"No," Hoshina said with a reluctance that indicated how much he would like to say he had. Arms folded, he blocked the door of the *ageya*. "But you've traveled here for nothing, because I already have an investigation underway. Whatever you want to know, just ask me."

The Miyako case had resulted in a truce between Sano and Yanagisawa—formerly bitter enemies—but Hoshina refused to let matters lie, because he viewed Sano as a threat to his own rise in the *bakufu*, the military government that ruled Japan. Now, having settled into his new position and cultivated allies, Hoshina had begun his campaign against Sano. Their paths crossed often when Sano investigated crimes, and Hoshina always sought to prove himself the superior detective while undermining Sano. He conducted his own inquiries into Sano's cases, hoping to solve them first and take the credit. Obviously, Hoshina meant to extend their rivalry into this case, and there was little that Sano could do to stop him. Although Sano was a high official of the shogun, Hoshina had the favor of Chamberlain Yanagisawa, who controlled the shogun and virtually ruled Japan. Thus, Hoshina could treat Sano however he pleased, short of causing open warfare that would disturb their superiors.

"I prefer to see for myself." Speaking quietly but firmly, Sano held his adversary's gaze.

Hirata and his detectives clustered around him, as the police moved nearer Hoshina. The wind keened, and angry voices yelled curses somewhere in the quarter. Then Hoshina chuckled, as though his defiance against Sano had been a mere joke.

"As you wish," he said, and stepped away from the door.

But he followed Sano's party into the *ageya*. Beyond the entryway, which contained a guard stationed at a podium, a corridor extended between rooms separated by lattice and paper partitions. A lantern glowed in a luxurious front parlor. There sat two pretty courtesans, eight surly-looking samurai, several plainly dressed women who looked to be servants, and a squat older man in gray robes. All regarded Sano and Hirata with apprehension. The older man rose and hurried over to kneel at Sano's feet.

"Please allow me to introduce myself, master," he said, bowing low. "I am Eigoro, proprietor of the Owariya. Please let me say that nothing like this has ever happened here before." His body quaked with his terror that the shogun's *sōsakan-sama* would blame him for the murder. "Please believe that no one in my establishment did this evil thing."

"No one is accusing you," Sano said, though everyone present in Yoshiwara at the time of the murder was a suspect until proven otherwise. "Show me where Lord Mitsuyoshi died."

"Certainly, master." The proprietor scrambled up.

Hoshina said, "You don't need him. I can show you."

Sano considered ordering Hoshina out of the house, then merely ignored him: Antagonizing Chamberlain Yanagi-sawa's mate was dangerous. But Sano must not rely on Hoshina for information, because Hoshina would surely mis-guide him.

Eyeing the group in the parlor, Sano addressed the pro-prietor: "Were they in the house last night?"

"Yes, master."

Sano ascertained that four of the samurai were Lord Mit-suyoshi's retainers, then glanced at Hirata and the detectives. They nodded and moved toward the parlor to question the retainers, courtesans, other clients, and servants. The propri-etor led Sano upstairs, to a large chamber at the front of the house. Entering, Sano gleaned a quick impression of burning lanterns, lavish landscape murals, and a gilded screen, before his attention fixed upon the men in the room. Two soldiers were preparing to move a shrouded figure, which lay upon the futon, onto a litter. A samurai clad in ornate robes pawed through a pile of clothes on the tatami; another rummaged in a drawer of the wall cabinet. Sano recognized both as senior police commanders.

"*Yoriki* Hayashi-*san*. *Yoriki* Yamaga-*san*," he said, an-gered to find them and their troops disturbing the crime scene and ready to remove the body before he'd had a chance to examine either. "Stop that at once," he ordered all the men.

The police halted their actions and bowed stiffly, gazing at Sano with open dislike. Sano knew they would never for-get that he'd been their colleague, nor cease resenting his promotion and doing him a bad turn whenever possible. He said sternly, "You will all leave now."

Hayashi and Yamaga exchanged glances with Chief Com-missioner Hoshina, who stood in the doorway. Then Yamaga spoke to Sano: "I wish you the best of luck, *Sōsakan-sama*, because you will surely need it." His voice exuded insolence.

He and Hayashi and their men strode out of the room.

The proprietor shrank into a corner, while Hoshina watched Sano for a reaction. Sano saw little point in losing his temper, or in regretting that his old enemies now worked for his new one. He crouched beside the futon and drew back the white cloth that covered the corpse of Lord Mitsuyoshi.

The shogun's heir lay on his back, arms at his sides. The bronze satin robe he wore had fallen open to expose his naked, muscular torso, limp genitals, and extended legs. A looped topknot adorned the shaved crown of his head. From his left eye protruded a long, slender object that looked to be a woman's hair ornament—double-pronged, made of black lacquer, ending in a globe of flowers carved from cinnabar. Blood and slime had oozed around the embedded prongs and down Mitsuyoshi's cheek; droplets stained the mattress. The injured eyeball was cloudy and misshapen. The other eye seemed to stare at it, while Mitsuyoshi's mouth gaped in shock.

Sano winced at the gruesome sight; his stomach clenched as he made a closer observation of the body and recalled what he knew about the shogun's cousin. Handsome, dashing Mitsuyoshi might have one day ruled Japan, yet he'd had little interest in politics and much in the glamorous life. He'd excelled at combat, yet there was no sign that he'd struggled against his killer. A reek of liquor suggested that he'd been drunk and semiconscious when stabbed. Sano also detected the feral smell of sex.

"Who was the woman with him last night?" Sano asked the proprietor.

"A *tayu* named Lady Wisteria."

The name struck an unsettling chord in Sano. He had met Lady Wisteria during his first case, a double murder. One victim had been her friend, and she'd given Sano information to help him find the killer. Beautiful, exotic, and alluring, she'd also seduced him, and memory stirred physical sensations in Sano, even though four years had passed since he'd last seen her, and he'd married the wife he passionately loved.

Hoshina narrowed his heavy-lidded eyes at Sano. "Do you know Wisteria?"

"I know of her." Sano wished to keep their acquaintance private, for various reasons. Now unease prevailed over nostalgia, because he had reason to know Wisteria had left Yoshiwara soon after they'd first met. He himself had secured her freedom, as compensation for wrongs she had suffered because she'd helped him. Afterward, he'd visited her a few times, but his life had grown so busy that he'd let the connection lapse. Later he'd heard that she had returned to the pleasure quarter, though he didn't know why. Now he was disturbed to learn that she was involved in this murder.

"Where is she now?" he said.

"She's vanished," Hoshina said. "No one seems to have seen her go or knows where she went."

Sano's first reaction was relief: He wouldn't have to see Wisteria, and the past could stay buried. His second reaction was dismay because an important witness—or suspect—was missing. Did her disappearance mean she'd stabbed Mitsuyoshi? Sano knew the dangers of partiality toward a suspect, yet didn't like to think that the woman he'd known could be a killer.

"Who was the last person to see Lady Wisteria and Lord Mitsuyoshi?" Sano asked the proprietor.

"That would be the *yarite*. Her name is Momoko." The man was babbling, overeager to please. "Shall I fetch her, master?"

A *yarite* was a female brothel employee, usually a former prostitute, who served as chaperone to the courtesans, teaching new girls the art of pleasing men and ensuring that her charges behaved properly. Her other duties included arranging appointments between *tayu* and their clients.

"I'll see her as soon as I'm finished here," Sano said, conscious of Hoshina listening intently to the conversation. The police commissioner was a skilled detective, but glad to take advantage of facts discovered by others. "Did anyone else enter this room during the night?"

"Not as far as I know, master."

But if Lady Wisteria had left the house unobserved, so could someone else have entered secretly, and committed murder. Sano drew the cloth over the body and rose. "Who found the body, and when?"

"Momoko did," the proprietor said. "It was a little after midnight. She came running downstairs, screaming that Lord Mitsuyoshi was dead."

All the more reason to question the *yarite*, thought Sano. She might have noticed something important, and in some murder cases, the culprit proved to be the person who discovered the crime. He bent to sort through the clothes on the floor, and found a man's surcoat, trousers, and kimono, presumably belonging to the victim, and a woman's ivory satin dressing gown. The gown was soft to his touch, and Sano recognized its odor of musky perfume. Closing his mind against memories of Wisteria and himself together, he moved to the dressing table behind the screen. The table held a mirror, comb, brush, jars of face powder and rouge. On the floor around the table lay a red silk cloth and a few strands of long black hair.

Sano addressed Hoshina: "What have you done to locate Wisteria?"

"I've got men out searching the quarter, the highways, and the surrounding countryside." Hoshina added, "If she's there, I'll find her."

Before you do, said his inflection. And Hoshina might indeed, because he had a head start. Sano felt an urgent need to find Wisteria first, because he feared that Hoshina would harm her before her guilt or innocence could be determined.

"Did Lady Wisteria often entertain clients here?" he asked the proprietor.

"Oh, yes, master."

Then she would have kept personal possessions at the Owariya, instead of just bringing a set of bedding with her for a night's visit, as courtesans did to houses they rarely used. "Where is her *kamuro*?" Sano said.

A *kamuro* was a young girl, in training to be a prostitute, who waited on the courtesans to learn the trade and earn her

keep. Her chores included tending the courtesans' possessions.

"In the kitchen, master."

"Please bring her up."

The proprietor departed, then soon returned with a girl of
perhaps eleven years. Small and thin, she had an oval face
made up with white rice powder and red rouge, and wispy
hair. She wore the traditional pine-leaf-patterned kimono of
her station.

"This is Chidori-*chan*," the proprietor told Sano, then addressed the *kamuro*: "The master wants to talk to you."

Her frightened gaze veered around the room, then downward; she bobbed a clumsy bow.

"Don't be afraid," Sano said in a reassuring tone. "I just
want you to look over Lady Wisteria's things with me."

Chidori nodded, but Sano saw her tremble. He pitied her,
trapped in Yoshiwara, destined for a life of sexual slavery.
She might someday attract a patron who would buy her freedom, but could instead end up begging on the streets, as did
many courtesans when they got too old to attract clients.
Sano gently led Chidori over to the cabinet, where they examined the folded garments and pairs of sandals on the
shelves. Hoshina watched, leaning against the wall, his expression attentive.

"Is anything missing?" Sano asked Chidori.

". . . The outfit Lady Wisteria had on last night." Chidori
risked a glance at Sano, seemed to discern that he wouldn't
hurt her, and spoke up more boldly: "She wore a black kimono with purple wisteria blossoms and green vines on it."

Her conspicuous costume would aid the search for her,
Sano thought, and saw the idea register on Hoshina's countenance. Opening the cabinet's other compartments, Sano revealed quilts, bath supplies, a tea service, a sake decanter
and cups, a writing box containing brushes, inkstone, and
water jar. A drawer held hair ornaments—lacquerware picks,
silk flowers mounted on combs, ribbons. Chidori attested that
all the possessions were present as she remembered from

when she'd tidied the cabinet yesterday. This left Sano one last task for the girl.

"Chidori-*chan*, I must ask you to look at the body." Seeing her blench, he added, "You need only look for a moment. Try to be brave."

The *kamuro* gulped, nodding. Sano stepped to the bed and peeled back the cloth just far enough to reveal the upper part of Mitsuyoshi's head. Chidori gasped; she stared in horror at the hairpin stuck in the eye.

"Does the hairpin belong to Lady Wisteria?" Sano said.

Emitting a whimper, Chidori shook her head. Sano experienced a cautious relief as he replaced the cloth. That Wisteria didn't own the hairpin was evidence that hinted at her innocence. "Do you know who it does belong to?"

"Momoko-*san*," the girl whispered.

The *yarite* again, thought Sano. Revealed as the last person to see Wisteria and Lord Mitsuyoshi, discoverer of the body, and now, owner of the murder weapon, she seemed a better suspect than Wisteria. He said to Chidori, "Look around the room again. Are you sure nothing is missing?"

"Yes, master." Then a frown wrinkled Chidori's brow.

Sano felt his instincts stir, as they did when he knew he was about to hear something important. Hoshina pushed himself away from the wall, eyeing the *kamuro* with heightened interest.

"What is it?" Sano said.

"Her pillow book," said Chidori.

A pillow book was a journal in which a woman recorded her private thoughts and the events of her life, in the tradition of Imperial court ladies. "What was in the book?" Sano said, intrigued to learn that Wisteria had followed the centuries-old custom.

"I don't know. I can't read."

More questioning revealed that the pillow book was a pack of white rice paper, bound between lavender silk covers tied with green ribbon. Wisteria wrote in it whenever she had a spare moment, and if she heard someone coming, she would quickly put it away, as though fearful that they might read it. She took the book with her whenever she left the brothel, and Chidori had seen her tuck it under her sash yesterday evening, but although Sano searched the entire room, the pillow book was indeed gone.

"Wisteria could have removed it when she left," Hoshina suggested.

Or someone had stolen the pillow book, Sano thought, resisting Hoshina's attempt to draw him into a discussion and elicit ideas from him. He considered possible scenarios for the crime. Perhaps the killer had entered the room while Wisteria and Mitsuyoshi slept, stabbed Mitsuyoshi, kidnapped Wisteria, and stolen the pillow book. But perhaps Wisteria herself had killed Mitsuyoshi, then fled, taking her book with her. Each scenario was as plausible as the other, and Sano realized how little he knew about his former lover. What had happened to her since they'd parted ways? Was she capable of such a grisly murder? The idea alarmed Sano, as did the suspicion that this case would bring him and Wisteria together again, with unpredictable consequences.

Hiding his uneasiness, Sano turned to the proprietor and said, "I'll see the *yarite* now."

2

Sano went outside, summoned the troops he'd banished from the *ageya*, and told them they could take Lord Mitsuyoshi's remains to the castle. He would have liked to send them to his friend and adviser, Dr. Ito, at Edo Morgue, but couldn't subject the body of an important person to such a desecrating, illegal procedure as a scientific examination. When Sano went back inside the *ageya*, Hirata met him in the corridor.

"We've interviewed everyone in the house," Hirata said in a low voice that wouldn't be overheard by Police Commissioner Hoshina, who loitered nearby. "The clients and courtesans say they were together in the bedchambers last night. There was a party here, and the servants say they and the proprietor and the *kamuro* were busy waiting on the guests the whole time.

"Nobody noticed anything unusual, until the commotion when the body was discovered. I'm inclined to believe they're telling the truth. They knew Lord Mitsuyoshi was in

the house, but they weren't personally acquainted with him.
I didn't find any reason why they would kill him."

"What about his retainers?" Sano asked.

"They were at the party, according to them and the other
guests. If they know anything about the murder, they're not
talking."

"We'll interrogate them again later," Sano decided.

Hoshina gave Sano and Hirata a faint smirk that said they
needn't bother trying to hide anything from him because he
could find it out on his own. Then he slipped away.

"It would have taken only a moment for someone at the
party to go up and stab Lord Mitsuyoshi, especially if he was
unconscious." Sano described the murder scene. "We'll have
to investigate all the guests."

Fortunately, Yoshiwara was a small, gossipy community,
and any hostilities involving Lord Mitsuyoshi shouldn't be
hard to discover. But the party complicated Sano's work by
increasing the number of potential witnesses and suspects.

"I sent the detectives to ask people in neighboring houses
if they observed anything that might help us," Hirata said.

"Good." Sano told Hirata that Lord Mitsuyoshi had spent
the evening with Lady Wisteria, who'd disappeared along
with the pillow book. As Sano described the book, he realized he should tell Hirata about his past relationship with
Wisteria, but now was not the time; he didn't want Hoshina
or the other policemen to overhear. "Please go out and see
if you can find any leads on Wisteria or the book."

"Yes, *Sōsakan-sama*. By the way, when I interviewed the
servants, they said Wisteria's *yarite* found the body. She'd
gone back to the Great Miura—the brothel where she lives—
so I brought her here because I knew you'd want to speak
with her."

"Well done," Sano said, grateful to have such a capable,
trustworthy retainer as Hirata. "Where is she?"

Somewhere in the house, a female voice burst into a stri-
dent harangue. Hirata rolled his eyes toward the sound. "Momoko made sure to tell me that she was once a great *tayu*,

but I can't imagine that her manner ever would have pleased many men," he said, then took his leave.

Sano followed the voice to the rear of the *ageya*, where a door stood open to a guest room. Inside were two women. The younger was in her teens, and Sano recognized her as one of the courtesans he'd seen in the parlor. She knelt on the floor before the older woman, who wore a brown kimono with the black girdle and cap of a chaperone. The latter, Sano deduced, was Momoko. She thrust a silk quilt at the courtesan's frightened, babyish face.

"You should be careful when you drink wine in bed!" she exclaimed, shaking the quilt, which exhibited a large purple stain. Her voice had a brassy edge, as if she often shouted. Her hair, knotted above her long, thin neck, was dyed a dull, unnatural black. "This will never come clean. You've completely ruined an expensive quilt, you little fool!"

The courtesan cringed and mumbled.

"Don't blame your client," Momoko said. Her profile was elegant, but vicious. "And how dare you talk back to me?"

She smacked the courtesan hard across the face. The courtesan shrieked in pain. Momoko hurled the quilt at her. "The price of this quilt will come out of the fee you earned last night. Forget about buying your freedom, because at this rate, you'll never leave Yoshiwara until you're so old and ugly they throw you out. Now go home!"

The courtesan sobbed as she scurried out the door past Sano. The *yarite* turned and saw him; the anger in her expression gave way to surprise, then dismay. "Oh! Are you the shogun's *sōsakan-sama*?" The words came in a gasp, and when Sano nodded, she quickly bowed. "I'm honored by your presence. Your retainer said you wanted to see me. How may I serve you?"

Sano noted that she must have once been beautiful, but the passage of perhaps forty years had sharpened the bones in her cheeks and narrow figure. Her coy smile showed decaying teeth and failed to hide her fear of Sano. Obviously, Momoko knew why he wanted to see her, and how precarious was her situation.

"I'm investigating the murder of Lord Mitsuyoshi," Sano said, "and I must ask you some questions."

"Certainly. I'll do my best to help you." Momoko minced closer to Sano, her posture sinuously provocative, her smile rigid as a shield. "Shall we go to the parlor? May I give you a drink?"

Perhaps her garrulity was merely an outlet for her nervousness, Sano thought, as might be her attack on the courtesan. Or was the *yarite* a cruel killer, chattering to hide her guilt? Reserving judgment, he accompanied Momoko to the parlor, where she seated him in the place of honor in front of the alcove. She bustled around, fetching the sake jar, warming it on the charcoal brazier, and pouring a cup for Sano.

"What a shame, the death of Lord Mitsuyoshi," she said. "He was so young, so charming. And how terrible, the way it happened!" Momoko talked faster and faster, alternately smiling and biting her lips, while darting frantic, coquettish glances at Sano.

"Let's go over what you did yesterday evening," he said.

"What I did?" Momoko froze, and panic leapt in her eyes, as if Sano had accused her of the murder.

"I'm trying to determine everyone's movements and learn about the events leading up to the crime." Sano wondered if her reaction indicated guilt, or the fear that he would think her guilty although she wasn't.

"Oh." Relief slackened the *yarite*'s face, but it immediately tensed again.

"Did you chaperone Lady Wisteria to the *ageya*?" Sano asked. When Momoko nodded, he said, "Tell me about it."

The *yarite* knelt before Sano, twisting her hands in her lap. "Shortly after the evening meal, the proprietor of the Great Miura told me that Lord Mitsuyoshi wanted an appointment with Lady Wisteria."

Every transaction in Yoshiwara was performed according to strict protocol. Sano knew that Mitsuyoshi would have gone to the *ageya* to ask for Wisteria's company, and the staff would have written a letter to the brothel, formally requesting the appointment.

"I helped Lady Wisteria dress," Momoko said, "and then she made her procession to the Owariya. We got there about an hour later."

A *tayu*'s procession to meet a client at an *ageya* was an elaborate affair that involved some ten or twenty attendants. It moved very slowly, so even though the brothel and the Owariya were but a few blocks apart, the journey would have been long. Sano had a sudden vivid image of Wisteria dressed in brilliant kimono, walking past admiring spectators, kicking each foot in a semicircular, ritualistic pattern as she stepped. She must be in her mid-twenties now, but still small and slender and graceful, with unusually round eyes that gave her delicate face an exotic charm. . . .

"What happened then?" Sano asked.

"I took Lady Wisteria to the parlor, where Lord Mitsuyoshi was waiting," Momoko said. "I served them their sake."

The greeting ritual between *tayu* and client resembled a wedding ceremony, in which the couple drank from the same cup to seal their bond. Sano pictured Wisteria seated at a diagonal from Mitsuyoshi, neither speaking to him nor showing emotion, as tradition required. She sipped her draught, while Mitsuyoshi gazed upon her with anticipation. . . .

Sano refocused his attention on the *yarite*. Her hands maintained their grip on each other, and the nervous movement of her eyes quickened. "It was their third meeting, so I took them upstairs," she said.

No *tayu* made love to a new client on his first visit, nor his second. Wisteria would have rejected Mitsuyoshi twice previously, as custom dictated. Sano envisioned Momoko, Lady Wisteria, and Lord Mitsuyoshi climbing the stairs to the bedchamber, where Mitsuyoshi would finally claim his prize. He imagined their expressions: Mitsuyoshi's eager, Momoko's sly, and Wisteria's carefully blank. Had any of them known how the tryst would end?

"I showed them into the room," Momoko said, "and Wisteria dismissed me. Lord Mitsuyoshi closed the door."

"Was there anyone else present then besides Wisteria, Lord Mitsuyoshi, and you?" Sano asked.

"No. I brought them up by myself. It's the custom."

And Yoshiwara custom was inviolable.

"Then I went downstairs. I had to watch over the courtesans who were entertaining the guests at the party. What a hard time I have with those wretched girls!"

Momoko's speech accelerated into chatter again, betraying her wish to avoid discussing what had later happened. But this was what most concerned Sano. He said, "Did you see Lady Wisteria again after you left the room?"

"No; that was the last I ever saw of her." The *yarite* interlocked her fingers so tightly they turned white.

"Have you any idea where she went?"

"No. She certainly wouldn't have told me, because she wasn't supposed to leave."

"Whom might she have told?" Sano said.

Momoko pondered, biting her lips. "Wisteria isn't close to the other courtesans. She keeps to herself." An aggrieved expression came over Momoko's features. "She never even speaks to me unless she has to, because she hates me. These girls today have no respect for their elders. I work hard training them, and how do they repay me? By treating me as if I were a mean old slave driver!" The brassy tone returned to her voice. "Well, of course I have to punish them for disobedience. And they suffer no worse than I did in my day."

The cruelty experienced by Yoshiwara courtesans at the hands of their chaperones was legendary, and the incident Sano had witnessed today was minor compared to the routine beatings and humiliation. Probably, former courtesans like Momoko enjoyed inflicting the same wrongs done to them upon the next generation. And Sano suspected that enmity lay on both sides of the relationship between courtesan and *yarite*—especially when one was beautiful and sought after, while the other had lost her glory.

"Do you hate Wisteria as much as she hates you?" he asked Momoko.

"Of course not. I love all the girls as if they were my daughters." But the *yarite*'s indignation rang false. She said sharply, "Something bad has happened to Wisteria, and you think I did it?"

Sano observed how quickly Momoko had responded to the implication that Wisteria had been hurt or killed, then perceived an accusation. "Did you?" he asked.

"No! I don't know where she is, or what's happened to her. I swear I never saw her after I left the room!"

"Let's talk about Lord Mitsuyoshi. How did you feel about him?"

"Feel about him?" The *yarite*'s face reflected puzzlement, although whether feigned or genuine, Sano couldn't tell. "Why, I hardly knew the man. I only saw him at parties, and when I brought courtesans to him for appointments."

"Did you see him again that night?"

"No—that is, not until I found him—" Momoko averted her gaze from Sano and murmured, "Dead."

"How did you happen to discover his body?" Sano said.

"Well, I went upstairs, and I noticed that the door to his room was open. I glanced inside, and I saw him lying there."

"Why did you go upstairs?"

"I needed to check on another courtesan who was entertaining a client. These girls behave better when they know someone is listening. And I wanted a moment alone. The party was noisy, and I had a headache, and it was quieter on the second floor."

That she'd offered multiple reasons when one would suffice warned Sano to doubt them all; yet Momoko was so agitated that he couldn't tell if she was lying, or just nervous. And anyone would be nervous while facing the threat of execution.

"Your hairpin was the murder weapon," Sano said. "Can you explain that?"

"My hairpin? It was?" Momoko gave a shrill titter of confusion and surprise, but Sano guessed she'd recognized the hairpin when she'd discovered Mitsuyoshi's body. "Oh, well,

I lost that hairpin ages ago—I don't remember when. I have no idea how it got there."

A scornful male voice from the doorway halted her stammering: "I suggest that you stabbed it through Lord Mitsuyoshi's eye."

Sano looked up to see Police Commissioner Hoshina stride into the room, followed by *Yoriki* Yamaga and *Yoriki* Hayashi. They must have been listening all along. Now Hoshina loomed over the *yarite*, who recoiled in terror.

"You went upstairs last night," he continued, "and when you saw that Lord Mitsuyoshi was alone and asleep, you killed him. Then you ran downstairs and pretended you'd found him already dead."

"No! That's not what happened!" Though clearly aghast, Momoko smiled and batted her eyes at Hoshina, employing flirtation in self-defense. "I didn't kill him!"

Anger rose in Sano, because he needed information from Momoko, not frantic denials produced by intimidation. He said evenly, "Hoshina-*san*, I am conducting this interview. Stop interfering, or leave."

Hoshina didn't bother to reply. "Arrest her," he told Yamaga and Hayashi.

The policemen advanced on the *yarite*, and she scuttled backward, crying, "No! I'm innocent." She simpered in a desperate attempt to ingratiate herself with them. "I've done nothing wrong!"

Sano stood between Momoko and the men. "The evidence against her isn't proof that she murdered Lord Mitsuyoshi," he said, glaring at Hoshina.

"It's enough for a conviction," Hoshina said.

This was an accurate statement: In the Tokugawa legal system, virtually all trials ended in guilty verdicts, sometimes based on less evidence than that against Momoko. Sano had to forestall persecution of someone who might be innocent. "She has no apparent motive for killing Lord Mitsuyoshi. You'll not arrest her, at least until I've finished questioning her."

A sneer twisted Hoshina's mouth. "I'll finish questioning her at Edo Jail."

At Edo Jail, prisoners were tortured into talking. "Forced confessions aren't always true," Sano said, enraged by Hoshina's attitude. Hoshina was well aware of the realities of Tokugawa law, but so eager to show Sano up and impress their superiors that he would risk mistakes. "And the investigation has barely begun. There may be more to this crime than is apparent, and other suspects besides Momoko." He saw the *yarite* looking from him to Hoshina, and hope alternating with fear in her eyes. "Lady Wisteria must be found and questioned, as must all the people who were in Yoshiwara last night. That will take time."

"All the more reason to speed things up," Hoshina retorted. "We both know the shogun expects quick action on this case, and what will happen if he doesn't get it." The shogun would punish everyone associated with failing to find his cousin's killer, and exile or death were likely penalties. "If you wish to drag your feet, don't expect me to follow your bad example. Besides, if this woman is guilty, I'm doing you a favor by applying pressure to her."

Hoshina nodded to his subordinates. They seized the *yarite* by her arms, dragging her upright. She didn't resist, but quaked in their grasp, her eyes wild with terror as she appealed to Sano: "I told you the truth about what happened last night. You believe me, don't you? Please don't let them take me!"

Sano found himself torn between prudence and his desire to conduct a fair, honest investigation. He risked incurring the shogun's wrath by showing sympathy toward anyone remotely connected with an attack on the Tokugawa, and therefore mustn't prevent the *yarite*'s arrest, even if he wasn't convinced of her guilt. Yet Sano believed that justice would be subverted unless he curtailed Hoshina's overzealous actions. Thus, he settled on compromise.

"Arrest her, then," he said.

Momoko let out a wail of despair. As Hayashi and Yamaga dragged her toward the door, Sano steeled himself against pity. "But if she's hurt—or if you send her to trial without my permission—I'll publicize that you are sabotaging my investigation because you'd rather find a scapegoat than allow me to identify the real killer."

Hoshina stared at Sano, his eyes black with anger because Sano had not only impugned his professional honor but threatened to bring their antagonism out in the open. And the latter was a step that neither of them could take with certainty of surviving. A long moment passed; the room seemed to grow colder. Sano waited, his heart racing with fear, because he had much to lose, while Hoshina had Chamberlain Yanagisawa's protection.

Then Hoshina reluctantly lifted his hand at the two *yoriki*. "Take her to jail," he said, "but make sure no one harms her."

As he walked out of the room with his subordinates and their prisoner, his malevolent glance backward said that Sano had scored only a temporary victory. Sano expelled his breath in a gust of revulsion for the strife that always complicated his duties. These seemed insurmountable because the Black Lotus case had severely reduced his stamina. The final disaster at the temple had comprised the worst violence he'd ever seen, a senseless carnage. His involvement made Sano feel sick, as though the spiritual disease of the Black Lotus had infected him. Sano couldn't even draw strength from a happy domestic life, for the Black Lotus had robbed him of that, too. Lately, the thought of Reiko caused him more worry than solace.

Now Sano mustered his flagging energy. With Hoshina probably thinking up new ways to plague him, he must move fast to prevent the investigation from slipping entirely out of his control. He set out to obtain the names of Wisteria's clients and the guests present at last night's party, and begin looking for other suspects besides the *yarite*.

He stifled the fear that he'd lost control of the investigation even before he'd begun.

3

News of the murder had reached the Large Interior—the women's quarters of Edo Castle—and interrupted an afternoon party hosted by Lady Keisho-in, mother of the shogun.

Moments ago, Keisho-in, her ladies-in-waiting, friends, some of the shogun's concubines, and their attendants had been talking, eating, and drinking while musicians played a flute and samisen. The news had sent Keisho-in rushing from her chamber to comfort the shogun; the musicians' instruments lay abandoned amid forgotten plates of food. Women now huddled in nervous clusters around the bright, overheated room. Servants rushed in and out, bringing rumors that incited much whispered chatter:

"The shogun is so furious about his cousin's murder that he won't stop ranting and cursing."

"He's sworn to execute the murderer with his own hands!"

Sano's wife, Lady Reiko, listened to the talk while holding her son, Masahiro. Not quite two years old, Masahiro didn't understand why the women had suddenly lost interest in him. He squirmed in Reiko's arms and whimpered, "Me want to go home!"

"Shh," Reiko said, wanting to hear more news about the murder.

Her friend Midori, a lady-in-waiting to the shogun's mother, hurried over to kneel beside Reiko. "Everyone says that the *sōsakan-sama* must find the killer fast," Midori said, breathless with excitement. At age eighteen, she was girlishly pretty, dressed in a red kimono. "If he doesn't—" Her dramatic pause and look of distress alluded to the persistent threat of death that shadowed Sano. "Oh, Reiko-*san*, how frightening! Can you help him?"

"Perhaps," said Reiko.

Around her, the buzz continued: "The enemies of Lord Mitsuyoshi had better beware." "Everyone in the *bakufu* is afraid they'll be blamed for the murder and executed."

Cuddling her son, Reiko listened to the rumors of intrigue, thinking how much she longed to be a part of it.

When she had married Sano, she'd persuaded him to let her help on his investigations instead of staying home as most wives of her class did. Sano had at first been reluctant to defy social convention, but he'd grown to appreciate Reiko's unusual nature. She was the only child of Magistrate Ueda—one of two officials responsible for maintaining law and order in Edo—and her father had given her the education normally accorded a son. Reiko had spent her girlhood listening to trials in the Court of Justice, learning about crime, and although her sex restricted her freedom, it conferred advantages. Reiko could move easily through the insular world of women, where clues and witnesses often abounded, but male detectives couldn't go. Her network of women associated with powerful samurai clans had provided crucial facts to Sano, and their unique partnership had nurtured a passionate love between them for three years of marriage.

Then had come the arson and triple murder at the Black Lotus Temple. Reiko had found herself and Sano on opposite sides of the case. The investigation had turned into a battle that had almost destroyed their marriage, and the repercussions still haunted Sano and Reiko.

Although they'd vowed to do better in the future, this was easier said than accomplished. They'd not worked together in three months because Reiko had avoided taking part in any new investigations. She had always valued her instincts, but the Black Lotus case had proved they could be wrong. She'd made up for her mistakes in the end, but she couldn't forgive them or trust herself again; and she was afraid Sano no longer trusted her, although he'd never said so.

Now Reiko and Sano lived suspended in a state of mutual caution. Their marriage reminded Reiko of a bubble, enclosing them in a surface that was shiny and perfect, yet so fragile that the slightest touch could rupture it. She longed to work with Sano again, and sensed that Sano was no happier than she, but feared upsetting their tenuous equilibrium for the worse.

"I hope the investigation won't take long," Midori said, her expression worried. "Hirata-*san* and I won't be able to marry until it's over."

Midori had been in love with Sano's chief retainer for years, but Hirata hadn't realized that she loved him and he loved her until recently. Having since declared their feelings for each other, they'd begun the process required to arrange their wedding.

"Just be patient," Reiko soothed her friend. Masahiro keened, and she bounced him on her lap. "There's no need to rush. You and Hirata-*san* have your whole lives to be together."

Inconsolable, Midori chewed her thumbnail; her other fingers were already bitten raw. "I can't wait," she fretted. "We must marry soon. But Hirata-*san*'s parents weren't very pleased when he told them he wished to marry me." Midori's round face was thinner, its usual rosy color turned pallid; her blissful glow had faded soon after she and Hirata had pledged their love. Her eyes were bright with anxiety instead of joy. "And my father wasn't pleased when I asked him for a *miai*."

A *miai* was the formal first meeting between a prospective bride and groom and their families. A ritual of exchanging gifts, negotiating a dowry, and eventually a wedding, would follow—if both families consented to the marriage.

"You know my husband has already arranged the *miai*," Reiko said. Sano, acting as Hirata's go-between, had convinced both families to attend.

"But it's scheduled for tomorrow. What if Hirata-*san* is so busy with the murder investigation that he can't go?" Midori wailed. "What if his family doesn't want me, and mine doesn't want him?"

These were distinct possibilities, given the circumstances, but Reiko said, "Just hope for the best. Don't worry so much." Though preoccupied with her own troubles, she tried to comfort Midori, and wondered why her friend was so upset.

The exterior door slid open, letting in a rush of cold air. A somber, elderly maid entered. She announced, "I present the Honorable Lady Yanagisawa and her daughter, Kikuko."

Conversations died as everyone turned toward the newcomers who stepped hesitantly into their midst: a woman in her mid-thirties, and a little girl of perhaps eight years.

"The chamberlain's wife and child?" Midori whispered.

"Yes." Curiosity leavened Reiko's spirits. "But why are they here? They've never attended these parties."

Lady Yanagisawa was utterly plain, with legs so bowed that they curved the skirt of her black brocade kimono, and a dour face so flat that all her features seemed to lie on the same plane. Her eyes were horizontal slits, her nostrils wide, her lips broad. In striking contrast, her daughter was a beauty, resplendent in a lavish pink kimono embroidered with silver birds. Kikuko had inherited her father's tall, slender body, luminous black eyes, and sculpted features. She gazed at the assembly, her face oddly vacant.

Women hurried forward to welcome the pair. They seated Lady Yanagisawa and Kikuko in front of the alcove, where maids served them tea and snacks. As the women went up one by one to meet the exalted guests, Reiko eyed Lady Yanagisawa with covert fascination, because she'd always wondered about the wife of the man who had often schemed against Sano. When her turn came, Reiko took Masahiro by the hand and led him to the alcove. They knelt and bowed; an attendant introduced them.

Lady Yanagisawa barely looked in their general direction. "It is an honor to meet you, Lady Reiko." Her soft voice was rusty as if from disuse, her expression downcast.

"The honor is mine," Reiko said, noticing that Lady Yanagisawa wore no makeup, except for the brows drawn upon her shaven forehead, perhaps to show off her one good trait—smooth, flawless, moon-white skin.

Masahiro gazed at Lady Yanagisawa with solemn childish scrutiny, and a fleeting smile rippled her somber aspect. He then thrust his chubby little hands toward Kikuko. "Hello," he said.

She giggled. Turning to her mother, she said in a high, sweet voice, "Mama, see boy. Nice boy. Funny boy." Saliva welled in the corners of her lovely smile. Kikuko acted and sounded much younger than her years, and Reiko realized with a shock that Chamberlain Yanagisawa's child was feebleminded. There was an uncomfortable silence until Reiko lit upon a topic for conversation.

"Your daughter is very beautiful," she said.

"A thousand thanks for your kind compliment." Lady Yanagisawa sighed as she watched Kikuko and Masahiro begin happily chasing each other around the room. "But alas, I fear Kikuko will never grow up."

Reiko felt a stab of pity for the woman, and ashamed of her own good fortune to have a normal child. "Masahiro is so glad to have Kikuko for a playmate," she said.

". . . Yes." Lady Yanagisawa's gaze followed Kikuko. "I am glad to have her, too." A fierce maternal love intensified her quiet voice. "Kikuko is a good, affectionate, obedient girl . . . in spite of everything."

Could she mean, *in spite of having Chamberlain Yana-*

gisawa for a father? The chamberlain usurped the shogun's authority; he'd slandered, persecuted, and assassinated his rivals. Did Lady Yanagisawa know? Did she wonder, as Reiko did, if his evils had damaged his child?

Courtesy forbade Reiko to ask these personal questions. "Kikuko-*chan* is the image of her father," she said, hoping that mentioning him would prompt revelations.

". . . Her father. Yes."

Lady Yanagisawa's expression was ambiguous, her tone neutral. Reiko supposed that the marriage between Chamberlain and Lady Yanagisawa had been arranged for the same social, political, and economic reasons as most marriages, yet she wondered whether the woman loved her husband. Despite the chamberlain's bad character, many women found him attractive, though it was no secret that he preferred men, and his status as the shogun's longtime lover had elevated him to power. Certainly Lady Yanagisawa must know about his affair with Police Commissioner Hoshina, who lived with him. Yet she must share some intimacy with him, for the marriage had produced a child. The couple's private life did indeed interest Reiko.

Masahiro had picked up a chopstick, and he wielded it like a sword, darting about on his short legs while Kikuko giggled and applauded.

Lady Yanagisawa said, "Your son is the image of his father." An inflection in her voice suggested to Reiko that Lady Yanagisawa was interested in her life, too. "I hope the *sōsakan-sama* is well?"

"He is, thank you," Reiko said. How much did Lady Yanagisawa know about her husband's relationship with Sano? This was another subject not easily broached. Kikuko and Masahiro began wrestling together, rolling on the floor and laughing. To fill the awkward silence, Reiko said, "Look at them—they're friends."

"As I hope we can be," Lady Yanagisawa murmured, and gave Reiko a look of cautious appeal. "In spite of everything."

Reiko realized that the woman did know about Sano and

her husband, and had a sudden flash of insight. Lady Yanagisawa obviously had no charm to attract friends, and she must be quite lonely if she welcomed an association with the wife of a man who had a history of conflict with the chamberlain. Reiko's heart went out to her, and to Kikuko.

"I hope so, too," Reiko said.

A timid smile and a flush of pleasure illuminated Lady Yanagisawa's plain face. "May I call upon you someday?"

"I would be honored. And Masahiro would love to see Kikuko again," Reiko said. But although she welcomed a chance to satisfy her curiosity about the woman, misgivings tempered her enthusiasm.

Lady Yanagisawa inclined her head, signaling her dismissal of Reiko, who politely withdrew. After the introductions concluded, the musicians began playing again, and the party resumed; but Lady Yanagisawa's presence inhibited festivity. The women made stilted small talk instead of discussing the murder, because everyone feared the powerful chamberlain and didn't want to say anything about a controversial subject that might get them in trouble if his wife reported it to him. Lady Yanagisawa maintained her dour countenance, only spoke when directly addressed, and showed no interest in anyone. She sat isolated in the crowd.

"Why did she come, if she thinks she's so superior to us?" Midori whispered to Reiko.

"I think she wants company, but is too shy to join in the party," Reiko said.

Presently, Lady Yanagisawa rose to leave and called to her daughter. As soon as they'd gone, the women burst into eager conversation about them. Masahiro, bereft of his playmate, hurled himself into Reiko's lap and pouted.

"Lady Yanagisawa is rather dull," Midori said. "Do you really want to see her again?"

"It might be better not to," Reiko said.

"Why?" Midori asked.

Reiko hesitated to speak of delicate matters in public, but the other women were talking loudly and paying no attention to her and Midori. "Even though my husband and hers are at peace for the moment, I don't trust anyone associated with the chamberlain," Reiko said. "And my husband might not approve of my befriending Lady Yanagisawa."

The Black Lotus case had taught her that an unwise attachment could wreak havoc upon a marriage.

"I hope Hirata-*san*'s family approves of me, and mine approve of him," Midori said, her attention focused on her own problems. "But what harm could the friendship do to you?"

"Maybe the war between my husband and Chamberlain Yanagisawa is about to begin again. Lady Yanagisawa could be a spy for her husband, and trying to get close to me, as part of a new plot against my husband."

"Maybe my family and Hirata-*san*'s will become friends at the *miai* tomorrow." While pursuing her own train of thought, Midori said, "But I didn't notice any sign that Lady Yanagisawa is mean enough to hurt you."

Nor had Reiko. But the Black Lotus had conditioned her to disbelieve what her own eyes, ears, and intuition told her. She'd begun to perceive threats everywhere, and hidden malice in everyone. Now Reiko experienced a stab of fear. How could she ever be a detective again, if she couldn't distinguish between imagination and reality?

The room around her suddenly seemed too small and full of noisy women. Was this trivial, petty, feminine world to be her whole life from now on? Fear turned to panic in Reiko; she involuntarily clutched Masahiro, until he yelped in protest. The craving for adventure remained in her blood, even after she'd faced her death at the Black Lotus Temple. She almost thought she would rather face death anew, in a thousand different ways, than resign herself to her present uneventful, suffocating existence.

"I must ask my husband if I can work with him again," she decided.

"I'll be happy for you if he says yes, because I know how badly you want that." Sighing, Midori contemplated the blood that welled from her bitten cuticles. "And you can be happy for me if my *miai* goes well."

Yet even as Reiko had spoken, opposing concerns agitated her. She yearned to resume her partnership with Sano, and she couldn't bear to sit by while a difficult case threatened their lives. She had useful talents that might help him, as they had in the past. She wanted excitement instead of boredom, action instead of idleness, renewed passion with Sano instead of cautious restraint. But the terror of making mistakes, and shattering what remained of their marriage, hollowed out a dark, ominous void in her heart.

"I hope Hirata-*san* and I can marry soon," Midori said.

Still, her samurai spirit wouldn't let Reiko bow to fear, nor accept defeat without a struggle. She said, "I hope I can join the investigation into the murder of the shogun's heir."

4

The hunt for Lady Wisteria led Hirata into areas of Yoshiwara that few visitors ever saw. Accompanied by the proprietor of the Great Miura—who would recognize Wisteria
on sight—Hirata searched every teahouse, shop, and brothel.

He saw *tayu* lounging in lavish chambers, and women of
the lower ranks crowded into dingy barracks. He saw bath-
tubs of scummy water crammed full of naked females. Little
girls toiled in kitchens, and courtesans wolfed down food in
storerooms because they weren't allowed to eat in front of
clients. Most of the women looked sullen, miserable, or resigned to their lot. In one house, they quarreled bitterly
among themselves, like caged cats; in another, a girl lay
moaning on a futon while a maid washed blood from between her legs. An odor of squalid humanity pervaded the
brothels, and Yoshiwara completely lost its glamour for Hirata. Everywhere he went, he crossed paths with Police Commissioner Hoshina's men, engaged in the same mission, but

Lady Wisteria was nowhere to be found. No one had seen her since her procession to the *ageya* last night. She'd apparently vanished without a trace, as had her pillow book.

Discouraged, Hirata made his way up Nakanochō. The quarter had grown colder and darker as the day waned. Snow continued to fall; white drifts lay alongside the buildings. Windblown flakes stung Hirata's cheeks and glinted in the light from windows. The streets were empty, except for patrolling police, because all the visitors, still imprisoned in Yoshiwara by the locked gates, had sought shelter indoors. Hirata approached the gate, where two guards paced, muffled in cloaks and hoods. They halted and bowed to him.

"Were you on duty last night?" Hirata asked them.

One guard was lean with rough-hewn features, the other solid and swarthy. Both nodded.

"Did Lady Wisteria go out the gate?" Hirata said.

The swarthy man laughed in disdain. "Courtesans can't sneak past us. They try, but we always catch them. Sometimes they disguise themselves as servants, but we know everyone here, and they can't fool us."

"Women have bribed porters to carry them through in chests or barrels," the lean guard said, "but we search every container before it leaves. They know there's little chance of escaping, but they keep trying."

After what he'd seen today, Hirata didn't blame the women. "But since Wisteria's not in Yoshiwara, she must have gotten out somehow."

He and the guards looked beyond the snow-laced rooftops at the wall that enclosed the pleasure quarter. It had a smooth, plastered surface, and alleys separated it from the buildings. "She would have had to climb on a roof, jump to the top of the wall, and cross the moat on the other side," said the lean guard. "No woman has ever managed that."

"What do you think happened to Wisteria?" said Hirata.

The men glanced at each other, then shook their heads. "We didn't let her out," the swarthy man said.

"We'll swear to it on our lives," said the other.

Their emphatic declarations didn't hide their fear that they would be punished severely for the disappearance of a suspect in the murder. Hirata sympathized with them, for his own future was threatened. If he and Sano failed in their duty to catch the killer, he would be demoted, exiled, or forced to commit ritual suicide; he would never marry Midori. Hirata thought of their upcoming *miai*, and joy and apprehension entwined inside him.

He had fancied himself in love many times during his twenty-five years, but never felt such affection or longing for any woman until Midori. They had come to believe they'd been lovers in a former life, and their souls destined to reunite. And spiritual affinity engendered physical passion. Desire for each other made them all the more impatient for marriage. However, marriage wasn't so easily accomplished as falling in love. Hirata hoped the meeting between his family and Midori's would have happy results, and feared that the case would prevent his attending the *miai*.

Banishing personal worries, he concentrated on the problem at hand. Maybe Wisteria had turned invisible and spirited herself away; but Hirata favored simpler solutions. Whether she'd left the pleasure quarter alive or dead, someone must have devised a practical way to smuggle a courtesan out of Yoshiwara.

"Lady Wisteria was last seen by her *yarite* sometime after the hour of the boar," Hirata said. "Who left Yoshiwara between then and the time Lord Mitsuyoshi's murder was discovered?"

The guards' postures stiffened. "No one did," said the lean man. "The gates are locked after curfew at midnight. Everyone who's inside Yoshiwara then has to stay until morning. It's the law."

"But not everyone stayed last night, did they?" Hirata said, for he knew that enough money could buy a passage out of Yoshiwara after curfew. Seeing the guards' expressions turn fearful, he said, "I won't punish you for taking bribes, so just tell me: Who left the quarter last night?"

The men exchanged leery glances; then the lean man said reluctantly, "There was Kinue the oil merchant, with some servants and friends."

Hirata knew that the merchant owned a major shop in Nihonbashi. "Who else?"

"A group from the Mori clan, and their bodyguards," said the swarthy man.

This news piqued Hirata's interest: The Mori were powerful gangsters, associated with trouble of all kinds.

"And Nitta Monzaemon, the treasury minister," said the lean guard, "with his retainers."

Hirata frowned, disturbed by the idea that high *bakufu* officials might be involved in Wisteria's disappearance and Lord Mitsuyoshi's murder. "How did all these people travel?"

"Kinue's party walked to and from the river ferries," said the swarthy guard. "The Mori group rode the causeway."

Because the law granted only samurai the right to travel on horseback, the merchant had gone on foot. The Mori, however, were *rōnin*—masterless samurai—and could therefore ride. It seemed unlikely to Hirata that Lady Wisteria had accompanied either party. Women didn't ride, and if Wisteria had done so last night, she would have risked notice by patrolling soldiers. A woman walking with a group of men would have been just as conspicuous. But a desperate fugitive courtesan might have taken the risk, if she'd found willing accomplices.

"Treasury Minister Nitta's retainers also rode," said the lean guard. "But he had a palanquin waiting for him outside the quarter."

Excitement warmed Hirata's cold muscles. The palanquin made Nitta a more promising lead than the others. However Wisteria had gotten out of Yoshiwara, the palanquin could have afterward carried her off, in safety and privacy, to a destination known to the treasury minister. Hirata thanked the guards and trudged through the swirling snowflakes to find Sano.

· · ·

The twenty other guests who'd attended last night's party at the Owariya were high-ranking *bakufu* members and their retainers. During a lengthy search of Yoshiwara, Sano and his detectives located six of the men, as well as the courtesans who'd entertained them at the *ageya*, and learned that they'd stayed together during the time when the murder occurred. Apparently, none of these people had left the party to slip upstairs, and none had reason to kill the shogun's heir. Sano then tracked down five more guests at the Tsutaya teahouse.

The Tsutaya occupied the ground floor of a building near the quarter's rear wall. A cylindrical lantern over the doorway bore the characters of its name; light gleamed between the slats of the closed shutters across the front. Sano dusted snow off himself and entered. Inside the elegant room, an alcove held a porcelain vase of bare branches, and maids served drinks to the five men. Charcoal braziers emitted warmth, but when everyone turned to look at Sano, their unfriendly expressions chilled the atmosphere.

A man seated before the alcove spoke: "Greetings, *Sōsakan-sama*."

Sano knelt and bowed. "Greetings, Honorable Senior Elder Makino."

The senior elder was one of five officials who advised the Tokugawa on national policy and comprised the *bakufu*'s highest echelon. He had an emaciated body, and his bony skull showed through the tight skin of his face; a black kimono accentuated his deathlike pallor. His retainers, who doubled as secretaries and bodyguards, sat grouped around him.

"I suppose you've come to question me in connection with Lord Mitsuyoshi's murder," Makino said.

"If you're willing." Sano replied cautiously, because Makino was no friend of his. The powerful senior elder had once accused Sano of treason, thereby almost ruining him.

"I might be willing to provide information to you," said Makino, "under certain conditions. Shall we drink?"

He gestured to a maid, who poured sake for him and Sano. They drained their cups, and Sano felt the heated liquor flush warmth through him. "What conditions?" he said. Survival in the *bakufu* required give-and-take, but Sano was wary of the terms Makino might offer.

"The other party guests can confirm that I was with them at the time of the murder." Makino inhaled on his tobacco pipe, and blew smoke through his brown teeth. "So can the staff of the Owariya. Hence, I couldn't have killed Mitsuyoshi. You'll find no evidence that I was in any way involved in his death."

Suspending judgment, Sano kept his expression neutral.

"I'm prepared to furnish evidence that might otherwise take you quite some time to find." Makino gave an ugly grimace that passed for a smile. "And time is critical, is it not?"

It was indeed. "In exchange for what?" Sano said.

"For keeping me out of your investigation."

The senior elder spoke calmly, but the sinews of his neck tightened like leather cords: He knew Sano could name him as a murder suspect and ruin him because he'd happened to be in the wrong place at the wrong time. For a moment Sano was tempted to take revenge for all the trouble Makino had caused him, but the impulse quickly passed. To use a murder investigation to further selfish interests would compromise his honor, and he was just as vulnerable to attack as Makino. Should he begin a campaign to advance himself at the expense of his enemies, the resulting bloodbath would probably destroy him. Besides, he needed all the information he could get.

"Very well," Sano said, "but if I find out that you are involved in the murder, our agreement is terminated."

Makino's hollow eyes contemplated Sano with disdain, but his relief was palpable. He signaled the maid to pour another round of sake. After he and Sano drank, Makino said, "There are three guests from the party whom you won't find in Yoshiwara."

"Who would they be?" Sano asked.

"The Honorable Treasury Minister, Nitta Monzaemon. And his two top retainers."

The treasury minister was the official charged with overseeing the collection of taxes on commerce, revenue from the landed estates of the daimyo—feudal lords who ruled Japan's provinces—and other monetary tributes paid to the Tokugawa. This was an important post and its incumbent one of the shogun's most trusted, powerful vassals.

"Where has Nitta-*san* gone?" Sano said, as he found himself facing the perils of an investigation that extended upward to the high levels of the *bakufu*.

"I've no idea, but he left the quarter with his men during the party." Makino grimaced, clearly perceiving and relishing Sano's discomposure.

"Why did he leave?"

"He was not in a festive mood." Inhaling on his pipe, Makino seemed ready to make Sano probe for every fact.

"Why not?" Sano asked patiently.

"Because of Lady Wisteria. He's her patron, and quite enamored of her." Makino shook his head, scorning anyone unwise enough to fall in love with a prostitute. "He is her sole client, now that Lord Mitsuyoshi is gone. She's very selective."

By custom, a *tayu* could pick and choose her clients, and her high price compensated for their small number.

"Nitta is so jealous that he reserves her services for every night. He pays her fee, whether he visits her or not, just so he knows she isn't with anyone else. But he'd learned that on two recent occasions when business kept him away from Yoshiwara, Lord Mitsuyoshi had obtained appointments with Lady Wisteria. Nitta was furious. Then, when he came to Yoshiwara yesterday, expecting to spend the night with Lady Wisteria, the proprietor of the Owariya told him that Lord Mitsuyoshi had requested her, and asked him to yield."

Yielding was the procedure by which one client preempted another's appointment with a courtesan. When a client had engaged a courtesan, and a second client asked for her company on the same night, the *ageya* would, under certain circumstances, ask the first client to yield his appointment to the second. The imposition might displease the first client; however, the polite code of behavior required him to concede if the second client was a special customer of the courtesan, or of higher social position than the first.

"How do you know all this?" Sano asked Makino.

"I make it my business to know all about my colleagues." In other words, Makino employed spies in the households of the treasury minister and other officials. "I also overheard Nitta arguing with the proprietor of the Owariya last night."

"What did he say?"

"Nitta objected to giving up Wisteria," said Makino, "especially since this was her third appointment with Lord Mitsuyoshi, and she would finally bed him. But Nitta didn't dare offend the shogun's heir apparent by refusing to yield. Instead, he consented, and he joined our party. He sat in a corner, drinking and sulking. When Wisteria arrived and met Lord Mitsuyoshi in the next room, Nitta watched them through a hole in the partition. When they went upstairs, he stormed out of the house. Obviously, he couldn't bear to stay while Wisteria pleasured another man right above his head."

"Did you see the treasury minister after that?" Sano said.

"No. I stayed at the party; he never returned."

But Nitta might have sneaked back to the house, gone upstairs, then stabbed the man who'd done him out of a night with his beloved. "While you were at the party, did you hear any unusual sounds from upstairs?" Sano asked Makino.

"I heard nothing whatsoever. The music was loud, and so were my fellow guests."

Sano wondered what had become of Wisteria. Was she also dead by the hand of her patron? The idea dismayed Sano, as did the possibility that he might soon find himself for the first time investigating the murder of a former lover.

"That ends my story," Makino said. "May I ask when I and my fellow captives might be allowed to leave Yoshiwara?"

"As soon as my men have finished taking everyone's names," Sano said.

The senior elder eyed him with veiled expectancy. "I've handed you a possible culprit in the murder. I trust that is a fair reward for your discretion?"

"Your evidence doesn't prove Treasury Minister Nitta's guilt," Sano said, "or explain how Lady Wisteria got out of Yoshiwara."

The door of the teahouse opened, and Sano turned to see Hirata, ruddy-faced and windblown, standing on the threshold. "Excuse me, *Sōsakan-sama*," Hirata said, bowing, "but I've discovered something of possible importance."

Walking down the street together, Sano and Hirata compared the results of their inquiries. "Jealousy gives Treasury Minister Nitta a motive for wanting Lord Mitsuyoshi dead," Sano said, "and his attachment to Lady Wisteria is a reason for him to remove her from Yoshiwara."

Ahead, beyond the rows of teahouses and brothels, the guards had opened the gates. Men emerged from the buildings and streamed out of Yoshiwara. The sky resembled an ink-wash spreading across damp paper; blustering wind and veils of falling snow promised an arduous evening's journey home.

"Nitta could have taken Lady Wisteria away in the palanquin," Hirata said. "He seems as good a suspect as the *yarite*."

Unless she confessed under torture, thought Sano. He wondered uneasily where Hoshina was. "We'll interrogate Nitta tomorrow—if he hasn't fled town with Wisteria."

As they reached the gates, where Sano's detectives awaited them, Sano noticed Hirata looking at him as if needing to speak, but reluctant to do so. "Was there something else?" Sano said.

"Oh, no," Hirata said nervously. "It's just that my *miai* is tomorrow . . ."

Caught up in the investigation, Sano had completely forgotten the *miai*, in which he, as Hirata's go-between, must play a key role. Distress flooded him. "Hirata-*san*, I'm sorry, but I'm afraid I won't be able to go."

"That's all right," Hirata said staunchly. "The *miai* can be rescheduled after the investigation is over."

They both recognized that duty took precedence over personal affairs; yet Sano knew how eager Hirata was to marry Midori. "Go ahead with the *miai*," Sano said. "I'll get someone to substitute for me."

Hope and concern mingled in Hirata's expression. "I appreciate your generosity, but you need me on the case. I can't take time away."

"Yes, you can," Sano said, although he was loath to lose the services of his chief retainer at a critical time. "The *miai* won't last long, and the detectives can help me until you're finished." Observing that Hirata was ready to refuse, he said, "You'll go to the *miai*. That's an order."

"Yes, *Sōsakan-sama*," Hirata said with heartfelt gratitude.

Sano hoped the *miai* would succeed without him, but he had more immediate concerns. "We'd better get back to the castle." On the way he must tell Hirata about his past relationship with Wisteria. He could trust Hirata to keep the information confidential. "The shogun will be expecting a report from us."

5

Sano and Hirata reached Edo just before the hour of the boar, when the gates to every neighborhood would close for the night, halting the movement of traffic through the streets until dawn. The snowfall had ceased; the indigo sky glittered with stars like ice crystals. A ride up the hill through the stone passages and guarded checkpoints of Edo Castle brought Sano and Hirata to the shogun's palace. Snow gleamed white upon the gabled roofs and transformed the garden's shrubs and boulders into ghostly shapes. Sano and Hirata trod softly in the eerie quiet, alone except for the sentries at the palace doors.

But the interior of the palace was a hive of activity. In the shogun's private chamber, a funeral altar held smoking incense burners, hundreds of lit candles, and a portrait of Lord Mitsuyoshi. Sano and Hirata entered to find Shogun Tokugawa Tsunayoshi hunched on his bed on a raised platform. Swathed in quilts, his face haggard, and his head bare of the black cap of his rank, he looked less like the dictator of Japan than like an old peasant. He moaned with every breath. Edo Castle's chief physician, dressed in a dark blue coat, felt the pulses of the shogun's body; two more doctors mixed herb potions. Attendants and guards milled about. Near the platform, Chamberlain Yanagisawa sat facing four members of the Council of Elders.

"What is your diagnosis, Dr. Kitano-*san*?" asked Yanagisawa. Tall and slender, with sharp, elegant features, he was a man of remarkable beauty, clad in brilliant silk robes. His intense, liquid eyes watched the shogun.

"The death of Lord Mitsuyoshi has caused His Excellency a severe shock," the doctor said gravely. "His emotions are out of equilibrium and threatening his physical health."

Anxious murmurs arose as the elders, all dignified samurai of venerable age, conferred among themselves. Conspicuously absent was Senior Elder Makino, who Sano supposed was still journeying home from Yoshiwara.

Dr. Kitano palpated the shogun's chest. "Do the pains persist here, Your Excellency?"

"Yes, ahh, yes!" Tokugawa Tsunayoshi groaned.

"He's taken neither food nor drink all day," the doctor informed the assembly. To the shogun he said, "You must keep up your strength. Won't you please try to eat?"

Servants proffered bowls of broth and tea, which the shogun waved away. "Alas, I cannot. Ahh, how I suffer!"

Sano registered alarm at how badly the murder had affected his lord's weak constitution, just as Tokugawa Tsunayoshi spied him and Hirata. "Ah, *Sōsakan-sama*, at last!" the shogun said; his swollen, red-rimmed eyes brightened. "Come here to me."

Everyone watched Sano and Hirata approach the platform, kneel near the other officials, and bow. As the officials bowed to the newcomers, Chamberlain Yanagisawa's face wore the deliberately bland expression with which he'd greeted Sano throughout their truce. The elders looked hopeful that good news would relieve the shogun's illness, and Sano felt apprehension tighten his nerves.

"Have you caught the, ahh, evil criminal who killed my beloved cousin?" the shogun said with eager anticipation.

"Not yet, Your Excellency," Sano was forced to reply.

Disappointment drew the shogun's features into a frown. "And why have you not?"

"I apologize for the delay, Your Excellency, but there's been insufficient time." Sano masked fear with a calm, polite manner. The shogun had no understanding of detective work, and thus expected that every killer should be caught within the day.

"This case is a complex one, with many people to interview."

"And many leads to pursue," said Hirata, the only person to come to Sano's defense.

"But I've got search parties looking for Lady Wisteria, the missing courtesan who was with the Honorable Lord Mitsuyoshi last night," Sano said, "and—"

An impatient gesture from the shogun cut him short. "At least you can tell me exactly how, ahh, Mitsuyoshi-*san* was killed. No one else seems to know."

Tokugawa Tsunayoshi cast an annoyed look at Yanagisawa and the elders, who turned to Sano. He understood that they did indeed know, but preferred not to deliver the news themselves.

"The Honorable Lord Mitsuyoshi died of a stab wound through the eye, inflicted with a woman's hairpin, probably while he was semiconscious," Sano said reluctantly.

The shogun drew a great inhalation of horror. "Merciful gods," he whispered, then began to pant, clutching his chest. "Ahh, ahh, ahh! I'm dying!"

Physicians hastened to his aid. Sano and Hirata exchanged stricken glances. Tokugawa Tsunayoshi often fancied himself on his deathbed, but perhaps he really was this time.

Dr. Kitano held a cup to the shogun's mouth and said, "Please drink this, Your Excellency." The shogun gulped, then flopped back on the bed, sighing.

"My poor cousin," he lamented weakly. "So beautiful and full of life one day, then dead and disfigured the next. The loss of his, ahh, companionship grieves me." Tokugawa Tsu-nayoshi liked handsome young men, and Lord Mitsuyoshi had won the position of heir apparent by flattering, amusing, and flirting with the shogun. "For such a cruel killer, no punishment is too harsh. *Sōsakan* Sano, have you any idea who committed this terrible crime?"

"So far there's one definite suspect: Lady Wisteria's *ya-rite*." Sano explained that the hairpin belonged to Momoko, and that she had found Lord Mitsuyoshi dead.

The shogun pushed himself upright. "Ahh, then this woman may be the culprit?"

"Yes. And I have arrested her," a masculine voice said from the doorway.

Police Commissioner Hoshina entered the room. He must have ridden as fast and hard from Yoshiwara as had Sano; yet he'd changed from traveling garb to a maroon silk ki-mono, and looked stylish and vigorous. As he knelt beside the chamberlain, they betrayed no sign of their intimacy. Yanagisawa's relationship with the shogun had never been exclusive, and it was no secret that they'd both enjoyed many other lovers, but Sano knew Yanagisawa never flaunted his affairs, lest their lord take unexpected offense. The elders' courteous bows to Hoshina acknowledged his special status. Sano's gut tightened: Hoshina's arrival boded no good for him.

The shogun responded to Hoshina's bow with a feeble smile. "Ahh, Hoshina-*san*, welcome. I was not aware that you were helping *Sōsakan* Sano with the, ahh, investigation."

"I'm always ready to help when I'm needed," Hoshina said in a humble tone that didn't hide his arrogance from Sano. "And I believe I am needed in this investigation, be-cause with all due respect to the *sōsakan-sama*, he appears determined to make slow progress."

Sano had expected trouble from Hoshina, but this was the first time Hoshina had attacked him in front of the shogun. His heart began to race, for he understood that his adversary had decided to make their rivalry public here and now.

Before he could counter the accusation, Hoshina said, "In

spite of all the evidence against the suspect, the *sōsakan-sama* would not arrest her. He preferred to give her the benefit of the doubt. I had no choice but to step in."

"You refused to arrest the person who killed my cousin?" The shogun gaped at Sano, appalled. "After I have elevated you, a former *rōnin*, to a high position and trusted you to do my bidding? Can this be true?"

"I am most grateful for your patronage, but I must say that the *yarite*'s guilt is by no means certain," Sano defended himself. "The evidence doesn't prove she's the murderer."

"Ahh, you are correct," the shogun said, his opinion always easily swayed.

While Sano detested squabbling for power, he had to strike back at Hoshina. He said, "The police commissioner would rather persecute a convenient suspect before all the facts are in than make any effort to identify the true culprit."

Now the shogun turned to Hoshina. "Would you indeed?" Angry color suffused his pale cheeks. "I allow you to, ahh, take over the police force, and you shirk your duty?"

"My duty is the reason I jailed the *yarite*," Hoshina said deferentially, but with a venomous glance at Sano. "If there's any chance that she killed Lord Mitsuyoshi, she shouldn't be left free to attack other members of the Tokugawa regime."

The shogun looked from Hoshina to Sano in confusion. The elders sat like stones, and Sano perceived their attention focused on Chamberlain Yanagisawa, though nobody looked straight at him. Yanagisawa, the power behind the shogun, usually took charge during meetings and settled arguments, but tonight he was in an aloof, enigmatic mood.

Smoking his pipe, his expression hooded, he merely said, "Have you anything else to report concerning your investigation, *Sōsakan* Sano?"

"I do," Sano said, uncertain whether to be thankful that Yanagisawa had changed the subject, or fearful of what his former enemy had in store for him. "I've identified another potential suspect. It's Treasury Minister Nitta Monzaemon."

The shogun exclaimed in surprise; the elders frowned, while Chamberlain Yanagisawa sat alert. As Sano told of

Nitta's history with Lady Wisteria and Lord Mitsuyoshi, his presence in the *ageya* at the time of the murder, and his suspicious departure, Hoshina narrowed his eyes. Apparently, the story was news to him, and he disliked that Sano had beat him to it.

"Nitta-*san* has served me well, and I never doubted his, ahh, loyalty to my clan. That he might have, ahh, killed my cousin is unthinkable!" The shogun's skepticism immediately turned to anger. "If he did, he shall die for his treason."

The reminder that a taint of suspicion could negate years of faithful service poisoned the air. Hoshina said to Sano, "How did you learn about the treasury minister?"

"From a confidential informant," Sano said, keeping his promise to Senior Elder Makino.

Hoshina glanced at Yanagisawa. When Yanagisawa didn't speak, a shadow of bafflement crossed Hoshina's face. Evidently, Hoshina couldn't fathom the chamberlain's mood any better than could Sano.

"Has Nitta been questioned?" Hoshina spoke cautiously, as if now less certain of victory over Sano without his lover's backing.

"I've sent troops to his estate." Sano had done this before coming to the palace. "If Nitta is there, he'll be under house arrest by now. If he's not, my men will send search parties after him. I'll interrogate him as soon as possible."

The shogun nodded in approbation, but Hoshina compressed his lips, clearly displeased by Sano's efficiency.

"What other plans have you, *Sōsakan* Sano?" Chamberlain Yanagisawa's bland manner gave no hint of what lay underneath.

While Sano was loath to reveal his strategy to Hoshina, he couldn't refuse to answer. "I'll call on the family and associates of Lord Mitsuyoshi and ask whether he had any enemies, and what he might have done to make someone want him dead."

Tokugawa Tsunayoshi lurched forward off his bed. "Lord Mitsuyoshi was a fine, honorable young man, beloved by all. He never, ahh, wronged anyone in his life!" The shogun sputtered in outrage; droplets of saliva flew from his mouth. "Are you saying you would, ahh, blame him for his own death?"

"Of course not, Your Excellency," Sano said, horrified that what he considered basic detective procedure had been misinterpreted. "I just think Lord Mitsuyoshi's background could provide valuable clues that we can't afford to overlook."

"Well, we shall overlook them because, I, ahh, won't let you cast aspersion upon Lord Mitsuyoshi." The shogun's red eyes smoldered at Sano. "And you shall not, ahh, bother his family with questions during their time of mourning."

The elders looked perturbed, as did Hoshina: He realized that the shogun's pronouncement applied to him, too. Yanagisawa alone remained nonchalant. Sano's heart plummeted as he saw an entire avenue of inquiry closed to him.

"But Your Excellency, unless we gather all possible clues, we may never find the killer," he said.

A lethal combination of fury and peevishness darkened Tokugawa Tsunayoshi's expression. "Do you dare suggest that the, ahh, killer is to be found within my clan?"

"No, Your Excellency," Sano said hastily, although experience had taught him that the murderer was often a person close to the victim. "A thousand pardons; I meant no offense."

"Well, just, ahh, remember that you are forbidden to investigate Lord Mitsuyoshi or intrude upon the person or property of any other Tokugawa clan member. You will therefore confine your detection to other people and places."

"Yes, Your Excellency." Sano surrendered with regret.

"You will also stop dallying and find my cousin's killer at once, or suffer the consequences!"

Sano experienced an antipathy so strong it bordered on hatred for the shogun. That all his efforts counted for nothing in the view of his lord! No matter how many cases he solved, any failure would doom him. He didn't expect gratitude or encouragement, but the Black Lotus case had diminished his tolerance toward the shogun's constant criticism and threats.

He must get away before he said something regrettable, or anything worse happened.

"Your Excellency, may I speak?" Hoshina said.

The shogun nodded indifferently as the doctors massaged pressure points on his limbs.

"Perhaps the *sōsakan-sama* has a particular reason for conducting his investigation in such a questionable fashion." Hoshina's eyes sighted on Sano like gun barrels. "Perhaps he would cast suspicion on the Tokugawa clan to protect himself."

"That's a lie," Sano burst out, shocked and infuriated that Hoshina had virtually accused him of the murder. The room had gone still, the faces turned to him frozen in surprise. Goaded into blunt speech, Sano said, "Perhaps you wish to sabotage me so that I won't discover that you were involved in the crime."

Hoshina's mouth curved in a satisfied smile, though he must know how dangerous was the game he played. Turning to Yanagisawa, he said, "Honorable Chamberlain, what do you think?"

Horror flooded Sano as he saw that Hoshina intended to break the truce between Sano and Yanagisawa by manipulating the chamberlain into taking sides in his war against Sano. A suspenseful hush quieted the room while the chamberlain pondered Sano and Hoshina, his expression unreadable.

Tokugawa Tsunayoshi suddenly clutched his chest and moaned, "I think I shall die unless my cousin's death is soon avenged!"

Dull-witted and self-absorbed, he'd missed the meaning of Sano and Hoshina's interchange. Spasms racked his body as the doctors laid him down on the bed. Hoshina frowned, his ploy thwarted; but Sano exhaled in gratitude for the distraction. The elders conversed in low, urgent tones.

"What if His Excellency does die?" "With the heir apparent dead, we can expect conflict over the succession." "If the *bakufu* and the daimyo form factions, there will be a battle." The elders turned in unison to Sano, their unspoken meaning clear: He had better avenge Lord Mitsuyoshi's death soon, or take the blame for the shogun's death and civil war.

Chamberlain Yanagisawa rose and calmly announced, "I think this meeting is over."

But Sano knew that his troubles had only begun.

Reiko sat in her parlor, wrapped in a quilt that spread over the square frame of a charcoal brazier. The chilly mansion creaked; distant temple bells heralded midnight. The servants had retired for the evening, and Reiko had put Masahiro to bed long ago. Now she waited, alone and anxious, in the light of the lantern she kept burning for Sano. Perhaps this was too soon after the Black Lotus case to ask him for a part in an investigation, and he would justify his refusal by mentioning her past faults. If another quarrel arose, reconciliation might be impossible this time.

The front door opened, and Reiko heard clattering in the entryway as Sano hung his swords on racks. Hastily she threw off the quilt and rose, her heartbeat accelerating. His footsteps padded down the corridor, and he entered the parlor.

"Hello," he said. Exhaustion shadowed his face; his proud posture seemed burdened by worry. "You didn't need to wait up for me."

"Yes, well. I wanted to." Reiko moved forward and helped him remove his cloak. Her smile felt stiff. "I'm glad you're home."

"Thank you. I'm glad to be back."

They embraced tentatively, the way thcy did nowadays— as though they considered each other too fragile to withstand much affection. "You're cold," Reiko said, feeling the winter on him. "Sit down. I'll make you warm."

He sat, and she wrapped him in the quilt, then draped it over the brazier. "That's better," Sano said. "Thank you."

Reiko wished she could as easily thaw the spiritual coldness that surrounded them. "Are you hungry? Would you like dinner?"

"Yes. Please. If it's not too much trouble."

This was typical of their interactions during the last three months. They were so polite to each other, so careful not to impose nor offend. Even their lovemaking was cautious, without joy. Sadness swelled in Reiko as she recalled their past intimate companionship. She went to the kitchen to warm the miso soup and rice she'd prepared for Sano, then carried the food and a pot of tea on a tray into the parlor, where she heated sake and cooked fish on a brazier.

Sano courteously thanked her for the meal. As he ate, she knelt opposite him. Neither of them acknowledged the fact that she'd never cooked for him until after the Black Lotus case. Reiko had always disliked domestic chores, but they were a way to placate Sano.

"How is Masahiro?" Sano said.

"He's fine. He's in bed, asleep."

Nights were the most difficult, because during the day, Masahiro filled the empty space once occupied by their work. They seemed to have nothing left in common except their son, and therefore nothing to share when he was absent.

"What did you do today?" Sano said.

Reiko could tell that his mind was on the events of his own day, and she wanted to ask about the investigation, but fear held her back. "Lady Keisho-in had a party. I met Chamberlain Yanagisawa's wife and daughter there."

"Did you?" Sano regarded her with scant but genuine curiosity. "What are they like?"

Describing Lady Yanagisawa and Kikuko, and her encounter with them, Reiko experienced more misgivings about her new friendship. "Do you think I should have tried to discourage Lady Yanagisawa?" she said.

She'd always done as she pleased, and enjoyed her independence, but now she was always seeking approval from Sano. He frowned, and she dreaded a reprimand. Then Sano's frown dissolved into a weary, harassed expression, as though he lacked the energy for another problem besides the ones he had.

"It would have been worse to snub Lady Yanagisawa,"

he said, "and you couldn't have refused to let her visit you without giving offense. And we mustn't offend a member of the chamberlain's family just now."

"Oh? Why not now, in particular?" Reiko said.

Sano told her about the crime scene, his inquiries in Yoshiwara, and the two suspects. Reiko listened eagerly, welcoming the start of renewed communication. How much she longed for a part in this challenging case! Still, she hesitated to ask. Then Sano described how Police Commissioner Hoshina had interfered with his investigation and threatened his truce with Chamberlain Yanagisawa.

"The shogun threatened to punish me, and die himself, if I don't solve this case fast enough," Sano finished.

"How unfortunate." Yet although Reiko was truly appalled, her hope flared. That things were this bad meant Sano needed all the assistance he could get. Opportunity beckoned. She drew a deep breath of courage, but Sano spoke before she could.

"Perhaps you would make a few inquiries for me?" He regarded her with somber caution.

The last thing Reiko had expected was for Sano to ask for her help, and glad surprise stunned her. But contradictory emotions forestalled the agreement she longed to give him. She wanted to restore the partnership that had been a cornerstone of their marriage, but she was terrified that she would make a mistake and cause Sano more trouble.

Now she saw disappointment, and guilt, in Sano's eyes. Averting his gaze, he stacked empty dishes on his tray. "I'm sorry. I shouldn't involve you in this bad business. After what happened to you at the Black Lotus Temple, I won't blame you if you want to give up detecting for good."

He thought the experience had scared her off detective work, Reiko realized. He thought her a coward! Anxious to correct his misperception, Reiko said, "I'm not afraid of what will happen to me. I'm afraid of what I might do!"

• • •

As Reiko poured out her fears and explanations, Sano saw how much their reticence had hidden from each other. They'd sworn to put the Black Lotus case behind them, but Reiko hadn't been able to do so any better than he had. Self-recrimination had eroded her spirit, and though she protested that danger didn't scare her, Sano believed that facing death at the temple had undermined his wife's valiant courage.

She abruptly fell silent, her head bowed in shame and anguish. Compassion toward her filled Sano.

"You need to make a fresh start," he said. "This investigation will give you the opportunity."

Reiko lifted her face to him, and he saw trepidation as well as hope in her eyes. "But I interfered with your investigation into the Black Lotus murders," she said. "I disobeyed you. I opposed you in public. Can you really forgive me enough to work together again?"

"I said I did, and I meant it." Sano trusted that her mistakes had taught Reiko a valuable lesson. What she needed was to go on from there. "Besides, if things had been the other way around, and I had made mistakes that upset you, I would want another chance."

A sigh issued from Reiko. She stood, and Sano could see yearning in her face, and apprehension like chains shackling her body.

"Women often know more about what goes on in Edo than do men," Sano said, "and you can get facts from them better than I can. Now that the shogun has forbidden me to interview the family and associates of Lord Mitsuyoshi, I need a discreet way to learn what enemies he had and what might have provoked his murder." Sano coaxed, "If you want to be a detective, you have to start again sometime. Please take the chance now, when I need you most."

"I suppose I could try." Eagerness vibrated beneath Reiko's tentative words. "Tomorrow I'll begin asking questions. Maybe I can also discover what became of Lady Wisteria. I know women who follow the Yoshiwara gossip, and they may have ideas where she could be."

The conversation suddenly became a landscape of perilous chasms around Sano. He'd never told Reiko about his affair with Lady Wisteria. He assumed that Reiko assumed he'd had lovers before her, because men enjoyed the freedom to satisfy their desires at will. However, he and Reiko had a tacit agreement never to discuss the women in his past, because they liked to believe they were kindred spirits bonded in exclusive togetherness. And although Sano didn't think an affair that predated their marriage should matter, he worried about how Reiko would feel if she learned about him and Wisteria at a time when their union was troubled. If he said he'd freed Wisteria, his wife might think there'd been more to the affair than just a few nights of sex. Furthermore, honesty was integral to their relationship, and keeping a secret from Reiko bothered him.

Reiko shimmered with an exuberance she couldn't suppress. "What is known about Lady Wisteria? Have you any information on what kind of person she is, or about her past, that might help us find her?"

Sano couldn't tell Reiko that he'd personally known Wisteria, because she would wonder why he hadn't mentioned it sooner, and might guess the reason. Now he had second thoughts about involving Reiko in the case. He got to his feet, stalling while he thought what to say.

"Wisteria came from Dewa Province," he said, remembering what Wisteria herself had told him, on their first night together. "Her father was a farmer who sold her to a brothel procurer because his crops failed and he couldn't support all his children."

These were facts he could have learned in Yoshiwara today, and Reiko seemed so absorbed in the case that she didn't notice his agitation. "Then Wisteria probably has no family in Edo," she said, "but since she's a popular *tayu*, her business must be the subject of much talk. I'm sure I'll find someone who can tell me about her."

Reiko embraced Sano with an ardor typical of happier days. "I'll help you solve this case, and things will be as they were before."

Sano held his wife, hoping that their bad experience on the Black Lotus case wouldn't repeat itself, and Reiko need never learn more about Wisteria than would benefit the investigation.

6

Unbroken snow covered the empty streets of Edo. Shutters sealed the windows and storefronts of buildings. Stray dogs cowered in alleys, where puddles glazed to ice as the night's cold deepened. On the banks of canals, itinerant beggars slumbered beside smoldering bonfires. Starlight shimmered along the black curve of the Sumida River, and boats moored at wharves stood as if frozen. Night had paralyzed most of the city, but in certain areas of the Nihonbashi merchant district, life flourished most busily after dark.

A ramshackle building situated between a public bathhouse and a noodle stand housed a nameless gambling den. Inside sat peasants and samurai, gangsters with arms and chests covered by tattoos, and even a few priests in saffron robes. They dealt, shuffled, and flung down cards. Shouts and laughter accompanied the games. Piles of coins shifted, while slovenly maids served sake. Tobacco smoke from the gamblers' pipes filled the room with an acrid haze that wreathed the ceiling lanterns.

Beyond a curtained doorway, in the dim back room of the gambling den, Lady Wisteria sat on a straw mattress. Her head was wrapped in a blue kerchief, and her lovely eyes gleamed with anxiety in the light that shone through the curtain. She shivered beneath her cloak as she listened to the clink of coins and the men's raucous voices. Whenever arguments and curses erupted, she winced. Her fearful gaze roved the bare rafters, the sake urns that lined the walls, and the barred window.

A day had passed since Wisteria had left Yoshiwara, and she'd traded one prison for another. This pause between her old life and new seemed almost harder to bear than had the prospect of years in the brothel. Impatience unfurled in her like a growing thistle plant. Her solitude frightened her, and she puckered her sensuous mouth in an ironic smile. How often had she yearned for solitude! She'd not anticipated how defenseless she would be.

The silhouette of a man appeared on the curtain. Alarmed, Wisteria shrank into the corner. Then he flung aside the curtain and entered the room, carrying a large bundle tied in a cloth. He was short but powerfully built, his shoulders broad beneath his cloak, and his calves knotted with muscles in his leggings. His neck resembled a stone column, and his face was all hard lines and angles: slanted brows that met over a bladelike nose; chin and jaws hewn; hair in a topknot crowning a slab of a forehead.

"That's a poor welcome," he said, striding toward Wisteria with a quick, animal grace. His eyes, dark gashes in his face, looked everywhere at once, watching for threats, calculating his next step. "Something wrong?"

Wisteria breathed easier, though not quite in relief. "Lightning," she said. "You startled me, that's all."

She rose to meet him, feeling the attraction that his strange, mercurial beauty inspired in her, and fear of his edgy temper. "Where have you been?"

"Out," he said curtly, his brows slanting farther downward. "I had business to take care of."

He didn't like accounting for himself to anyone, Wisteria knew. "I'm sorry for asking," she said. "It's just that you were gone all day, and I'm afraid to be alone." In the outer room, a brawl had started; the sounds of punches, crashes, coins scattering, and loud cheering clamored.

Lightning laughed. "You're safer than you were last night."

Wisteria wished she could believe him. Though she'd traveled far away from the room where Lord Mitsuyoshi had died, life outside the walls of Yoshiwara promised new hazards. The police would have begun looking for her by now. And while she'd escaped her brothel master, she was now at the mercy of Lightning, nicknamed for the way no one knew what he was going to do until it was too late.

"What's the matter?" He regarded her suspiciously. "You don't like it here?" Hurling down the bundle, he advanced on Wisteria. "Don't like the company either? Miss your fine rooms and fancy friends?"

"No, it's fine," Wisteria said, stumbling backward from the menace in his voice. "I'm happy to be here, with you—"

"Do you know what would have happened to me if I'd gotten caught smuggling you out of Yoshiwara?" He seized her wrist, and his painful grasp provoked a yelp from Wisteria. "I'd have been arrested, beaten, maybe even killed. I risked my life for you, and you ought to be satisfied with whatever I give you, and not complain."

"I am satisfied." Wisteria hastened to placate Lightning. "I thank you for all you've done for me." Lowering her eyelids, she smiled provocatively and dropped her voice to a husky whisper: "A man as strong and brave as you can satisfy me in every way."

Years of practice had made her adept at coaxing men, and as she grazed her fingertips across Lightning's cheek, lust replaced the anger in his eyes. "That's better," he said.

"Please let me show my appreciation by satisfying you." Wisteria didn't have to pretend eagerness, for Lightning's touch, his strength, and his flashing gaze awakened in her an urgent need for him.

His sardonic smile acknowledged his power over her. Releasing her wrist, he said, "Later." He squatted and opened the bundle. "I've got food here, and I'm hungry. Let's eat."

He'd brought cooked rice, smoked eel and salmon, pickles, grilled prawns, steamed dumplings, and different kinds of sweet cakes. Wisteria had spent much of the day sleeping, and the rest too nervous to eat; but now the sight and smell of the food made her ravenous. She and Lightning sat on the floor, gobbling with their fingers, gulping sake between bites. This seemed the best meal she'd ever eaten, with no need to mind her manners as a *tayu* should, and no brothel master tallying the cost of what she ate and adding it to her debt. Giddy with pleasure, she laughed. She fed morsels to Lightning. He grinned and sucked her fingers.

When they finished, he took the remaining, largest package from the bundle and tossed it in her lap. "Here's a present."

Wisteria opened the package and found a kimono of crimson satin, lavishly brocaded with waves and swimming carp in rainbow-hued metallic thread.

"How beautiful!" she exclaimed in delight.

"Sure it is." Lightning smiled proudly, but his tone distrusted her reaction. "It's as nice as anything those other men have given you—isn't it?" He was jealous of her high-class lovers, who often brought her expensive gifts.

"Yes, yes," Wisteria assured him. Stroking the kimono, she didn't ask where he'd gotten it; knowing how he earned his living, she could guess. Yet she didn't care, because the kimono was hers now, a promise of a brilliant future.

"You can show me your appreciation now," Lightning said.

Lust gleamed in his eyes as he swept aside the remains of their meal. He tore off her garments. The cold raised bumps on her skin, but Lightning opened his own clothes and pulled her against his warm flesh. Wisteria moaned, overwhelmed by desire for him. Lightning was her own age of twenty-four, instead of decades older, as were most men who could afford the services of a *tayu*. Caressing him, Wisteria reveled in the feel of him, so firm and strong instead of pudgy or emaciated like her typical client. His hands on her breasts, her buttocks, and between her legs caused her pleasure instead of disgust. When Lightning climbed atop her, his manhood was erect. No over-refined, impotent gentleman was he!

"I want you inside me." Gasping, Wisteria wrapped her legs around his waist. "Take me now!"

Lightning reared up from her in sudden anger. "Impatient, are you?" He slapped away her hands and wrenched free of her. "I'm the one who says when and how, not you!"

In her passion, Wisteria had forgotten that he never liked being told what to do. "I'm sorry," she said hastily, for last night had proven his contrary nature and shown her the peril of trying to impose her will upon him. "Please forgive me."

His face blazed with bestial rage and desire; he was panting and perspiring, literally steaming in the chill air. He roughly turned Wisteria over on her stomach. His hands jerked her hips upward and pushed her face to the floor. Frightened, though aroused by his brutality, Wisteria cried out in protest.

"Don't you dare resist me," Lightning shouted as cheers and laughter exploded in the gambling den. "You're mine, and I'll treat you as I wish."

Mounting her, he yanked her buttocks against his loins; his manhood entered her with a friction that drew moans from them both. "Did Lord Mitsuyoshi take you this way?" he gasped out. He began thrusting deep and fast into Wisteria. "Did you enjoy it with him?"

The floor's rough planks scraped Wisteria's knees and forearms. Her pride rebelled against this mistreatment, and she hated that the gamblers would hear her degradation. Her inner flesh swelled with excitement born of pain and pleasure.

Lightning abruptly withdrew from her body. Unable to bear the cessation, Wisteria gave the answer he wanted: "No.

No!" She knew he'd hated Mitsuyoshi more than any of her other clients. She wriggled backward, trying to regain him.

"Did you want Lord Mitsuyoshi?" Breathless, Lightning shuddered with his own passion, but he held her away from him while she struggled. "Did you love him?"

"I didn't want him. I didn't love him," Wisteria said, sobbing in her desperation to have Lightning. "Please—"

He reentered her, and as she keened in joy, he said, "Tell me you love me."

"I love you!" At this moment, with him moving inside her, and the world reduced to the two of them, Wisteria did love Lightning passionately, truly, devotedly.

"Tell me I'm the only man you'll ever love."

"You're the only one," Wisteria cried. Eyes shut, she concentrated on their climb to pleasure. She lost awareness of the rough floor, the cold, and the other people nearby.

Thrusting harder and quicker, Lightning growled like a wild beast. "If anyone else dares look at you, I'll kill him. And if you ever shun me or betray me—if you ever cross me in any way—I'll kill you, too!"

His threats terrified Wisteria, for she knew he spoke the truth. Terror increased arousal, and her climax struck her in waves of ecstasy. She screamed. Lightning's growls culminated in a triumphant roar, and she felt him release inside her. They collapsed together in heaving exhaustion, and Wisteria's spirits slid into a black pit of distress.

She realized that her liberator had become her captor, and one more prone to cruelty than any brothel master. Wisteria had extricated herself from financial debt, but she now owed Lightning, whom she must repay in flesh and blood. She'd hoped to harness his strength and daring to further her own aims, yet he was untamable. Last night marked the point at which her control over her destiny had shattered.

No one would know whether she was an innocent witness to murder, or an accomplice in crime. If only Lord Mitsuyoshi hadn't died! Had things worked out differently, she might now be free to enjoy the fruition of her secret plans.

However, there seemed no use dwelling upon the past.

Wisteria recognized that she'd bound herself to Lightning, for good or bad, and she was dependent on him for survival.

She hoped she could survive his jealous rages, his volatile, unpredictable behavior.

And he was still crucial to her plans, which had hinged on him from the beginning.

Closing her eyes, imprisoned in Lightning's possessive embrace, Wisteria prayed they would escape Edo alive.

7

Treasury Minister Nitta lived in the Edo Castle official district, in a street higher on the hill and closer to the shogun's palace than Sano. His estate had the same style of architecture as all the others in the district, with barracks enclosing courtyards, garden, stables, and a low mansion raised on a stone podium and crowned by a brown tile roof. But Nitta's estate was on a larger scale, befitting his exalted rank.

When Sano and a team of his detectives arrived to call on Nitta the next morning, a hard, brilliant blue sky arched over the castle. The sun melted the snow on the roofs, but the intense cold froze the dripping water into icicles that glittered on the eaves. The snow in the roads turned grimy under the horses' hooves. But in spite of the weather, the treasury minister emerged from the shelter of his house to meet Sano's party as soon as it reached the front door.

"*Sōsakan-sama*. How dare you send troops to invade my home and wake me up in the middle of the night?" He gestured at Sano's men, standing guard in the courtyard. "This is an execrable offense."

Nitta was a pallid, gaunt samurai whom Sano knew to be fifty years of age, though he seemed older because of his prematurely silver hair. Silver brows bristled over eyes that seemed too dark in contrast; ire compressed a mouth so thin that it appeared lipless. Clad in a kimono, surcoat, and trousers in shades of gray, he looked like a figure in a monochrome painting. He stood on the veranda, hands on his hips and feet pointed outward, glowering down at Sano.

"Would you now kindly explain why you have placed my entire household under arrest?" he said.

"I apologize for the disturbance." Sano bowed low, as did his men. "But I need to question you regarding the murder of Lord Mitsuyoshi."

"Murder? Lord Mitsuyoshi?" Surprise inflected Nitta's high-pitched voice and sharpened his eyes. "How and where did it happen?"

Sano explained, wondering if the treasury minister's reaction was genuine, or feigned. Then Nitta's expression turned disdainful.

"And you obviously consider me a suspect. How ridiculous. Well, I suppose you are desperate to find the culprit, but there was no need for you to treat me, or my family, in such a rude manner."

Yet Sano saw fear beneath his disdain. Nitta was clearly aware that the murder of the shogun's heir, and a visit from Sano in connection with the murder, posed him great danger. "I did not kill Lord Mitsuyoshi," Nitta declared, "and all I know about his death is what you've just told me."

"If that's the case, then we can conclude this matter quickly." Sano kept his manner deferential, because if Nitta proved not to be the murderer, he could become a formidable enemy. Nitta could retaliate by withholding the treasury funds that financed Sano's detective corps and investigations. Yet if Sano hadn't placed Nitta under guard, he would have opened himself to accusations of leniency toward a suspect—and allowed Police Commissioner Hoshina to interrogate

Nitta first. It had been a difficult choice, and Sano hoped he'd made the right one.

"Take yourself and your thugs away," Nitta said. "I shall let you know when an interview is convenient for me."

Sano stood his ground. "I have my orders to investigate the murder with all due haste. And I respectfully advise you to cooperate, because otherwise, you'll displease our lord."

The treasury minister's dark eyes flared like live coals; then a guise of indifference veiled their angry light. He said, "Come inside."

In the reception room of the estate, screens painted with lush green forest landscapes enclosed an area around a sunken brazier, sealed out cold drafts, and created the illusion of a warmer season. There, Nitta performed the ritual of welcoming Sano and serving tea with an elaborate courtesy that conveyed his antipathy more clearly than could blatant insults. They sat opposite each other, tea bowls in their hands, and Nitta's contemptuous gaze challenged Sano to speak.

"Please describe what you did the day before yesterday," Sano said, "beginning with your arrival in Yoshiwara."

"It was late evening when my men and I got there. We went to the Owariya because I had an engagement with a courtesan." Nitta's statement had an artificial, rehearsed quality; he spoke in the tightly modulated voice of a man conscious that a wrong word could doom him. "Upon arriving at the Owariya, I learned that the courtesan had been requested by another man, and I was asked to yield my appointment. I complied, and my men and I joined a party in the *ageya*. But after a while, I recalled some business in town that needed my attention the next morning, so I decided to leave. I paid the Yoshiwara guards to let my men and myself out the gate."

He added, "Bribing the guards and leaving Yoshiwara after curfew are but minor, common transgressions of the law. They do not implicate me in murder."

That the treasury minister had omitted compromising details from his recitation intrigued Sano. That Nitta would expect him to believe this limited version of events, and never find out that there was more to the story, insulted his professional honor and goaded Sano to speak boldly.

"What does implicate you are the facts you left out of your story," he said, and watched caution hood Nitta's expression. "Or were you going to tell me that the man to whom you yielded your appointment was Lord Mitsuyoshi?"

"I did not consider that fact important." Nitta calmly sipped from his tea bowl. "Preemption of appointments is common in Yoshiwara, and it would be absurd to think that a man would kill someone for doing him out of one night with a woman."

"Men have killed because of rivalry over courtesans," Sano said, remembering duels fought during recent years. "And in this case, the courtesan was Lady Wisteria, the woman you love so much that you reserve her company every night because you're jealous of her other clients."

Nitta flapped a hand in impatient dismissal. "Some folk have nothing to do but spread foolish, inaccurate gossip. While it's true that I did go to see Lady Wisteria that night, and I am her patron, she is just a prostitute, and only one of many that I use." A brief, vain smile quirked his lipless mouth, and Sano recognized him as the kind of old man who liked to flaunt his sexual potency and needed young, beautiful women to feed his pride. "Wisteria is not an object of my love or jealousy. You should know better than to believe everything you hear."

Sano felt his patience slipping; his ire flared as it had last night, when the shogun had berated him. He willed himself to remain calm, because losing his temper with a suspect would harm his investigation, and he didn't want to antagonize Nitta any more than necessary. "So you didn't care if Wisteria entertained Lord Mitsuyoshi instead of you?" he said.

"Her business was of little consequence to me."

"You weren't angry at Lord Mitsuyoshi for taking your place?"

"Not in the least." Nitta set down his tea bowl and rose.

Turning away from Sano, he faced the painted forest on a screen, his shoulders rigid.

"Then why were you so upset about yielding to Lord Mitsuyoshi that you argued with the proprietor of the *ageya*?"

Nitta whirled, his face suddenly taut with alarm. "Who told you?" Sudden, angry enlightenment flickered in his eyes. "Senior Elder Makino, that old sneak. He was at the party. He must have been eavesdropping, the way he often does." Though Sano gave no sign of confirmation, Nitta nodded in certainty. "Well, I must warn you against listening to anything Makino says about me. Some years ago, he asked me for a huge loan from the treasury. I declined because his credit is bad. Ever since then, Makino and I have been enemies."

Had Makino consequently lied to frame the treasury minister? Sano had heard nothing of a feud between the pair, and feuds involving such high officials were hard to keep secret. However, Nitta had a reputation as one of the few honest men in a corrupt bureaucracy.

"I did argue with the proprietor of the *ageya*," Nitta said, "but not because I was upset about Wisteria or angry at Lord Mitsuyoshi. My concern was strictly financial. I had paid Wisteria's fee for the night, and so had Lord Mitsuyoshi. I asked the proprietor for a refund, but he insisted on keeping both fees because it's the custom." Nitta puckered his mouth, as if at an unpleasant taste. "I lost my temper with the greedy lout. After I threatened to close down his establishment, he agreed to give me my next appointment free, to compensate for the one I'd lost."

Sano began to doubt the treasury minister's veracity and put more faith in Senior Elder Makino because this story seemed so implausible. The samurai class disdained money as sordid and beneath their dignity, and a man of Nitta's wealth and position shouldn't have minded losing a much greater sum than the price of a *tayu*, let alone quibbled over it.

"What did you do after the argument?" Sano asked.

"I stayed for a few drinks. Around midnight, I went home."

"You walked out of the *ageya* and straight to the gate, you bribed the guards, then left Yoshiwara?"

Nitta's gaze turned wary and speculative, as though he was trying to determine how much Sano already knew. Sano kept his countenance opaque. After a moment, Nitta gave a faint grimace, signaling his capitulation to Sano's bluff.

"No," he said. "I told my men to wait for me at the gate. Then I went through the back entrance of the *ageya*, and upstairs. I thought I might be able to have a moment with Lady Wisteria. I didn't want to leave Yoshiwara without seeing her."

A crimson flush colored Nitta's pale cheeks, like blood dropped onto the surface of virgin snow. This first sign of passion in him told Sano that the man had feelings for Wisteria, in spite of his denials, and that he craved more from her than just carnal satisfaction.

"I stood at the door of the guest chamber and listened," Nitta continued. "Lord Mitsuyoshi was known to drink heavily, and I thought that perhaps he would be asleep, and I could speak to Wisteria."

Sano pictured the treasury minister hovering outside the chamber, his face engorged with desire and jealousy, longing for his lady while she pleasured his rival.

"I heard her whispering. And him whispering in reply. They laughed together." Nitta's eyes burned fever-bright with outrage, as if he thought the couple had been mocking him, the cheated lover. "I couldn't bear to listen anymore."

Then he seemed to realize that he'd exposed his private feelings. His expression turned deliberately neutral. Squatting, he gazed past Sano. "I stole out of the *ageya*, then joined my men at the gate. We paid the guards and began the journey home."

Excitation quickened in Sano, because Nitta had placed himself at the scene where the murder had occurred, at the crucial time. "You didn't go into the chamber?" he said.

"I did not," Nitta said with asperity. "Haven't I made that clear enough?"

"Did you see Lord Mitsuyoshi at all?"

"I did not. But the fact that I heard them means Lord Mitsuyoshi was alive when I left." Nitta arranged his body in a kneeling posture, his complexion its normal hue again, his emotions hidden behind a smug smile. "Therefore, I am not the killer you seek."

The male voice Nitta had heard might have belonged not to Lord Mitsuyoshi, but to his murderer. "Was there anyone present who can confirm what you heard and did?" Sano said.

Nitta shook his head. "The corridor was quite empty."

So he could have entered the room, Sano thought, and stabbed Lord Mitsuyoshi. The treasury minister could have lied about hearing a man's voice. Sano had only Nitta's word as proof that he'd left Mitsuyoshi alive, and no witnesses to say otherwise.

"What about Lady Wisteria?" Sano said. "Did you see her that night?"

"I already told you I'd given up my appointment with her, and I left without seeing her." Nitta's look accused Sano of denseness. "Furthermore, what difference does it make whether I saw her or not?"

"Lady Wisteria is missing," Sano said. "She seems to have vanished around the time of the murder."

A heartbeat passed. "Indeed," Nitta said. His silver eyebrows lifted; his tone reflected concern. "And no one knows where she is?"

"I was hoping you could tell me." Sano couldn't determine whether Nitta really hadn't been aware of Wisteria's disappearance, or was pretending surprise.

"Unfortunately, I've no idea." Now the treasury minister regarded Sano with incredulity. "*Sōsakan-sama*, do you harbor the absurd notion that I am responsible for Wisteria's disappearance, as well as the murder of the shogun's heir?" His voice rose on a shrill note of scorn. "Such acts would be pure stupidity, and no man rises to my position by being stupid. Even if I did love Lady Wisteria, I would never steal a courtesan from Yoshiwara. Nor would I commit treason on her account. Even if I'd hated Lord Mitsuyoshi, I would never risk my life and honor just to eliminate him."

Yet a man in a jealous rage could act on violent impulse, regardless of his intelligence or desire for self-preservation. And Sano could well believe that Wisteria was a woman capable of inspiring violent impulses. He'd not loved her himself—their relationship had been primarily physical—but he guessed that a man who did love her would do anything to gain exclusive possession of her.

"What route did you take to the gate?" he asked Nitta.

"I walked up Nakanochō."

"Did you pass anyone who knows you?"

"Perhaps. But I didn't notice, because I was in a hurry." Nitta laughed, a dry, mirthless chuckle. "Surely you don't think that I abducted Lady Wisteria and hid her somewhere? Or that I killed her and hid her body?"

Someone had done one of those alternatives, Sano believed. "If you didn't, then you'll permit me to search your property and question your household."

Nitta looked affronted. "As you wish," he said, rising. "But you'll discover nothing worth your while."

Sano and his detectives searched the whole estate, including offices, parlors, bathchambers, cellar, and kitchen, barracks, storehouses, stables, garden pavilion, and the family's and servants' quarters. They opened chests, barrels, and cabinets large enough to contain a person, and hunted for secret rooms. But they found no sign of Lady Wisteria, nor any evidence to connect Treasury Minister Nitta to her or the murder. They questioned Nitta's retainers, wife, concubines, relatives, and servants—some eighty people in total—and all told the same story: Nitta had arrived home from Yoshiwara with the retainers who'd accompanied him there, and no one else. Finally, Sano and his men regrouped in the courtyard.

"Maybe everyone's lying to protect Nitta," said Detective Fukida, a serious young man. "Their first loyalty is to him, not the Tokugawa regime."

"Ask the checkpoint guards whether he brought a woman into the castle when he came home," Sano said. "He might have bribed them to ignore Wisteria."

"But if she's here, Nitta must have made her invisible, because otherwise, we'd have found her." Detective Marume had the strong build of an expert fighter, and a jovial manner now sobered by disappointment. "Did he seem upset to learn that she's missing?"

"Not very," Sano said.

"Maybe he knows where Wisteria is," Fukida said.

"He could have had an accomplice remove her from Yoshiwara and shelter her away from here," Sano said.

"That would have posed less risk to him than smuggling her out of the pleasure quarter and into the castle," Marume agreed.

"And if he did, Wisteria would be someplace nearby, where he can have easy access to her," Sano said. He gave orders to his other detectives: "Watch Nitta. Follow him wherever he goes, and perhaps he'll lead us to Wisteria. Order troops to begin searching Edo. They should go neighborhood-by-neighborhood and arrest any women who aren't listed on the residential records kept by the headmen."

The door of the mansion opened, and Nitta emerged. His face wore a look of vindication. "Are you finished here, *Sōsakan-sama*? Am I free to go about my business?"

Sano nodded; he and his men bowed, conceding defeat.

"His Excellency won't be pleased to hear that you've wasted so much time on me, instead of pursuing his heir's killer," Nitta said with sardonic pleasure. "But just to show you that I bear no hard feelings toward you, I shall give you a bit of advice. If you're looking for a likely culprit, you might consider a *hokan* named Fujio."

A *hokan* was a male entertainer who sang and played music for guests in Yoshiwara and for wealthy nobles and merchants around Edo. "Why should I?" Sano said.

"Fujio was a client of Lady Wisteria when she first became a courtesan. His love for her is the subject of his most popular songs. But when Wisteria rose to the rank of *tayu*, she rejected him in favor of samurai clients. This made Fujio very angry at her, and jealous of her new lovers, who included Lord Mitsuyoshi."

The treasury minister spoke in a tone heavy with significance, as if to make sure Sano understood that Fujio had reason for killing Mitsuyoshi and Wisteria. However, it was obvious to Sano that Nitta sought to divert suspicion from himself by implicating the *hokan*.

"Fujio performed at the party in the Owariya," Nitta continued. "He could have slipped into the bedchamber, stabbed Lord Mitsuyoshi, and abducted Lady Wisteria."

Yet perhaps Nitta had killed Lord Mitsuyoshi himself, and now wished to destroy another man who'd enjoyed the favors of his courtesan.

"Thank you for the information," Sano said, keeping his expression neutral. Though he didn't trust Nitta, he desperately needed leads. He intended to pay Fujio a visit, whatever Nitta's motive for casting suspicion on the *hokan*.

As Sano rode down the street with his men, a clatter of hoofbeats caused him to look backward. He saw Police Commissioner Hoshina and a squadron of troops arriving outside Treasury Minister Nitta's gate.

8

The Saru-waka-cho theater district had been selected as the location of the *miai*.

Hirata and his father, wearing their best silk robes and finest swords, walked up the street with Segoshi, a palace guard captain whom Sano had engaged as a substitute go-between. Behind them followed two family retainers, Hirata's mother, and her maid.

The district sparkled with life in the bright, clear weather. Theater buildings sported colorful banners that announced the current plays. Bursts of song and applause emanated from windows. In towers on the roofs, men beat drums to attract customers. People jammed the teahouses or queued at ticket booths, lugging quilts to keep them warm during the performances that lasted all day. Fragrant smoke wafted from outdoor braziers where vendors roasted chestnuts. But Hirata and his party walked in somber quiet. As they neared their destination, anxiety clenched his stomach tighter and tighter.

They stepped aside to let a wedding procession pass. A palanquin carried the bride in her white kimono. Friends, relatives, and lantern-bearers accompanied the palanquin.

"What an auspicious sign for the day of a *miai*," said Captain Segoshi. A good-natured older samurai, he obviously wanted to lighten the mood of his companions.

"As far as I'm concerned, the sight of a wedding procession is a bad-luck omen," Hirata's father said in a grumpy tone. He walked with a severe limp, caused by an accident that had necessitated his retirement from the police force. "I attend this *miai* against my wishes, and I'd rather turn around and go home before we take a step we'll regret."

"But everything has been arranged," Hirata said, alarmed by his father's attitude. "Backing out now would be a terrible breach of courtesy. And you won't regret beginning my marriage negotiations. Midori-*san* is a good, honorable match for me, for our family."

This was but another argument in the dispute that had begun three months ago, when Hirata had told his parents that he wished to marry Midori and asked their permission. They opposed the idea, and had only consented to the *miai* because the formal request had come from Sano, whom they couldn't refuse.

Disapproval darkened the broad, lined face of Hirata's sire. "Honorable matches can only occur between families of similar tradition, and that's not the case here. We are *hatamoto*—hereditary Tokugawa vassals. Lord Niu is an outside daimyo. His clan didn't swear allegiance to the Tokugawa until after it was defeated at the Battle of Sekigahara."

"That battle ended almost a hundred years ago," Hirata said. "Ever since then, the Niu have been loyal subjects of the Tokugawa, just like us. Can't we forget the past?"

"Tradition is too important to forget." His father's voice sharpened with reproach. "It's the mainstay of our society. And surely the Niu clan desires this alliance no more than I do. If you marry this girl, you'll never really be accepted by her kin, nor she by ours."

Hirata glanced backward at his mother. Small though

sturdy, dressed modestly in gray, she gave him a smile that said she sympathized with him, but agreed with her husband. Captain Segoshi looked embarrassed to be caught in a family dispute.

"Why can't you be satisfied to marry into one of the suitable families who've offered their daughters to you?" Hirata's father said.

When Hirata had left his lowly position as a *doshin* and become chief retainer to the *sōsakan-sama*, his status in the marriage market had soared. His family began aspiring to a better match for him than they could have expected before his promotion. After Hirata gained a place in the shogun's inner circle, proposals from high-ranking clans had inundated Hirata and his parents. They'd attended many *miai*, but Hirata had spurned all the fine young ladies introduced to him.

"Niu Midori is the woman I want to marry," he said now. "I love her. She loves me."

His father gave a disgusted snort. "Love is unimportant in choosing a bride. Social position and duty to your family are what really matter. If you marry a woman who's right for you, then the two of you will learn to love each other after the wedding, as your mother and I did." He halted in the street. "I can't approve of this match, even though the *sōsakan-sama* does. You should marry someone I choose for you, because you're unable to choose wisely for yourself."

Hirata's mother bowed her head, silently seconding her husband's words. Desperation forced Hirata to employ the one argument that could aid his cause.

"I respect your opinion, Honorable Father," he said, "but I must remind you that my marriage to Niu Midori would solve a big problem for us."

That problem was their chronic shortage of money. Hirata had elderly, ailing grandparents, two widowed sisters with small children, and many destitute relatives, as well as long-time retainers and servants to support. Unfortunately, Hirata's father earned little by teaching martial arts to police officers. Hirata contributed as much to his family as he could, but even his generous stipend didn't go far enough. He needed to make a financially advantageous marriage, and he'd hoped that this need would convince his parents to allow him to wed Midori.

Although the Niu clan had been subjugated and stripped of its ancestral fief after the Battle of Sekigahara, it remained one of Japan's most powerful families. The first Tokugawa shogun had realized that unless he pacified his conquered foes, they might later rebel. He'd granted the Niu a fief in Satsuma, and the right to rule that entire province. Lord Niu Masamune, the current daimyo, possessed huge wealth, and whoever married a daughter of his would gain a valuable dowry.

Now Hirata's father glowered at the knowledge that he needed this match he repudiated. "That's the only reason I'll even consider a marriage between you and this girl," he said, resuming his awkward, limping pace down the street.

"Here we are," Captain Segoshi said cheerfully, as though determined to get the family through the *miai*. "The Morita-za Theater." This was a large building with painted scenes from plays above the entrance. Outside stood a squadron of soldiers who wore a dragonfly crest on flags attached to their backs. "Look: Lord Niu has arrived. He and his daughter must be already inside, waiting for us."

"Such an ostentatious display," muttered Hirata's father. "Typical of his kind."

Hirata cast him a look that begged him to put aside his envy and prejudices. Captain Segoshi bought tickets from the attendant in the booth, and the party entered the Morita-za.

Inside, a drafty, cavernous room echoed with a roar of voices. A play had just ended, and on the stage, a lone musician plinked a samisen. Tiers of box seats along the walls held crowds of people awaiting the next performance. More people occupied the floor, which was divided into compartments, separated by raised dividers. Hirata scanned the audience, then saw Midori in a compartment near the stage. The light streaming through windows along the upper gallery illuminated her scarlet kimono. As their gazes met, his heart lifted. She smiled, but quickly turned away. The *miai* was supposed to seem like a chance encounter, so that if it failed, both families could pretend it had never occurred, and thus save face.

Hirata led his party along the dividers, past refreshment sellers bearing trays of drinks and food. He halted above the compartment where Midori sat with an elderly woman, two slightly younger female attendants, and two middle-aged samurai. Stricken by nervousness, Hirata knelt on the divider and bowed to the group, as did his companions. Midori darted a wide-eyed, solemn glance at him, then looked at the floor.

"Greetings," Hirata said in a voice that quaked.

The group bowed and murmured in polite reply. Captain Segoshi said, "What a coincidence that we should meet."

As he ably assumed the role of go-between and managed introductions, Hirata learned that the crone dressed in black was Midori's paternal grandmother, and the other women her ladies-in-waiting. The elder of the samurai, a dour man named Okita, was Lord Niu's chief retainer. Hirata barely noticed these people because his attention focused on Lord Niu.

The daimyo was small, but his torso was broad, his posture regal in maroon garments emblazoned with his dragonfly crest in gold. His tanned, square face disturbed Hirata. Its two sides didn't match. The right half was slightly askew; the eye gazed off into space.

"Please join us," Lord Niu said. Only the left half of his mouth smiled at Hirata.

As Hirata and his family settled into the compartment, Midori sat rigid with panic, her heart hammering, not daring to look at anyone. *Please*, she prayed inwardly; *please make our families consent to our marriage!* If they didn't, she was doomed, because love wasn't the only reason she must wed Hirata.

During their courtship, they'd enjoyed more time together, and more freedom, than was usual for unmarried young gentlemen and ladies. Their connection with Reiko and Sano placed them in constant proximity, and they'd taken advantage of their situation. While Reiko thought Midori was busy waiting on Lady Keisho-in, and Keisho-in thought Midori was with Reiko, Midori was actually meeting Hirata in deserted gardens or empty storehouses. There, chaste embraces had led to things less than chaste.

A flush of pleasure and guilt enflamed her as she recalled lying naked with Hirata beneath pine trees at dusk. How much she'd wanted to satisfy him, and to experience the rapture of having him! And how much she now wished they'd exercised self-control, for soon afterward had come the cessation of her monthly blood, a continual nausea, a fullness in her abdomen. Midori had threaded a needle with red thread and stuck it in the wall of the privy, hoping that this ancient folk remedy would cause the blood to come, but to no avail. She was pregnant.

Now she listened to her companions exchanging courteous pleasantries. None of them knew her problem, not even Hirata. She hadn't told anyone. She couldn't admit her shame, or admit that if she and Hirata didn't marry, she would bear an illegitimate child, disgrace her honor, and ruin herself.

"Your family has a proud tradition, does it not?" Lord Niu said to Hirata's father. "I understand that your people have served the shoguns since the Kamakura regime four hundred years ago."

"Yes, that's correct."

Hirata's father looked stern and intimidating to Midori, but also gratified that the daimyo recognized his heritage. She relaxed as she began to think that her father would continue to behave properly.

"And you've made a name for yourself in the police force." Lord Niu smiled his peculiar half smile. "It's men like you who've kept society under control and made Edo the great capital it is."

"That's high praise, coming from the ruler of an entire province," Hirata's father said, obviously warming toward the daimyo. "Your kindness is more than I deserve."

Lord Niu gave a self-deprecating chuckle. "Oh, I'm just the humble overseer of a country estate that the Tokugawa deemed fit to give me." He turned to Hirata. "So you're chief retainer to the shogun's *sōsakan-sama*."

"Yes, my lord." Hirata sat stiffly, his expression serious. Midori felt a rush of tenderness toward him for trying so hard to appear a suitable husband for her.

"That the *sōsakan-sama* trusts you with so much responsibility at your youthful age speaks highly of your character," said Lord Niu. His left eye studied Hirata; his right wandered. "And I hear you're looking into Lord Mitsuyoshi's murder. What have you discovered so far?"

Blushing, Hirata gave an account of the investigation, mentioning the suspects and the missing courtesan and pillow book.

"Cunning and initiative," Lord Niu said jovially. "That's exactly what I expected to find in you."

Hirata's parents beamed with pride. Captain Segoshi smiled. Midori and Hirata exchanged quick, elated glances.

"I understand that your daughter is a favorite lady-in-waiting of His Excellency's mother," Hirata's father said to Lord Niu, then addressed Midori: "Can you play music?"

Midori tensed, realizing that he wanted to know whether she possessed the accomplishments required of a lady, and that this was a test she must pass. "Yes," she said, hesitantly, "I've played the samisen since I was a child."

"Have you learned calligraphy and flower arranging and tea ceremony?"

"To the best of my humble ability." Midori chewed her fingernail; seeing her grandmother frown, she dropped her hand and tried to look the modest, feminine, perfect daughter-in-law.

Hirata's father nodded, and she could tell she'd favorably impressed him. Giddy delight filled her.

Then Lord Niu said, "Yes, my daughter is a prize. And you would steal her from me the way the Tokugawa stole my family's ancestral lands after the Battle of Sekigahara."

He spoke with a sudden rancor that completely dispelled the harmonious atmosphere. Midori saw puzzlement on the faces of Hirata and his party, and consternation on those of her grandmother and Okita. Her heart sank, for this was exactly what she'd feared would happen.

Lord Niu, a shrewd, competent leader of his subjects, had one eccentricity—his unreasonable obsession with injustices done to his clan. Now Midori realized that his compliments to Hirata's family had been veiled expressions of hostility toward them, and he'd meant from the beginning to oppose the marriage.

"You should be .satisfied that your ancestors helped the Tokugawa trample my clan in the dust," Lord Niu said bitterly to Hirata and his father. "You should be satisfied that the *bakufu* extorts millions of *koban* in taxes from me every year. But no—you greedy louts want my flesh and blood!"

For as long as Midori could recall, her family had carefully avoided mentioning the Tokugawa or the Battle of Sekigahara to Lord Niu, for fear of rousing his violent temper. But they couldn't prevent him from thinking of those topics at inopportune times and angering himself. And although his relatives limited the time Lord Niu spent in public, lest his behavior shame them or create problems, they couldn't always restrain him. Once, after the Tokugawa revenue agents had collected a large tribute from him, Lord Niu had mounted his horse and ridden through a village, shrieking and cutting down innocent peasants. The clan had so far managed to hush up his bad spells, and neither the *bakufu* nor the general public knew of them—yet. What a disaster that his obsession should interrupt the *miai*!

"Master," Okita said cautiously to Lord Niu, "perhaps this isn't a good time to dwell on the past."

Ignoring his retainer, Lord Niu again addressed Hirata and his companions: "It's clear to me that you are plotting with the Tokugawa clan to take over my province, steal my money, and destroy my whole clan."

Hirata and his father gaped in shock. Midori huddled in fear, and her grandmother sadly shook her head. Hirata's father blurted, "With all due respect, Honorable Lord Niu, that's absurd. We came in peace, to consider the possibility of joining our families together through a marriage between your daughter and my son."

Midori longed to explain the daimyo's behavior and beg the forgiveness of Hirata and his family, but she was too afraid to do anything but watch helplessly as Lord Niu stood.

"I'll never allow a daughter of mine to marry the spawn of a scoundrel like you!" he shouted at Hirata's father. People in other compartments fell silent and stared at Lord Niu. His skewed face twitched; his eyes glittered with hatred. "You're a dirty thief, and a treacherous sneak, and a foul murderer!"

Hirata's mother and Captain Segoshi looked aghast. Hirata's father surged to his feet. "How dare you insult me?" he demanded. Anger reddened his complexion. "I'm a man of honor, and I'll not tolerate this disgraceful treatment from an outside lord. Take back what you said, or I'll—"

Sneering in contempt, Lord Niu smacked Hirata's father on the cheek. Then the two men were wildly hitting and kicking each other. Midori and the other women cringed away from the combatants. Hirata cried, "Father, stop!" while Okita begged, "Master, please control yourself."

The musician onstage halted his performance as the audience stood up to watch the commotion. Lord Niu jumped up on a divider and drew his sword. Hirata's father also drew his weapon, but his bad leg hindered his climb onto the divider. Men in the audience stamped on the floor, shouting, "Fight! Fight!"

Hirata grabbed his father, and, with Segoshi's help, pulled him back inside the compartment and restrained him. Okita wrestled Lord Niu, grappling for the sword. The audience booed.

Lord Niu yelled, "I'll get you yet, you despicable villain!"

Okita, panting from his effort to hold the daimyo, addressed Hirata: "You'd better go."

As Hirata hurried his family out of the theater, he looked briefly back at Midori. His face reflected the despair in her heart. She buried her face in her hands and wept.

9

Sano, accompanied by Detectives Fukida and Marume and some troops, again rode to the pleasure quarter, this time in pursuit of the entertainer whom Treasury Minister Nitta had implicated in the murder. Arriving in late afternoon, Sano found that Yoshiwara had undergone a striking change since his last visit.

Gone was the dismal atmosphere. The rooftops gleamed bronze in the light of the descending sun, while in through the gates swarmed hundreds of men eager for sensual delight. Some wore basket-shaped rush hats that concealed their faces. Sano recognized these as samurai, whom the law prohibited from visiting Yoshiwara. Though many samurai disregarded the law, and virtually no one cared, the most upstanding or cautious came in disguise. Along Nakanochō, the lanterns on the eaves burned brightly. Courtesans sat in the window cages of the brothels. Visitors ogled the courtesans, jammed the teahouses, and thronged shops that sold souvenirs and guidebooks to the quarter. As Sano entered Yoshiwara with his men, he imagined all the money that would change hands in the morning, when the customers paid the exorbitant fees that the brothels charged for food, drink, service, and women.

"We'll stop in a teahouse and ask where we can find Fujio," Sano said to his detectives. "He's sure to be performing somewhere." Sano wasn't personally acquainted with Fujio, but he'd watched the *hokan* play at parties and knew his reputation as an acclaimed entertainer.

Just then, two boys marched up the avenue, beating drums. "Hear the magnificent Fujio play at the Atami Pleasure House tonight," they called.

Spared the trouble of hunting the suspect, Sano and his men walked to the Atami, located on Edochō, a side street bordered by rows of brothels. The recessed entranceway of the Atami held a low table. On it sat three folded futon, a quilt, and a coverlet, all made of rich colored silk.

"*Tsumi-yagu no koto,*" Sano said.

This was the practice by which a courtesan showed off her patron's wealth and devotion. The patron would supply a small fortune for the courtesan to buy elegant bedding. She would place it outside her brothel for all to admire. Even if the women would prefer to use their patrons' money to pay their debts and shorten their term of service, Yoshiwara custom required them to display a carefree, impractical attitude. A courtesan who didn't spend lavishly would appear stingy, become unpopular, and never free herself.

Sano glanced at the paper label attached to the quilt, which bore a date three days before the murder, and an inscription. " 'This bedding was presented to Lady Takane by the Honorable Nitta Monzaemon,' " Sano read.

"Then the treasury minister is patron to at least one other courtesan besides Lady Wisteria," said Detective Marume. He fingered the coverlet. "Pretty expensive goods."

"Maybe he's not really in love with Wisteria," Sano said. "A client devoted to a particular woman will usually confine his spending to her."

"Maybe he dallies with other women to cover his feelings for Wisteria," Fukida suggested.

"Or maybe Senior Elder Makino lied," said Marume.

This was a real possibility, given Makino's nature. "If he did, and Nitta told me the truth," Sano said, "then Nitta had no apparent reason to abduct Wisteria or kill Lord Mitsuyoshi." And Nitta had seemed like a promising suspect this morning. "Marume-*san*, check into Nitta's relations with the courtesans and find out whether he does spread his attention around. The Introducing Teahouses would be a good place to start." These establishments matched clients with courtesans, arranged appointments, and negotiated fees.

"Fukida-*san*, look for witnesses who saw Nitta on the night of the murder," Sano said. "We want to know everything he did. I'll handle Fujio myself." He hoped that if his case against Nitta dissolved, the *hokan* would prove to be the culprit.

The detectives bowed and departed. Leaving his troops outside, Sano went into the pleasure house. A guard stationed in the entryway greeted him.

"Welcome, master," the guard said. "Have you an appointment with one of our ladies?"

Sano introduced himself, then said, "I'm looking for Fujio."

"He's about to perform in the banquet room."

Sano walked down the corridor toward the sound of voices and laughter. In the banquet room a party of samurai and courtesans lounged and chatted. *Kamuro* served roasted sardines, salted ferns, quail eggs, steamed clams, and sake to the men. As Sano paused in the doorway, a man strode through a curtained entrance at the far end of the room. He carried a samisen in one hand and a large folding fan in the other. He snapped the fan shut with a loud, ritualistic flourish, and all heads turned toward him.

"Thank you, everyone, for your favor," Fujio said.

The party cheered. As Fujio knelt, positioned his samisen, and played a cascade of notes, Sano studied the *hokan*. Fujio was perhaps thirty-five years old, tall and slender, and handsome in a raffish way. He had bold, sparkling eyes, a mischievous set to his features, and sleek hair knotted at his nape. He wore the traditional *hokan*'s black coat printed with crests, over a beige kimono.

"With your kind permission, I shall perform my new song, 'The Mysterious Flood,' " he announced.

The audience eagerly settled down to listen. Fujio played a gay tune and sang in a smooth, vibrant voice:

> *"A big spender from Ōsaka,*
> *Weary of the pleasures of his hometown,*
> *Came to Yoshiwara with his entourage*
> *To pluck some fresh blossoms.*
>
> *All eager for conquest,*
> *The men courted the best* tayu,
> *Sake flowed, and they made flattering*
> *   talk, but alas!*
> *The proud beauties scorned them.*
>
> *But the men would not accept*
> *   disappointment,*
> *For thirty nights they engaged the same*
> *   courtesans,*
> *Attempting to win favor,*
> *For thirty nights they failed, their desire*
> *   thwarted.*
>
> *At last they decided to return to Ōsaka,*
> *But so aroused were they,*
> *That they paused by the Dike of Japan,*
> *And each caressed his own manhood,*
> *   spurting a mighty fountain of seed.*
>
> *The torrent overflowed the dike,*
> *The peasants in neighboring villages beat*
> *   the flood-warning drums,*
> *For many years they wondered,*

*What caused a flood on that rainless
      night?"*

The samurai in the audience guffawed; their female companions tittered; Sano smiled. Lewd songs were Fujio's specialty, and he performed with sly humor. The *hokan* bowed to enthusiastic applause. Then he caught sight of Sano. Recognition and stark fear erased his smile.

"Please excuse me," he said to the audience.

Dropping his samisen, he fled out the curtained exit, amid protests from the samurai. Sano hurried after Fujio, but so did the courtesans, who clustered at the exit, crying, "Come back!"

By the time Sano pushed past them into the corridor, Fujio was gone. A door stood open to the night. Sano sped outside and found himself in a shadowed alley that ran along Yoshiwara's eastern wall. He saw the *hokan* running past stinking privy sheds, toward the back of the quarter. Sano took off in pursuit, his feet skidding on the damp, slimy paving stones.

A small crowd of women gathered in the distance. They surrounded Fujio, crying, "Come with me, master, and I'll make you happy!"

This area of Yoshiwara was known as Nichome—"Wicked Creek"—a name derived from a legend about a warrior attacked by an ogre. Here, low-class courtesans, desperate for customers, would accost men, pull them into squalid brothels, and service them in rooms shared by many couples. Now they clutched at Fujio, who shouted, "Let go!"

Sano caught up with the *hokan*, grabbed him by the front of his coat, yanked him away from the women, and shoved him against the wall. The women scattered in fright. Fujio flung up his hands in a gesture of surrender.

"No need to hurt me, *Sōsakan-sama*," he said, flashing the smile that had charmed many female admirers. "Whatever business you have with me, we can settle it without a fight."

Sano released Fujio, but stood ready to catch him should

he flee again. "Why did you run when you saw me?"

"I was afraid," Fujio confessed sheepishly.

"Afraid that you were wanted for the murder of Lord Mitsuyoshi?"

"Well, yes." Fujio laughed, making a joke of his predicament, though Sano perceived how much he wished he'd gotten away. "If you're looking for the killer, you've got the wrong fellow." His mobile face assumed a humble, sincere expression. "But I'll be glad to help in any way I can."

There was something irresistibly likable about Fujio, and Sano couldn't be angry at his obvious attempt to beguile his way out of trouble. "In that case," Sano said, "you can tell me what were your relations with Lord Mitsuyoshi."

"He was a patron of mine. I performed for him and his friends here, and in town." A *hokan* lived on money from his patrons and depended on them to recommend him to new customers. "So you see that Lord Mitsuyoshi was worth more to me alive than dead," Fujio said, turning his palms up as he smiled. "I wouldn't kill him, and I didn't."

His nimble, eloquent hands pantomimed innocence, and Sano remembered hearing that Fujio had once been a Kabuki actor. "But you hated Lord Mitsuyoshi because he was your rival for the affections of Lady Wisteria," Sano said.

"That would have been true once, when I was madly in love with Wisteria. She made me jealous by carrying on with samurai in front of me. But someone is telling you ancient history." Condescension tinged Fujio's smile. "I ended that affair last year, when I married the daughter of the proprietor of the Great Miura. Now I couldn't care less about Wisteria."

He leaned nonchalantly against the wall. "But it's interesting that she should disappear on the same night when her lover was murdered in her bed. Do you know where she's gone?"

"I was hoping you could tell me," Sano said.

"Sorry. I've no idea."

"Then you won't mind if I search your home?"

Fujio's eyebrows shot up. "Not at all."

When asked where his home was, the *hokan* readily said

he lived in Imado, a nearby village. But Sano had a distinct feeling that Fujio was hiding something, even if it wasn't the missing courtesan.

"Where were you and what did you do on the night Lord Mitsuyoshi died?" Sano said.

"I performed at a party. But you've already found out that I was in the house where Lord Mitsuyoshi died, haven't you? That's why you came for me. Nothing stays a secret for long in this place." Fujio slumped in gloomy resignation; then he brightened, raising a finger. "But I was entertaining the guests from the time dinner was served at the hour of the dog, until after midnight, when we learned that Lord Mitsuyoshi was dead."

"Did you leave the room at any time?"

"No, master."

Though his position as the focus of people's attention provided him a good alibi, Sano again sensed that Fujio was dodging. "Are you sure you never took a break?"

A peculiar look came into the *hokan*'s eyes, as if he'd just realized something that simultaneously disconcerted and gratified him. He said, "I went to use the privy in the back alley. But you needn't take my word for it. Treasury Minister Nitta saw me. He was standing in the alley outside the back door of the Owariya."

Surprise jolted Sano. Before he could respond, Fujio said, "Nitta put you onto me, didn't he? He's the one who told you the old gossip to get me in trouble. Aha, I thought so. But I bet he didn't say he saw me in the alley, because he would have had to admit he was there, too. He must have just killed Lord Mitsuyoshi when I saw him." Fujio grinned in triumph.

But perhaps Fujio was the killer and sought to incriminate Nitta the way Nitta had tried to incriminate him, Sano thought. "Why would the treasury minister kill the shogun's heir and try to frame you?" he said. "Because he loves Wisteria and was jealous of you and Lord Mitsuyoshi for having her?"

The *hokan* dismissed the idea with a flick of his hand.

"Oh, Nitta likes exclusive use of his courtesans, but this isn't about love—it's about money." He jingled the leather coin pouch he wore at his waist. "How do you think Nitta covers the huge expenses he runs up in Yoshiwara? The last night I spent with Wisteria, she said Nitta has been stealing gold from the treasury."

"How did she know?" Sano said, shocked by this accusation of embezzlement, which constituted treason.

Fujio shrugged. "She didn't say. But I think she blackmailed Nitta, and he killed her to keep her quiet."

Blackmail was a new motive for the murder, and Sano knew he must check into it, though he wouldn't put it past Fujio to have improvised the story on the spot. Sano dreaded confronting Nitta, and the upheaval that an investigation of treasury affairs would cause in the *bakufu*. Still, this development offered a possible explanation for the missing pillow book.

"I also think Wisteria wrote about Nitta's embezzlement in that book she always carried around with her—the one everybody says is missing," Fujio said, echoing Sano's thoughts. "Nitta probably destroyed the book so that his crime wouldn't come to light after she was dead."

Now Sano needed more than ever to find the book. "That's an interesting story," he said. "How does Lord Mitsuyoshi fit into it?"

"He was in Wisteria's bedchamber, and probably drunk by that hour. When Nitta got there, he thought Mitsuyoshi was asleep, and he killed Wisteria. But then he discovered that Mitsuyoshi was awake and had seen the whole thing. Wisteria was a peasant, and Nitta could have gotten away with her murder, but he was afraid that if the *bakufu* found out what he'd done, his stealing would be discovered. So he killed Mitsuyoshi to get rid of the witness." Fujio nodded, certain of his reasoning.

"How would he have gotten rid of Wisteria's body?" Sano said.

"Oh, well, he probably ordered people to help him and keep silent afterward," Fujio replied.

The story was plausible, though based on dubious assumptions. Willing to play along for now, Sano said, "How do you explain the hairpin that was used to stab Lord Mitsuyoshi? Why should Nitta choose it instead of his sword? Or would you like to change your story and blame the murder on Wisteria's *yarite* because the hairpin belonged to her?"

"No, no, no." Fujio waggled his hands. "Momoko didn't do it. Even though she's a mean old hag, according to what I hear. Do you want to know what she does when she shaves courtesans?" Yoshiwara custom dictated that all prostitutes must shave their pudenda. "She yanks out hairs one by one, from the most sensitive spots."

He winced; so did Sano.

"And if the courtesans complain, Momoko adds false charges to their account, to keep them in the brothels longer. In my opinion, she's more likely to be murdered herself than kill anybody," Fujio said. "She must have dropped the hairpin in Wisteria's room. Nitta used it on Lord Mitsuyoshi to direct blame from himself onto someone else." The *hokan* gave Sano a significant look. "As he tried to do with me."

"And you're returning the favor," Sano said, as frustration welled in him. That both Fujio and the treasury minister were anxious to protect themselves discredited their statements against each other.

Mischief gleamed in Fujio's eyes. "A bad deed deserves payment in kind, I always say." Edging away from Sano, he said, "Are you going to arrest me, or may I go? There's a roomful of customers who'll be furious at me if I don't play for them."

"You can go," Sano said, "for now."

Watching Fujio hurry off, Sano wondered if he'd been handed the solution to the case, or conned by the *hokan*. He had difficulty imagining Fujio as a killer; yet charm could mask deceit and murderous rage, and Sano decided to assign detectives to watch Fujio. Sano's frustration increased as he acknowledged that tonight's inquiries had, instead of bringing him closer to success, created more work for him. He must now hunt for witnesses to confirm or contradict Fujio's story as well as Nitta's, and the web of personal relationships associated with the crime had grown more complex.

Dusk was falling upon the quarter; the western sky glowed copper. As Sano walked up a road of brothels toward Ageyachō, the lanterns seemed brighter, the crowds louder, and the music gayer in the gathering darkness. He saw *Yoriki* Yamaga and a group of other police officials, presumably hunting the same facts he needed. He thought of Reiko, who'd gone out this morning in search of clues to the whereabouts of Lady Wisteria. He hoped that Wisteria was still alive, because she might be the only person who could tell him what had really happened in that bedchamber.

10

Inside the courtyard of Sano's estate, bearers set down a palanquin, and Reiko alighted in the chilly dusk. Midori burst out the door of the mansion and ran toward Reiko, sobbing.

"What's wrong?" Reiko said, embracing her friend.

"Oh, Reiko-*san*, it was awful!" Midori poured out the tale of her *miai*, and Reiko exclaimed in dismay at how Lord Niu had insulted Hirata's father and the two men had fought. "They're enemies now," Midori mourned. "They'll never allow my marriage to Hirata-*san*."

Although Reiko feared this was true, she said, "Don't give up hope yet. I'll ask my husband to speak to your families and help make peace between them."

"Oh, thank you!" Smiling, Midori wiped her nose on her sleeve and hugged Reiko. Then more tears flowed. "I spent the afternoon at my father's estate. He kept raving about how Hirata-*san*'s family is trying to destroy him and he must fight back. Then he locked himself in his chamber. I didn't have a chance to beg him to make amends to Hirata's father or reconsider the match."

A sob choked Midori. "And I haven't seen Hirata-*san* since he left the theater. No one here knows where he is. Why doesn't he come to me? I'm afraid he doesn't love me anymore."

"Of course he does," Reiko said soothingly. "Hirata-*san* is faithful. He'll understand that your father's behavior wasn't your fault. He's probably just busy working. Now cheer up—you don't want him to come in and see you like this."

Midori bit her quivering lips and breathed deeply in a visible attempt to pull herself together. "Please forgive me for imposing my troubles on you, when you've just gotten home. Were you out investigating the murder of Lord Mitsuyoshi?"

Nodding, Reiko felt the despair in her own heart.

"And you've discovered lots of clues?" Midori said with flattering confidence in Reiko's ability.

"I wish it were so." Reiko sighed. "I've spent the whole day visiting my cousins and aunts and friends, talking to servants and shopkeepers. Everyone is so afraid to speak ill of the shogun's dead heir that no one will talk about Lord Mitsuyoshi. And as for Lady Wisteria, everyone was full of gossip about the clothes she wears and the lavish parties she gives. Everyone has a theory of how she got out of Yoshiwara—she turned into a bird and flew away, she drank a magic potion that made her small and she sneaked under the gate. But no one has any real idea where she went."

"Oh, Reiko-*san*, that's too bad," Midori said.

Reiko dreaded admitting her failure to Sano. Cold, tired, and hungry, she couldn't bear to think about what that failure meant. "Let's go inside where it's warm," she said. "Have you eaten yet? We can have a meal together while you wait for Hirata-*san*."

Midori looked tempted, then shook her head regretfully. "I'd better go. Lady Keisho-in will be looking for me."

They parted, and Reiko entered the house. There, Masahiro toddled down the corridor, calling, "Mama, Mama! Come see what I made." He grabbed her hand and tugged.

One of his nursemaids, a girl named O-hana, trailed after him. "The young master has been working hard today," O-hana said. She was nineteen and pretty, with a glint of cleverness in her eyes and a pert smile shaped like an inverted triangle. Though she wore the customary indigo kimono of a servant, she always added a personal, stylish touch. Today it was a paper butterfly perched on her upswept hair.

"Let's go see what you've done, Masahiro-*chan*," said Reiko.

The three went to the nursery. On the floor stood colored building blocks arranged in the rudimentary shape of a house.

"That's wonderful!" Reiko exclaimed, as her pleasure in her son eased the disappointment of the day.

"Now the young master is the little lord of his own castle," O-hana said fondly.

Masahiro laughed and jumped up and down. Reiko wished she had as much accomplishment to boast. She was so afraid she would let Sano down and prove herself unworthy of his trust.

"Excuse me, mistress," said the housekeeper, entering the nursery, "but you have visitors."

"Who are they?" Reiko said, surprised because she wasn't expecting anyone.

"Lady Yanagisawa and her daughter, Kikuko."

"Merciful gods."

Reiko hadn't thought the chamberlain's wife would call on her this soon. Now she jumped up in a flurry of agitation, for she'd never received such an important guest. She smoothed her hair and clothes as she hurried to the parlor, where she found Lady Yanagisawa and Kikuko kneeling side by side.

"Good evening." Reiko knelt opposite them and bowed.

Lady Yanagisawa echoed the greeting. She wore drab, brownish mauve, and her plain face was as dour as before.

"My apologies for arriving without notice," she murmured. "I hope I am not inconveniencing you?"

"No, not at all," Reiko said nervously. "I'm glad you came. Hello, Kikuko-*chan*. My, how pretty you look."

The little girl giggled and hid her face behind the sleeve of her aquamarine kimono.

"Say, 'You are too kind, Honorable Lady—I am not worthy of your praise,'" Lady Yanagisawa gently instructed her daughter.

Kikuko obeyed, stumbling over the words. When Reiko provided refreshments, the girl slurped the tea and spilled some on her kimono. She gobbled the cakes and got sugary crumbs all over her face and the floor. Lady Yanagisawa wiped Kikuko's face with a napkin, picked up crumbs, and gave Reiko a look of embarrassed apology.

"This winter is particularly harsh," Reiko said, seeking to initiate a conversation and put her guest at ease.

". . . Yes."

Lady Yanagisawa cupped her tea bowl in her hands; her gaze flitted around the room, taking in the wall mural, the alcove where a scroll of calligraphy hung above a celadon vase of dried flowers, and the shelves that held figurines. Reiko wondered whether she didn't realize she was supposed to say something to keep the talk going, she couldn't think what to say, or she expected other people to carry the burden of conversation.

"Having to stay indoors in cold weather makes me restless," said Reiko. "How do you pass the time?"

"I read poetry. I sew clothes for Kikuko. I try to teach her a little reading and writing. We play together." Long pauses separated Lady Yanagisawa's sentences. "Sometimes we go out to a temple."

"How nice." Reiko thought Lady Yanagisawa's life sounded circumscribed, dull, and lonely. Perhaps she didn't want to expose Kikuko to people who might mock her.

Lady Yanagisawa glanced at Reiko, then away, then back again, repeatedly, scrutinizing her hair, figure, clothes, and face. Although Reiko could detect no malice in Lady Yanagisawa's narrow eyes, she grew uneasy.

"Does your husband share your interest in poetry?" Reiko said.

"My husband is very busy."

This reply told Reiko that the chamberlain, like many a man, paid his wife little attention, but Lady Yanagisawa gave no hint of whether she minded. Reiko began to feel as though the other woman's gaze were taking small bites out of her, and at a loss for how to entertain Lady Yanagisawa. Then Reiko noticed Kikuko fidgeting restlessly with her hair ornaments.

"Maybe Kikuko-*chan* would like to play with my son," Reiko said. "Shall we take her to the nursery?"

"That would be fine." Lady Yanagisawa spoke in a tone of indifference, but rose and held out her hand. "Come, Kikuko-*chan.*"

The way to the nursery took them past Sano's office, Reiko's study, and the bedchamber. Lady Yanagisawa paused at each doorway to peer inside, her face expressionless, her gaze unblinking. Kikuko imitated her mother's pose, and Reiko's uneasiness burgeoned. Their behavior seemed intrusive, but Reiko dared not object. With considerable relief she ushered Lady Yanagisawa and Kikuko into the nursery. There, Masahiro had dismantled his block house and begun building another while O-hana watched.

"Masahiro-*chan*," Reiko said, "look who's here."

He saw Kikuko and gave a happy chortle. The girl smiled. Letting go of her mother's hand, she hurried over to kneel beside Masahiro and his blocks. O-hana bowed to Lady Yanagisawa, who studied the maid for a moment, then ignored her.

"Me do," Kikuko said, piling blocks in an untidy heap.

"No," Masahiro said. "Here. Like this."

He showed her how to build a wall, and they began working together. Kikuko, docile and clumsy, chewed on a block. Lady Yanagisawa impassively observed the game without a change of expression, but Reiko feared that the glaring contrast between their children would upset her guest.

"Masahiro-*chan*, how about showing Kikuko-*chan* some of your other toys?" Reiko said.

The little boy went to a cabinet and took out wooden animals and soldiers. Kikuko examined each with lively curiosity. Lady Yanagisawa knelt, apparently content to watch the children, and Reiko relaxed, spared the onus of making conversation and glad not to be the focus of her guest's attention. Soon the children began tumbling and wrestling. Now Kikuko's greater age and strength showed to advantage. She picked up Masahiro and spun around with him until he whooped in joyous excitement, while a slight smile leavened Lady Yanagisawa's stern aspect.

A pleasant hour passed in this manner. Then Lady Yanagisawa said, "I am afraid we've outstayed our welcome. Kikuko-*chan*, it's time to go home."

The little girl obediently rose from the floor, where she and Masahiro were turning somersaults. "Good-bye," she said to Masahiro.

Reiko escorted her guests to the entryway. Lady Yanagisawa donned her sandals and cloak and helped Kikuko put on hers. "Many thanks for your hospitality," Lady Yanagisawa said, bowing.

"Your presence did me an honor." Reiko also bowed, thinking that Lady Yanagisawa seemed as aloof and unfathomable as when they'd first met.

"Perhaps you will bring your son to see Kikuko-*chan* and me someday," Lady Yanagisawa said.

"Yes. I will." Though Reiko still had doubts about the prudence of associating with the chamberlain's wife, courtesy required her agreement.

"The days are often long and melancholy when one is alone, and your company is most cheering. . . . I must thank you for your friendship."

The pauses in Lady Yanagisawa's speech lengthened the farewell ritual. Reiko, suddenly overwhelmed by fatigue, wished to be alone, but waited politely.

Then Lady Yanagisawa said, "This business of Lord Mitsuyoshi's death . . . Please excuse my candor when I say that I know you collaborate with your husband on his inquiries into such matters, and I know the peril that now threatens you both." Face averted from Reiko, she hushed her voice. "I shall do whatever I can to assist you in your endeavors."

"Your generosity is much appreciated." Reiko hid her surprise: Nothing had prepared her to expect that the chamberlain's wife would offer help in the investigation. "A thousand thanks."

As Reiko stood in the doorway and watched her guests climb into their palanquin, she wondered if a woman like Lady Yanagisawa, isolated in her home, with few friends and no talent for talking to people, could possibly provide any worthwhile information. Reiko sighed and returned to the nursery, where she sat watching Masahiro play and waited for Sano to come home.

11

Music and laughter drifted across the dark countryside from Yoshiwara, while latecomers queued at the gate. Through the streets of the pleasure quarter marched a long procession. Lantern-bearers led a shy young girl dressed in elaborate kimono, female attendants, and a horde of spectators eager to see the young courtesan make her debut. More spectators craned their necks from balconies as she stopped at teahouses to solicit business. But Hirata paid scant attention.

He walked alone down Nakanochō, his mind preoccupied. After the *miai*, he'd escorted his parents to their home in the *hatamoto* district north of Edo Castle. He'd tried to talk to them about what had happened at the theater and persuade them to allow his marriage to Midori in spite of it; but they had proved intractable.

"Lord Niu is a vile monster," his father had said. "Never mention him or anyone connected with him to me again."

Hirata's mother had bowed her head in assent.

"You've wasted far too much time on your foolish romance," Hirata's father said. "Go back to your work and forget that girl."

The impossibility of their marriage had only shown Hirata how much he loved Midori. But although he longed to see her and hated to leave matters as they stood, he decided to resume the murder investigation. He felt he'd already shirked his duties today, and he mustn't let Sano down.

But when Hirata had gone to Edo Castle, he'd been unable to find Sano or any of the detectives assigned to the case. He didn't know what they'd learned during his absence, or what he should do. Feeling left out and guilty, Hirata had come to Yoshiwara in the hope of catching up with the investigation. Yoshiwara was a gathering place for people from all around Edo as well as points distant, and thus a lode of news that Hirata had often mined for tips about crimes and criminals during his career as a *doshin*. Now he strolled along Nakanochō, seeking acquaintances who'd been helpful in the past.

Loud drumming throbbed from a teahouse. Hirata peered under the doorway curtain and saw a group of men seated in a circle, clapping in time to the drummer's beats. In the center of the circle, three young women dressed alike in red kimono minced, whirled, and gestured in a flirtatious dance. Their tense smiles and awkward movements told Hirata that they weren't courtesans. They were *odoriko*—girls from peasant families who scrimped and borrowed to buy dance and music lessons for their daughters, then put them on display. The object was to attract rich men who would marry the girls or hire them as household entertainers. At the edge of the audience Hirata saw an older woman he recognized, a gossip who had her nose in all the business of Yoshiwara.

He entered the teahouse and knelt beside her. "Hello, Nobuko-*san*," he said.

She turned a homely, pleasant face to him. "How nice to see you again," she said with a bucktoothed smile.

"What brings you here?" Hirata gestured toward the dancing girls. "More daughters to marry off?"

"Yes, indeed," Nobuko said with a gloomy sigh. "Why was I cursed with five girls? If they don't marry soon, we'll all starve." She ventured hopefully, "Do you need a wife?"

"No, thank you. But I do need your help." Hirata explained that he was investigating the murder of Lord Mitsuyoshi. "What have you heard?"

Though usually glad to share gossip, Nobuko hesitated. She held up her fan to shield her mouth, and whispered in Hirata's ear: "They say that Lord Mitsuyoshi owed money all over Yoshiwara because his family cut off his spending allowance. But nobody could refuse to serve him, or force him to pay."

Because he was a Tokugawa clan member and the shogun's heir, thought Hirata. Had an angry proprietor killed Mitsuyoshi to punish him and stop his freeloading?

"Who in particular had a grudge against him?" Hirata asked.

Nobuko turned away and fixed her gaze on her dancing daughters. "I've already said too much."

Clearly, she didn't want to incriminate the owners of the establishments where her daughters performed. And although Hirata welcomed a new clue, his heart sank because pursuing this one would take him into dangerous territory. The shogun had forbidden Sano to investigate Lord Mitsuyoshi, and hunting the dead man's enemies would constitute disobedience. Regretting the shogun's orders, Hirata thanked Nobuko and left the teahouse.

Through the crowds ambled a man clutching a bucket filled with jars and cloth soap bags in one hand, and a wooden staff in the other. A bell hanging from the top of the staff tinkled as he stepped. His head was bald, his gaze sightless.

"Yoshi-*san*," Hirata called. "Isn't it a little late for washing hair? All the courtesans must be dressed by now."

The blind shampoo man paused, and recognition illuminated his face. "Ah, it's you, Hirata-*san*. I was just heading home. Is there something I can do for you?"

Hirata knew that Yoshi was privy to many secrets because

he worked inside the brothels. The courtesans seemed to think blindness equaled deafness and talked in front of him. When Hirata asked him for news associated with the murder, the blind man replied with the same caution as had Nobuko.

"A certain young dandy made himself unpopular among my customers," he said, avoiding the use of Mitsuyoshi's name and protecting himself from accusations of treasonous slander. "He would promise to free a courtesan and take her home as his wife if she satisfied him. She would do her best, but when he tired of her, he would drop her."

Hirata wondered whether Mitsuyoshi had tricked Lady Wisteria. Had she killed him in revenge for his faithlessness?

"I know *tayu* who must now spend years longer in Yoshiwara because they refused other clients to serve him," Yoshi said.

"Give me their names," Hirata said, and pressed coins into the blind shampoo man's hand.

"Thank you, master. They are Lady Columbine, Lady Takao, and Lady Kacho."

"Not Lady Wisteria?"

"I don't know, master."

Yoshi trudged off, his bell tinkling. Hirata bought rice dumplings from a street vendor and leaned against a wall, eating as he watched drunks flirt with courtesans seated in the window cages, and reviewed what he'd just accomplished. He'd identified three more suspects and could probably find others by canvassing the quarter; yet the shogun's prohibition seemed like a stone wall protecting the murderer. Hirata must find a different path to the truth.

A stout man dressed in a thick padded cloak and wicker hat rushed by. Fast on his heels followed a younger, smaller man with a wiry frame and pugnacious expression.

"Get lost, you scum!" the first man shouted over his shoulder.

"There's only one way to get me off your tail," the second man shouted back.

Hirata recognized the pursuer as a "following horse"—a debt collector hired to hunt down people who owed money in Yoshiwara and chase them day and night until they paid. And he recognized this one as his old friend Gorobei.

The following horse grabbed hold of the debtor, who turned and began throwing punches. While they scuffled, pedestrians gathered round, egging them on. Hirata, anxious to prevent a brawl, wrenched the combatants apart. The debtor escaped into the crowd, and Gorobei faced Hirata.

"You let him get away!" he said, his jaw jutting in rage. "I've just lost my commission." Then, as he recognized Hirata, dismay came over his face. "Oh. It's you. What do you want with me? I've done nothing wrong."

"Maybe not this time." Hirata had once arrested Gorobei for his sideline occupation—selling stolen goods. Gorobei made a habit of carrying small items on his person, in case he happened to meet a customer, and Hirata noticed an unnatural bulge at Gorobei's waist, under his coat.

"What have you got in there?" Hirata said.

Gorobei leapt away from Hirata's reaching hand. "Nothing. I'm just getting fat in my old age."

"Give it over." Hirata yanked on Gorobei's coat, and out dropped a gold Buddha statue. "Ha! Either you've just given birth to the Buddha, or you're up to your old tricks."

"I bought and paid for that with my own hard-earned money," the following horse exclaimed, picking up the Buddha and dusting it on his sleeve.

"A likely story. You're under arrest."

Panic gleamed in Gorobei's eyes. "Can't you give me a break this time?"

Hirata wasn't really interested in small-time theft, or in arresting Gorobei. The following horse collected something else besides debts: information that he picked up around town.

"That depends on you," Hirata said.

Gorobei's expression turned cunning. "I can give you something you need more than my pitiful self."

"Oh?"

"Your master wants to find the person who killed the shogun's heir, doesn't he?"

"So what if he does?" Hirata feigned indifference, but his heartbeat quickened.

Gorobei thrust out his jaw and looked wise. He spoke in a low voice so passersby wouldn't hear: "Maybe I can tell you something about that."

"Then tell," Hirata said, "before I haul you off to jail."

Holding out his palm, Gorobei said, "A man's got to live."

The nerve of him, expecting payment in addition to his freedom! "Well, I've got the law to uphold," Hirata said, resting his hand on the hilt of his sword. "Come along."

"Wait! What I have is so good, you should be glad to pay what it's worth." Gorobei added slyly, "If you don't, I bet Police Commissioner Hoshina will."

Hirata puffed out his breath. Clearly, Gorobei knew about the rivalry between Sano and Hoshina. If Hirata didn't pay, Hoshina would jump to buy information that might help him solve the case before Sano did. Hirata couldn't let that happen. Nor did he want to leave Yoshiwara empty-handed.

"All right," he said grudgingly.

They went into an alley behind a cookhouse where men labored over steaming pots, preparing food for brothels. Smoke that smelled of garlic and roasting fish drifted through the alley. Hirata and Gorobei haggled over the price. The following horse insisted Hirata pay cash in advance. Hirata reluctantly agreed; coins changed hands.

"This had better be good," he said.

Gorobei rummaged inside his coat and removed a wad of papers, which he handed to Hirata.

In the dim light from the cookhouse doors, Hirata examined the papers. They consisted of small pages of fine white rice paper, covered with black characters and folded in half. When Hirata unfolded them, he saw that their edges were ragged, as though they'd been torn out of a binding. Oily stains blotched the outer sheet.

"A beggar I know found it the morning after the murder," Gorobei said, "while he was scavenging food out of the garbage containers behind the Owariya."

Hirata read the beginning of the top page:

Life in Yoshiwara can be such a bore. Even though I am Lady Wisteria, the favorite of the quarter, I see the same people and do the same old things time after time. But last night, something interesting happened.

A thrill of excitation coursed through Hirata. This was a segment of the missing pillow book.

12

The Pillow Book of Lady Wisteria

Life in Yoshiwara can be such a bore. Even though I am Lady Wisteria, the favorite of the quarter, I see the same people and do the same old things time after time. But last night, something interesting happened.

I was at a party, playing cards with the guests, and I was tired and wishing I could just go to bed, when I felt someone watching me. I looked up and saw a man standing in the doorway. He was so handsome that my heart began beating fast and hard. I stared at him. He stared back, with a little smile on his face. I turned away because I was ashamed that this stranger had seen my feelings. But I can tell when a man wants me, and I knew he did. While I dealt cards, I waited for him to approach me.

"Who is that man in the doorway?" I whispered to one of the other courtesans.

"What man?" she said.

When I looked up again, he was gone.

I have seen him often since that night. Three days ago he was standing on a balcony, watching me promenade to the *ageya*. Two days ago he came to another party where I was entertaining. Yesterday, while I was dressing in my room, I looked out the window and saw him pacing the street in front of the house. But he always vanishes as soon as he knows I've seen him! He never speaks to me. No one seems to know who he is, and I've asked everyone. What does his strange behavior mean? I fear him, but not as much as I want to know him. I, who have known so many men and never cared about any of them!

Today I was shopping with my *yarite* in the marketplace, when I sensed him near me. Instead of looking at him, I turned and hurried away through the stalls. I heard him following, but I didn't look back. I didn't stop until I reached the alley inside the back wall. I turned around. There he stood, so handsome and strong, his smile so mysterious.

"Who are you?" I said, frightened and out of breath. "Why are you doing this?"

"I am the Herd Boy," he said in a strange accent. "You are the Weaver Girl. Today we finally meet on the River of Heaven."

He was referring to the legend about two constellations that are supposed to be lovers. They cross once a year in autumn. Well, I've heard a lot of poetic speeches from men, including that one. Usually I just laugh inside because they sound so silly. But there was something about him that made my legs go weak and my heart pound. We stood there gazing into each other's eyes. Then I heard my *ya-rite* calling me.

"I must go," I said.

He nodded and bowed, and I left.

But we had already fallen in love.

He's from Hokkaido, in the far north, and that's why his accent is strange. I won't write his name, because someone might read this, and I would rather keep him as much to myself as I can. I don't want every nosy gossip in Yoshiwara chattering about us. Since that day in the alley, we've been meeting often, always in secret, because he has no money for appointments with me. I sneak out of parties to the alley where he waits. When my clients fall asleep, I steal downstairs and let him in the back door. We make love behind the screen in my room, careful to be quiet so we won't wake up my client.

Yesterday, after we'd finished and were lying together in the moonlight, he whispered: "When winter comes to Hokkaido, the snow piles up in deep drifts that almost bury the houses."

He ran his hand along my hip. "Your body is as white and pure and beautiful as those snowdrifts. I wish I could show them to you. How would you like to see Hokkaido?"

My heart filled with joy, because I knew he was asking me to go away with him.

"In Hokkaido you'll be my wife," he said. "You'll never come back to this place of shame and suffering."

"But you can't afford to buy my freedom," I said. "And there's no escape from Yoshiwara."

"Love will find a way," he said, and he smiled.

Tonight is the night. All our plans are made. I will put the sleeping potion in Lord Mitsuyoshi's wine. After he's asleep, I will steal outside to my beloved. We will flee Yoshiwara forever. I know this is a dangerous undertaking. But he's clever. He has friends to help us. There's a man who owns a teahouse in Suruga. He'll let us stay there until I can buy new clothes and my beloved gets money and provisions for the journey. If the teahouse turns out to be unsafe, there's a noodle shop in Fukagawa that will take us in. But we won't stay around Edo for long. Soon we'll be on the northern highway, bound for the snows of Hokkaido.

I tremble with excitement.

How can I bear to wait the long hours until night, when my beloved will come for me?

Ah, freedom!

The excerpt from the pillow book lay in Sano's office, on the desk where Sano, Reiko, and Hirata had placed it after reading Lady Wisteria's story. They sat in silence, looking expectantly at each other.

"This could be the key to finding Lady Wisteria and solving the case," Sano said as his hope vied with caution.

"Just when we need it most," Hirata said.

Sano had come home from Yoshiwara late that evening to find Reiko waiting for him. Hirata had arrived moments later, and they'd discussed the other results of their inquiries, which had reached a dead end. Sano had questioned the owner and employees of the Owariya, and they'd confirmed Fujio's story that he'd left the party for only an instant—not long enough to go upstairs, stab Lord Mitsuyoshi, and abduct Wisteria. Detective Fukida had turned up witnesses who'd seen Treasury Minister Nitta on the street in Yoshiwara, but none besides Fujio who could place Nitta near the Owariya after he'd left the party. Detective Marume had learned that Nitta was patron to many courtesans besides Wisteria. Sano had searched Fujio's home in Imado and found nothing. He and Hirata had reluctantly agreed that they couldn't pursue the leads on Lord Mitsuyoshi's enemies without angering the shogun. And since Reiko's efforts had failed to produce clues, the discovery of the pillow book was a welcome development.

"It seems almost too good to be true," Reiko said, voicing the thought on everyone's mind. "And we've encountered false clues in the past."

"I did think it was too coincidental that I ran into Gorobei and he happened to have the pages," Hirata said. "But after I bought them, I showed them to people at Wisteria's brothel. They thought the pages resembled what they'd seen in her book, but she was careful to keep anyone from getting a close look at it. Besides, most of the courtesans there can't read. Nor can any of the servants. They wouldn't recognize the text. But there's no reason to believe the pages aren't from Wisteria's book."

He spoke as if trying to convince himself in spite of the lack of proof, and Sano guessed why Hirata wanted so much for his clue to be genuine. They'd not yet talked about the *miai*, but Hirata's careworn face told Sano that the marriage negotiations had gone wrong. Hirata must be anxious to make up for taking time off from his duties, and to succeed at his work even in the midst of a personal crisis.

Reiko held a page closer to the lantern, examining it carefully. "The language is simple. The calligraphy is crude. And look at all the crossed-out mistakes. This is what one would expect of a peasant woman who'd learned a little reading and writing but had no formal education."

Sano heard uncertainty in her voice. In the past Reiko had been quick to make up her own mind, and he realized how much self-doubt the Black Lotus case had instilled in her. During that investigation he'd battled her convictions and wanted her to yield to his; yet he now regretted that she was deferring to his judgment at a time when he needed an independent opinion. Sano wished he could be sure of the pillow book's authenticity, for he had his own doubts about it.

"Would you please read a page aloud?" he said to Reiko.

She complied. Sano listened, frowning because what he'd noticed while reading the words grew more apparent upon hearing them. They didn't sound like Wisteria, though he couldn't define exactly why not.

Reiko ceased reading. "What is it?" she said, looking curiously at Sano.

What he'd omitted telling Reiko about the case now enmeshed him in a thickening tangle of deceit. He couldn't voice his concerns about the pillow book without admitting he'd known Wisteria. If he did admit he'd known the courtesan, Reiko would ask why he hadn't said so before. And if she learned the reason now, his evasiveness would hurt her more than honesty would have at the start.

"It's too bad the pages came without the cover," he said. "That would have been easily recognized by people who'd seen Lady Wisteria's pillow book."

Reiko wore a quizzical expression that told him she knew he hadn't said what he was really thinking and wondered why. But she didn't ask. Sano saw Hirata watching him. Hirata had known about Sano's relationship with Wisteria since Sano had told him on the way home from Yoshiwara that first day, and Sano was glad he could trust Hirata to keep the secret, even from Reiko.

"I searched for the cover," Hirata said, "but the garbage had been taken away and burned, and the alley swept clean. If the cover was ever there, it's gone now."

"That brings us to the question of why the pages were in the alley," Sano said.

"Wisteria could have thrown them away," said Hirata. "Maybe she didn't need to write anymore because she was starting a new life. But she didn't want anyone to read her private thoughts, so she tore up the book, then put the pages in the garbage as she and her lover were leaving the Owariya."

"But she was a runaway courtesan," Reiko said, "and she would know her master would look for her." Brothel proprietors hired searchers to track down fugitives, and added the cost of the search to the debt of women who got caught. "Why would she leave clues to where she planned to go? Why not take the book with her, or burn it?"

"Maybe she wasn't smart enough to think of that," Hirata said.

"The book could be a fake, with misleading details about her lover and her plans, that she put in the alley, to thwart anyone looking for her," Reiko said.

Hirata defended his find: "Maybe she just didn't think anyone would care enough about getting her back that they would bother looking for her pillow book."

"Probably no one would have cared that much, if Wisteria hadn't left Lord Mitsuyoshi dead in her room." Sano followed this line of reasoning to a thought that disturbed him. "What if she didn't know he'd died? That would explain why she carelessly tossed away the pages—if indeed she did. Maybe she'd already left Yoshiwara by the time Mitsuyoshi was stabbed. Certainly, there's nothing in the pillow book to indicate that she witnessed the murder."

Reiko and Hirata's somber silence acknowledged the possibility that he was right.

Sano picked up the pages, then set them down. "In that case, these would do us no good, even if they're for real, because finding Wisteria won't help us identify the killer."

The house was so quiet that they could hear the coals in the braziers crumbling into ash. The lantern's flame flickered as the oil burned low. Yet Sano needed to keep hope alive.

"Still, I believe Lady Wisteria was in some way involved with the murder and does have knowledge that's critical to our investigation," he said. "The pillow book could be a genuine clue to her whereabouts. We'll treat it as such, while we try to verify whether it is or isn't.

"Hirata-san, tomorrow I want you to check out the Suruga teahouses and the noodle shops of Fukagawa. Also, send out a notice to the neighborhood headmen throughout Edo, ordering them to report any men from Hokkaido seen in their areas. I'll send search parties out on the northern highway to look for a traveling couple, in case Wisteria and her lover have already left town."

"Shall I find out if any of the women I know have heard anything about Wisteria's secret lover from Hokkaido?"

Reiko said. She looked chastened by her failure to learn anything today, and eager for a second chance.

"That's a good idea," Sano said. "The lover is a potential witness, and his name, or even a description of him, would help us find him and Wisteria."

Nodding, Reiko smiled in thanks.

"We'll keep the pages a secret," Sano said. "Police Commissioner Hoshina is shadowing every bit of ground I cover, interrogating the same people. The pillow book is the one clue we have that won't fall into his hands."

Sano rose, adding in grim conclusion, "It could also be our only hope of beating him to the solution to the case before he sabotages us."

13

Chamberlain Yanagisawa's estate was isolated in a separate compound in Edo Castle, high on the hill and near the palace. Around this fortress within a fortress, spikes protruded from the top of the stone wall to discourage trespassers, and the cold, clear night vibrated with the alertness of many guards at the gates, perched on the roofs of the buildings, and hidden in the grounds. The mansion they protected was a maze of interconnected wings, with soldiers' barracks surrounding principal retainers' quarters. At the center lay the private domain of the chamberlain.

Here, Police Commissioner Hoshina stood at the threshold of the bedchamber. The doorway framed a view of Yanagisawa, who reclined on cushions inside, his elegant profile outlined by the lantern-light. With his silk kimono, trousers, and surcoat arranged in still, lustrous folds, he looked as perfectly composed as a painting. Deep in thought, he didn't appear aware that Hoshina had come. Yet Hoshina knew

Yanagisawa had heard the alarm given by the nightingale walk—the specially constructed floor that emitted loud chirps under approaching footsteps. Yanagisawa knew whose arrival the alarm signaled, because Hoshina was the only person welcome in his bedchamber.

But their relations had been strained since the murder of Lord Mitsuyoshi, and Hoshina hesitated, wondering whether to interrupt Yanagisawa's reverie.

Then Yanagisawa lifted a silver tobacco pipe to his lips. He exhaled smoke, and turned toward Hoshina. As their gazes met, Hoshina felt his heartbeat quicken and his senses come alive, as they always did when he was with Yanagisawa, even after two years together. But Yanagisawa wore an air of abstracted calm; he merely gestured for Hoshina to join him.

"I looked for you earlier," Hoshina said, entering the room and kneeling near Yanagisawa.

"I had business to attend to," Yanagisawa said.

That he didn't say where he'd been irked Hoshina. Although Hoshina accepted that he was accountable to Yanagisawa while the chamberlain owed him no explanations, Hoshina often found his subordinate status difficult to bear. His passionate love for Yanagisawa only worsened the damage to his pride and the hurt caused him by Yanagisawa's cool greeting.

Nonetheless eager to please his master, Hoshina said, "I spent the day investigating the murder, and I've turned up some interesting facts. Treasury Minister Nitta has implicated a *hokan* named Fujio. Unfortunately, Sano got to Fujio before I did. But what Sano doesn't know is that one of my spies—a maid at the Owariya—saw Fujio on the stairway just before the murder was discovered. She saved the information for me."

The chamberlain nodded as if he'd not really listened, his expression inscrutable. During their affair, Yanagisawa had been generous about sharing his money, his authority, and his bed with Hoshina; yet sometimes he became aloof and taciturn. Hoshina never knew when these moods would occur, or what caused them. He suspected that his lover adopted the moods to keep him at a distance, because a man so powerful yet so insecure as Yanagisawa didn't like anyone to get too close.

"Nor does Sano have the facts that my other spies have uncovered about Treasury Minister Nitta and Lady Wisteria's chaperone." Hoshina heard himself speaking louder to bridge the distance between him and Yanagisawa. "When Nitta left Yoshiwara the night of the murder, he didn't go straight home. He rode a short distance with his entourage, then returned alone to the quarter and bribed the guards to let him back in. The guards didn't tell Hirata when he interviewed them, because he only asked whether they'd let Nitta out, and they're in my pay. Nitta could have sneaked back inside the Owariya and stabbed Lord Mitsuyoshi."

Instead of replying, Yanagisawa gazed into space, smoking his pipe. Hoshina wondered whether the mood indicated boredom with their affair. Was he about to become one of Yanagisawa's many cast-off paramours? Hoshina experienced a pang of dismay, because his career, as well as his happiness, depended on Yanagisawa.

"And Mitsuyoshi had been carrying on a flirtation with the *yarite*." Hoshina, aware that he'd begun nervously clenching and unclenching his muscles, stilled himself. "It seems that he promised to take Momoko as his concubine. He liked to toy with people, but the old fool took him seriously, and when she found out he'd been joking, she was furious. So she did know him, and she had good reason to want him dead, which contradicts what she said earlier."

"So you have incriminating evidence against all three suspects," Yanagisawa said. "That makes one as likely a culprit as any other. Therefore, you're no closer to solving the case than you were yesterday."

Praise from his lover always exhilarated Hoshina; criticism like this was torture. As he gazed at Yanagisawa, resentment tinged his desire, because their sexual bond gave Yanagisawa all the more power over him.

"Sooner or later, my evidence will accumulate and point

to the killer," Hoshina defended himself. "Don't you care?"

"I care as much as the case deserves," Yanagisawa said.

"What's that supposed to mean?" Hoshina demanded, stung by his lover's indifference. That they'd often exchanged private confidences seemed forgotten now; Yanagisawa was deliberately shutting Hoshina out. Hoshina rose, unable to sit still any longer. "Are you saying that the murder of the shogun's heir doesn't matter to you? That you don't care whether the killer is caught? After I've been chasing clues and witnesses for the past two days?"

He saw a warning gleam in Yanagisawa's eyes, but plunged recklessly ahead: "Or don't you care whether it's Sano or I who solves the case?"

Yanagisawa tilted his head, regarding Hoshina with detachment. "Why are you so angry at me?"

"I'm not angry." Turning away, Hoshina took a deep breath, swallowing his emotions. "Just confused. I expected you to take my side in the meeting with Sano and the shogun. But you left me flapping in the wind like a flag on the back of a soldier who rides into battle thinking he's leading a charge, while his army sits on the sidelines. Why didn't you join my attack on Sano?"

Whining like a petulant woman was no way to retain Yanagisawa's interest or respect; but Hoshina couldn't help himself. He heard the rustle of silk as Yanagisawa came to stand behind him. Their closeness increased his agitation.

"I'm sorry if you feel hurt because you think I deserted you," Yanagisawa said, "but remember that I'm the one who leads the charges. If you dash off on your own, don't expect me to follow. That was the wrong time to expose your rivalry with Sano. My silence should have made that obvious to you. If you're disappointed by the results of your actions, that's what you deserve."

The rebuke struck fear into Hoshina, for he had much more to lose than Yanagisawa's affection. The chamberlain had ruined men unwise enough to cross him, and those banished, executed, or assassinated included former partners. Though their affair had begun with mutual expectations of true, eternal love, and Yanagisawa had at first seemed happier and more tolerant than before, Hoshina knew old habits died hard.

"I don't understand your objections," Hoshina said, facing Yanagisawa. "I came to Edo to advance my career in the *bakufu* and prove myself capable of managing the police force." While he enjoyed his privileged status as Yanagisawa's lover, he needed to show he was worthy of his post and hadn't just seduced his way to a high rank. "But Sano is a constant hindrance. How will I demonstrate what I can do, while he and his private army of detectives are always getting the important cases, winning the major victories, and reaping all the shogun's esteem? Don't you want me to succeed in the job you brought me to Edo to do?"

"I thought you came here to serve me as my chief retainer," Yanagisawa said, and disapproval shadowed his face.

Hoshina involuntarily retreated a step as he perceived how selfish his aims had sounded. "Yes, of course I did. Serving you is my first wish." He hastened to appeal to Yanagisawa's interests: "Don't you want Sano out of the way? Forgive me if you think I've gone against your wishes, but I'm only continuing what you started years ago. This may be the best opportunity to get rid of Sano forever."

"Now is not the time," Yanagisawa reiterated. "Lord Mitsuyoshi's murder has created many opportunities besides the one you're so eager to seize. You are viewing the situation with too narrow a focus. You've not been in Edo long enough to see the larger picture, or appreciate serious concerns that extend beyond the present time." Impatience colored his voice. "I'm not trying to cheat you of what you want—far from it. So believe me when I say that if my plans go as well as I expect, Sano will become a matter of insignificance to us both."

"What plans?" Hoshina was completely perplexed; yet he could appreciate the irony of his situation. Night after night, they lay together, naked and vulnerable. Yanagisawa trusted Hoshina with his body—but not all his secrets. He considered knowledge the ultimate power, which he never yielded.

Hoshina understood this, but Yanagisawa's distrust hurt him deeply.

"I went to see my son today," Yanagisawa said.

The abrupt change of subject disconcerted and baffled Hoshina. Frowning as he attempted to follow the twists and turns of his lover's devious mind, Hoshina said, "Which one?"

He knew the chamberlain had at least four sons, all born to different women other than his wife. They lived with their mothers in estates outside Edo. Hoshina had learned of their existence via gossip in the *bakufu*, not from Yanagisawa. He'd heard Yanagisawa periodically visited the children, though the chamberlain had never before mentioned that to Hoshina either.

"Yoritomo. The eldest. He's sixteen years old now," Yanagisawa said.

That boy was the child of a former palace lady-in-waiting, Hoshina recalled. The lady, a Tokugawa relative, had been a beauty with whom Yanagisawa had enjoyed a brief affair.

"Is something wrong? Is your son ill?" Hoshina hoped that a mere family problem, and not dissatisfaction with their life together, had turned Yanagisawa cold toward him.

"Quite the contrary." A faint, proud smile touched Yanagisawa's mouth. "Yoritomo is the image of myself when I was young. Not as clever or strong-willed, of course. He'll do very well indeed."

Jealousy pierced Hoshina like a hot needle in his heart. He'd never cared much about the relationship between Yanagisawa and his sons; yet he hated for Yanagisawa to praise anyone after criticizing him.

"I'm glad you're pleased by your son," Hoshina said stiffly, "but what has he got to do with the murder case? Why is he more important than destroying a man who's defeated and humiliated you so many times?"

Yanagisawa lifted his eyebrows in surprise. "I've just told you."

"But I don't understand."

"You will."

Yanagisawa's expression softened, but Hoshina perceived this as condescension rather than love. He dreaded offending Yanagisawa, yet couldn't relinquish his campaign against his rival.

"Sano's influence in the *bakufu* grows daily," Hoshina said. "His allies include many high officials. And if he solves this case, he'll rise another notch in the shogun's estimation—while everyone else, including us, moves down. He could eventually take your place. Your treatment of him has given him ample cause to hate you. I think he's biding his time until he gains enough power to strike."

"He won't," Yanagisawa said with offhand confidence.

"Because of the truce between him and you?" Hoshina couldn't keep the scorn out of his voice. "Your truce is but an unspoken agreement that will last only as long as you both honor it. I say we should take the offensive, break the truce before Sano does, and strike at him now, while he's vulnerable."

"I'm aware of the hazards of a truce," Yanagisawa said, reproachful. "At present they're of minor concern to me, because I have the advantage over Sano."

"What advantage is that?" Baffled beyond endurance, Hoshina burst out, "I hate it when you speak in riddles! Why won't you explain what's going on?"

The chamberlain appeared unaffected by Hoshina's anger. "Certain things are best not spoken outright," Yanagisawa said. "Not even my house is free of spies. I've told you my plans, and it's up to you to figure them out. But I will make one thing clear: You shall not break the truce."

Hoshina started to protest, but the adamant expression on Yanagisawa's face silenced him. Then Yanagisawa chuckled.

"Don't look so disappointed," he said. "Just be patient, and I promise you'll be quite satisfied with what happens."

Although Hoshina wished he could believe Yanagisawa, he couldn't place his faith in schemes he didn't understand, or his trust in a man so unpredictable as his lover. He still considered Sano a threat to the chamberlain's power and his own rise in the *bakufu*. Hoshina must find a way to advance himself at Sano's expense, without defying his master. But how? Frustrated ambition roiled inside him.

Yanagisawa smiled; his dark eyes kindled like liquid fire. "That's enough talk of politics for tonight," he said.

Whatever of his lover's other hints had evaded Hoshina, he could interpret very well the innuendo in Yanagisawa's voice, the curve of his mouth, and the hand he extended. Desire flared in Hoshina; yet he resisted surrender even as he grew erect. How he hated for the chamberlain to rebuke, baffle, taunt, and thwart him, then expect pleasure from him! Hoshina's pride rebelled. For a moment he hated Yanagisawa.

But need prevailed over resentment. Hoshina craved sex as proof that Yanagisawa still loved him. He let Yanagisawa draw him down onto the bed, the only place in the world where they were equals.

Outside their chamber, Lady Yanagisawa stood peering in through a chink in the wall. She watched the naked bodies of her husband and his lover entwine, grapple, and heave. Her face remained impassive while she listened to their gasps and moans. As they convulsed in climax, a silent breath eased from her. Then she turned and walked away down the dark, vacant corridor.

14

Troops marched through the Nihonbashi merchant district. Their torches smoked in the night air; their footsteps shattered the quiet. They stopped at each house and pounded their fists against closed doors and shutters.

"Open up!" they shouted. "By orders of the shogun's *sōsakan-sama*, come outside and show yourselves!"

Men, women, and children, dressed in their nightclothes, poured into the street. They shivered with cold and fright. The neighborhood headman herded them into a line. He and the captain of Sano's search team walked down the line, matching each person to a name on the official neighborhood roster, looking for unlisted women. Soldiers raided the buildings in search of anyone hidden there. They burst into a gambling den, interrupting card games and hustling the gamblers outside.

The commotion roused Lady Wisteria and Lightning from their slumber in the back room of the gambling den. Lightning threw off the quilt that covered them and leapt upright, fully alert, while Wisteria lay in groggy confusion.

"What is it?" she mumbled.

"Get up," Lightning ordered in a hoarse whisper. "Those are soldiers out there. We have to go."

Terror jolted Wisteria awake, for she understood that the soldiers had come for her. Lightning grabbed her hand, yanking her to her feet.

"Hurry!" he urged.

Wisteria was glad they'd slept in their clothes in case of an emergency. While she scrambled for her shoes, he snatched up her bundle of possessions. He hurried her outside to the alley, just as the soldiers rushed through the curtained doorway between the gambling den and their room.

The bitter cold immediately chilled Wisteria. Her cloak billowed open in the wind, but she had no time to fasten it. Lightning raced along the alley, towing her by the hand. She tripped and fell, emitting a shriek of dismay.

"Quiet!" Lightning whispered furiously.

His speed kept her moving. Her knees scraped painfully against the rough ground until she regained her footing. They veered into another alley, then stumbled through the ruins of a burned house. Wisteria could no longer hear the soldiers, but still Lightning dragged her onward. A thick crescent moon above the roofs illuminated their way along a route that he followed with the ease of an animal that knows its territory.

They clambered down the bank of a narrow canal, and as they plunged waist-deep through frigid water, the muddy bottom tugged off Wisteria's shoes. Barefoot because courtesans never wore socks, she limped up the opposite bank. Stones and debris hurt her feet. She and Lightning ran through a maze of more dark alleys that stank from privies, garbage, and night soil bins. Wisteria was freezing, her wet garments clinging to her like a coat of ice. Her heart pounded; gasps heaved her chest. But Lightning wasn't even breathing hard. His hand around hers was warm. Would they keep running until she died?

At last Lightning halted at a building. Wisteria squatted, breathless and limp with exhaustion. Barred windows flanked a door. Lightning knocked: two slow beats, a pause, then three quick ones. The door opened a crack, and light shone into the alley. A man's face, thuggish and unshaven, appeared in the crack. The man eyed Lightning, then opened the door. As Lightning pulled Wisteria into a passage with an earth floor and bare rafters, she saw that the man held a dagger; tattoos on his arms marked him as a gangster. But Wisteria was too glad for sanctuary to care that she recognized this place and knew its evils.

"Have the soldiers searched this neighborhood yet?" Lightning asked the man.

The man shook his head. Lightning muttered a curse, and Wisteria feared they must go back out in the night. But Lightning took her down the corridor, past rooms enclosed by partitions. Lamplight shining through the tattered paper silhouetted pairs of embracing, writhing human figures. Wisteria heard moans and grunts; she smelled urine, sweat, and sex. As she and Lightning entered a room where a torn lantern hung above a floor made of wood slats that bordered a large, round, sunken tub of water, Wisteria wanted to laugh and cry. This place was a public bath that doubled as an illegal brothel. She'd escaped one whorehouse, only to take shelter in another.

But Wisteria was so cold that she trembled uncontrollably, her teeth chattering. The steaming water in the tub seemed like a vision of heaven. Lightning had already begun shedding his wet, filthy garments. Wisteria tore off hers as fast as her shaking hands could manage, but kept the cloth around her head. Her battered feet left bloody spots on the floor. She and Lightning scrubbed themselves with bags of soap, poured buckets of water over their bodies, then sat in the tub, immersed up to their shoulders.

The hot water engulfed Wisteria; she sighed in bliss. She ignored the scum floating on the water and the room's odor of mildew. Too overwhelmed by relief and fatigue to care what happened next, Wisteria closed her eyes, leaned back against the rim of the tub, and drowsed.

"Don't get too comfortable," Lightning said. "We can't stay. The soldiers will come eventually. We'll have to leave before then."

"Please, let's wait just a little while longer," Wisteria murmured.

Lightning shifted restlessly; the water bobbed. "No place in Edo is safe. We should have taken to the highway this morning, like I wanted to. But no—you wanted to stay."

His accusing tone set off a warning signal in Wisteria's head and jarred her out of a doze. She saw the malevolent gleam in Lightning's eyes, which shifted rapidly as he stared at her.

"Because of you, we're being hunted like animals," he said. "Because of you, we may not live to enjoy your freedom."

Wisteria sat up straight, clasping her knees to her chest. "But we have to stay," she said, needing to justify herself, though fearful of defying him. "That was part of the plan."

"Your plan. Not mine. I was a fool to agree to it." Lightning snorted in derision. "Why should we care what happens about the murder? We'll leave tonight."

"I care. I have to know," Wisteria said. "We can't go yet!"

Earlier today, Lightning had fetched her a news broadsheet containing a story about the *sōsakan-sama*'s investigation. She'd read that her *yarite* had been arrested. She needed to find out what happened to Momoko, and whether other people became implicated in the crime. And she might never hear the news in the distant province where she and Lightning planned to settle. She must watch events unfold—in spite of the danger.

Ire darkened Lightning's face. "Is satisfying your curiosity more important to you than my life?"

"No! Of course not!" Wisteria squirmed away, but her back struck the wall of the tub.

A bitter laugh burst from him. "I should have known. You're just using me. You don't really care about me."

"But I do care," Wisteria said. Under the water she reached for him, and her hand found his leg. It flinched at her touch. "I love you." If this intense, fearful attraction equaled love, then she did love Lightning. "Your safety is more important to me than my own." Because without him, she couldn't survive.

He shook his head, spurning persuasion. But as she coiled her hand around his manhood and stroked him, she felt him swell and harden. Arousal parted his lips and arched his neck.

"If you love me, you wouldn't have gotten me into all this trouble," Lightning said, his voice harshened by desire and anger at her attempt to manipulate him.

Disbelief startled Wisteria. She withdrew her hand. "*I* got *you* in trouble?" Indignant, she forgot caution. "Excuse me, but I'm not the reason we're being hunted. I'm not the one who almost ruined everything for us."

"Oh, so you're blaming me?"

The water sloshed as Lightning moved toward her. "Well, let me remind you that it was your plan that started everything."

"My plan would have worked fine if you'd stuck to it." Wisteria felt his hand close around her ankle, and she pulled back in alarm. "Let me go."

"You don't tell me what to do," he said, holding tight. As she tried to kick loose from him, his breaths came faster and harder. "I make my own decisions. I'm not your servant. I don't have to listen to you or anyone else."

Now Wisteria's own temper sparked. The water seemed to grow hotter; sweat trickled down her face. "You should listen," she cried. "Because this time you made a terrible mistake. Our problems are all your fault."

"Our problem is that you got carried away by anger," Lightning said. "Your grudges will be the death of us."

There was truth in what he said, Wisteria knew. The same outrage and self-righteousness that had inspired her plan was surging through her now. The bitter animosity that filled her heart now focused on Lightning.

She shrilled, "What about your grudges? Anyone who offends you had better watch out, because you don't think before you act. You're like a wild beast with no sense!"

"What did you call me?" His face distorted, teeth bared in a snarl, and his nostrils flared, Lightning indeed looked more animal than human. "You think I'm stupid? You're the one who's stupid if you think I'll let you insult me. I'll show you who's in charge around here."

Lightning jerked on her ankle, pulling her underwater. Wisteria shrieked as her head submerged. The hot water burned her eyes, filled her nose, gurgled in her mouth. She flailed her arms, fighting to raise herself above the surface, but he had hold of both her legs now, and he was too strong for her. Desperate, Wisteria writhed. Her body smacked against the hard bottom of the tub. She resisted the terrible urge to take a breath. Then Lightning let go. She burst up into the steamy air, gulping for breath. Rivulets streamed off her drenched head-cloth and over her face. In her blurred vision, Lightning loomed huge and monstrous.

"Apologize for what you said!" he commanded.

"No!" Wisteria was too incensed by his treatment of her. "You are a beast. I hate you!"

He planted his hands on her shoulders and shoved her downward. She strained against him while her neck, then her chin, sank beneath the water. "Somebody please help me!"

The noises from the couples in the brothel continued; no one answered her call. Forced below the surface, Wisteria clawed and kicked Lightning. Her heel found his groin, and she heard him yell, the sound distorted by the dark, turbulent water that surrounded her. His body heaved up, then crashed down upon her with a tremendous splash. His solid, muscular limbs imprisoned her. An airless vacuum trapped her screams in her throat and constricted her lungs. Her heart felt ready to explode. Panic filled Wisteria. Helpless, she tossed her head from side to side.

Lightning hauled her up from the water. Her head broke the surface and she inhaled a huge, gulping breath. Then he flung her out of the tub. Her right side hit the slatted floor.

Pain jarred her elbow and hip. As she rolled, stunned and gasping, onto her back, Lightning straddled her. He shook her so that her head repeatedly bumped the floor.

"Are you sorry you insulted me?" he demanded.

"Yes!" Wisteria screamed, her defiance at last subdued by his brutality. "Please don't hurt me!"

"Do you love me?"

"I love you!"

"From now on you'll do as I say?"

"Yes!"

"Because if you don't, I'll kill you. Do you understand?"

And he would. Wisteria hadn't fully appreciated his capacity for violence until now. "Yes. Yes!" she cried.

Climbing off her, Lightning stood. His wet, naked bulk heaved with his breaths. He grinned in cruel triumph.

"Next time I won't forgive you so easily," he said, then picked up his clothes and stalked out of the room.

Wisteria lay bruised and aching and shivering. How much she wished she'd never met Lightning! Whatever mistakes he had made, she'd made the most serious one— thinking she could handle him. Tears seeped from her closed eyes. The final stages of her plan required Lightning's cooperation, but she had serious doubts about her ability to manipulate him anymore. If she couldn't, what would she do?

She knew now that in spite of her passion for Lightning, they couldn't live together. She must get away from him before they disagreed again and he made good on his threat.

15

"Excuse me, *Sōsakan-sama*, but you have visitors."

Sano looked up from his desk, past the detectives gathered in his office for the morning meeting at which he issued orders for the day. In the doorway stood the manservant who'd interrupted the meeting.

"Who are they?" Sano asked, surprised because callers rarely arrived so early.

"The Council of Elders."

"The Council of Elders!" Sano rose in amazement. He dismissed his men, then hurried to the reception room. There he found three of the five officials seated in a row before the alcove. Pallid daylight and cold air seeped through the windows; the charcoal braziers emitted whiffs of heat that dissipated at waist level. Sano knelt and bowed.

"Welcome," he said. "This is an honor."

The elders had never called at his house. Whenever they wanted to see him, they summoned him to their chamber at the palace. This visit had a clandestine air, underscored by the absence of Senior Elder Makino.

The man at the center of the row spoke: "I hope we are not inconveniencing you." This was Ohgami Kaoru, in charge of the regime's relations with the daimyo. He had white hair and pensive, youthful features.

"Not at all," Sano said.

"How kind of you to receive us so promptly," said the elder seated at Ohgami's right. Uemori Yoichi was short and squat, with baggy jowls. He was the shogun's chief military adviser.

"It's my privilege," Sano said, as he wondered why the council had come, particularly the third man, Kato Kinhide, who was an expert on national finance. Ohgami was Sano's sometime ally, and Uemori had never overtly opposed him, but Kato was an outright foe. Sano turned to Kato, appraising the broad, bland face with eyes and mouth like slits in worn leather. A suspicion formed in Sano's mind.

"We're glad you're available," Kato said, "when you must be very busy with the murder investigation."

Sano saw his suspicion confirmed. Kato would never favor Sano with his presence, unless to talk about the important topic of the moment.

After tea and cakes had been served, pipes lit, and pleasantries exchanged, Ohgami said, "Sōsakan-sama, we've come to bring you news."

This surprised Sano, because information customarily flowed from him to the elders, not the other way. He understood why Ohgami might help him, but not the others. And why did they want to talk here instead of at the palace?

Ohgami carefully tapped ashes out of his pipe, forming a line on the smoking tray in front of him. He looked toward Uemori, who said, "You may be aware that Lord Matsudaira Dakuemon was in Yoshiwara the night of the murder."

Sano nodded, because Lord Dakuemon was on his list of people to interview.

"Dakuemon is a member of a Tokugawa branch clan," Uemori continued. He sucked greedily on his pipe, and a deep, phlegmy cough shook his loose jowls. "He's a bit older than Mitsuyoshi was, and not quite as personable nor favored by the court." Uemori paused, then spoke in a tone laden with significance: "But now that Mitsuyoshi is dead . . ."

Lord Dakuemon was a strong contender for the position of heir to the regime, Sano thought.

"Perhaps you should pay special attention to Lord Dakuemon's movements on that night," Uemori said.

That Uemori had handed him a new suspect alarmed as much as intrigued Sano, since this one was a Tokugawa clan member and therefore off-limits to him because of the shogun's prohibition against investigating Lord Mitsuyoshi's family, background, or enemies.

"You might also check into Sugita Fumio," said Kato. He refilled his pipe, measuring in the tobacco grain by grain.

"The head of the Judicial Council?" Sano said. This was the body that ranked just below the Council of Elders and supervised various government departments. "But Sugita wasn't in Yoshiwara that night."

"Perhaps you missed him," Kato said.

"Why might he be considered a suspect?" Sano hid his dismay at seeing another prominent man implicated in the murder.

"Many years ago Councilman Sugita wanted to marry a certain lady, but her family married her off to Lord Mitsuyoshi's father." Kato used the tongs on his smoking tray to search through the metal box of hot coals and drop precisely the right size ember into his pipe. "But Councilman Sugita still loves the lady and bears a grudge against her husband. Might his grudge not have extended to Mitsuyoshi, the offspring of her marriage?"

This story sounded far-fetched. "Is there other evidence to say that Councilman Sugita killed Lord Mitsuyoshi?" Sano turned to Uemori. "Or any that Lord Dakuemon did?"

"It's your duty to find evidence," Uemori said with stern reproof.

That personal interests lurked behind the men's guise of altruism became obvious to Sano. He knew that Sugita wanted a promotion to the Council of Elders, and had begun a campaign to oust Kato and take his place. What better way for Kato to defend himself than by incriminating Sugita in treasonous murder? Sano also knew that Uemori had a long-standing feud with Lord Dakuemon's father, who constantly lobbied the shogun to expel him from the council. Uemori wouldn't like Dakuemon to become the shogun's heir, because his father would gain power to ruin Uemori. That the elders wanted to enlist Sano in their war against their enemies didn't necessarily mean he should disregard their theories; yet he foresaw difficulties in determining whether Councilman Sugita or Lord Dakuemon were involved in the murder.

"You're aware that His Excellency has forbidden me to investigate Lord Mitsuyoshi's connections," Sano said. Of course the elders knew: They'd been present when the shogun issued the order. "How am I to use the information you've given me?"

A smile shifted the baggy skin of Uemori's face. "That is for you to decide."

Ohgami nodded. He'd added more ash to his smoking tray, in a pattern of crisscrossed lines.

A rush of anger flashed through Sano as he comprehended the elders' intentions toward him. They knew his tendency to place justice above duty. They expected him to defy the shogun's order and pursue Councilman Sugita and Lord Dakuemon as suspects. Whether or not either man was guilty, the scandal would ruin the reputations of both. Whether or not Sano solved the case by investigating them, he would suffer harsh punishment for his disobedience. But the elders would manipulate him without caring what happened to him.

Stifling his resentment, Sano addressed Ohgami: "Is there another suspect that you want to bring to my attention?"

"Oh, no," Ohgami said mildly. He regarded his ashes with the air of an artist contemplating his creation. "My only purpose here is to help my colleagues help you."

Sano's resentment turned to indignation because he understood Ohgami's real purpose. Ohgami was battling Senior

Elder Makino for control of the Council. He must have promised his two colleagues that he would help them destroy their enemies if they allied with him. Hence, he'd brought them here, safely away from Makino and the shogun, to draw Sano into his scheme.

"Many thanks for your concern," Sano forced himself to say.

He wasn't surprised that his ally would exploit him so callously, for self-interest dominated all relationships in the *bakufu*. Yet a powerful rage clenched his hands on the empty tea bowl he held. Sano stared at his guests, sitting smugly confident before him. He'd saved them and the entire city from the Black Lotus, but they would use him as if he were a rag for cleaning up messes, then crumple him and throw him away! Hatred tinged his vision with blood.

But his habit of maintaining outward calm was so strong that the men seemed to notice nothing amiss. They took their leave, and Sano sat alone, immobilized by fury, until a sharp pain in his left palm startled him. He looked down and saw that he'd crushed the fragile porcelain tea bowl. Blood oozed from his cut hand.

"Excuse me, *Sōsakan-sama*," the manservant said, bowing and entering the room.

"What do you want?" Sano said. His rage dissipated, leaving him shaken by his near loss of control. Since the Black Lotus case, his temper had gained a force that he found increasingly harder to discipline.

"More visitors are here to see you."

The women's quarter of the palace hummed with the chatter and bustle of the concubines and ladies-in-waiting as they bathed, dressed, and groomed themselves. Midori sat in the chamber of the shogun's mother, Lady Keisho-in. While other attendants combed Keisho-in's hair, Midori applied a mixture of white rice powder and camellia wax onto the old woman's face. Her hand automatically smeared and dabbed the makeup, but her thoughts centered on her urgent need to see Hirata. He'd not come to her last night, and the hours since she'd seen him at the *miai* yesterday seemed like an eternity.

"Aaghh!" Lady Keisho-in cried, recoiling from Midori; her round, wrinkled face bunched up in pain. "You've gotten makeup in my eye again. Can't you pay attention to what you're doing?"

"I'm sorry!" Midori snatched up a cloth and wiped at her mistress's eye, but Lady Keisho-in shoved her away.

"You're so absentminded lately," Keisho-in complained. "I can't bear to have you around me." She made a shooing gesture. "Get out!"

Glad of a reprieve from duty, Midori fled the palace. She was racing across the garden when she saw Hirata coming toward her.

"Hirata-*san*!" she called. He smiled; she hurled herself into his arms. As they embraced, she burst into tears. "I thought you would never come. I was so afraid you'd changed your feelings about me."

"Why would you think that?" Hirata said, his voice roughened by affection.

In this chill early morning, they had the garden to themselves, but he drew her into the pine grove where they'd met so many times before. The air was redolent with the clean, tangy scent of resin, the ground covered with a soft blanket of pine needles upon which they'd lain.

"You're shivering," Hirata said. He wrapped his own cloak around Midori and held her tight.

She basked in his nearness, sobbing. "After what my father said to yours, I was sure you must hate me."

"Nothing can change my love for you." Hirata held her shoulders and gazed at her with a sincerity that banished her fear. "What happened at the theater wasn't your fault." As she wept in relief now, he said, "Please believe that my family means no harm to yours. Why does your father think we're his enemies?"

Overcome by shame, Midori pulled away from Hirata, averting her face. "He gets all upset when it comes to the

Tokugawa or anyone associated with them," she whispered. "Because of what they did to our clan in the past."

"I see." Hirata's dubious tone said he didn't understand the eccentricity that made Lord Niu resent what other daimyo accepted. "Would he really try to kill my father?"

A sob choked Midori.

"Oh." Hirata paused. "Is he always like that?"

"Not always." Midori couldn't bear to tell Hirata that Lord Niu's bad spells were often worse. "Is your father still angry, do you think?" she ventured timidly. "Is he very much against the match?"

". . . I didn't have much chance to talk to him."

She could tell Hirata was trying to shield her from painful truth, and panic filled her because their marriage seemed even more impossible than ever, despite the increasing necessity of it. Every day Midori suffered from nausea; every day her body swelled larger with the new life growing in her.

"What are we going to do?" she cried.

"Maybe if we wait awhile," Hirata said, "the whole thing will blow over."

He spoke without hope, and the idea of delaying alarmed Midori. "How long should we wait?"

"At least a few days. Or maybe a month would be better."

"A month!" By then the pregnancy would be apparent to everyone. Midori feared that her disgrace would make both families even less amenable to the marriage. "That's too long!" Her voice rose in hysteria. "We have to do something now!"

"Forcing the issue right away would only hurt our chances." Hirata looked puzzled by her agitation. "We must be patient."

"I can't!"

"It's no use getting so upset," Hirata said. Taking her in his arms, he caressed her hair, her face, her bosom; passion strengthened his grip. "Calm down."

The amorous attentions she'd once welcomed now alarmed Midori. "No! Don't!" She tore free of Hirata.

"I'm sorry," Hirata said, chastened. "Forgive me."

She saw that he didn't understand why she'd rejected him, and she'd hurt his feelings. But she was scared to tell him about the child, or let him touch her and guess. Although refusing him now wouldn't protect her from what had already happened, she couldn't bear more forbidden intimacies.

"I should go," he said, backing out of the pine grove.

"No. Wait!" Midori lurched after Hirata and clung to him, weeping again.

He held her cautiously, but he spoke with a determination that gave her hope: "I'll be back soon. Don't worry. I'll find a way to make everything all right."

Hirata climbed off his horse beside a wooden notice board that stood at the foot of the Nihonbashi Bridge. As pedestrians streamed across the bridge, he pinned up a notice that read, "Anyone who has seen, heard of, or knows any man from Hokkaido, presently living in or formerly a resident of Edo, is ordered to report the information to His Excellency the Shogun's *Sōsakan-sama*."

Contemplating the notice, he frowned in frustration, because he'd already spent hours searching teahouses in Suruga for Lady Wisteria and her lover, but found naught. He began to doubt that the many notices he'd posted along the way would bring success. Tired, cold, and hungry now, he bought tea and a lunchbox of sushi from a passing vendor and perched on the bridge's railing.

Barges drifted down the canal below him. Crowds thronged the lanes and stalls outside the fish market on the bank. The smell of rotting fish permeated the moist, gray air; seagulls winged and squawked in the overcast sky. As Hirata ate, the problems of love and work weighed upon his spirits. He had little hope that time would heal the offense caused his father by Lord Niu, and if he didn't find Wisteria's lover, he and Sano might never solve the murder case.

A commotion on the bridge diverted Hirata's attention

from his gloomy thoughts. He looked up to see what was happening, and his spirits rose. The man walking toward Hirata had coarse black hair that sprang from his head and grew in a thick beard upon his cheeks, chin, and neck. Beady eyes peered from under shaggy brows. He wore a padded cotton cloak that was too large for his small stature. His pawlike hand held one end of a rope. The other end circled the neck of a large, snarling brown monkey with a red face. As man led beast along the bridge, pedestrians laughed, pointed, and exclaimed.

"Rat!" Hirata called, beckoning.

The man ambled up to Hirata and grinned, baring feral teeth. "Good day," he said in an odd, rustic accent. He bowed, and at a command from him, the monkey followed suit. "How do you like the latest addition to my show?"

The Rat operated a freak show that featured peculiar animals as well as deformed humans, and he roamed all over Japan in a continuous search for new attractions.

"He's amazing." Hirata reached out to pet the monkey's head. "Where did you get him?"

"Don't touch him—he bites," the Rat warned, jerking on the rope as the monkey screeched at Hirata. "He's from Tohoku. One might almost say our kinfolk are neighbors. I grew up in Hokkaido, you know."

Hirata had known of the Rat's origin in that far northern island known for cold winters and the copious body hair of the natives. "Speaking of Hokkaido," he said, "I'm looking for someone from there." He wondered if Lady Wisteria's lover was as hairy as the Rat, and shaved to blend with the Edo locals. "Have you come across any of your countrymen around town?"

Because the Rat collected news and had served as a reliable informant in the past, Hirata hoped for a lead on Wisteria's lover, but the Rat shook his head.

"Haven't seen or heard of any Hokkaido folk in these parts for years," he said. "Far as I know, I'm the only one in Edo now."

An idea occurred to Hirata, and though it seemed ludicrous, he had to ask: "Have you been seeing a courtesan named Wisteria?"

"Me? Why, no." The Rat looked dumbfounded, then guffawed. "Oh, you're joking. Even if I could afford Yoshiwara, those women would run screaming from me."

Hirata experienced discouragement, because if the Rat knew nothing of Wisteria's lover, then the man had kept himself well hidden. Or perhaps the pages he'd bought from Gorobei were a false clue, as Reiko had suggested. "Let me know anything you hear about a Hokkaido man, particularly one traveling with a woman," Hirata said.

"Will do." The Rat ambled away with his monkey.

Impatient for action, Hirata decided to press onward to Fukagawa and search the noodle shops where Lady Wisteria and her lover might have taken refuge. But first he would visit his family and test the chances of his marriage to Midori.

16

A horde of bureaucrats paraded in and out of Sano's mansion, all with the intent of heaping suspicion on their enemies. They besieged Sano with unsubstantiated accusations until his mind whirled. By mid-morning he couldn't endure any more self-serving attempts to manipulate him. Finally, during a break between calls, Sano donned his outdoor clothes and swords, then left the house in search of the one person who could tell him which rumors were true or false.

The day was cold and bleak, the sky like raw, soiled cotton, the moist air gritty with soot. Below Edo Castle, the steel-gray river and canals carved a monotone cityscape. The hazy peaks of the hills outside town smudged the distance. Sano passed hurrying officials and patrolling troops as he ascended through the castle's stone-walled passages. Everyone's expression appeared as dismal as the weather. Sano walked faster, uneasy in the tension created by Lord Mitsuyoshi's murder; he could almost smell the impending purge in the air. Entering the palace, he proceeded to a secluded area in which he'd first set foot a lifetime ago.

Here, hidden within a labyrinth of corridors, government offices, and reception rooms, lay the headquarters of the *metsuke*. The Tokugawa intelligence service occupied a room whose mean proportions belied its power. In compartments divided by paper-and-wood screens, men smoked tobacco pipes and studied maps hung on the walls; they conversed together or pored over papers at desks laden with scrolls, message containers, books, and writing implements. As Sano passed, heads turned toward him, and voices lowered.

Inside the last compartment knelt a samurai dressed in black. He looked up from reading a ledger and bowed to Sano. "Greetings, *Sōsakan-sama*."

Sano returned the bow. "Greetings, Toda-*san*."

Toda Ikkyu was a senior intelligence agent, and of such nondescript appearance that Sano might not recognize him if they met anywhere else. Neither short nor tall, fat nor thin, old nor young, Toda had weary eyes set in a face that no one would notice in a crowd. Sano had consulted Toda on past cases, and Toda had once described how he'd spied on an official suspected of treason. The official never recognized Toda, although they both worked in the palace and passed each other in the corridors daily. He went to his death on the execution ground without knowing who'd sent him there.

"Can you spare me a moment of your time?" Sano asked, imagining that he might someday find himself the unwitting prey of the *metsuke* agent.

"Certainly." Toda motioned for Sano to sit near him. His languid voice and gesture belonged to a man who seldom roused from a natural state of ennui. "I suppose this visit concerns your investigation of Lord Mitsuyoshi's murder?"

"Yes," Sano said.

"And you've come to me because you're deluged with rumors."

Sano chuckled, because the extent of Toda's knowledge never ceased to amaze him. Toda also chuckled.

"It never ceases to amaze me how far you've risen in the world since we first met," Toda said.

They'd met during Sano's first murder case, when Sano had discovered a plot against the shogun and had come to Edo Castle to report it to the *metsuke*.

"To go from renegade policeman on a personal crusade to Most Honorable Investigator for His Excellency is no small accomplishment," Toda said. "That you've kept the post for four years is a miracle, considering all the troubles you've had."

"Is it any more a miracle than that you've kept your post in spite of all your troubles?" Sano couldn't resist saying.

Toda had disbelieved Sano's story about the plot, and later, the shogun had punished the entire *metsuke* for failing to take the threat seriously. Agents had been demoted, banished, and executed, yet Toda had somehow survived. Sano suspected that Toda knew the secrets of many members of the *bakufu*'s upper echelon, and had blackmailed them into protecting him.

Now Toda smiled complacently. "We've both been fortunate," he said.

"Good fortune is an impermanent condition," Sano said, "but perhaps we can maintain ours by working together."

Toda's expression didn't change, but Sano felt the man's resistance to the hint that he'd better grant the favor Sano was about to ask. *Metsuke* agents had a habit of hoarding facts. They liked to know things that others didn't, they jealously guarded their unique power, and they wanted sole credit for keeping Japan under the *bakufu*'s control. But sometimes their habit backfired on them.

After the Black Lotus crisis, a disturbing fact had come to light: The *metsuke* possessed years of records that described the sect's illegal practices, yet had not only failed to prevent the sect from gaining an immense, dangerous following but had withheld their records from the Minister of Temples and Shrines, who'd tried to thwart the Black Lotus and asked the *metsuke*'s help. Further investigation revealed sect members within the ranks of the *metsuke*. Toda had survived the purge that ensued, but even he wasn't invincible. The murder of Lord Mitsuyoshi was such a politically sensitive issue that for Toda to refuse to cooperate with Sano's investigation equaled suicide.

"What can I do for you?" Toda said with weary capitulation.

"Let's start with Treasury Minister Nitta," Sano said.

The agent looked around the office, then rose and said, "Let's go elsewhere, shall we?"

Soon they were walking along the Edo Castle racetrack. In summer, this was the scene of samurai riding horses at a furious pace, while palace officials cheered. But now the track was a bare strip of earth, the benches vacant; only a faint smell of manure lingered. An empty meadow, surrounded by pine trees and stone walls, isolated Sano and Toda.

"Is it true that Nitta embezzles from the treasury?" Sano said.

Toda looked as though he'd guessed what Sano would say, but frowned, nonetheless perturbed. "Where did you hear that?"

"Nitta seems to have mentioned it to Lady Wisteria, who told another client," Sano said.

"Well, he's the subject of a highly confidential investigation," Toda said. "I'm surprised that Nitta would incriminate himself, but men are sometimes careless about what they tell courtesans."

"Then Nitta was embezzling," Sano inferred.

Toda nodded, gazing over the walls at the rooftops of the palace stables. A flock of crows perched in the pine trees. "There have been discrepancies between tributes sent from the provinces and the money in the treasury accounts. After we investigated, our suspicion settled on Nitta. He'd always been honest before, but Yoshiwara is an expensive habit. We placed him under secret surveillance and observed him taking gold from the storehouse at night. He alters the entries in the account books to hide the missing money."

The agent gave Sano a sharp glance. "How does Nitta's

embezzlement fit into the murder case? Is he a likelier suspect because of it?"

"That's possible," Sano said. "Maybe he killed Wisteria because he regretted telling her about his embezzlement and wanted to prevent her from reporting him. Even if she didn't have proof, and she was just a prostitute, her accusation could have hurt him."

"Perhaps Wisteria told Lord Mitsuyoshi," said Toda. "In his hands, the knowledge could have been most dangerous to Nitta because he and Mitsuyoshi were on bad terms. Nitta wrote a report about how much money Lord Mitsuyoshi squandered and sent it to his family. His father was shocked by his extravagance, and cut his allowance. Mitsuyoshi blamed Nitta for impoverishing him. He believed Nitta did it so he couldn't afford appointments with Wisteria."

They reached the end of the racetrack and turned, retracing their steps. The crows swooped over the meadow like black kites, their caws loud in the still air. Sano pondered the fact that Toda had just contradicted the treasury minister's claim that he didn't love Wisteria and wasn't jealous of her other clients, but confirmed Senior Elder Makino's statement. "Then you think Nitta killed Mitsuyoshi and Wisteria both?"

"He could be behind the murder and her disappearance," Toda said, "but he's not the type to dirty his hands by stabbing a man or abducting a woman."

"Could his retainers have done the dirty work?" Sano said.

"Unlikely. They're loyal to Nitta, but I doubt if their obedience extends to murdering the shogun's heir. Nitta has a wide acquaintance among the ruffians he meets in Yoshiwara. If I were you, I'd look into them."

Sano would. Yet he had misgivings about the scenario he and Toda had devised. "If Wisteria was murdered in her room, there should have been some evidence of it, but I found no indication that anyone except Mitsuyoshi had died there. If she was abducted, then killed someplace else, where is her body?"

"I understand you're still searching the area around Yoshiwara, and along the highways," Toda said.

"We've yet to find a corpse."

"She could have been dumped in the Sumida River, the Sanya Canal, or one of the smaller waterways."

But Sano's instincts told him that Wisteria was alive, and he had additional reason to discount the likelihood of her murder. The pillow book provided a scenario that didn't involve the treasury minister, and indicated that Wisteria's disappearance had been a voluntary elopement. However, Sano understood that even if the book was genuine, and Lady Wisteria had written the truth in the pages he'd read, they were only part of the whole book. Perhaps the unnamed lover from Hokkaido was just as possessive toward Wisteria and jealous of her clients as Nitta seemed. Perhaps he'd murdered the last client she'd entertained before they left Yoshiwara.

"You might be interested to know that Treasury Minister Nitta was arrested early this morning," Toda said.

"What?" Sano halted in surprise.

"For his embezzlement," Toda explained. "By now, his trial should be underway." With a sly smile, Toda added, "If you need any further information from him, you'd best get over to Magistrate Aoki's Court of Justice."

"But my investigation isn't finished. Nitta can't be tried now." Sano knew what would happen to the treasury minister. That Nitta had earned his fate didn't ease Sano's horror. Sano urgently beseeched Toda, "Please call off the trial!"

"I'm sorry, but the matter is out of my hands." Shrugging, Toda contemplated the crows. They alighted in a black horde in the meadow, where they squawked and fluttered, squabbling over some bit of food. "And I venture to say that the murder investigation is out of yours."

Hirata's family home was in the *bancho*, the district west of Edo Castle where the Tokugawa *hatamoto* occupied estates surrounded by live bamboo fences. Although these vassals had served the shogun's clan long and faithfully, they lived in conditions modest at best and often near poverty because of rising prices and the falling value of their stipends. Today the crowded neighborhood of ramshackle buildings looked drab indeed, with the bamboo withered and leafless. Hirata rode amid other samurai, along narrow, muddy dirt roads. He dismounted outside his parents' house, one of the poorest in the district.

Entering the plain wooden gate, Hirata found the court-yard occupied by four horses, decked with fancy saddles and bridles, which didn't belong to his family. Three of his small nephews raced around the side of the low, weathered house, shouting. Hirata secured his own horse and went into the house. When he hung his swords in the entryway, he noticed four ornate sets of swords, presumably belonging to the visitors, on the racks with the plain weapons of his father and grandfathers. He entered the corridor and found the house full of people and noise. His grandmothers sat in the main room, smoking while they scolded the toddlers playing near them. Hirata heard the maids banging dishes in the kitchen, and a baby crying. Every time he came home, the place looked smaller and dingier. Today it was also chilly because his family needed to conserve fuel. Greeting his grandmothers, Hirata experienced guilt that his kin must endure this, while he enjoyed the quiet luxury of Sano's estate.

His eldest widowed sister came carrying the baby. "How nice to see you, Brother," she said. "Many thanks for the clothes you sent the children."

Spending most of his stipend on his family didn't ease Hirata's guilt. Before he could ask who was visiting them, his father's voice called from the parlor: "Is that you, Son? Please come in."

Curious, Hirata obeyed. In the parlor sat his parents and a middle-aged samurai garbed in opulent robes. Near the samurai knelt three men in plainer dress, evidently his re-tainers. Hirata's mother was serving tea with her best uten-sils.

"How fortunate that my son should arrive while you're here," Hirata's father said to the guest, then turned to Hirata.

"You remember the Honorable *Yoriki* Okubo."

"Of course." Hirata knelt beside his father and bowed to the guest. *Yoriki* Okubo had been his commander when he was a police officer, and his father had served under Okubo's. But the two clans had never been on intimate terms, and Hirata wondered why the *yoriki* had come. He said politely, "It's an honor to see you again. I hope you are well?"

"Yes, thank you." *Yoriki* Okubo had fleshy, down-turned features. He observed Hirata with shrewd approval. "I can see that you are also well. Life in the *sōsakan-sama*'s employ suits you." After questioning Hirata about his duties, Okubo said, "That you make time in your busy day to visit your parents is a mark of good character."

Hirata cast a puzzled glance at his father, who avoided his eyes and addressed Okubo: "My son is always conscientious about his duties to both his master and his family." Still without looking at Hirata, his father said to him, "Okubo-*san* has come on behalf of his colleague, the Honorable *Yoriki* Sagara."

"My colleague has an unmarried daughter," Okubo said.

Alarm struck Hirata as he comprehended that Okubo was here as a go-between, bearing him a marriage proposal from the other police commander. Since his parents clearly welcomed the proposal, it was obvious that they'd rejected the idea of his marriage to Midori.

"A match between my son and the Sagara girl would be most suitable," said Hirata's father. "Their common heritage in the police force would be a foundation for a harmonious life."

"There would be other benefits for both sides," Okubo said. "Speaking frankly, your son's status in the *bakufu* is valued by the Sagara clan. And their fortune is considerable."

Hirata opened his mouth to protest; but his father spoke: "What about the girl herself? Is her character pleasing?"

"Quite," Okubo said. "She is modest, obedient, and dutiful." He turned to Hirata. "She is also sixteen years old and very pretty."

Hirata didn't care how wonderful the Sagara girl was. "Father," he said.

An ominous look from his father and a frantic shushing gesture from his mother forestalled his protests. He squirmed in wordless agitation as the talk proceeded.

"The next step is a *miai*, I presume?" said his father.

"That can be arranged," Okubo said. "The Sagara are most eager for a meeting."

Polite farewells ensued. Afterward, Hirata's father said to his wife, "My leg hurts from kneeling so long. I must have my medicinal bath."

Hirata helped his mother fill a tub with hot water and herbs. His father sat on cushions with his thin, crooked leg immersed in the water.

"Father, I don't want to go to that *miai*," Hirata said.

"You must, because we've already committed ourselves." The older man spoke offhandedly, as though manners were their sole concern and he'd decided to pretend that Hirata had no serious reason for objecting to the *miai*. "For us to back out now would offend *Yoriki* Okubo and the Sagara clan."

"Well, I won't go," Hirata said. His voice shook even as he folded his arms and planted his legs wide. He, who supervised Sano's hundred detectives and troops, still quailed before paternal authority; he hated to defy his father. "I'm upset that you began this marriage negotiation behind my back."

A glint of anger sparked in the older man's eyes. "It's my right to make arrangements on your behalf, and your duty to obey me," he said. "You will go to the *miai* and fulfill our obligations. Then, if you don't like the Sagara girl, we can politely refuse the proposal. There are plenty of other good clans eager to wed a daughter to you."

"Father, I don't want anyone but Midori. I beg you not to force me into a marriage with another girl." Desperate, Hirata dropped to his knees. "Please reconsider allowing me to marry the woman I love. Please forgive Lord Niu and resume our marriage negotiations."

"If you came here hoping to change my mind, then you've wasted your time." His father flexed his leg in the tub and glowered. "I forbid you to marry Lord Niu's daughter. I order you to choose one of the girls whom I consider suitable."

"But, Father—"

The older man angrily waved away Hirata's protest. "Your desire to marry the Niu girl is selfish. It shows a disrespect toward me, and a deplorable lack of consideration for our family." He addressed his wife, who was stirring more herbs into the tub: "Let it alone! Stop fussing!" To Hirata he said, "We have too many mouths to feed and too little space. For you to expect your parents and grandparents, your sisters and their children, to live off crumbs from your stipend is disgraceful, when the Sagara girl's dowry would fill our rice bowls in the comfort of a bigger house."

Hirata felt his cheeks flush and his spirit contract with shame at the idea that he placed his personal needs above his family's welfare. "The Niu have far more money than the Sagara. If I marry Midori, you'll want for nothing."

His father's expression turned grave. "For you to marry her and us to share her clan's wealth is impossible, and not just because I oppose the match." Turning to his wife, he said, "Mother, bring the letter that came from Lord Niu today."

She hurried from the room, then returned bearing a scroll, which she gave to Hirata. He read:

This is my official notice that I am ending the marriage negotiations between our clans. That I should wed my daughter to the son of a rascal like you, who are my sworn enemy, is preposterous!

I warn your son to sever all contact with my daughter. His inferior person shall not be allowed to defile Midori. He shall suffer severe misfortune for daring to court her. And if he so much as goes near her, I shall slay him with my own sword and mount his head over my gate as a warning to other unwelcome suitors.

> Niu Masamune
> Daimyo of Satsuma Province

As Hirata stared at the letter in shock, his father exclaimed, "Not only did Lord Niu threaten me in public, he now threatens you! You must do as Lord Niu says and keep away from his daughter."

Never to see Midori again! The thought horrified Hirata. "Perhaps there's been some misunderstanding that could be cleared up if we all sat down together and talked—"

"I'll not see Lord Niu again and invite more of his vicious insults," Hirata's father declared. "And I refuse to reconsider this match."

Though his father's face wore a stony aspect that repelled further argument, Hirata had promised Midori that he would find a way for them to marry. He spoke in desperation: "If Lord Niu were to make amends for insulting you, take back his threats, and welcome me as a son-in-law, would you change your mind about the marriage?"

His father regarded Hirata with a torn, wistful expression. Though he didn't speak, Hirata understood that his father loved him and wanted him to be happy. Hope leapt in Hirata, then died as his father shook his head.

"If Lord Niu did as you suggest, I might be persuaded," the older man said. "But you might as well pray for a miracle as expect him to change his feelings about the match, because he seems bent on hating us. You must learn to live without that girl and accept the idea of marrying another."

He raised his leg from the tub. As his wife dried it with a cloth, he said to Hirata, "This whole business has distracted you from duty. The last thing you need is for the *sōsakan-sama*'s investigation to suffer because of your personal concerns. You had better get back to work."

"Yes, Father," Hirata said dejectedly. He left the house with his hope of marrying Midori seeming as futile as locating Lady Wisteria's lover.

17

"Be very quiet, Kikuko-*chan*," Lady Yanagisawa whispered.

Crouching beneath low, sloped rafters, mother and daughter crept across the floor joists in the attic between the second story and the roof of the chamberlain's mansion. This attic, which ran above all the interconnected wings of the house, was a dim, unfurnished labyrinth. Cobwebs festooned the rafters; dust, mouse droppings, and dead insects littered the floors. The only light came from grills set in the peaked gables.

Kikuko tiptoed, a finger pressed to her lips, her eyes dancing in enjoyment of what she thought was a game. They lay down on a futon set upon a tatami mat, and Lady Yanagisawa covered them with a quilt to protect them from the damp cold in this place where they alone ever came. She positioned herself on her stomach, chin propped on her folded arms, and peered through a palm-sized hole in the floor.

This hole, bored through the ceiling below and concealed by intricately carved and painted woodwork, gave Lady Yanagisawa a view of the chamberlain's office. Years ago she'd discovered the hidden route from her wing of the house to his. She'd cut the hole at night while everyone else slept, so that she would have this window into the life of her husband.

He never told her about his business; he rarely spoke to her at all, and if she wanted to hear his voice or learn what he did, she had to eavesdrop. And because he spent virtually no time with her, when she wanted to lay eyes on him, she watched him in secret. Perhaps he was unaware of what she did; probably he knew and didn't care.

Now she saw him at the desk, smoking his pipe while he wrote. His oiled hair and silk robes gleamed. He sat alone, though bodyguards lurked in the adjacent rooms, behind the moveable wall panels. As Lady Yanagisawa beheld him, a profound, familiar adoration clenched her heart.

He was as beautiful as on the day they'd met. She had wondered then how she could deserve a husband like him. She should have known that their marriage would turn out to be exactly what a woman like her should have expected.

The knowledge that she was ugly seemed to have always been with her. Born the middle of three children, she'd grown up in Kai Province, in a mansion owned by her parents, who were both distant relatives of the Tokugawa. Her household had been lively and gregarious, and she a shy, retiring outcast. Mocked by her pretty sisters, criticized by her mother and the servants, and ignored by her father, she'd spent most of her days alone. Her only companion was a doll with a chipped porcelain head, whom she loved all the more for its imperfection.

When she reached a marriageable age, her parents took her to many *miai*. She couldn't look at the prospective bridegrooms because she feared to see disgust in their eyes. No proposals came of those meetings. She resigned herself to spinsterhood . . . until that fateful *miai* with the shogun's young chamberlain.

It had taken place ten springs ago. As the party strolled

through the grounds of Kannei Temple, she kept her head bowed and eyes downcast, listening to the conversation. The smooth, vibrant voice of Chamberlain Yanagisawa stirred something in her. Curiosity overcame her shyness. She risked a glance at him, and their gazes met. He dazzled her. It was like looking at the sun after living in darkness. Heat flushed her body as though his image had burned her. Then he smiled, and she experienced the giddy, heart-pounding sensation of first love.

That he agreed to marry her seemed a joyous miracle. Exchanging ritual cups of sake at their wedding, she dared to dream of happiness. But their first night together at his mansion showed her the cruel reality of her marriage.

"These are your chambers," Yanagisawa said in a cold, impersonal manner. "I'll leave while you undress and get in bed."

Trembling in fearful anticipation, she obeyed. Soon Yanagisawa returned. Without a glance at her, he extinguished the lantern, and his garments rustled in the dark as he shed them. He slipped under the quilt with her. She felt a welling of desire, but after a few perfunctory caresses, it was over. He rose and departed. She lay alone, weeping as the soreness between her legs oozed blood. She and her husband hadn't exchanged a single word during their union; she'd not even seen his body. And she knew he'd put out the light so he wouldn't have to see her.

In the months that followed, the chamberlain paid her hardly more attention. She felt like a ghost haunting his house. She saw few people besides the servants and made no friends at Edo Castle; she uttered hardly a word. His absence increased her love and longing for Yanagisawa. Every few nights he came to her bed, and she always hoped that this time he would treat her with affection and she would experience fulfillment. But he always behaved as he had that first time.

A need to understand her husband had initiated her habit of watching him and listening to the servants gossip about him. She learned that he'd attained his position by seducing the shogun, with whom he had a longtime sexual liaison. She learned that he'd only married her because he wanted a wife with family connections to the Tokugawa. He had many lovers, both male and female, whom he discarded so fast that she considered them meaningless entertainment, unworthy of her jealousy. She fantasized that someday the chamberlain would love her.

The arrival of Kikuko had at first fueled her hope.

After their daughter's birth, Chamberlain Yanagisawa would stand in the nursery door, watching her tend the baby, and although she was too shy to talk to him, she thought surely he must value her as the mother of his child. But soon Kikuko's defects became apparent.

"Why doesn't she walk? Why doesn't she speak?" the chamberlain had demanded when Kikuko reached the age at which other children could do those things.

He'd stopped visiting Lady Yanagisawa's bed when she got pregnant, and he never came again. She heard the servants say he blamed her for breeding an idiot and didn't want another. He ignored Kikuko.

Now, lying in the attic above the chamberlain's office, Lady Yanagisawa hugged the little girl close. Kikuko was so good and obedient; she would lie quietly here in the attic for as long as necessary, instead of squirming and complaining the way other children would. Kikuko, beautiful on the outside and flawed within, was all Lady Yanagisawa had. Her affection would compensate Kikuko for her father's cruel rejection. Despite it, Lady Yanagisawa had continued in love with her husband. For almost six more years she'd believed that he would come to care for her, until two events shattered her faith.

The first was the marriage of *Sōsakan* Sano. She'd heard of Sano when he'd come to Edo Castle and her husband had deemed him a rival and begun spying on him and plotting against him. But Sano hadn't interested Lady Yanagisawa until the day when she and Kikuko had gone riding in their palanquin and returned to the castle to find a procession lined up outside the gate.

"It's Ueda Reiko, the *sōsakan-sama*'s bride," said someone in the crowd of spectators.

Curious, Lady Yanagisawa had peered at the bridal palanquin. Its window opened, and Reiko lifted her white head drape to look outside. Her beautiful face caused Lady Yanagisawa a piercing stab of envy. Reiko was everything that she herself was not. Seeing Reiko showed her the only kind of woman who might win her husband, and the futility of her love for him.

Envy fostered in Lady Yanagisawa an obsessive desire to know more about Reiko. She listened to the chamberlain's spies report that Reiko helped her husband with his investigations. She ordered the servants to find out from Reiko's servants what Reiko did and when she went out. Following Reiko at a distance, Lady Yanagisawa learned that Reiko led an active, interesting life. She herself had only the bitter pleasure of vicarious experience. Her envy had turned to hatred two summers ago when the *sōsakan-sama* took his wife to Miyako.

Lady Yanagisawa had hidden in the crowd that watched the procession exit the castle, and seen Sano riding alongside Reiko's palanquin. Reiko spoke to him; he smiled at her. This brief glimpse of them together had told Lady Yanagisawa they shared a love that her own marriage lacked. Lady Yanagisawa gazed after them while her fingernails gouged bloody crescents in the palms of her hands. This seemed the culmination of her woes, for she couldn't have known that the Miyako investigation heralded the second calamity to befall her.

A knock at the door broke the silence in the office below. Chamberlain Yanagisawa called, "Enter!"

Into the room *Yoriki* Hoshina walked, his step cautious and his countenance somber. Lady Yanagisawa experienced the turmoil of emotion that Hoshina always aroused in her.

Hoshina knelt opposite the chamberlain. He said, "I've been thinking about the conversation we had last night."

"Oh?" Yanagisawa laid down his writing brush. Both men behaved with reserve, but Lady Yanagisawa felt the heat between them. She could almost smell the quickening of their blood, breath, and desire.

Her husband had also gone to Miyako, and he'd brought Hoshina back to live with him. He had fallen in love with this man instead of her! Night after night she suffered the agony of watching them in the throes of sexual passion that Yanagisawa had never shown toward her. How she despised Hoshina, who had stolen what she wanted! Hatred for her husband entwined her love for him, like a thorny vine growing up around a tree.

"I've figured out what you meant when you said that Lord Mitsuyoshi's murder created more opportunities besides the chance to depose Sano." Eagerness crept into Hoshina's voice.

The chamberlain smiled in expectancy. "Go on."

Lady Yanagisawa tried to suppress her emotions and listen, for she wanted to understand what her husband had said when she'd eavesdropped on him and Hoshina last night. She wanted to hear her husband's plans because they might affect her and Kikuko, but also because these tidbits of illicitly gained knowledge were all she had of him.

"Now that Mitsuyoshi is gone, the shogun needs a new heir." Hoshina hesitated, watching the chamberlain for a reaction. When Yanagisawa's smile broadened, Hoshina continued: "The new heir must be a young man of pleasing appearance and manner."

"Indeed." Stroking his chin, Yanagisawa regarded Hoshina with the veiled approval of a teacher beholding a clever pupil.

"He must also have a blood connection with the Tokugawa so that the succession will stay within the clan." Hoshina let a beat pass, cut a meaningful glance at Yanagisawa, then spoke in a tone replete with insinuation: "Next time you visit your son, please convey to him my best wishes for a prosperous future. May he be as malleable in your hands as the man I won't name."

The chamberlain laughed; fondness shone in the proud look he gave Hoshina. "I knew you would understand."

He was plotting to install his son on the throne and rule through the boy! The breadth of her husband's audacity stunned Lady Yanagisawa.

"But how would you achieve this, when there's so much competition?" Hoshina said. "The Tokugawa branch clans will bring forth their relatives as candidates for the succession. Anyone with any claim to the dictatorship is either on his way to Edo or already at the palace seeking an audience with the shogun. Have you seen the crowd in the antechamber?"

"I've already persuaded the shogun to grant Yoritomo an audience," Yanagisawa said, his confidence unshaken. "The boy's resemblance to me will remind His Excellency of when he and I first met. He'll feel young again, and ripe for seduction. Memory and desire should render him quite cooperative."

He would pander his own flesh and blood to the shogun! Yet even this depravity didn't lessen Lady Yanagisawa's love for him. She didn't care what he did with the bastards he'd fathered on other women.

"Would you have your son follow in your footsteps?" Hoshina said. He drew back and folded his arms, displaying the qualms that Yanagisawa lacked.

Yanagisawa smoked his pipe in momentary silence, his air troubled now. "It may seem cruel, but it's imperative for Yoritomo as well as myself. I can give him a good position in the *bakufu*, but there's a limit to how high he can go without a special advantage."

He would never become shogun, Lady Yanagisawa knew, unless Tokugawa Tsunayoshi took him on as lover and adopted son.

"And unless I can extend my influence into the next generation, neither of us will survive a change in regime," the chamberlain continued.

Lady Yanagisawa also knew that her husband's many enemies would welcome the opportunities posed by the death of the shogun. If the chamberlain lost power, they would rush to execute him and his sons. And what would become of her and Kikuko? Would they be executed, too?

"Unless my plan succeeds, you won't last long in a new regime, either," Yanagisawa told Hoshina. "But if things go well, then Sano will be mine to command—as will everyone else. You'll not need to worry that he'll surpass you or prevent you from having anything you want."

If her husband managed to install his son as the next shogun, he and Hoshina would enjoy vast power and wealth. But Lady Yanagisawa expected no rewards for herself. Probably, she and Kikuko would go on living as they always had. The prospect seemed almost as terrible as death.

Hoshina's expression was thoughtful, perturbed. "His Excellency may rule for many more years."

"And we should pray that he does," Yanagisawa said, "because present conditions are a much surer thing than future ones may prove to be, no matter how carefully we plan."

"Then you expect me to honor your truce with Sano and wait for however long it takes until conditions change and bring him under your control?" An aggrieved note tinged Hoshina's voice.

The chamberlain only smiled. "Or until I decide it's time to break the truce. But otherwise, you're free to challenge Sano and cause him as much trouble as you wish."

Hoshina rose, his face unhappy. Lady Yanagisawa could almost pity him because he, too, was in thrall to her husband. Yet she gloated over Hoshina's disappointments. When he'd come to live in her home, she'd thought of poisoning him, or sneaking into his bedchamber at night and cutting his throat. Someday she might find the courage to kill him, even though she feared punishment from her husband and couldn't expect him to turn to her just because Hoshina was gone. For the present, she channeled her ill will toward Reiko.

Reiko had become the mother of a son at the time when Lady Yanagisawa realized that Kikuko would never be normal. One day this summer, when Lady Yanagisawa took Kikuko on a pilgrimage to Zōjō Temple, seeking a spiritual cure for her daughter, she spied Reiko and Masahiro in the temple grounds with a party of the Edo Castle women. As she watched Masahiro chatter and romp, her bitterness overwhelmed her because he was everything that Kikuko would never be.

Why did some women have so much, and others so little?

That day, Lady Yanagisawa had developed a vague but compelling notion that the world contained a limited amount of good fortune and Reiko had more than her share. The idea turned to certainty that Reiko was an enemy who had stolen the luck that Lady Yanagisawa deserved, and that only if Reiko lost her happiness could Lady Yanagisawa claim her rightful due. Lady Yanagisawa didn't know how to achieve this, but forming an acquaintance with her enemy seemed a good first step. Hence, Lady Yanagisawa had gone to the party at the palace . . . where something unforeseen had happened.

At first Lady Yanagisawa had seethed with ire at discovering that Reiko was even more beautiful up close, and Masahiro made Kikuko seem more deficient. Yet Reiko had been so kind to Lady Yanagisawa that her resolve wavered. When she asked to visit Reiko, she wasn't sure whether she sought a way to attack Reiko or win her friendship.

Below, the chamberlain and Hoshina rose and left the room. Kikuko stirred under the quilt, knowing it was safe to move now. Although there was nothing more to hear, Lady Yanagisawa lay immobile, thinking of that visit to Reiko's house. She recalled seeing a toy horse in the *sōsakan-sama*'s office, and a man's dressing gown on a stand in Reiko's chamber. That house was a place where husband, wife, and child lived in togetherness, and she might find comfort as well as food for envy. Lady Yanagisawa didn't know whether to seek happiness by hurting Reiko or by attaching herself to Reiko in the hope that some good luck would rub off on her. But she was certain of one thing.

If she could help Reiko with the murder investigation, she must, because that would give her the opportunity to follow whichever impulses prevailed.

18

Reiko walked from her palanquin into her house, and sighed in frustration as the maids removed her cloak. Despite her hope of finding Lady Wisteria and her Hokkaido lover, the morning's inquiries had ended in failure.

None of the women she'd visited seemed to know anything of the mystery lover. Reiko had then gone to her father's estate in the official district near Edo Castle. Magistrate Ueda, who alternated duty with Edo's other magistrate, was spending a month off, while his colleague, Magistrate Aoki, presided over trials. Reiko had asked her father if a man from Hokkaido had ever come to his attention. He consulted his records and his staff, but none of them produced any clues. She began to think that the pillow book Hirata had found was a fake.

Disconsolate now, Reiko wandered into the nursery and found Masahiro napping. The maid O-hana sat beside him, looking bored, but when she saw Reiko, she perked up.

"Lady Reiko-*san*! You're back at last," she said, smiling. "Are you cold from being outside? Shall I bring you hot tea?"

"Yes, please, that would be nice," Reiko said.

The maid hurried off. Reiko sat watching Masahiro sleep while she wondered how to proceed now that none of her usual sources had yielded clues. Soon O-hana returned and placed a steaming bowl of tea in her hands.

"Thank you," Reiko murmured absently.

"You and the *sōsakan-sama* are looking for Lady Wisteria, aren't you?" O-hana said.

"Yes." Reiko eyed the nursemaid in surprise. She never discussed Sano's cases with servants, and though she supposed they eavesdropped, they'd never crossed the bounds of propriety by mentioning what they'd heard.

"Maybe I can help you," O-hana said.

Reiko took a closer look at O-hana, appraising her cunning smile, eyes bright and sharp as black quartz, and stylish red sash. O-hana was Reiko's least favorite of the nurses, although the girl was an efficient worker, kind to Masahiro, and he liked her. Reiko had always thought O-hana a little conceited, a little too eager to ingratiate herself with her employers.

"How could you help?" Reiko said.

"I know Wisteria's family."

"How can you know them?" Reiko said, recalling what Sano had told her about the courtesan. "They live far away in Dewa Province." She also recalled that O-hana was a native of Edo and had never been outside the city.

"Excuse me, but I must disagree," O-hana said. Her tone was humble, but her faint smirk showed her enjoyment of pointing out someone else's mistake. "Lady Wisteria isn't from the country, even though that's what she tells people. Her parents live right in Nihonbashi. My mother used to be a maid in their house. I knew Wisteria when we were children."

"Why would she lie?" Reiko was skeptical of O-hana's news even as it intrigued her.

O-hana's smile turned mysterious. "Lies sometimes sound better than the truth."

And the truth about Wisteria's past might reveal truths about the murder, Reiko thought. Excitement quickened her heartbeat. "Might her family know where Lady Wisteria went?" she speculated aloud.

"I could introduce you to them," O-hana suggested eagerly. "We could ask. Shall we go now?"

She leapt to her feet, and Reiko noted how quick O-hana was to abandon her nursemaid duty and presume a closer relationship between them. Reiko liked her less for it, and didn't trust O-hana. Yet she had to stop distrusting people just because her trust had once been abused. Just because the evil influence of the Black Lotus had threatened her didn't mean everyone meant her harm. She couldn't disregard an opportunity to help Sano solve a case because she disliked the person who offered it. And there seemed no other opportunities at hand.

"All right," Reiko said. "Let's go."

"There it is," O-hana said as the palanquin carried her and Reiko down a street lined with large houses. "The next one on the left."

Reiko called to the bearers to stop. She was glad they'd reached their destination, because the trip from Edo Castle to the Nihonbashi merchant district had been unpleasant. The cold had seeped into the palanquin and through the quilts that covered Reiko and her companion. And O-hana had chattered all the way here, clearly enjoying her ride in the palanquin, and striving to rise above her station by attaching herself to Reiko. Stifling her dislike and trying to feel grateful toward the poor nursemaid, Reiko climbed out of the palanquin. She and O-hana walked up to the house.

The house and its neighbors were residences of the affluent merchant class. Built of wood and whitewashed plaster, they fronted directly onto the street. Heavy brown tile roofs peaked above their second stories and sheltered recessed entrances. The district wasn't what Reiko had expected, because Sano had said Wisteria came from a poor family who had sold her into prostitution.

A young maid, dressed in a blue kimono and carrying a broom, appeared in the doorway. She gazed in surprise at O-hana, Reiko, and the troops who'd escorted them. "O-hana? Is that you? What's going on?"

"My mistress wants to see yours," O-hana said in a self-important tone. "Go tell her that the wife of the shogun's *sōsakan-sama* is here."

The maid hurried to comply. Soon two older maids seated Reiko and O-hana in a warm, stuffy parlor full of ornate lacquer tables, chests, and screens, silk floor cushions, shelves of porcelain vases.

"Isn't this beautiful?" O-hana whispered to Reiko as they waited for Lady Wisteria's mother.

Reiko nodded, although the decor exemplified the vulgar taste of the merchant class.

Into the room minced a small woman perhaps forty years old, trailed by two different female servants. Her face, round with a pointed chin, was covered with heavy white powder. Rouge dotted her cheeks; scarlet paint brightened her thin, prim lips. Painted brows arched over unusually round eyes. Clad in a gaudy red floral kimono that would have better suited a younger woman, she was pretty in the same vulgar way as her parlor.

"Welcome, Honorable Lady!" Bowing to Reiko, she smiled, revealing teeth cosmetically blackened in the manner of highborn wives. She ignored O-hana. "This is an unexpected honor."

"Allow me to introduce Madam Yue-*san*," O-hana said to Reiko, looking miffed at their hostess's slight.

Madam Yue knelt near Reiko and offered refreshments; maids served tea and expensive cakes on fine dishware. Reiko had counted six attendants by now. If this family could maintain so high a standard of living, how could they not have afforded a daughter's keep? Was this really the home of Lady Wisteria?

While Reiko and O-hana ate and sipped, Madam Yue chatted with Reiko about the weather. She spoke and smiled with affected elegance. Presently she said, "May I ask what brought you here to see me?"

"I've come about your daughter," Reiko said.

The woman's smile vanished; displeasure thinned her lips. "My daughter isn't here. It's been many years since she's lived in this house."

"She is Lady Wisteria, the courtesan?" Reiko said, wanting to make sure they were both talking about the same person.

Madam Yue looked away and nodded.

"You know she disappeared from Yoshiwara the night when the shogun's heir was murdered?"

Another nod from Madam Yue; she twisted her dainty hands together at her bosom and frowned into space.

"My husband needs to find Wisteria," said Reiko. "I was hoping you could help us."

"I haven't seen her, and I don't know where she's gone," Madam Yue said. Her elegance had deserted her; she spoke in a flat, common voice. "I'm not surprised she's in trouble, though. If you find her, I would appreciate it if you would tell her not to expect any help from me."

Though Reiko was disappointed that this expedition wouldn't reveal the location of Wisteria, the woman's attitude intrigued her. Clearly, there had been trouble between Wisteria and her mother. "Maybe if you tell me about your daughter, that will give me a clue to where she is," Reiko said.

Madam Yue's mouth twitched and her gaze darted. She looked anxious to avoid speaking of Wisteria, yet afraid to offend the *sōsakan-sama*'s wife. She sighed in resignation.

"How did Wisteria come to be a courtesan?" Reiko asked.

"That kind of thing doesn't usually happen in our family," Madam Yue burst out. "But she deserved it. I'm glad I sold her to the brothel!"

This woman had willingly delivered her own daughter

into a life of degradation. Reiko was horrified into speech-lessness.

"When she was a little girl I loved her so much, but she went bad." Madam Yue spoke in a rush, her round eyes glittering with shame, tears, and a need to justify herself. "I did without things so I could buy pretty clothes for her, and she repaid good with evil!"

The woman sniffled angrily and wiped her nose on her sleeve. "It started when she was thirteen, after her father died. He was a laborer in a boatyard. He hurt his leg there, and it festered, and the sickness killed him. I didn't know how Wisteria and I would live, because we had no money or family. But then the owner of the boatyard offered me a job as a maid—in this house. He let me bring my girl to live here with me and help with the work. It turned out that he fancied me. The next year we were married. I became the mistress of the house."

She smiled through her tears, proud of her advancement in society, but then her expression turned bitter. "I should have noticed how Wisteria looked at him, and how he looked at her, and bought her things, and paid more attention to her than to me. But I never suspected. Then one night I was wakened by noises in the house. You'll understand what I mean when I say they were the kind of noises that shouldn't have been coming from anywhere except the room where my husband and I sleep. He was supposed to be working late that night. I thought one of the maids had sneaked in a man. So I got up and went to throw them out.

"But I discovered that the noises were coming from Wisteria's room. I looked inside. And I saw them. They were in bed together—Wisteria and my husband!" Indignation blazed in Madam Yue's eyes. "I grabbed him and pulled him away from Wisteria. I began hitting him, and I shouted, 'Leave my girl alone, you beast!' "

Pantomiming her actions, Madam Yue beat her fists at the air. Reiko winced, imagining the innocent child mistreated by her stepfather.

"He fell on the floor," Madam Yue continued. "I hurried

to Wisteria and said, 'Are you all right?' And the sight of her froze my heart. I expected her to be frightened and crying. But she stood up, stark naked, with her head high." Madam Yue rose, her manner cruelly triumphant. "She said, 'I love him, Mother. And he loves me, not you. He only married you so he could have me, because I'm the one he's always wanted. And now that I'm old enough, he's going to marry me.'

"I couldn't believe what she said. I was so shocked that I stood there gaping at her, shaking my head." The woman's attitude altered to suit her words. "Then Wisteria said to my husband, 'Tell her it's true. Tell her you're going to divorce her, like you promised, so we can marry.'"

While Reiko sat amazed by this story, Madam Yue said, "I turned to my husband. 'She's lying,' I said to him. 'Tell me she's lying.' But he just hung his head and sat there. And I realized that Wisteria had seduced him into betraying me. I rushed at her and shouted, 'Wicked slut! How dare you steal my husband?' I slapped her face. I pulled her hair. I threw her to the floor and trampled her. She called to my husband to save her. But he didn't move, he wouldn't look at us. Wisteria started crying. I cursed and beat her until my strength gave out. We all sat in that room, without speaking, for the rest of the night."

Madam Yue sank to her knees, her expression murderous. Reiko pictured the guilty man, the raging wife, and the weeping girl, characters in a tragic play.

"You can see why I had to get rid of my daughter." Madam Yue turned a defiant gaze on Reiko. "My husband wasn't really going to marry her and throw me out, but if she stayed, she would make him always want her instead of me." Bitterness curdled the woman's voice. "I couldn't just put her out of the house, because she would come back and persuade my husband to take her in again. And she deserved to be punished.

"When morning came, I told them what we were going to do. Wisteria begged my forgiveness, but I ignored her. My husband took us in a ferry up the river to Yoshiwara.

We walked to the gate, and I said to a guard, 'I want to sell my daughter.' He fetched the brothel-masters. They fought over Wisteria because she was so pretty. I sold her to the one who offered me the most money. It was enough that I thought she'd be trapped in Yoshiwara forever. As the man took her into the quarter, she begged my husband not to leave her. She cursed me and screamed that I would be sorry for what I'd done, but I just walked away. My husband followed me. We went home."

Reiko was appalled. What Madam Yue had done was worse than poor peasants selling children they couldn't afford to raise. Those peasants gave up the children so they would be fed and clothed at the brothels, while Madam Yue had sought to condemn Wisteria to a lifetime of prostitution. Reiko glanced at O-hana, who gave a smug nod, as if to say, *I told you that lies sound better than the truth.* Wisteria must have created a new personal history for herself because she didn't want to tell people that she'd brought about her own disgrace and her mother had won their battle for the man they both wanted. Reiko pondered what implications the courtesan's falsehood had for the murder case. At the very least, it suggested that Wisteria was a more complex woman than Reiko or Sano had thought.

A man dressed in the dark, respectable cotton robes of a successful merchant peered through the parlor doorway. Madam Yue saw him, and a look of guilty chagrin came over her face. "Honorable Husband. You're home early." Flustered, she introduced him and Reiko.

They bowed to each other, murmuring polite greetings. Reiko noted that the man was some years younger than his wife, and handsome. His diffident manner suggested weakness of personality, and Reiko perceived that he would always yield to the person with the strongest will. His young stepdaughter hadn't stood a chance against her outraged, overpowering mother.

The man withdrew. A moment passed in uncomfortable silence while Madam Yue twisted her hands nervously. She said, "I don't like to talk about the past when my husband is around," then forced a bright, artificial smile at Reiko. "Many thanks for the honor of your visit. I hope you have a pleasant trip home."

She was obviously eager to see her guests gone. Reiko thanked Madam Yue for her cooperation and allowed the woman to escort her and O-hana outside. The afternoon continued sunless and bleak; moisture in the air condensed into icy droplets that chilled Reiko's face. Pausing before she climbed into her palanquin, she turned to Madam Yue.

"Was that day at Yoshiwara the last time you saw your daughter?" Reiko asked.

Madam Yue hardened her mouth. "I wish it had been. But Wisteria came back here about four years ago."

"She did?" Reiko said, surprised. "How?"

Courtesans were forbidden to leave Yoshiwara, except in special cases. A *tayu* could only go home to visit fatally ill parents, and that circumstance didn't apply to Wisteria.

"I came home from shopping," Madam Yue said, "and I found Wisteria in my room. She was all grown up, and beautiful, and dressed in the highest fashion." The murderous look darkened the woman's features again. "She was slashing my clothes with a knife. There was a big pile of shredded fabric on the floor around her.

"I said, 'How did you get here? What do you think you're doing?' Wisteria said, 'I've been freed. And I'm paying you back for what you did to me.' Then she urinated on my ruined clothes. I shouted, 'Get out of here!' She laughed and said, 'May you be reborn into the life of degradation that I suffered.' And she swept out of the house. That was the last I've seen of her. And good riddance!" Madam Yue snorted; fury glinted in her eyes.

Though Wisteria's violence and crudity disgusted Reiko, she could sympathize with the courtesan's need for revenge. And the story offered a possible clue.

"Who was it that freed Wisteria?" Reiko asked.

"She didn't say. Later I heard he was a wealthy, high-ranking official."

One aspect of the story perplexed Reiko. She said, "If this

man freed Wisteria, why did she return to Yoshiwara?"

"I don't know." An unpleasant smile twisted Madam Yue's lips. "But I'm glad she did."

Reiko decided she must find out the identity of the man. Perhaps he and Wisteria had kept in contact, and he knew where she was. "Did Wisteria have any close friends I might talk to?" Reiko meant to continue probing Wisteria's past, which seemed a rich source of enlightenment.

"There was a girl named Yuya. She lived down the street when she and Wisteria were young. I heard she went bad, too, but I don't know what became of her."

"If you should see Wisteria, or hear from her, will you please send a message to my husband's estate at Edo Castle to let me know?" Reiko said.

"Oh, I certainly will," Madam Yue replied, with a nasty chuckle that conveyed how much she would like to turn her daughter in to the shogun's *sōsakan-sama*. "Does your husband think Wisteria killed Lord Mitsuyoshi?"

"He's investigating the possibility," Reiko admitted.

"Well, you can tell him that she's mean and spiteful and cunning enough to be the murderer," Madam Yue said. "And when he catches her, I'll be plenty glad to say so at her trial."

19

The guards at the Court of Justice opened the broad, carved door for Sano. He and four of his detectives entered the cavernous room, which was filled with men kneeling in rows all the way up to the *shirasu*, an area of floor covered with white sand, symbol of truth. There knelt Treasury Minister Nitta. Head bowed, his wrists shackled, he faced the low dais at the front of the room. On the dais, flanked by two secretaries stationed behind desks equipped with paper and writing implements, sat Magistrate Aoki.

Sano and his men knelt at the back of the audience. The magistrate addressed Nitta in a cracked but resonant voice: "We have just heard evidence that you stole from the treasury." His face reminded Sano of a bitter-melon—tapering and deeply wrinkled, his eyes like black stones embedded in furrows. He wore black ceremonial robes adorned with gold crests. His bald scalp reflected light from the lanterns above the dais. "You may now speak for yourself if you wish."

"I confess that I took the money, betrayed my lord's trust, and dishonored myself," Nitta said. His quiet words conveyed no feeling, but his shoulders slumped in despair. The penalty for stealing from the Tokugawa was death, as everyone knew.

"I hereby pronounce you guilty of embezzlement and treason," said Magistrate Aoki.

Sano drew a breath to ask that Aoki delay the execution until he solved the murder case. He might need more information from Nitta, and he wanted all the suspects alive until he determined who was the killer. But the magistrate spoke first.

"I will wait to sentence you because you are accused of yet another serious crime," he said to Nitta. "You will now undergo trial for the murder of Lord Mitsuyoshi."

The treasury minister jerked upright, as if pierced by shock. Disbelief stunned Sano. Magistrate Aoki intended to try Nitta here, today, for the murder, and hadn't even notified Sano! Then Sano realized he should have expected this. The magistrate aspired to a loftier status than his present post, and he never gave up trying for a promotion. He always insinuated himself into high-level *bakufu* business, hoping to impress the shogun. Unsatisfied with condemning Treasury Minister Nitta for embezzlement, he'd seized the chance to prosecute Nitta as the murderer of the shogun's heir.

Magistrate Aoki now stared across the room at Sano, defying him to object.

"Honorable Magistrate, with all due respect, I must ask that you postpone the murder trial." Despite his anger, Sano spoke politely because he knew the danger inherent in his request. Heads swiveled toward him, and he recognized important *bakufu* officials among the audience. "I also ask you to defer Treasury Minister Nitta's sentence for embezzlement and keep him under house arrest for now."

"Why is that?" Magistrate Aoki's stony eyes glinted.

Sano saw the treasury minister gazing at him in avid hope of reprieve. Nitta's normally pale skin had acquired the same gray color as his hair; he looked to have aged a decade since Sano had last met him.

"The murder investigation isn't finished," Sano said, although alarmed to take the dubious position of protecting a criminal from the law. "It hasn't yet been established whether Treasury Minister Nitta or someone else is the killer. And I need him to be available for interrogation."

"Your request is noted—and regretfully declined." Magistrate Aoki's manner was deferential, but laced with enjoyment. "I remind you that a magistrate has the right to schedule trials and sentences at his discretion."

While Sano enjoyed high status in the *bakufu* because he belonged to the shogun's inner court, his actual rank was ambiguous. Whether he had authority over other officials was a matter of constant debate.

"The court shall proceed," Magistrate Aoki continued. "Whatever punishment I deem appropriate for Treasury Minister Nitta shall be meted out today."

"His Excellency the Shogun has given me the responsibility for identifying the killer of Lord Mitsuyoshi," Sano said, struggling to control his rage. "For Treasury Minister Nitta to be tried for murder and punished for embezzlement today will interfere with my duty."

"I begin to think that you wish to delay justice for your own sake." Menace lurked beneath Aoki's even voice; the audience stirred in uneasy anticipation. "Would you rather see the murderer of His Excellency's heir go unpunished than have someone other than yourself determine whether Treasury Minister Nitta is guilty?"

This was tantamount to an accusation of treason, and Sano knew that if he persisted in opposing the trial, the accusation might stick. Defeated, he shook his head and seethed in silence. What bad luck that Aoki was on duty this month, instead of Reiko's father! Magistrate Ueda wouldn't place self-aggrandizement before reason.

"We shall hear the first witness," Magistrate Aoki said.

Mixed feelings beset Sano. He didn't want to see Aoki prove Treasury Minister Nitta's guilt when he himself couldn't; but if the magistrate served justice by convicting Nitta, then Sano had no right to complain. Much as he would hate to lose face and the shogun's regard if Aoki solved the mystery, an end to the investigation would quiet the unrest in the *bakufu* and save Sano trouble even if his reputation suffered. Furthermore, Sano was curious to see what the trial revealed.

One of the secretaries said, "Kacho, courtesan of Yoshi-wara, is ordered to come forward."

In the front row of the audience, a woman shuffled forth on her knees and stopped near the *shirasu*. Sano recognized her as one of the courtesans who'd entertained party guests at the Owariya the night Lord Mitsuyoshi died.

"Are you acquainted with Treasury Minister Nitta?" the magistrate asked her.

She bowed and replied meekly: "Yes, Honorable Magistrate."

"Was he so much in love with Lady Wisteria that he reserved all her appointments because he didn't want any other man to have her?"

"Yes, Honorable Magistrate."

"Let it be noted that Treasury Minister Nitta is a jealous man who went to great lengths to keep Lady Wisteria all to himself," Magistrate Aoki said to the assembly. "This witness is dismissed. We shall hear the next one."

Sano's objection to the trial gained force because Magistrate Aoki had used the witness as a puppet to confirm his own statements, which set Treasury Minister Nitta up as the murderer. Virtually all trials in Japan ended with a guilty verdict, and this one was looking to be an example of how Aoki maintained the trend.

The second witness was the proprietor of the Owariya. Magistrate Aoki asked him, "Did Treasury Minister Nitta keep his appointment with Lady Wisteria the night of the murder?"

When the proprietor replied in the negative, Magistrate Aoki said, "Why not?"

"Lord Mitsuyoshi requested Lady Wisteria's company,

and Treasury Minister Nitta yielded to him," said the proprietor.

"Was the treasury minister angry and upset because Lord Mitsuyoshi took his appointment with the woman he loved?"

"Very angry. Very upset."

"Let it be noted that Treasury Minister Nitta's anger toward the victim and bad mood were ample reasons for murder," said Magistrate Aoki.

Sano experienced a sense of vindication because Magistrate Aoki hadn't produced any new evidence against Nitta, and dismay that he sought to convict a man based on evidence that Sano had discovered and thought inadequate.

"How long was Treasury Minister Nitta in the Owariya that night?" the magistrate asked.

"Several hours, Honorable Magistrate," said the proprietor.

"Even though he couldn't have Wisteria and he knew she was upstairs with Lord Mitsuyoshi?" The wrinkles in Magistrate Aoki's face expressed feigned surprise.

"Yes."

The magistrate nodded in satisfaction. He said to the assembly, "Treasury Minister Nitta stayed because he wanted revenge on Lord Mitsuyoshi. He had ample opportunity to sneak upstairs and kill his rival."

The next two witnesses were the guards from the Yoshiwara gate. Under Magistrate Aoki's questioning, they testified that Nitta had bribed them to let him out after curfew.

"Obviously, Treasury Minister Nitta broke the law and left because he was anxious to flee the scene of his crime." Turning to Nitta, the magistrate said, "Have you anything to say in your own defense?"

"I didn't kill anyone." Nitta's high-pitched denial trembled with vehemence. "I'm a thief, but not a murderer."

"A samurai who is depraved enough to rob his lord is capable of murdering his lord's cousin," Magistrate Aoki said. "I pronounce you guilty of the murder of Lord Mitsuyoshi."

Nitta clambered to his feet, scattering the white sand. "I

didn't kill him!" he shouted. A ripple of excitement passed through the audience. "Whatever else I've done, I'm innocent of that!"

Two courtroom guards grabbed him and forced him to his knees. Whether Nitta was telling the truth, or was just trying to avoid further dishonor to his family name, Sano could keep silent no longer.

Rising, he said, "Honorable Magistrate, you mustn't convict on such meager evidence."

Magistrate Aoki glared as if he would like to throw Sano out of the court, but he couldn't because of Sano's high status. "It is the right of a magistrate to appraise evidence. I have decided that the evidence against Treasury Minister Nitta is worthy to convict him of the murder."

"You can't convict me!" Nitta struggled against the guards. "I'm innocent. I swear on my ancestors' honor!"

"You've not even presented the evidence which indicates that he is innocent," Sano protested.

He heard murmurs in the audience, saw faces avid with interest turned on him, and sensed the officials speculating on what would happen to him for taking the side of a confessed traitor. He knew there were people who would be eager to see him executed along with Nitta. His pursuit of the truth always led him into such peril! Yet he couldn't allow the investigation to end with Nitta's conviction and significant odds that the real killer might escape justice.

"I've presented all the evidence I deem relevant," the magistrate said. "It's more than enough to satisfy the law."

This was true: Countless defendants were condemned, wrongly or rightly, on the basis of less evidence than Aoki had presented against Nitta, with the full sanction of the *bakufu*.

Sano said, "You've no witnesses to say that Treasury Minister Nitta went inside the room where Lord Mitsuyoshi died. And there was nothing in that room to prove he did."

The magistrate dismissed this argument with an impatient wave of his hand. "Either he removed all traces of his presence, or you failed to find them. His love for Lady Wisteria is enough evidence that he seized his opportunity to murder the rival who spent that night with her."

"I don't love her!" Nitta wailed in desperation. "If I'd wanted her so badly, I would have bought her freedom and married her. She wanted me to, but I refused. And I would never kill my lord's cousin for a prostitute!"

"There's reason to believe he's telling the truth," Sano said, aware that his every word allied him more strongly with Nitta and impugned his loyalty to the regime. "The treasury minister enjoys other courtesans besides Wisteria. He even financed a ritual bedding display for one of them."

"You see?" Nitta demanded of the magistrate.

"Quiet," Magistrate Aoki said, then turned to Sano. "Whether he enjoys a million other courtesans is irrelevant. Yielding Wisteria to Lord Mitsuyoshi upset him enough to argue with the proprietor, then kill in revenge."

"I was upset because the Owariya charged me for the appointment I lost," Nitta said furiously.

"The musician Fujio is also a suspect, as is Wisteria's chaperone, Momoko, who is under arrest for the murder." Sano advanced up the aisle between the rows of seated men, toward the dais. "You could just as well have prosecuted one of them."

"But neither of them is a convicted traitor." Magistrate Aoki regarded Sano with veiled glee.

That the treasury minister's bad character made him a likelier culprit wasn't the main reason Aoki had chosen him instead of the others, Sano understood. Magistrate Aoki wasn't evil enough to condemn someone on a whim, and he didn't want the blood of Fujio or Momoko on his hands because he realized they might be innocent. Treasury Minister Nitta, who'd already earned the death penalty by embezzling, was a safe scapegoat. The magistrate could tack a murder conviction on him with a clear conscience—and without much concern that the real culprit could be still at large.

If Lord Mitsuyoshi had been the killer's sole target, the killer would have no reason to kill again. The shogun would be satisfied by the conviction of Treasury Minister Nitta. The magistrate would win the promotion he craved.

His ruthless scheming chilled Sano's blood.

"Then condemn Treasury Minister Nitta if you will," Sano said, "but delay the execution." Given some time, he could learn the truth about the murder, and refute Nitta's conviction if necessary. "A few days is all I ask."

"You have already trespassed too far into the purview of the court," Magistrate Aoki said, vexed. "Justice will not be delayed on your account." Turning to Nitta, he said, "I sentence you to death by ritual suicide," then nodded to the guards. "Take him to the execution ground."

A series of gasps and moans came from Nitta. His eyes went wide with horrified realization that all hope was lost. As the guards hauled him toward the door, his legs crumpled; he dangled between the guards like a corpse.

In desperation, Sano stood in the aisle, blocking their progress. "Stop," he commanded.

His four detectives rose and joined him. The guards halted, looking to Magistrate Aoki for orders, as more guards rushed to their aid. Confused murmurs swept the audience.

"I'm taking Treasury Minister Nitta into my keeping," Sano told the magistrate.

He grasped the hilt of his sword; his detectives and the courtroom guards followed suit. As the two sides faced off, the spectators leapt up and pressed themselves against the walls, clearing space for a battle.

Magistrate Aoki's eyes blazed with an ire that told Sano he'd made a permanent foe. "I'll not allow bloodshed to foul my court," he said. At a gesture from him, the guards let go of their weapons and released Nitta, who collapsed on the floor. "You can prevent his death by force if you wish. But I advise you to think hard before you do."

Deadly quiet stilled the courtroom while Sano foresaw the potential consequences of his actions. Taking Nitta seemed the only way to buy himself time to solve the case. But he would face severe criticism for protecting a traitor. Whether Sano had the power to overrule Magistrate Aoki was beside the point. Interfering with the legal process would brand him an opponent of justice. His own loyalty to the regime would be questioned, his reputation ruined. The treasury minister was officially guilty of the murder of the shogun's heir, and many people would therefore believe Nitta really was the killer. If the shogun believed it, Sano would be exiled at the least, but more probably executed. Even if the shogun spared Sano's family, Reiko and Masahiro would share his disgrace. Their lives would be ruined.

For the sake of Treasury Minister Nitta, who might eventually prove to be the murderer after all.

Anger and frustration boiled within Sano. He shook his head at his detectives. Then, while Magistrate Aoki gloated, they all stood aside to let the guards bear Treasury Minister Nitta from the room.

20

"Treasury Minister Nitta has committed *seppuku*?" said Hirata.

Sano nodded unhappily. "The news is official." Some two hours had passed since the trial. Now Sano, Hirata, and Reiko sat in Sano's office. Reiko poured steaming tea into bowls for the three of them.

"What's going to happen?" she said.

"The best outcome is that I can persuade the shogun to let me keep investigating the murder until I prove whether Treasury Minister Nitta really was the killer or Magistrate Aoki made a mistake." Sano sipped tea; it scalded his mouth. "The worst is that the shogun will decide *I* made a mistake, failed in my duty, and offended the regime."

He didn't have to elaborate the consequences for Hirata and Reiko; their expressions said they understood.

"But we won't know which it will be for a while yet," Sano said. "The shogun is ill, and has issued orders that he doesn't want to be disturbed. I wrote a report explaining what I did at the trial and left it with the shogun's secretary. But Magistrate Aoki will have sent a report, too. We'll just have to wait and hope that when the shogun reads the reports, he likes my side of the story better than Aoki's."

Dread pervaded the atmosphere as they sat holding their tea bowls. To boost morale, Sano said, "For now we'll proceed as if the investigation will continue. I've got some new leads." He told of his visits from officials who wanted to incriminate their enemies. "They may be spurious, but we'll have to check them. What have you learned today?"

"I've found no trace of Lady Wisteria or her Hokkaido lover," Hirata said, eyes downcast. "They weren't at any of the Suruga teahouses or Fukagawa noodle shops, and I searched them all. I'm beginning to wonder if the man doesn't exist, and the pillow book isn't genuine."

Disappointment burdened Sano's spirits, because if he was to convince the shogun that the inquiries should go on, he needed better justification than a lot of dead ends. "It's too early to give up," he told Hirata. "Keep looking."

Reiko said, "I may have found something important." Her manner was cautious but hopeful. She described meeting Lady Wisteria's family, and what she'd heard at their home. "That Wisteria tried to steal her mother's husband, and ruined her mother's clothes as revenge for selling her into Yoshiwara, shows her to be a selfish, mean person."

"And therefore a good murder suspect, even if what happened when she was young has no direct bearing on Lord Mitsuyoshi's death," Hirata said, looking cheered by the new development.

However, Reiko's description of Wisteria disturbed Sano profoundly. The courtesan had lied to him about her past, and he realized that he knew even less about her than he'd thought. The idea that his former lover was the killer revolted Sano. But if he proved that Treasury Minister Nitta was innocent, the list of suspects would shrink, and the odds that Wisteria was guilty would rise.

"I may also have some clues to where Lady Wisteria has

gone," Reiko said. "She had a childhood friend named Yuya. After I left her mother's house, I questioned the neighbors. They said Yuya works in a bathhouse somewhere in town. Maybe Wisteria took shelter with her."

"I'll have my detectives search the bathhouses," Sano said.

"A man bought Wisteria's freedom about four years ago," Reiko said. "Her mother doesn't know how Wisteria got back in Yoshiwara, or the name of the man. But he was rumored to be a high-ranking samurai official. I think I should try to find out who he is, because he might be able to lead us to Wisteria, if Yuya can't."

Dismay jarred Sano. A hum of alarm began in his head as a bad day turned worse. Just as he'd feared, Reiko's inquiries concerning Lady Wisteria had led to him.

A little frown of uncertainty puckered Reiko's forehead as she sensed the change in atmosphere. "Is something wrong?"

Sano noticed Hirata watching him to see whether he would tell Reiko about his relationship with Lady Wisteria. Must he now reveal what he'd hidden from his wife? If they were to proceed with the investigation together, what choice had he? Panic besieged him.

Just then, a manservant appeared in the doorway. "Excuse me, master," he said to Sano, "but a letter has just arrived for you. The messenger said it's urgent." He proffered a scroll case made from a short cylinder of bamboo, sealed with wooden plugs at the ends.

"Thank you," Sano said. Never had an interruption been so timely. Awash in relief, he opened the case, unrolled and read the letter.

If you want to learn something important about the murder of Lord Mitsuyoshi, go to the house in the hills that belongs to the *hokan* Fujio.

There was no signature on the message, but it did include directions to the house.

Sano, Hirata, and a squadron of detectives and troops followed the directions into the hills north of Edo. They rode along a winding highway that climbed the forested slopes. Frigid wind ripped the smoke from their lanterns and the breath from their lungs. The horses galloped on hard earth that had borne little traffic since summer, when Edo's citizens took to the hills for relief from the heat. The cold fire of sunset burned above the leafless trees; patches of snow reflected pink upon the ground. In the darkening sky rose the moon, a radiant silver crescent filigreed by shadows, suspended amid stars.

"When I told Fujio that I wanted to search his house, I had a feeling he was hiding something," Sano said to Hirata. "Now I think he didn't want me to know he has another house besides the one in Imado where he lives."

"I hope we find something worthwhile." Hirata echoed Sano's hopes.

Yet they both harbored skepticism about the clue. Before leaving town, they'd tried to discover who had sent it. A castle messenger had delivered the letter, which the guards at the main gate had given him. The guards said a man had brought them the letter; but they couldn't recall anything about him because they took so many messages from so many people. The letter was written on cheap, common paper, in a hand unfamiliar to Sano. Although he and Hirata feared a trick, they couldn't afford to ignore the message.

The sunset faded to a dull red edge on the horizon, and darkness clothed the hills. Sano saw the shape of a house with a peaked roof and jutting veranda, clinging to a nearby hillside. "There it is," he called to his companions.

They left the horses, with two soldiers to guard them, at the bottom of a steep, narrow trail. As Sano climbed the trail with Hirata, the detectives, and his troops, the cold worsened; curves in the path obscured what lay ahead. Tree trunks and underbrush confined the light from the lanterns in a minuscule space around Sano and his men. Nothing else moved in the forest; the only sounds were their footsteps in the rocky path, the huffing of their breath, and the distant ripple of a stream. But Sano recalled the many attacks on him since he'd become the shogun's *sōsakan-sama*.

Was the anonymous message the lure for an ambush?

The trail abruptly ended in a clearing. There stood the house, a dilapidated shack. It appeared to be an ordinary, cheap summer retreat, yet Sano's instincts prickled, sensing evil.

"Beware," he whispered to his men.

The guards led the advance, cautiously panning their lanterns as they stole through knee-high grass that rustled underfoot. Sano and Hirata followed, while the detectives brought up the rear, their alert gazes sweeping the area for signs of trouble. A lull in the wind stilled the forest; the stream rippled. Somewhere, a dog or wolf howled. As the group neared the house, the lanterns revealed weathered plank walls, a thatched roof, latticed windows, and a door framed by a webbing of vines.

Pausing near the threshold, Sano motioned for the guards to circle and scout the building. They obeyed, then returned, shaking their heads to indicate they'd seen no threats. At a gesture from Sano, they opened the door and shone the lanterns into the dark space within. The light penetrated a narrow, empty passage. Sano nodded; the guards preceded him and the others inside, along a bare, creaking wooden floor, beneath low rafters. The lanterns splashed their shadows across paper walls. Sano inhaled, trying to scent danger, but the cold had numbed his nose: He smelled nothing.

"There's nobody here," Hirata said, voicing what Sano perceived.

A slithering sound caused Sano's heart to lurch; everyone started. Hands grasped swords. A guard flashed his lantern into a kitchen furnished with cooking utensils on shelves, and a plaster-encased hearth. It was vacant, the sound probably caused by vermin seeking food. Breaths fogged the air as everyone relaxed; yet as they moved to the doorway of the opposite room, Sano's instincts blared a continuous warning.

Inside the room, tatami covered the floor; dried flowers

bloomed from a vase in the alcove. A table held a cricket cage, sake jar, and folding fan—relics of summer. On a lacquer chest lay a few papers. Hirata fetched them and gave them to Sano.

They were musical scores, signed by Fujio.

One more room remained. As the group approached this, dread slowed Sano's steps. Whatever he was meant to find must be there.

The cramped space he saw from the threshold appeared as abandoned and lifeless as the rest of the house. A swath of white muslin mosquito net hung from the ceiling and draped a futon. The futon held what at first looked to be a large, crooked bundle of fabric. Then Sano saw, protruding from one end of the bundle and out of the mosquito net, an arm that extended to a hand with curled fingers. The bundle was a human body, slender and curved and female, dressed in a patterned kimono and sprawled on the futon. That she lay so still, in this freezing, isolated house, could mean only one thing.

"Merciful gods," Sano said.

He and his comrades rushed into the room. Sano flung back the mosquito net, and everyone exclaimed in horror. The body was headless, the neck an ugly stump of mangled flesh, clotted blood, and hacked bone. In his memory Sano heard a girlish voice saying, "She wore a black kimono with purple wisteria blossoms and green vines on it." The garment on the dead woman was surely the one described by the *kamuro*, Chidori.

"Lady Wisteria," Sano said, aghast.

Reiko lay in bed, where she'd fallen into a restless sleep hours after Sano left for Fujio's house. Quiet footsteps in the corridor impinged on her consciousness, and she jerked awake, breath caught, eyes wide open in the darkness of her room.

She knew the estate was well guarded, but ever since the Black Lotus case, noises at night conjured up terror of attack.

She snatched up the dagger she kept beside the bed. Silently she crept down the corridor, shivering with cold and fear. Lamplight glowed from the bathchamber; a human shadow moved inside. Peering cautiously through the open door, Reiko saw Sano. He was undressing. Her body sagged in relief. She lowered the dagger and entered the room.

"I'm glad you're home," she said.

Sano nodded without looking at her, his features set in a frown. He dropped his sash on the slatted wooden floor, then stripped off his trousers. He tore off his robes and socks. Reiko noticed his hands shaking; the sculpted muscles of his stomach contracted in spasms as he shed his loincloth. He squatted, emptied a bucket of water over himself, and shuddered in the icy splash.

Worried by his strange behavior, Reiko laid down the dagger and crouched near Sano. "What happened at Fujio's house?"

Sano picked up a bag of rice-bran soap and violently scrubbed his torso. His voice emerged from between chattering teeth: "We found the dead body of a woman."

"Oh." Reiko now understood why Sano would bathe in the middle of the night. He wanted to cleanse himself of the spiritual pollution from his contact with death. Postponing more questions, she said, "Let me help you."

She lit the charcoal braziers. Luckily, the water in the round, sunken wooden tub was still warm, heated earlier for her own bath. She washed Sano's back and rinsed him. He climbed into the tub, groaning as he immersed himself up to his chin and closed his eyes. Reiko knelt beside the tub. Moments passed. Gradually Sano ceased shuddering.

"The body was wearing the kimono that Lady Wisteria had on the night she vanished," he said wearily.

Dismayed, Reiko said, "But you don't know for sure if the body is hers?"

"The woman's head was missing."

Reiko sucked air through pursed lips. "Did she die from decapitation?"

"I don't know yet. I had my men take the body to Edo

Morgue for Dr. Ito to examine. But this clearly wasn't a natural death. She was murdered."

"Was there a weapon?"

Sano opened hollow eyes that looked unfocused, as if he saw the murder scene instead of Reiko. "We searched the house," he said, "but we didn't find anything. Her killer could have taken the weapon, or thrown it away in the woods. The same possibilities apply to her head."

A feeling of distance between her and Sano troubled Reiko. Tonight the investigation, which she'd hoped would unite them, seemed to have separated them further. But perhaps this was just a temporary effect caused by Sano's upsetting experience.

"Do you think Fujio killed Wisteria?" Reiko asked.

"She was in his house," Sano said. "That implicates him."

Reiko sensed that Sano was upset about more than discovering the body and losing a witness. She wanted to ask what it was, but his reticence prevented her. Instead she said, "How did Wisteria get there?"

"Fujio could have smuggled her out of Yoshiwara and hidden her in his house." Sano spoke as if forcing out each word; he stared at the water before him.

"Wouldn't he have known better than to kill her on his own property, leave her corpse there, and incriminate himself?"

"He might have thought no one would find her there. I never would have, if not for that message."

Reiko also sensed that Sano wasn't telling her everything. "If Fujio did kill Wisteria, does that mean he also killed Lord Mitsuyoshi?"

"Perhaps."

"Could someone else have found Wisteria and killed her?" Reiko hated coaxing Sano to talk when he would obviously rather not; but they needed to determine what the new murder meant to the case.

"Anything is possible," Sano said in that same reluctant tone. "But who besides Fujio would have known she was in the house?"

"Perhaps a traveler who happened upon her?" Reiko said.

"There aren't many travelers in the hills this time of year, though she could have been killed by bandits robbing summer homes. Her death must be connected with Lord Mitsuyoshi's murder, and so must the killer."

Reiko had hoped that if they kept talking, Sano would open up about what was bothering him. "Who would want Lady Wisteria dead and Fujio blamed?" When Sano didn't answer, Reiko suggested, "It could be the person who sent the message."

Sano rested his head against the rim of the tub and closed his eyes, exhaling a tremulous breath.

Increasingly worried, Reiko said, "Are you ill? Shall I prepare you a medicinal tea?"

His throat muscles clenched as he swallowed. "No. I'm fine."

"If you'd rather be alone . . . ?" Although unwilling to leave him like this, Reiko rose.

"Don't go." With an obvious effort, Sano opened his eyes, lifted his head, and met her gaze. "We need to talk."

Reiko waited, nervous about what she might hear. A heartbeat passed in ominous suspense. Then Sano said, "Maybe the dead woman isn't Wisteria, and the scene at the house was arranged to mislead me."

"And her head could have been removed so you would think she was Wisteria." Reiko guessed that this topic wasn't the one Sano had originally intended to broach. "But if it isn't Wisteria, then who is it?"

"I hope Dr. Ito can provide some answers," Sano said.

"Doesn't this murder cast doubt on Treasury Minister Nitta's conviction?" Reiko asked.

"If the victim is Wisteria, and it happened after Nitta was arrested, yes. Her disappearance from Yoshiwara and Lord Mitsuyoshi's death are linked, and if Nitta is innocent of one thing, he may not be guilty of the other."

Sano's melancholy seemed unrelieved by this theory that justified continuing his investigation. "All this time I've felt so sure Wisteria was alive," he said.

Reiko detected in him a concern that seemed deeper than she would expect him to feel about a stranger who was a murder suspect. A vague, disturbing notion crossed her mind.

Sano's shoulders moved in a gesture that expressed doubt and anxiety. "Whether or not this murder is what it seems, there's no use drawing conclusions until we hear what Fujio has to say about what we found."

He climbed out of the tub, and as Reiko draped a cloth around him, she rejected her notion. It was surely a product of the distrust instilled in her by the Black Lotus. Whatever secret Sano was keeping from her, that couldn't be it.

"Let's go to bed and try to sleep for what's left of the night," Sano said. "In the morning, Hirata will question Fujio while I go to Edo Morgue and see what Dr. Ito's examination of the corpse can tell us. What we learn might help me persuade the shogun to let the investigation go on."

His face was haggard with exhaustion. "Or it might not."

21

The village of Imado, home to various Yoshiwara merchants and workers, lay across rice fields and marshes from the pleasure quarter. It contained a few streets of houses, shops, inns, and teahouses. Upon arriving in Imado with two detectives, Hirata proceeded to one of several villas on the outskirts, built by wealthy brothel owners.

A thatched roof spread over the interconnecting wooden structures that comprised Fujio's house; a stone wall enclosed the surrounding garden and courtyard. Beyond the wall stretched fallow brown earth dotted with farmers' cottages. Gauzy bands of white cloud streaked the pale blue sky. Sunlight brightened a chill, blustery morning as Hirata and the detectives dismounted outside Fujio's gate and walked into the courtyard.

When Hirata knocked on the door, a boy answered. Hirata said, "We're here to see Fujio."

Eventually, the *hokan* came to the door, yawning. His

handsome face was puffy, his hair mussed. He wore a blue-and-red checked dressing gown, and reeked of liquor and tobacco smoke. His bloodshot eyes blinked in puzzlement at Hirata; but he smiled and bowed gallantly.

"Sorry for my miserable appearance," he said, "but I was out late last night. What can I do for you, masters?"

Hirata introduced himself, then said, "I need to talk to you. May we come in?"

"If this is about what happened to Lord Mitsuyoshi, I've already told the *sōsakan-sama* everything I know." Fujio rubbed his temples and winced. "Merciful gods, what a headache! I really shouldn't drink while I perform."

"It's about your house in the hills," said Hirata.

Dismay cleared the sleepiness from the *hokan*'s face. "Uh," said Fujio. He took a step backward and bumped into two women who appeared in the entryway behind him. One was young, pretty, and pregnant, the other middle-aged and scowling.

"Who are those men?" the younger woman asked Fujio in a shrill, petulant voice. "What do they want?"

"It's none of your business," Fujio told her with obvious irritation.

"How can you be so rude to let your guests stand outside?" the older woman chastised him. "Invite them in."

Fujio rolled his eyes. "My wife and her mother," he explained to Hirata. "Could we please talk somewhere else?"

Hirata agreed. Fujio went to dress, and returned wearing a brown cloak and kimono over wide, striped trousers. He and Hirata walked down the lane toward the village, while the detectives trailed them. Ducks huddled in a ditch alongside the lane; in the distance, a peasant drove oxen across the sere landscape.

"My wife and in-laws don't know I own the house, and I don't want them to know. I bought it years ago, as a summer retreat." Fujio eyed Hirata. "You married?"

"No," Hirata said. After reading Lord Niu's letter yesterday, he doubted he ever would be, unless he accepted his father's choice of a bride. But he couldn't give up on finding some way to make peace between the two clans so he could wed Midori.

"Well, when you do marry, you'll understand that having a wife can really tie you down," Fujio said. "Especially if you live with her parents. A fellow needs a place where he can have a little privacy."

"And the company of lady friends?" Hirata said.

Fujio cracked a mischievous grin. "Well, yes. That house comes in handy for entertaining my female admirers. But I'd be ruined if my father-in-law ever learned that I was unfaithful to his daughter. He would throw me out. Besides, he owns the Great Miura brothel and has a lot of influence in Yoshiwara. I would never get any work there again."

Was this the only reason Fujio wanted to keep the house a secret? Hirata said, "Tell me about the woman you've been keeping in the house."

"What?" Fujio halted. "Nobody's there now. I only use the place in the summer." The daze from his hangover dissipated; he looked puzzled but sober. "Say, how did you find out about my house, anyway?"

"The *sōsakan-sama* got a letter," Hirata said. "We went there last night and found a dead woman in your bed."

A cloud of breath puffed out of Fujio's mouth, but no sound emerged. His surprise seemed genuine, though Hirata knew Fujio was an entertainer and skilled at dramatics.

". . . A dead woman? In my house?" After a few more stammers, Fujio recovered enough composure to say, "Who was it?"

"We don't know. Her head had been cut off and removed from the premises," Hirata said, closely watching Fujio. "But she was dressed in what appear to be Lady Wisteria's clothes."

"Wisteria? Merciful gods." Fujio staggered backward, as if physically shaken by the news. "What was she doing there?"

"You tell me."

"Wait." The *hokan* raised his hands palm-up. "If you think

I killed Wisteria, you've got it all wrong. I don't know how she got in my . . ."

A look of comprehension sharpened his eyes. "But I can guess. When we were lovers, I told her about my house. She must have remembered, and gone there because she knew it would be empty. She did it without my knowledge or permission. I had nothing to do with her dying."

He could be telling the truth, Hirata thought—or improvising an explanation to protect himself.

"Tell me everything you did from the time Lord Mitsuyoshi's murder was discovered, up to last night," Hirata said.

The *hokan* pondered with intense concentration, clearly recognizing his need to demonstrate that he'd been nowhere near his secret house. "I was performing in the Owariya when Momoko ran into the party screaming that Lord Mitsuyoshi was dead. The Yoshiwara gate was shut, and before it opened in the morning, the police came and locked everyone in the quarter. When they let us go, I went home."

"What did you do there?" Hirata said.

"I had dinner with my family," Fujio said, "then went to sleep." He added with pointed emphasis, "I was in bed all night, beside my wife."

Hirata intended to check this story with the *hokan*'s wife and in-laws, although they might confirm what Fujio said whether it was true or not, to protect him. "And in the morning?"

"I went to Yoshiwara. There wasn't much going on, so I sat around the teahouses, drinking and playing cards with friends."

"Were you with them the whole time?" Hirata said.

"Not every moment, but I was never out of their sight long enough to go to the hills." Yet Fujio slowed his speech, as if he saw danger looming ahead in his tale. "That night I performed at a party. The *sōsakan-sama* met me there. After we talked, I entertained the guests until dawn. Then . . ."

From a distance echoed the ring of an axe, chopping wood. "Then what?" Hirata prompted, eager because they'd reached a critical time period. This morning he'd learned that

Fujio had managed to shake the detectives assigned to watch him, and he'd been out of their sight from dawn until afternoon of that day, when they'd caught up with him in Yoshiwara.

"I visited a friend," Fujio said reluctantly. "I was with . . . my friend until yesterday afternoon, when I went back to Yoshiwara to perform."

"Who is this friend?"

"A woman." Despite the cold, Fujio's face was slick with sweat. "I can't tell her name. She's the wife of a patron." He shook his head, deploring his own rakish behavior. "How do I get myself into these things?"

"If you want me to believe you were with this woman, she must verify what you've told me," Hirata said.

"But I can't let her," Fujio protested. "Her husband is a prominent samurai. He has a bad temper. If he finds out about us, he'll kill me."

Tokugawa law permitted a samurai to kill a peasant and escape punishment. Fujio seemed caught between the threat of his mistress's husband on one side and execution for murder on the other. The story sounded credible to Hirata, who began to doubt that Fujio had killed the woman. Fujio was clever; if he'd committed the crime, wouldn't he have invented a better alibi? Furthermore, Hirata's examination of the crime scene last night argued that Fujio could be innocent.

There was no evidence that Fujio had been in the house recently. The woman could have gone there by herself. Hirata even wondered whether she'd been hiding there at all. The stove and braziers had contained no sign of recent fire, the only food in the house was some old dried fruit, and the privy didn't smell as if anyone had used it lately. The woman could have been taken there and immediately killed—by someone who wanted to frame Fujio.

Yet perhaps Fujio was guilty, but hadn't expected the body to be found, and therefore had thought he wouldn't need an alibi. The story about a secret mistress might have been the best he could do when caught off guard.

"I think you went to see Wisteria at your house yesterday," Hirata said. "Maybe she didn't like being alone, in the cold, and she complained. Maybe you were desperate because you had nowhere else to put her. There was an argument. Things got out of control. You killed her."

"That never happened." Fujio shifted his stance, planting his feet firmly on the ground.

"Or maybe you intended to kill her all along," Hirata said, "because she saw you kill Lord Mitsuyoshi."

"Treasury Minister Nitta did it." Triumph tinged Fujio's declaration. "I heard the news."

"You killed Wisteria before you knew Nitta was convicted," Hirata guessed. "You were afraid she would tell the police that you're the killer, and you couldn't let her live."

In Fujio's eyes dawned the realization that this was exactly how it looked—and how a magistrate who tried him for the murder would interpret the crime scene.

"I didn't kill Lord Mitsuyoshi," Fujio said hotly. "And I didn't kill Wisteria. Someone put her body in my house to make it look like I killed her!" A visible current of panic tautened his slim figure. Hirata sprang forward to grab Fujio, at the same instant that the *hokan* turned and bolted across the rice fields.

"Hey! Come back here!" Launching himself in pursuit, Hirata called to the detectives: "Stop him!"

Fujio stumbled over dirt clods, his garments flapping, legs and arms pumping furiously. Hirata panted as he labored to catch up. But soon Fujio's pace slowed; fatigue hobbled his gait. Hirata closed the distance between them and lunged, seizing Fujio around the waist.

The *hokan* fell forward and slammed to the ground. Hirata landed with a thud on top of him. Fujio lay limp and wheezing.

"You're under arrest," Hirata said.

After the treasury minister had died with his guilt or innocence undetermined, Hirata couldn't risk allowing one of Sano's only two other suspects to escape. And even if Fujio proved not to have killed the shogun's heir, he was still the primary suspect in the murder of the woman at his house.

"Silly habit of mine, running away when I'm sure to get caught," Fujio said, managing a wry laugh. "But this time it was worth a try."

Although Sano usually traveled with an entourage to assist him and uphold the dignity of his rank, Edo Jail was a place he preferred to go alone.

Edo Jail, a fortified dungeon surrounded by deteriorating stone walls and watchtowers, reigned over the slums of northeast Nihonbashi. Inside, jailers tortured confessions out of prisoners, and convicted criminals awaited execution. The jail also housed Edo Morgue, which received the bodies of citizens who perished from natural disasters or unnatural causes. There Dr. Ito, morgue custodian, often lent his medical expertise to Sano's investigations. Because the examination of corpses and any other procedures associated with foreign science were illegal, Sano wanted as few people as possible to know about his visits to Edo Jail.

Dr. Ito met him at the door of the morgue, a low building with flaking plaster walls. "What a pleasure to see you," Dr. Ito said.

In his seventies, he had white hair like a snowfall above his wise, lined face and wore the dark blue coat of a physician. Years ago he'd been caught practicing forbidden foreign science, which he'd learned through illicit channels from Dutch traders. The *bakufu* had forgone the usual sentence of exile and condemned him to work for the rest of his life in Edo Morgue. There Dr. Ito had continued his scientific experiments, ignored by the authorities.

"However, I might have wished for a better occasion than another violent death," he said.

"I, too," Sano said. "I wouldn't ask you to examine another body now if I had any choice."

The Black Lotus disaster had taken its toll on Dr. Ito even though he hadn't been at the temple that night, when over seven hundred people had died. Their bodies had been taken directly to a mass funeral outside town, but many nuns and priests had died from injuries or committed suicide in jail, and Dr. Ito had prepared their corpses for cremation. His horror at the Black Lotus carnage had put a halt to his work—the one solace that made his imprisonment bearable—and the spiritual pollution from so many deaths had weakened his health.

Dr. Ito smiled reassuringly and gestured for Sano to enter the morgue. "Justice for a murder victim takes precedence over personal feelings."

Inside the morgue, a large room held stone troughs used for washing the dead, cabinets containing tools, a podium stacked with papers and books, and three waist-high tables. Upon one table lay a figure draped by a white cloth. Beside this stood Dr. Ito's assistant, Mura, a man of some fifty years, who had bushy gray hair and an angular, intelligent face.

"We're ready to begin, Mura-*san*," said Dr. Ito.

Mura was an *eta*, one of the outcast class from which came the wardens, torturers, corpse handlers, and executioners of Edo Jail. The *eta*'s hereditary link with death-related occupations such as butchering and leather tanning rendered them spiritually contaminated. Most citizens shunned them, but Dr. Ito had befriended Mura, who performed all the physical work for Dr. Ito's studies.

As Sano went to stand near the table, he battled an impulse to run away. He'd not yet recovered from the horror and nausea he'd experienced upon finding the body. He dreaded examining the corpse of a woman he'd known intimately.

Mura peeled off the white cloth from the corpse, beginning at the feet. The rigidity of death had passed, and the woman lay flat on her back, limbs straight. Her feet were bare, their skin a bluish white; dirt and cuts marked the soles. As her clothes came into view, Sano observed red-brown splotches on the kimono's purple and green floral pattern. The woman's fingernails were broken and crusted with dried blood. Mura uncovered her top half, exposing the hideous mutilation where her head should have been. The sweet odor of rotting meat struck Sano; his stomach lurched.

"Where did you find her?" Dr. Ito asked.

Sano related the details of the murder investigation, explained how he'd discovered the body, and described the scene.

"Was there blood around the body?" Dr. Ito said.

An indelible picture of the room haunted Sano's mind. "Not much. Some spatters on the floor, the wall, the futon, and the mosquito net."

He knew Reiko was worried about him, and he'd wished to act normal in front of her last night, but all his energy had gone toward keeping sickness and emotion at bay. Closing himself off from Reiko would drive them farther apart, but he couldn't explain the murder's extreme effect on him without telling her what would make matters worse.

"To determine exactly what happened, we must view the rest of her." Dr. Ito gestured to Mura.

The *eta* fetched a knife and cut the kimono off the woman. He removed the white under-kimono, exposing her naked body. It was an ugly patchwork of huge red and purple bruises that had erupted under the pale skin on her abdomen, breasts, and ribcage. Smaller bruises blotched her neck, arms, and thighs. Sano inhaled sharply through his teeth; Dr. Ito murmured in dismay, and even the stoic Mura looked shaken.

"Please turn her on her side, Mura-*san*," said Dr. Ito.

Mura obeyed, and they silently viewed the bruised back and buttocks. Then Dr. Ito walked around the table, his expression pitying as he studied the corpse. "This brutality indicates a male rather than a female attacker, because it required considerable strength. Those bruises were made by fists. The small ones on the arms and neck are fingerprints."

"She fought back," Sano said, observing the woman's hands. "Her fingernails are broken and bloody because she clawed her attacker."

In his mind he saw the blood on the floor and walls, smeared with two sets of handprints and footprints, one large, one small—the victim's and the killer's. If this was Wisteria, what responsibility did he bear for her death?

"Note these dark, deep bruises along her back. After she fell, he kicked and trampled her," Dr. Ito said. "She probably died from the rupture of internal organs."

"So he beat her to death."

Sano wished more than ever that he'd bothered to find out what had become of Wisteria after their affair ended, and not just because he might have saved her life. His sense of responsibility extended to what she might have done, as well as what had been done to her.

"The removal of the head was performed after death," said Dr. Ito, "because otherwise, there would have been copious blood in the room."

"The dead don't bleed," Sano concurred, forcing a matter-of-fact tone even as he saw bits of gore clinging to mosquito net. "After he killed her, he laid her on the bed, then decapitated her."

"And see how the neck is hacked and ragged at the edges." The concern in Dr. Ito's eyes said he guessed that something troubled Sano. "Whoever did this must have been in a violent frenzy of rage."

From the jail drifted the howls of the prisoners. Sano envisioned Wisteria, her beautiful face contorted in terror, trying to ward off a shadowy attacker. He heard her scream as fists hit her, saw her clutch the wall as she went down under a storm of blows and kicks . . .

With an effort Sano said, "Now that we know how she died, we just have to figure out if this really is Lady Wisteria, and whether Fujio killed her."

"Let us first determine whether this woman matches the missing courtesan's description." Dr. Ito paused, clearly on the verge of asking Sano what was wrong; but either Sano's expression stopped him, or courtesy precluded prying. "How old is Wisteria?"

"Twenty-four years," Sano said. Her age was the one thing she'd told him that he thought he could take as fact.

"This woman was young," Dr. Ito said, studying the corpse. "Her flesh is smooth and firm. Twenty-four years is a reasonable estimate of her age."

The similarity in age could be a coincidence, Sano thought; but the spreading hollow in his stomach said otherwise.

"What is Wisteria's physical size and shape?" Dr. Ito said.

"She's small." Sano raised his hand at shoulder height, assailed by a memory of embracing Wisteria. He tried to compare his knowledge of her naked body to the dead woman's, but the absence of a face, as well as the bruises and the pall of death, made recognition impossible. He swallowed and forced himself to continue: "She's slim, with narrow hips and small breasts."

"As is the victim." Dr. Ito glanced at the part of the woman's body where Sano had avoided looking and said, "Her pubis is shaved. She was a prostitute."

So many points of resemblance indicated that the dead woman was Lady Wisteria, even if they weren't final proof. Sano felt his hope that Wisteria was still alive yield to desolation; he turned away from the body.

"Cover her, Mura-*san*," Dr. Ito said quietly.

Whatever lies Wisteria had told or evils she'd committed, she'd been a proud, courageous woman. Sano recalled her aloof behavior the last time he'd seen her. Might she have had a premonition that her remaining time on earth was short?

"Do you think the *hokan* killed her?" Dr. Ito asked.

"It's hard to imagine Fujio being capable of such brutality. Hirata went to question him this morning. We'll see what happens."

Sano stared grimly out the window as he pondered the consequences that the second murder held for him. His investigation could now continue, because even if the shogun believed that the killer of his heir had already been punished, he would expect Sano to solve the case of the decapitated woman. New inquiries might turn up new evidence to prove who had killed Lord Mitsuyoshi. Yet this prospect caused Sano dread as well as satisfaction.

"Mura-*san*, please leave us," Dr. Ito said. The *eta* complied, and Dr. Ito stood near Sano. "Can I be of further assistance?" he said gently.

The need to confide overcame Sano's reserve. "I knew her," he blurted, then told Dr. Ito his secret. "It's hard to be objective when the victim could be someone who was once my lover," he admitted. "But if I go on with this investigation, I'll have to keep my mind open to the possibility that the dead woman is Lady Wisteria—and that Wisteria was a murderer."

Dr. Ito nodded in somber understanding. "If the treasury minister was innocent, then Wisteria, Fujio, and Momoko are the only suspects left. Wisteria may have stabbed Lord Mitsuyoshi."

"In other words, my former lover killed my lord's heir."

Sano felt sicker than ever. "There's another problem. My wife doesn't know any of this. I never told her about Wisteria and me because I thought it wouldn't matter. But if Reiko keeps on with her inquiries, she may find out that I freed Wisteria and think I haven't told her because I have something to hide."

Fraught with anxiety, Sano clenched his hands around the window bars. Never had he expected his minor omission to grow into a major threat to his already shaky marriage. "I wish I'd told her at the start. What should I do now?"

"A tiny pebble rolling down a mountain can start a landslide," Dr. Ito reminded him. "I suggest you tell your wife as soon as possible, because the longer you wait, the worse your problems may get."

22

The palanquin carried Reiko out the gate of Edo Castle's official quarter. Huddled beneath a quilt, she brooded as she rode along the stone-walled passage leading toward the palace.

Sano's behavior last night disturbed her, as did the fact that he'd left home this morning before she'd awakened. Perhaps this latest murder was too much for him? She feared for his spirit. And at any moment the shogun might condemn him for interfering with Treasury Minister Nitta's trial and failing to solve the murder case.

Reiko also worried about Midori, who'd come to the house earlier to announce that she'd received a message from Lord Niu, ordering her to come to him. Midori was now headed to Lord Niu's estate, while Reiko traveled toward the palace women's quarters, where her cousin Eri was an official. Eri, the center of Edo Castle's female gossip network, could perhaps identify the samurai who'd freed Lady Wisteria. Finding him seemed more important to Reiko than ever. If Wisteria was still alive, he might know where she was. If she was the corpse in the summer house, he might have information relevant to her murder.

The thought of Wisteria caused Reiko more worry about Sano. She'd guessed that he didn't want her investigating the courtesan's background. Was there something he didn't want her to discover?

Suddenly Reiko heard hoofbeats and footsteps approaching. Her palanquin rocked to a standstill as her guards, bearers, and maids halted. Reiko put her head out the window to see who was blocking the passage. She saw a procession of troops and attendants facing her, escorting a large black palanquin. Out of its window popped two heads. One belonged to Lady Yanagisawa, the other to her daughter, Kikuko.

The girl smiled and waved. As Reiko waved back and bowed, Lady Yanagisawa murmured something to her escorts. Her guard captain addressed Reiko's: "The wife of the Honorable Chamberlain wishes to visit the wife of the *sōsakan-sama*."

Reiko was surprised that Lady Yanagisawa wanted to see her again so soon. Though reluctant to delay her inquiries, she had no choice except to tell her attendants, "Take me home."

Inside the reception room of Sano's estate, Lady Yanagisawa and Kikuko knelt opposite Reiko. Lady Yanagisawa politely declined Reiko's offer of refreshment.

"We won't stay long," she said. Suppressed emotion ruffled her composure, and a blush tinged her flat cheeks. She held in her lap a small bundle wrapped inside a square of dark blue silk printed with white leaves. "I'm sorry to bother you when you were on your way somewhere."

"Oh, it's no bother," Reiko said. "I'm glad to see you again."

Yet she feared that their acquaintance would become an onus if her new friend wanted more attention than she wanted to give. The peculiar sheen of Lady Yanagisawa's narrow eyes made Reiko uneasy.

"Please believe that I wouldn't have interrupted your business except . . . except for the most urgent reason." Lady Yanagisawa's voice dropped; she paused, fingering the tied ends of her bundle. Then she blurted, "Last time we met . . . I said I would do whatever I could to assist you with your husband's inquiries. That's why I've come today."

Kikuko hummed a tuneless song, turning her head from side to side. Reiko regarded Lady Yanagisawa with surprise.

"You've found information that will help the murder investigation?" Reiko said. Eyeing the package her guest held, she wavered between skepticism and hope.

A brief frown shadowed Lady Yanagisawa's aspect. "I wish I could say that my discovery will benefit your husband . . . but I fear the opposite is true. May I please explain?"

When Reiko nodded, Lady Yanagisawa said, "Yesterday this came for my husband."

She untied the bundle, revealing a flat, rectangular package wrapped in rough brown paper and bound with coarse string. Reiko saw the words, "For the Honorable Chamberlain Yanagisawa. Personal and Confidential," written on it in simple black characters.

"My husband wasn't home," Lady Yanagisawa said. "I overheard his secretaries saying they didn't know who sent the package and discussing whether to open it. Finally they decided not to, and left the package on my husband's desk. My curiosity was aroused. I went into the office, slipped the package into my sleeve, and took it to my room."

Reiko sat speechless with amazement that anyone would dare steal from the chamberlain.

Lady Yanagisawa sighed. "If my husband finds out what I've done, he'll be very angry with me. But when I looked inside the package . . . I knew I must risk his displeasure."

Her intense, yearning gaze flitted over Reiko. "You've been so kind to me, and I shall now repay you. This package represents a terrible threat to your husband. I brought it to you so that he will understand the danger . . . so that he can protect himself, and you."

"What danger?" Reiko asked in alarmed confusion.

Kikuko emitted a loud keening sound, made faces, and rocked back and forth. Lady Yanagisawa put a hand on the girl's shoulder, quieting her. "Perhaps it's better that you see for yourself than that I should tell you. Please accept this with my sincere wishes for your good fortune, and allow me to bid you farewell until we meet again."

Extending the package on her palms, she bowed to Reiko.

"Many thanks," Reiko said, accepting the gift.

As soon as her guests had gone, she took the package into her chamber and closed the door. Eager yet fearful, she untied the string and unwrapped the paper. Inside was a book covered in lavender silk, bound by a green ribbon threaded through holes near the spine. A thrill of recognition and disbelief shot through Reiko. She opened the book.

The first of some twenty pages of thin white rice paper bore an inscription: *The Pillow Book of Lady Wisteria.*

The daimyo maintained great fortified estates in the district east and south of Edo Castle. Here the provincial lords resided during the four months they spent in the capital each year. Here Tokugawa law required them to leave their families as hostages when they returned to their provinces, to prevent them from staging a revolt. Here Midori rode in a palanquin down a wide avenue crowded with mounted samurai.

Lines of barracks, their white plaster walls decorated with black tiles arranged in geometric patterns, surrounded each estate and housed thousands of retainers who served the daimyo. Elaborate gates boasted multiple portals, tiered roofs, and guardhouses occupied by sentries. As Midori's palanquin halted outside the gate that bore the Niu dragonfly crest, her chin quivered with apprehension.

This had once been her home; but the place harbored bad memories, and she never came back unless it was absolutely necessary. If not for her father's summons and the hope of salvaging her chance of marrying Hirata, she would have avoided the estate forever.

Inside the estate, multitudes of samurai patrolled a large courtyard or sat in guardrooms. Barracks for the officers formed an inner wall around the daimyo's mansion, a vast complex of half-timbered buildings joined by covered corridors and intersecting tile roofs and elevated on granite foundations. At the door to Lord Niu's private room, Midori met Okita, her father's chief retainer.

"He's waiting for you," Okita said.

His dour face and neutral tone gave no hint of what Midori should expect. "How is he?" she said.

"Slightly better." That meant Lord Niu had calmed down. "I advise you not to upset him."

"Why does he want to see me?" Midori asked.

In answer, Okita opened the door. Reluctantly Midori entered the room. Okita followed, closing the door behind them.

The room could have belonged to any noble, but for features known only to those familiar with Lord Niu. Cabinets, chests, and secret compartments in the walls and under the floor contained hidden weapons, as Midori was aware. A mural bore dents and stains from objects hurled by her father during fits of rage. The two guards stationed inside the door were there to protect Lord Niu from himself, and everyone else from his bad spells. The room had a peculiar sweet smell, as if tainted by poison in his blood.

Lord Niu knelt on the dais, sharpening a dagger. The motion of his blade against the grindstone produced metallic rasps. He didn't immediately acknowledge Midori's presence. As she knelt before the dais, she thought how ordinary he appeared today, like any other noble who spent his leisure time tending his weapons. Then Lord Niu raised his skewed face to her.

A tremor of dread passed through Midori. Hastily lowering her gaze, she bowed.

"Little whore. Little traitor." Lord Niu spoke the insults in a pleasant, ordinary tone of voice that made them all the more chilling to Midori. His hand continued swiping the dagger across the grindstone. "How could you betray your own father to consort with the son of the enemy?"

Too frightened to answer, Midori pressed her lips together to still their trembling. Her hope that he'd changed his mind about the marriage seemed ludicrous now.

"I ought to kill you for your treason," Lord Niu said.

The rasp of his blade quickened, as did Midori's heartbeat. Glancing at Okita and the guards, she saw them move closer to the dais. Lord Niu had never yet killed a family member, but this was no guarantee that he wouldn't.

"But you're my flesh and blood, no matter what you've done," Lord Niu said. "I'll give you a chance to atone for your evil." His left eye twinkled at Midori. The right eye dreamed. "Tell me everything you know about the Hirata clan's strategy for destroying me."

Midori wished she could run away, but her father's will held her captive, and she must defend Hirata. "But I don't—they're not—I can't—"

"Don't pretend to be ignorant." The rasping ceased as Lord Niu stopped sharpening the dagger. His hands were black with grit; his expression scorned Midori. "You and that boy are lovers. What secrets does he whisper to you when you lie together?"

Midori hoped her father didn't really know the things she and Hirata-san had done, or suspect she was pregnant.

"Speak!" Lord Niu ordered.

Desperation loosened Midori's tongue. "There's nothing to tell. Hirata-san and his father aren't making war on you."

Lord Niu snorted in disgust. "They're trying to lull me into believing I'm safe. And they're using my own daughter as a messenger for carrying their lies to me."

"I'm telling the truth!" Midori cried. "They're good, honorable men who came to you in peace."

The grindstone suddenly flew out of Lord Niu's hand and crashed against the wall. Midori shrieked. Okita and the guards started.

"Do you take me for a moron?" Lord Niu shouted. "My enemy wants to sneak his son into our clan, to cause discord among us and weaken us so we'll be vulnerable. I should cut off your head and send it to him as proof that I'm onto his scheme!"

Midori whimpered as he brandished the dagger. He crawled to the edge of the dais, tilted his head, and scrutinized her. She recoiled in terror from his fierce, distorted gaze. Then the left side of his mouth curved upward in a pitying smile.

"Ah. I see," he said. "You really don't know anything. You're too innocent to recognize my enemies for what they are."

Rage suffused his features. "That boy has tricked you into thinking he loves you, all the while he's used you for his evil purposes. That dirty, vicious scoundrel!"

Lord Niu jumped up and stalked around the dais; he slashed the dagger at the air. "Son of a snake! Demon from hell! I'll see him destroyed before long!"

Cowering, Midori put her hands over her ears to block out her father's voice, but Lord Niu shouted more curses against Hirata. Wild, reckless terror overcame her.

"Stop!" she screamed.

Lord Niu abruptly fell quiet. He stood still, weapon dangling, as he and his men regarded her in surprise that she dared command him. Midori quailed at her own boldness; yet her love for Hirata and need to marry him inspired courage. She said what Reiko had suggested might bend Lord Niu to her wishes: "Do you want to be safe from your enemies?"

Caught off guard and startled out of his rage, Lord Niu said, ". . . Yes?"

"Do you want to make sure that the Hirata clan will never attack ours?" Midori's voice quavered; she pressed her thighs together, fighting an urge to urinate.

Lord Niu looked wary, but nodded.

"Then the best thing to do is unite our two clans in a marriage between Hirata-*san* and me," Midori said in a rush. "The wedding would mean a truce. We'll be allies, not enemies."

A thoughtful look came over Lord Niu's face. Its two halves seemed almost to align.

Midori took heart because in spite of his peculiarities, Lord Niu wasn't entirely impervious to logic. She remembered what else Reiko had told her to say, when they'd met earlier that morning: "The union will also protect you from the Tokugawa. They won't attack a lord whose daughter is married to the chief retainer of the shogun's *sōsakan-sama*."

Lord Niu pondered; something awakened in his dreaming eye. He wasn't completely out of touch with the world, either, Midori knew. Even if he didn't realize that the Tokugawa wouldn't start a war and disrupt the peace they'd maintained for almost a century, he understood the benefit of marrying a daughter to someone with a Tokugawa connection. And he had a clever instinct for seizing chances to serve himself. A short eternity passed. Midori held her breath. Then Lord Niu hopped off the dais and crouched in front of her.

"Do you want so badly to marry?" he said.

He appeared so concerned about her that Midori's heart leapt. "Yes," she breathed.

"Well, I suppose that can be arranged." Rising, Lord Niu beckoned to his chief retainer, who came to him. Lord Niu whispered in Okita's ear; Okita listened, nodded, then left the room. Midori wondered what was going on. She prayed that her father would change his mind about Hirata.

"Are you in love with this boy?" Lord Niu said.

Midori thought she felt her father relenting. Could this possibly mean he'd sent Okita to apologize to Hirata's father and ask for another *miai* so the marriage negotiations could start fresh?

"Yes," Midori said, poised between fear and joy.

A gradual frown eclipsed Lord Niu's face; his right eye veered slowly. "I shall permit you to marry, and I desire that you should make an advantageous match. But I forbid you to wed the Hirata boy."

Midori's mouth fell open in stunned disappointment.

"Whatever his high connections, I don't trust him or his

father," Lord Niu said. "A marriage is no guarantee of their good behavior toward me. They would cut my throat as soon as the wedding was over, and sack my province. You shall marry an ally I can trust. I shall begin seeking prospective husbands at once."

Midori didn't want to bear her baby out of wedlock, but neither did she want Hirata's child born into a marriage between her and a stranger. "Please, Honorable Father, I don't want to marry anyone but Hirata-*san*." Frantic, she prostrated herself at Lord Niu's feet. "He loves me as much as I love him. We must be together!"

"Shut up!" Lord Niu raged. "You'll do as I say!"

"If I can't marry Hirata-*san*, I'll die!" Midori wept now.

"I order you to renounce him."

"No. Please!"

"Do it, or I'll kill you."

Lord Niu grabbed her hair, forced her head back, and held the dagger to her throat. Midori sobbed in terror and panic. She didn't want to give in, yet as she felt the cold steel against her skin, she knew her father was serious. She would rather let him kill her than give up Hirata, but she must protect her unborn child.

"All right," she cried. "I renounce Hirata-*san*. Just please don't hurt me!"

"That's better." Lord Niu smiled, released her, and stood. Midori collapsed in a miserable heap. "Now you'll promise to accept a husband I choose for you, or marry the first man that Okita sees passing my gate."

"No!" Fresh horror reawakened Midori's defiance.

Lord Niu cocked his head, listening as footsteps came down the corridor. "Ah. Here he is now."

Okita entered the room, bringing another man with him. The man had straggly hair and missing teeth, and wore filthy rags. He carried a begging bowl that held a few coins. Okita pushed him face-down in front of Lord Niu.

"Greetings," Lord Niu said as though the beggar were a visiting dignitary. "Many thanks for coming."

"It's a privilege," the beggar stammered, clearly awed and puzzled at being summoned by the daimyo.

Lord Niu hauled Midori close to the beggar. She gagged on his stench. "This is my daughter," Lord Niu said. "How would you like to marry her?"

The beggar looked dumbfounded by what must have seemed to him a stroke of unbelievable luck. "I would like it very much, master, if that's your wish."

Lord Niu glared at Midori. "Do you promise?"

Hope died in her, as did the will to resist. "I promise," she whispered.

23

The Pillow Book of Lady Wisteria

As I sit writing by my window, I look down at the street filled with merrymakers. The potted cherry trees are pink with blossoms whose petals fall like snow. How fleeting is their beauty! And how fleeting was the happiness that I hoped would last forever.

Four years ago I stood beside Sano-*san* in the parlor of the brothel. He said to the proprietor, "I redeem Lady Wisteria from her servitude to you."

His attendants paid a chest of gold coins in exchange for my freedom. I was so overwhelmed by love for Sano-*san* that tears poured from my eyes. His eyes shone with desire for me. We were eager to flee Yoshiwara together, but the departure rituals had to be performed, and such a momentous occasion as the end of my suffering deserved proper celebration.

The next day I dressed in fine new robes that Sano-*san* had bought me, then I distributed the farewell gifts he'd provided. My attendants and I promenaded through Yoshiwara, visiting all my friends and giving them packages of boiled rice and red beans. I gave smoked bonito to the teahouses and *ageya* where I'd entertained clients. All the entertainers and servants received tips from me. Everyone wished me a long, prosperous life. Then Sano-*san* and I hosted a lavish banquet. I was drunk on wine and joy. Ah, to have the powerful, wealthy *sōsakan-sama* as my lover! I would be safe and want for nothing.

At last we were escorted to the gate. Sano-*san* helped me into a palanquin. He and his entourage escorted me all the way to Edo. I laughed, sang, and never looked back at the wicked pleasure quarter.

I thought Sano-*san* would take me to Edo Castle, but we stopped in a neighborhood in Nihonbashi. His attendants carried my belongings into a house.

"I rented this place for you," Sano-*san* told me.

Though I was disappointed, I supposed that a man of his rank couldn't marry a courtesan straight out of Yoshiwara; some time must pass before I gained enough respectability to be his wife. And the house would suit me fine until we could live together. It was small, but clean and prettily furnished, and Sano-*san* had hired servants to wait on me.

I said, "A thousand thanks for your generosity. Will you stay awhile?"

His ardent gaze moved over me. "Oh, yes."

He drew me close. His hands slipped inside my robes. They fell away. I sighed with delight as he caressed me. I loosened his sash and parted his garments and unwound his loincloth. His organ sprang erect. Dropping to my knees, I worshipped him with my mouth. I licked and sucked and stroked him. He threw back his head, moaning, growing larger and harder.

He raised me and led me to the bed. He sat propped against the cushions, and I straddled him. I rode him slowly and gently, then faster and harder. We breathed and moaned together. As he grabbed my hips and thrust into me with mounting urgency, I leaned toward him and pressed my mouth to his.

I had taught Sano-*san* and many other men this lewd, exotic technique. The warm, wet joining of our lips, tongue, and spit drove him wild. He bucked, shouting as he released inside me. His rapture brought on mine. I floated on waves of ecstasy. We were one, our bodies and spirits inseparable.

Reiko sat holding the book, her lips parted and eyes glazed with shock at what she'd read.

The story couldn't be true!

Sano had never said he even knew Lady Wisteria; he couldn't have been the lover who'd freed her from Yoshiwara. And there couldn't be two pillow books. This one was surely a forgery.

Yet even as Reiko tallied the reasons to disbelieve the story, a cold, sick feeling gathered in her stomach. This second pillow book matched the description of Lady Wisteria's, while the first was just a handful of papers. Worse, the passage in which Sano coupled with Wisteria had struck an ominous chord in Reiko.

Sano liked to make love to her in the position described in the book. He also liked pressing their mouths together during sex. Reiko had never questioned how Sano had developed this practice she'd never heard of; she'd assumed it was something all men did in secret. Had Wisteria really taught it to him?

Despite her fear of finding proof that Sano had withheld information from her, or more descriptions of his past amorous adventures, irresistible curiosity compelled Reiko to turn the page.

Spring warmed into summer before I began to suspect that I was merely Sano-*san*'s mistress, not his betrothed. He visited me every other night or so, and we coupled as passionately as ever, but he never mentioned marriage. He seemed content, while I grew bored with sitting alone in my little house and waiting for him. Anxious about my future, I began dropping hints.

"It's so lonely when you're gone," I would say.

"Partings are necessary," he would say with a mischievous smile. "Without them there would be no joyous reunions."

"How I'd like to see Edo Castle," I would say.

"Someday you shall," he would say.

Autumn came, then winter. The passing seasons made me too desperate to be subtle any longer. One night, as we lay together, I blurted, "When are we going to marry?"

Sano-*san* looked surprised. "Marry? You and me?" He laughed and shook his head. "We're not."

I was shocked. "I thought you loved me," I said. "I thought you freed me so we could be together."

"I do love you," Sano-*san* said, "and I'm sorry you got the wrong idea. But a man of my class can't marry a woman of yours. I thought you understood."

He meant I would always be a whore, good enough for bed, but not for matrimony. I was crushed!

"Besides, I'm engaged," Sano-*san* said with a sheepish grin.

"Engaged?" I gasped. "You never told me."

"I didn't want to upset you," he said. "And it didn't seem that important."

Not important! His news hurt as if he'd stabbed me in the heart.

"Who is she?" I demanded.

"Magistrate Ueda's daughter."

To hear more about her would worsen my pain, but I had to ask: "Is she beautiful?"

Sano-*san* gave me that flirtatious look of his. "Not as beautiful as you. She's nobody special. But her father is an important man. It's a good match for me. The wedding will be sometime in the New Year."

I rose and staggered backward, clutching my chest. "You're going to take this girl into your home, into your bed." Tears filled my eyes. "Oh, I can't bear it!"

Now Sano-*san* seemed puzzled. "Why are you so upset? My marriage needn't change anything between us." He stood up and put his arms around me. "I'll come and see you as often as ever."

He meant that I must share him with the magistrate's daughter, and he would enjoy us both! I felt chilled by his callousness, then hot with rage.

"If you marry her, you'll never touch me again!" I cried, pushing him away.

Sano-*san* laughed. "Don't be silly," he said.

He grabbed my arm, pulled me close, and pressed his mouth to mine. I bit his lip. He shouted and reared back. Blood ran down his chin, and I tasted it on my own tongue.

"Witch!" he yelled. He slapped my cheek so hard I fell to the floor. "Don't you ever hurt me again. And don't ever tell me what I can do or not."

I hated him then as much as I loved him. "I'll leave you," I sobbed.

"Really?" he jeered. "Where will you go? How will you live without the money I give you?"

"I'll get another man," I said.

His face turned dark and terrible with rage. "Oh,

no, you won't," he said. "You're mine. I paid for you. And I'll have you however I want."

Then he was upon me, yanking up my skirts, weighing down my body under his. "Stop!" I screamed, furious that he would treat me so.

I tried to push him off. I beat my hands at him, I tried to squirm away, in vain. Finally I gave up and surrendered. His organ was hard against my loins. He shoved it into me, and oh, the hurt!

"Please have mercy," I sobbed.

But Sano-*san* laughed and groaned and thrust and enjoyed my suffering. When at last he finished, he climbed off me. As I lay sore and weeping and humiliated, he wiped himself on my kimono.

"That should teach you your place," he said.

Revulsion halted Reiko's reading. She uttered a sound of indignant denial. This wasn't her husband described in the pillow book. The Sano she knew was good and kind, not mean nor violent as the story portrayed him. He would never mistreat a helpless woman nor take pleasure in forcing himself on her. But doubt eroded Reiko's disbelief.

She realized how little she knew about Sano's relations with other people. His personality might have a different side that he kept hidden while at home. Nor did Reiko know anything about women in his past. She'd never wanted to find out and shatter her fancy that Sano had never loved a woman until her. Now her ignorance left her defenseless against suspicion, and her inexperience with men made her a poor judge of male character.

Had Sano really spoken so disparagingly of her to Lady Wisteria?

Had he indeed loved Wisteria and meant to keep her as his mistress after he married?

Reiko swallowed the sickness that rose in her throat. Bracing herself, she resumed reading.

We quarreled again and again. My rage annoyed Sano-*san*, but I couldn't give up trying to convince him to break his engagement, even though nagging would drive him away.

The day before his wedding, I made such a scene that he left in disgust. And he didn't come back. A month passed. I thought my heart would break from missing him. Another month went by, and the landlord threatened to evict me because Sano-*san* hadn't paid the rent. The servants left because they hadn't received their wages, and I had to feed myself on tea and noodles from a nearby stall. The little money Sano-*san* had left me was running out. I wrote his name on a paper and hid it, but the old charm didn't work. Sano-*san* didn't come. I would starve to death in the streets!

Then one night three months after his marriage, as I huddled over a fire made from the last of my coal, the door opened, and there he was. I was so overjoyed that I threw myself into his arms and wept.

Sano-*san* laughed. "This is a nice welcome. Maybe I should have stayed away longer."

His mocking hurt, but he made love to me with such ardor that I knew he'd missed me. He also paid the landlord, rehired the servants, and gave me money. His visits resumed, and I realized that unless I wanted to lose him entirely, I shouldn't nag him. I must use better means of persuading him to divorce his wife and marry me.

Whenever he was with me, I dedicated myself to his satisfaction. I caressed the nether region between his buttocks with my tongue. I paid a hunter to bring me a live wolf and hold it while I coupled with it and Sano-*san* watched. Often I would hire young girls to join us in the bedchamber. When we were apart, I worked a charm to make him faithful to me. I drew a picture of his private parts and boiled it with sake, vinegar, soy sauce, tooth-blackening dye, dirt, and lamp wick. But a year passed, and although

Sano-*san* always came back to me, I seemed destined to spend my life on the fringes of his.

Still, I forced myself to be patient, even on the night when he said his wife had just given birth to their son. This was proof that he bedded his wife even though he said he didn't love her. How jealous and miserable I was that she had borne him a child, while my love for him was barren! And the child bound him more tightly to her, dividing us.

But I smiled and congratulated Sano-*san* and hid my feelings. Patience and perseverance were my only hope of winning him, and eventually they paid off.

It was in the year that the child was born, during the month of leaves, while Sano-*san* and I sat on the roof viewing the full moon. He was in a thoughtful frame of mind.

"I've accomplished more in my life than I ever expected," he said, "but it's not enough. The shogun treats me like a flunky. That despicable idiot will never give me a higher rank, more wealth, or my own province to rule because he likes keeping me where I am. When he dies and I lose his protection, my enemies will jump at the opportunity to destroy me. My only hope of survival is my son."

A cunning look came over his face. "The boy is strong, bright, and handsome. The shogun has no sons of his own, and therefore no one to succeed him. I shall persuade him to adopt my son as his official heir to the regime. It will take time, of course. My son must grow up and earn the shogun's affection. There are obstacles to clear out of the way. One of them is Lord Mitsuyoshi, the shogun's current favorite. But I know just how to deal with him. Eventually my son will be dictator, and I, who raised him to power, will be secure for the rest of my life."

I was shocked by Sano-*san*'s nerve, then delighted at my good luck. Sano-*san* has put himself under my power! All I need do is play my cards right, and he will give me everything I wish.

Reiko closed the pillow book. She sat paralyzed, her heart drumming while she envisioned Sano indulging in sexual depravity. Feverish waves of horror assailed her. To think that Sano's liaison with Lady Wisteria had continued after their marriage! Perhaps it had continued until Wisteria disappeared.

But this was unthinkable to Reiko. Sano did love her. She recalled their first months together, and their passionate lovemaking. Sano couldn't have committed adultery, not then, not ever. A unique spiritual bond joined them; they belonged only to each other.

Then Reiko remembered the many times they'd spent apart. Sano could have visited Wisteria during his absences. And one of those absences had occurred the night Reiko gave birth to their child. Sano had gone away on business for the shogun . . . or so he'd said. Was their love a sham, and her trust in Sano misplaced?

A stinging onslaught of tears rushed upon Reiko; she felt like vomiting. Sano had always seemed a loving father, incapable of trading Masahiro for political security. That he would give their son to the shogun, who used young boys as sexual playthings, was beyond belief. Yet Reiko knew how precarious was Sano's position at court, and what a toll his constant struggle to stay in the shogun's good graces took upon him. The honorable samurai she knew would never insult his lord nor plot to usurp power, but perhaps Sano had grown desperate and wayward enough to do both.

She couldn't know for certain that he hadn't, because they'd grown apart and he didn't confide in her. And if he would betray her, then why not Masahiro?

Clutching the pillow book, Reiko glanced around the room, which looked unfamiliar, as if transformed into an alien place. Her mind went on adding links to a terrible chain of logic.

Sano had been hiding something from her.

He didn't want her to investigate Wisteria.

He'd behaved strangely after discovering the corpse—as if someone he knew and cared about had died.

She had already begun to suspect that there had been something between him and the missing courtesan.

With an anguished cry, Reiko hurled the book across the room. It fell behind a gilded screen; yet she could not ignore the book. Nor could she escape realizing that it was as much of a threat to Sano as Lady Yanagisawa had claimed, and not just because it jeopardized his marriage. She felt helpless in her fear and misery.

There was nothing she could do until Sano came home.

24

Various inquiries took Sano from Edo Morgue to the palace, to the official quarter and daimyo district, and finally to Yoshiwara. Now a sentry at the gate clapped two wooden blocks together to signal midnight and curfew. Lanterns still blazed along the streets; hawkers called customers to tea-houses and brothels; samurai and commoners still loitered, flirting with courtesans in the window cages. Gay music spangled the air. A small group of men who didn't want to spend the whole night in Yoshiwara streamed out a small door in the gate. Among these were Sano, Hirata, and the eight detectives they'd brought. As they rode along the dark causeway toward the city, Sano and Hirata exchanged news.

"The woman we found in Fujio's house was beaten to death," Sano said. "She may or may not be Lady Wisteria." But he'd grown more certain that the dead woman was indeed the courtesan.

"Fujio may not be the killer." Hirata described how he'd

interviewed, then arrested the *hokan*. "Today I talked to his wife, in-laws, friends, and mistress. They confirmed that he was with them when he says he was. Unless they're lying, he couldn't have committed murder in the hills."

"Maybe Fujio didn't kill Lord Mitsuyoshi either. Maybe Treasury Minister Nitta was guilty, and a third party murdered Wisteria." Sano had difficulty believing that the murders were unconnected. Still, he couldn't ignore the possibility.

"I've checked the stories I heard from the Council of Elders and other officials," he said. "It's been hard to investigate Mitsuyoshi's background without appearing to do so. But I learned that Lord Dakuemon and several other men mentioned to me were in Yoshiwara the night of Mitsuyoshi's murder. Some are former clients of Lady Wisteria. The next step is to determine where they were during the time between Wisteria's disappearance and the discovery of the body."

This would be simple if not for the shogun's orders. Sano regretted that he couldn't directly interrogate the new suspects instead of working through spies and informants, a laborious, time-consuming process.

"If the killer isn't Fujio or a *bakufu* official, there's still Lady Wisteria's Hokkaido lover," Hirata said. "But no one in Yoshiwara seems to know anything about him, and I haven't gotten any response to the notices I posted."

Sano gripped the reins; the icy wind penetrated his garments as his horse's hooves pounded the ground under him. The landscape of fields and starlit sky flowed past, so unchanging that he couldn't gauge the progress of his journey.

"Things will look more promising after a good night's rest," he said.

Hours later, Sano arrived home, frozen and exhausted, to find that Reiko had waited up for him. She was standing in their bedchamber, and one look at her face told Sano something was amiss. Her jaw was set, her gaze simultaneously frightened and accusing.

"What's wrong?" Sano said, afraid that something bad had happened to her or Masahiro.

She stepped back to avoid the hand he extended to her, and thrust a small book toward him. "Will you please explain this?" Her voice was brittle, stretched between dread and reproach.

Puzzled, Sano took the book, opened it, and frowned in surprise at the inscription. *"The Pillow Book of Lady Wisteria*? Where did this come from?"

Reiko didn't answer. Unnerved by her strange expression, Sano began reading the pages. His surprise turned to alarm, then horror at the mixture of fact and fabrication. Lady Wisteria couldn't have written such disgusting slander about him! The book must be a forgery. But while he read, it was as if he could hear Wisteria's voice speaking the words, and who except she could have known intimate details of their relations?

If only he'd already told Reiko about the affair! How could he now persuade her that most of the story was a lie while he admitted concealing from her the parts that were true?

Sano read the last passage, which showed him insulting the shogun and plotting to make Masahiro the next dictator. His blood boiled with outrage. Feeling shamed and trapped, he slowly closed the book, delaying the moment when he must face Reiko. When he at last raised his eyes, she regarded him with the brave caution of a warrior encountering a stranger who may be friend or foe.

"Where did you get this?" Sano asked.

"From Lady Yanagisawa." Reiko explained how the anonymous package had arrived for the chamberlain, and her friend had brought it to her. "Is the story true?"

Nerves raised sweat on Sano's brow. "Let's sit down and talk," he said.

Reiko didn't move, but her eyes went round, and Sano saw her pride crumble. "Then it is true," she whispered. "She was your lover. I thought we were—all the while you—" Abruptly Reiko looked away.

"It was over before we married," Sano said.

"Then why didn't you tell me about her at the start of the investigation?"

"I didn't want to upset you." Sano ached with guilt. The brief pleasure he'd gotten from Lady Wisteria wasn't worth this.

"That's what you said to her when she was upset to learn you were engaged." Reiko was afire with hurt, suspicion, and anger. She gestured toward the book that Sano still held. "She was beautiful. You loved her. She did everything for you that a man could want." Bitterness twisted Reiko's mouth. "You only married me because I'm from a high-ranking samurai family instead of a brothel."

"I didn't love her," Sano protested. "There was nothing between us but sex." He saw Reiko's eyes narrow. "It was just a brief affair that had no future."

"Then why did you free her?" Reiko retorted. "Or didn't you?" she added in a querulous tone that bespoke her need to believe he hadn't performed this act that signified deep commitment to a courtesan.

"I did," Sano said, though aware that the admission made him look guiltier.

Reiko briefly closed her eyes.

"But it wasn't because I wanted the affair to go on." Regretting to hurt her more, Sano nonetheless realized that he must tell her the whole story, and hastened to explain: "I met Wisteria on a case I investigated while I was on the police force. She gave me information. We spent a night together."

"During which she taught you the art of lovemaking?"

Hearing the pain behind Reiko's sarcasm, Sano nodded reluctantly. "Certain people were displeased that Wisteria helped me. She was punished. Her suffering was my fault, and I had to compensate her." He described the events that had made this possible. "But I didn't go to Yoshiwara to take her away." Leafing through the book, he said, "There was no departure ceremony, no trip together to her new home. The *bakufu* provided the money and handled everything. Wisteria wasn't my mistress. I never intended her to be."

"So you were never together again?" Eagerness underlay Reiko's skeptical query.

Though he hated to disappoint his wife, Sano said, "We were, but only twice—before you and I met. Wisteria was unfriendly to me. I was busy working for the shogun, and I never bothered going back to Wisteria. There were no violent quarrels, no reunions, no perverted sex, no insults toward the shogun, and certainly no scheme to use Masahiro-*chan* for my own benefit."

Sano flung down the book, incensed anew by its portrayal of him. He was relieved that his secret had come out, but upset that it had come out this way. Gazing upon Reiko's rigid, unhappy face, he said, "I love you. I've always been faithful to you." Sincerity and tenderness hushed his voice: "I swear it on my life."

Reiko looked torn between wanting to believe and wanting not to be deceived. Then she turned away. Sano inwardly cursed the Black Lotus for her morbid distrust that extended to him and what she knew in her heart about him.

"You're always telling me that a good detective bases judgment on evidence," she said. "What evidence is there to prove you're not an adulterer?" She swallowed hard, as if to forestall crying. "What evidence is there to prove you weren't involved in Lord Mitsuyoshi's death?"

She even suspected him of murdering Mitsuyoshi so that Masahiro could take his place as the shogun's heir! Sano lifted his eyes to the ceiling as despair filled him. He had nothing to prove the pillow book was a fraud. The only person who could say for a fact that he'd never done the things described in the book was Lady Wisteria. Sano thought of the mutilated corpse and shook his head. Then his gaze lit on the book, which lay on the table where he'd thrown it. A phrase that hadn't registered while he read now jarred his memory. He snatched up the book and whipped through pages until he found it.

"Reiko-*san*, look," he said.

She didn't move. Eagerly Sano read aloud: " 'It was in the year that the child was born, during the month of leaves, while Sano-*san* and I sat on the roof viewing the full moon.' But I couldn't have been with Wisteria on the night of the full moon in the seventh month after you gave birth to Masahiro-*chan*. I was with you. Don't you remember?"

Now Reiko did remember. She also remembered the passage in the book that she'd overlooked because she'd been too upset to read objectively. A rush of confused emotions made her feel faint. Stunned, she turned to Sano.

"Yes," she said, and heard breathless relief in her voice.

Her distrust and his confession had transformed her husband into a stranger capable of adultery and treason; but now Sano looked his familiar self. An encouraging smile dawned through the worry on his face.

"The shogun had given you a holiday that month," she said. "You took Masahiro-*chan* and me on a religious pilgrimage." The temple where they'd stayed was a three-day journey from Edo, their holiday had lasted ten days total, and therefore Sano could not have gone to Wisteria in Nihonbashi at any time near the full moon.

"After you put Masahiro-*chan* to bed, you and I watched the moon from the garden," Sano said.

"And we made love there." The tears Reiko had been holding back now spilled. She wept with gladness that one small, false detail had shown the pillow book to be an elaborate lie, and shame that she'd not immediately recognized it as such. "Will you forgive me for doubting you?"

"If you forgive me for keeping a secret I should have told you," Sano said.

He looked so earnest and chagrined that Reiko's lingering anger melted away. Unaware of whether she moved toward him, or he toward her, she found herself and Sano embracing. She felt her sobs resonate through him, and the wetness on her cheek that could have been her tears or his. Sano's hands caressed her with a tenderness that she could tell Lady Wisteria had never known from him. Her body responded with a welling of desire. His breath quickened and his grasp on her tightened.

Lovemaking would have followed, but they moved apart because they had serious matters to discuss. Reiko heated a vessel of sake, and they knelt with the pillow book and the tray of cups before them.

"If Wisteria didn't write the book, who did?" Reiko said, pouring the steaming liquor.

Sano's expression turned grim as he accepted a cup. "I can think of one person who would like me implicated in the murder and branded a traitor."

"*Yoriki* Hoshina?"

Sano nodded. "Hoshina knows about the pillow book, and what it looks like, because he heard Wisteria's *kamuro* describe it to me. Maybe he forged his own version and had it delivered anonymously to Chamberlain Yanagisawa. After that, all he had to do was wait."

"For the chamberlain to use the book against you?" Reiko warmed her hands on her cup of sake before she drank. "But what about your truce with him?"

"The truce wouldn't protect me in this case," Sano said. He drained his cupful and poured himself another. "No matter if Yanagisawa wants us to remain at peace, he couldn't ignore evidence that I insulted and plotted against the shogun or had reason to kill Lord Mitsuyoshi. He would have to give the book to the shogun, whether he believes I'm guilty or not."

Now Reiko understood. "For him to shield a possible traitor would make him a traitor as well."

"He might hesitate to act if he were the only one who knew about the evidence," Sano said, "but he's not. The author of the book also knows. And the author knows that Yanagisawa received the book. While Yanagisawa and I are no longer at war, we're not exactly friends. He would never conceal the book and endanger himself for my sake. And Hoshina knows how his lover thinks. He's been looking for a way to attack me." Sano eyed the pillow book. "That must be his doing."

In spite of the strong reasons to believe Hoshina had written the book, a different possibility occurred to Reiko.

"If Hoshina isn't the author . . ." Her voice trailed off because the idea seemed at once plausible and outlandish.

"Do you have someone else in mind?" Sano said.

"I'm thinking of Lady Yanagisawa," Reiko said.

Sano regarded her with surprise. "How could she have known Wisteria had written a pillow book, or that it was missing?"

"Maybe she overheard the chamberlain and Hoshina discussing the case."

"Even if she did, how would she have known what to write?"

Reiko saw that he didn't think Lady Yanagisawa could be familiar with Yoshiwara customs, what went on between prostitutes and clients, or political ploys. "*Yoriki* Hoshina might have learned about you and Wisteria from *metsuke* spies, but women have their own ways of finding out things," Reiko said. "Maybe Wisteria told her friends or clients about her affair with you, and gossip traveled from Yoshiwara to Edo Castle, where Lady Yanagisawa heard it from her servants. She must also hear plenty that the chamberlain and his men say about *bakufu* business."

"That's possible. But the story in the book seems so real that the author must be a clever writer and have experience with the situations in it," Sano said. "That description would fit Hoshina better than Lady Yanagisawa."

"I think she's smart enough to write a good story," Reiko said, "and imagination can make up for lack of experience."

Sano's expression conveyed doubt. "Supposing Lady Yanagisawa did manufacture the pillow book, she could have also invented the story about the anonymous package to fool you. But you said she wants to be your friend. Why, then, would she try to hurt you by writing slander about me?"

Here Reiko's logic foundered. "I don't have a good reason. But Lady Yanagisawa is odd. I don't like the way she looks at me, or the way she sought my acquaintance at this particular time."

Instinct told Reiko that the chamberlain's wife had befriended her for some secret, nefarious purpose. But instinct had also encouraged her to trust a suspect in the Black Lotus murders, and to doubt Sano's fidelity to her and loyalty to the shogun. Reiko was more afraid than ever that the Black Lotus investigation had permanently damaged her judgment.

She saw her fear reflected on Sano's face. He said, "If Lady Yanagisawa does want to get me in trouble, why did she do you the favor of bringing you the book instead of leaving it for her husband and letting matters take their course?"

Reiko sighed in dejection. "I don't know." Yet her suspicions about the chamberlain's wife nagged at her. Wishing she'd kept them to herself, she changed the subject: "If the second pillow book is a forgery, then maybe the book Hirata found is Lady Wisteria's genuine one. Nothing in the first book has proved to be untrue, even though we haven't been able to find the Hokkaido man. What are you going to do about the second pillow book?"

Sano picked up the volume and weighed it in his hand for a moment, his expression perturbed. "I hate to destroy evidence. But the only information in here is false information about me."

"There may be clues we don't recognize yet," Reiko said. "And the fact that the book says you plotted treason on a night for which you have an alibi reveals that the story is slander. You may need the book as proof of your innocence."

"Maybe." Still, Sano was more certain of the book's threat to him than willing to bet it would turn out to be useful. "But whether the book has any value, it's too dangerous to keep."

He untied the ribbon binding and fed the pages one by one into the brazier. They flamed, shriveled, and blackened. At last Sano laid the lavender covers and green ribbon on the coals.

"I wish I could believe this is the end of the matter," Reiko said, opening a window to clear out the smoke.

"So do I," said Sano, "but unfortunately, it's not. Whoever wrote that book will be waiting for Chamberlain Yanagisawa to act on it and me to be ruined. When that doesn't happen, he'll know his plan went wrong."

"And try again to implicate you in the murders?"

Sano nodded. "I must find out who the author is before he manufactures more false evidence against me. And I must find out as soon as possible who killed Lord Mitsuyoshi, so that if suspicion does fall on me, I can prove I didn't do it."

The second pillow book complicated the investigation and raised the price of failure; yet Reiko tried to be optimistic. "We're safe for now," she said. "Maybe the author of the book is the murderer of Lord Mitsuyoshi and Lady Wisteria. If that's true, we need to find only one person to solve the case and avoid danger."

25

Although exhausted from a tumultuous day and night, Sano and Reiko rose early the next morning, cognizant of how much work awaited them. As they sat eating a meal of rice, broth, and fish, Hirata came to the door of their chamber.

"There's been a new development," Sano said. "We have something to tell you."

He described the second pillow book. After they'd discussed its ramifications, Hirata said, "I came to tell you that Magistrate Aoki has had Fujio taken out of jail and delivered to his court. Our informant there just brought the news. And the shogun wants to see you immediately."

"The magistrate is interfering again," Reiko said in dismay.

"As if that wasn't bad enough, the shogun must want me to explain why I defended Treasury Minister Nitta at his trial." Unpleasant foreboding stole through Sano. He rose and told Hirata, "You go to the court and find out what's going on. I'll be at the palace."

When Sano arrived in the shogun's reception hall, he found the Council of Elders aligned in their customary two rows on the upper level of the floor. The shogun sat on the dais, with Chamberlain Yanagisawa kneeling below at his right and Police Commissioner Hoshina at his left. Tokugawa Tsunayoshi looked ill, his features fragile as crumpled paper, his eyes rimmed with red and shadowed underneath. Trembling visibly, he glared at Sano.

Dread chilled Sano as he knelt and bowed. Just as he'd feared, the shogun was furious with him.

"How could you?" demanded Tokugawa Tsunayoshi. "After all I've, ahh, given you, after I've trusted you, how could you do such a, ahh, cruel, disgraceful thing?"

"A million apologies for displeasing you, Your Excellency." Quaking, Sano tried to stay calm. "I couldn't let Magistrate Aoki condemn the treasury minister and end the investigation while there was a strong chance that Nitta was innocent."

"Of course Nitta was innocent!" The shogun's voice rose to a high pitch of hysteria. As Sano listened in surprise, Tokugawa Tsunayoshi said, "He didn't kill my cousin. You did!"

Sano felt shock resonate through his body. The shogun was accusing him? What was going on? Aghast, he looked around at the other men, and his gaze lit on Hoshina.

"The *sōsakan-sama* appears bewildered, Your Excellency." Hoshina's expression was smug, gloating. "If I may enlighten him?"

Tokugawa Tsunayoshi nodded as a sob wracked his body. Hoshina said to Sano, "I've located the missing pillow book of Lady Wisteria. It contains a description of a sordid love affair between her and you. She wrote that you used her for pleasure, then mistreated her. She also wrote that you called

His Excellency a despicable idiot, and you intended to murder Lord Mitsuyoshi so His Excellency would adopt your son as his successor.

"I showed the book to the Honorable Chamberlain. We agreed that we must show it to His Excellency, and we have done so."

Yanagisawa inclined his head, silently concurring with his lover. Alarm and confusion beset Sano. Lady Yanagisawa had told Reiko that her husband had gotten the book from an anonymous sender. Had she lied, or had Hoshina secretly opened the package, then pretended he'd found the book somewhere, to impress his superiors?

But however the book had come to light, the shogun had read it before Lady Yanagisawa stole it. Her attempt to do Reiko a favor had failed. Sano had destroyed the book too late, and Hoshina had used it against him.

"I have never insulted His Excellency," Sano said, his panic balanced by anger at his foe. "Nor have I ever expressed threats toward Lord Mitsuyoshi. I didn't kill him, and I'm not plotting to put my son in power. The book is a fraud."

Hoshina gave him a cocksure smile. "Residents of the Great Miura brothel have identified it as Lady Wisteria's."

"Did you bribe them? Or did you threaten to kill them unless they said what you wanted? You wrote the book yourself, to ruin me." Sano grew certain this was true. "Admit it!"

The shogun's puzzled gaze flicked from Sano to Hoshina, who said ruefully, "I'm not the author of the book. The *sōsakan-sama* is trying to save himself by accusing me."

"Let's examine this book and compare the calligraphy to yours." Knowing the book was in ashes, Sano hoped that forcing Hoshina to admit it no longer existed would lessen the harm it could do him.

"The book has vanished," Hoshina said, unperturbed.

"How convenient for you that no one can scrutinize it too closely," Sano said.

Hoshina's gaze rebuked him. "How much more convenient for you if you'd had it stolen before we read it instead of afterward."

Hoshina dared frame him for theft along with murder and treason! "I didn't know the book had turned up until now," Sano said. "How could I have stolen it?" Yet he feared everyone could see through his pretended ignorance. He addressed the shogun: "Even though you're understandably upset by what the book said about me, please consider that there's no other evidence that anything in it happened."

"That is, ahh, true." Realization eclipsed the anger on Tokugawa Tsunayoshi's countenance. "You've always been loyal to me in the past. And the, ahh, man in the story was a cad who didn't, ahh, resemble you at all."

His unexpected good sense relieved Sano, but Hoshina said, "The affair between the *sōsakan-sama* and Lady Wisteria was verified by my informants. And here's a page of the account book from the brothel, showing a sum paid by Sano Ichirō for the discharge of Lady Wisteria." Hoshina held up a paper.

"That proves nothing except that I freed her," Sano said, appalled by the thoroughness of Hoshina's effort to authenticate the book.

"Any verified detail lends credibility to the others," Hoshina said. "Besides, I've located the house where Wisteria lived after she left Yoshiwara. The neighbors say she had a samurai lover. Their description of him fits the *sōsakan-sama*. They also say that he and Wisteria quarreled frequently and violently, as the book describes."

Sano couldn't admit he'd visited Wisteria at all, and make himself look guiltier. "I never quarreled with her. Either those witnesses are lying, or you are," he told Hoshina. "Your evidence is slander woven from a few innocuous facts!"

The shogun recoiled from Sano's vehemence.

"See how he rages when someone irks him," Hoshina said to the assembly, his face alight with vindication. "This is the bad temper that caused him to hurt Lady Wisteria."

Further incensed, Sano looked at the chamberlain. Yanagisawa met his gaze with a warning expression that said their truce didn't make them allies and Hoshina had free rein here. The elders watched with a detachment that fueled Sano's anger. They expected him to destroy their enemies for them, at his own risk, and now they were doing nothing to help him. The contemptible wretches!

Stifling an impulse to rage at them, Sano mustered his self-control. He said to the shogun, "That Police Commissioner Hoshina has demonstrated an association between Lady Wisteria and me isn't proof that I'm a murderer or traitor."

"That the *sōsakan-sama* attempted to conceal the association indicates that he's guilty," Hoshina said quickly.

Sano turned on his foe. "Just when does the book say I plotted against His Excellency and Lord Mitsuyoshi? Or is the story as vague about dates as it is untrue?"

Caution narrowed Hoshina's eyes. "Lady Wisteria marked the date as Genroku Year Five, the seventh month, on the night of the full moon."

"You mean *you* did. When you wrote the book, you made the mistake of specifying an exact time. My wife will swear that I was with her that night," Sano said.

"I certainly did not write the book. And the wife of a liar is no more honest than he," Hoshina scoffed. "Everyone knows Lady Reiko is very fond of her husband and would do or say anything to protect him. She's an untrustworthy witness."

"Do you have any witness at all who can confirm that I said the things in the book?" Sano demanded.

"Your Excellency, the only witness to his statements was Lady Wisteria, who's been murdered. Her body was discovered the night before last." The crime hadn't escaped the notice of Hoshina and his spies. "How convenient for the *sōsakan-sama* that she can't speak against him." Hoshina flashed a sardonic glance at Sano.

"The body may not even be Wisteria," Sano said, "and it was found in a house belonging to Fujio the *hokan*. He's the primary suspect in that murder, and also in Lord Mitsuyoshi's. There are other suspects, including Wisteria's chaperone, and maybe more we don't know about because the investigation isn't finished."

"The investigation has been controlled by the *sōsakan-sama* from the start," Hoshina said with disdain. "The suspects he mentions are only people who can't prove their innocence. He persecuted them to shield himself."

"You were the one who arrested Momoko," Sano pointed out.

"Because he tricked me into it," Hoshina told the shogun. "He even defended Treasury Minister Nitta at his trial to make everyone believe he cares about justice. But his investigation is a farce, and his good character a disguise.

"Lady Wisteria wrote in her pillow book that she wanted to force the *sōsakan-sama* to marry her. He gave her the weapon she needed when he insulted Your Excellency and threatened Lord Mitsuyoshi. It's obvious that Wisteria tried to blackmail the *sōsakan-sama*, and he killed her so she could never tell anyone what he'd said. He's a traitor who killed once to place his son in line for the succession, and again to cover up his crime."

"Indeed." Tokugawa Tsunayoshi glowered at Sano.

Sano felt the escalating pulse of panic along his nerves. Whatever he said in his own defense, Hoshina twisted to make him appear guiltier. Terrified by the nightmare that enmeshed him, furious at Hoshina, the elders, the shogun, and the injustice he faced, Sano resorted to guile, his only means of survival.

"Your Excellency," Sano said, "please allow me to remind everyone here that you are the ultimate authority. Your wisdom and powers of judgment surpass those of lesser humans. Police Commissioner Hoshina owes you an apology for trying to impose his feeble opinions on you."

Dismay wiped the self-satisfaction off Hoshina's face. "He's trying to flatter you into thinking better of him and worse of me, Your Excellency."

But the shogun, clearly eager for praise, frowned in resentment at Hoshina and waved a hand to silence him. "Go on," Tokugawa Tsunayoshi ordered Sano.

"You are a judicious ruler with a unique ability to distinguish right from wrong. Would you condemn a man just because a mere subordinate said you should?" Sano went on, though ashamed of manipulating his lord. "Would you let the real killer go free because Hoshina-*san* wants me blamed for Lord Mitsuyoshi's murder?"

While Hoshina stared in helpless outrage, indecision creased the shogun's brow. "I, ahh, guess not," the shogun said, looking to Sano for approval.

"Of course you wouldn't." Heartened that he'd gained the upper hand, Sano said, "Your strong sense of honor requires more than just a book of dubious origin and Hoshina-*san*'s accusations before you decide whether a man you've trusted is a criminal. You require facts."

"Facts. Ahh, yes." The shogun seized upon the word, as though delighted to see a complex situation reduced to one simple idea. Then his face clouded with confusion. "But how do I get them? What, ahh, shall I do?"

"Since you ask my humble opinion," Sano said, "I suggest that you order me to continue investigating the murders until I find the real culprit and prove my claim that I am innocent and have been framed by my enemies."

Enlightenment cleared the confusion from the shogun's face; but before he could speak, Hoshina said, "Please excuse me, Your Excellency, but the *sōsakan-sama* mustn't be allowed to search out an innocent person to blame for his crimes." Hoshina's tone was fervent, desperate. "If you agree to what he asks, you'll be abetting the man who killed your cousin!"

"In the interest of fairness, Police Commissioner Hoshina should be permitted to look for evidence that I'm guilty," Sano said.

Hoshina's mouth opened in incredulity. The shogun considered. He looked toward Chamberlain Yanagisawa, whose shoulders moved in a slight shrug that disclaimed responsibility for the decision. The shogun then turned to the elders, but they sat still and impassive, like trees motionless until the prevailing wind blows.

At last Tokugawa Tsunayoshi nodded. "That sounds, ahh, reasonable," he said. The elders also nodded, their heads moving in unison.

Sano experienced a deluge of relief that didn't quench his rage at everyone in the room. He'd won a chance to save himself, but it was far less than he deserved.

Indignant, Hoshina turned to Yanagisawa. The chamberlain looked straight at Sano. Was that respect, and a gleam of amusement in Yanagisawa's eyes? Sano had learned from the chamberlain's example how to manipulate the shogun. Did Yanagisawa enjoy watching Sano stoop to his own level?

Sano suddenly understood why Yanagisawa didn't care who had killed Lord Mitsuyoshi—or if the killer was caught—and chose to stay out of the argument. Yanagisawa had his mind on the future rather than the immediate controversy.

Tokugawa Tsunayoshi flapped a hand at Sano and Hoshina. "I, ahh, order you both to go and do what *Sōsakan* Sano suggested. But remember this." He focused his bloodshot eyes on Hoshina. "If you fail to prove that Sano-*san* is guilty, you will be punished for, ahh, slandering him." The shogun's warning gaze moved to Sano. "And unless you prove your innocence, you will be executed for killing my heir."

26

A large, noisy crowd filled the courtyard of Magistrate Aoki's mansion and overflowed into the street. Hirata, accompanied by three detectives, had to push his way through the gate. People jostled him, craning their necks toward the mansion. Some were young men whose raffish clothing marked them as entertainers, artists, hustlers, or other denizens of the fashionable low life, but most were women.

Samurai ladies, dressed in silk and guarded by troops, clustered around an iron vat, where a fire had been lit to heat the courtyard. In the outer reaches of the fire's warmth, nuns with shaven heads knelt chanting prayers. Beyond them stood gaudily dressed wives and daughters of merchants. The largest contingent, huddled against the wall and buildings, looked to be servants, teahouse girls, and disreputable females. Some of the women wept; others whispered together, clearly distraught. Several *doshin* kept order among the crowd.

"Who are all these people?" Hirata asked a *doshin* he knew.

"Family, friends, and admirers of Fujio the *hokan*."

And probably his lovers, too, Hirata thought, all come to stand vigil during his trial.

Upon walking into the Court of Justice, Hirata found old Magistrate Aoki and his secretaries already seated on the dais before an audience of officials. Fujio knelt on the *shirasu*. He wore a ragged hemp robe; chains shackled his hands and bare feet. As the door shut behind Hirata and his detectives, Fujio turned. His handsome face was drawn with misery, but he gave Hirata a brief, valiant smile.

"Fujio, you are accused of the murder of the courtesan Lady Wisteria," said Magistrate Aoki.

Hirata wasn't surprised; knowing how Aoki had rushed Treasury Minister Nitta to trial, he'd anticipated this. But as he and his men knelt at the side of the room, he noticed a woman on the *shirasu* near Fujio. She, too, wore a hemp robe and chains. Her drab hair hung in a braid down her thin back. Her elegant profile seemed carved by despair. It was Lady Wisteria's *yarite*, Momoko. Shock jolted Hirata. Why was the chaperone here?

"Momoko, you are accused of abetting Fujio in the murder." Magistrate Aoki's wrinkled bitter-melon face wore a prideful, smug look. "The pair of you shall therefore be tried together."

Hirata and his detectives exchanged glances of amazed consternation. The corpse in the cottage still hadn't been definitely identified as Wisteria. The evidence against Fujio had weakened when his family and friends confirmed that he'd been far from the cottage during the crucial time period. And there was no evidence at all to implicate Momoko in the crime. What on earth was Magistrate Aoki doing?

Then Hirata understood. Aoki had had second thoughts about convicting the treasury minister, and believed he might have erred. As long as other suspects existed, Aoki faced the chance that Sano would prove one of them guilty of Lord Mitsuyoshi's murder and him guilty of subverting justice.

Aoki wanted to eliminate Fujio and Momoko so that even if the shogun decided Nitta had been wrongly condemned, Magistrate Aoki would have already executed the only other possible culprits. He would be safe because Sano's investigation would have no reason to continue. And the second murder had given Aoki the opportunity to fulfill his corrupt aims at the expense of two people who might be innocent. Outrage filled Hirata.

"In the interest of saving trouble, I shall dispense with the usual formalities and summarize the relevant facts of the case," Magistrate Aoki said to the assembly.

"Fujio had a love affair with Wisteria that continued in secret after he married a daughter of the man who owns the Great Miura brothel. Wisteria threatened to tell Fujio's father-in-law about the affair unless Fujio got her out of Yoshiwara. But he didn't have enough money to free her, and he didn't want to lose his wife, his home, and his livelihood, as he would if his father-in-law learned he was an adulterer. Hence, Fujio decided to kill Wisteria to keep her quiet."

Hirata listened, incredulous. However likely a story this sounded, Magistrate Aoki offered no evidence whatsoever that it was true. And he apparently didn't intend to present any witnesses. None existed, as far as Hirata knew.

"Fujio told Wisteria he would help her escape," Magistrate Aoki continued. "He hired a palanquin and bearers to wait outside Yoshiwara. He planned to sneak Wisteria out of the *ageya*, and the sentries at the gate would let her through if he bribed them. The palanquin would carry her to his secluded cottage, where he could murder her."

But of course, Magistrate Aoki had the authority to dispense with legal protocol if he chose, Hirata realized. Watching the defendants, he pitied them even while he acknowledged the possibility that they were guilty. Fujio sat quiet and composed, but Momoko looked shrunken like a wounded animal, and Hirata could hear her quick, rasping breaths. This was a mere case of two commoners accused of conspiring to kill another. Fujio and Momoko were powerless to resist, and the *bakufu* didn't care what happened to them.

From outdoors came shrill yells, and thumps against the wall of the building. Magistrate Aoki ignored the sounds. "However," he intoned, "Fujio couldn't manage his crime by himself. He had to perform at the *ageya* that night. He couldn't risk getting caught helping his father-in-law's courtesan run away because his secret would come out. And performing would give him an alibi for Wisteria's disappearance. So he engaged an accomplice."

The magistrate gestured his wizened hand at Momoko. "This *yarite* was jealous of Wisteria and hated her. Momoko was also a friend of Fujio, and when he told her his plan, she was glad to help him. While he sang at the party, Momoko crept upstairs to the room where Wisteria was entertaining Lord Mitsuyoshi. The hour was late, and the lovers had been drinking. Momoko arrived to find them both asleep—or so she thought, until she saw that Mitsuyoshi was dead. Treasury Minister Nitta had sneaked into the room and stabbed him while Wisteria slept."

Momoko whimpered, shivering; her chains clinked.

"She was horrified," Magistrate Aoki said, "but she went through with Fujio's plan. She awakened Wisteria and dressed the frightened courtesan in a hooded cloak she'd brought to disguise Wisteria. Then Momoko hurried Wisteria downstairs, out the back door, and through the streets to the gate."

Shrieks erupted outside the courtroom. The door shuddered under furious banging. On the far side of it, female voices pleaded; male voices threatened. The audience and guards turned in alarm.

"What is that infernal racket?" Magistrate Aoki demanded.

"It seems that the women from the crowd outside have gotten into the building," one of his secretaries said, "and they want to see the accused man."

Fujio looked over his shoulder and gave Hirata a rueful

but proud grin: Even when he was facing certain doom, he enjoyed his celebrity.

"Well, they shan't interrupt this trial." Magistrate Aoki pitched his voice over the rising din: "Momoko bribed the gate sentries with money Fujio had given her. They let Wisteria out of the pleasure quarter, and she rode away in the palanquin. Then Momoko rushed back to the *ageya*. She told Fujio that Wisteria had escaped safely, but Lord Mitsuyoshi had been murdered. She was terrified that she would be blamed because her hairpin was the weapon.

"Fujio cleverly told Momoko to go back upstairs, then come running down, screaming that Lord Mitsuyoshi was dead, as if she'd just discovered the body. Momoko was later arrested, but Fujio had evaded suspicion and was free to do as he pleased. He traveled to the cottage where Wisteria was hiding. He beat her to death and left her body to rot."

The story was plausible enough that Fujio and Momoko might really have contrived the murder as Magistrate Aoki claimed. Yet Hirata wouldn't believe it without proof that Aoki hadn't invented the whole tale.

Now the magistrate gazed sternly at the accused pair. "Have you anything to say in your own defense?"

Hirata lost all tolerance for this travesty of justice. Before Fujio or Momoko could answer, he rose and strode toward the dais. Everyone stared. "Honorable Magistrate, I'm stopping this trial until you show some real evidence that these people did what you say they did," he said.

Magistrate Aoki's eyes glittered like dark, flinty pebbles as he gave Hirata a contemptuous look. "Your master tried to stop one of my trials. You won't succeed where he failed. And unless you want a reputation for interfering with the law, you'd best keep quiet."

The door burst open. A horde of women stampeded into the courtroom. "Fujio-*san*! Fujio-*san*!" they screamed. Possessed by hysteria and ardor, samurai ladies, nuns, merchant women, and servant girls rushed toward the *hokan*. Fujio waved and beamed at them.

"Stop!" Magistrate Aoki shouted at the women, then ordered the guards, "Get them out of here!"

The guards pushed back the mob. Women moaned, struggled, tore their hair, and wept. They overwhelmed the guards and fell to their knees, occupying every empty space on the courtroom floor. Magistrate Aoki grimaced in disgust, then returned his attention to Fujio and Momoko.

"Have you anything to say in your own defense?" he asked, clearly determined to ignore the interruption.

"I didn't do it!" Momoko's desperate wail rose over the noise.

Hirata, still standing near the dais, watched with horror and pity as the *yarite* simpered at Magistrate Aoki. Fluttering her eyelids, she wriggled her body in a grotesque attempt to seduce, and cried, "Please believe that I'm innocent!"

The magistrate's flinty gaze was merciless. "I pronounce you guilty as an accomplice to murder. You are sentenced to death."

Guards bore the weeping, swooning Momoko through the crowd, out of the room. Magistrate Aoki addressed Fujio: "What do you say for yourself?"

The room fell silent as the women waited for their idol to speak. Fujio said in a clear, ringing voice, "I confess."

An uproar of screaming and weeping burst from the women. Young girls beat their heads on the floor; the nuns chanted prayers. Magistrate Aoki yelled orders for the women to be quiet and the guards to remove them. Fujio struggled to his feet, weighted by the shackles. Slowly he turned toward the crowd. His noble, somber mien quieted the women. Tearful adoration shone on their faces as they beheld him.

"Thank you, Hirata-*san*, for trying to help me," Fujio said. "Thank you, honorable ladies, for your favor. But I know when I'm beaten, and I'd like to leave this life with grace. Therefore, I will sing my confession in a song I've written."

He looked to Magistrate Aoki, who frowned but nodded. Inhaling deeply, Fujio donned a look of intense concentration. He paused on the verge of the performance of his career, as suspense hushed the court. Then he sang in a stirring, melancholy voice:

> *"Love is a garden of many flowers,*
> *Where the rose, peony, and iris unfurl*
> *their petals to the sun.*
> *My life was a garden of beautiful women,*
> *Which I wandered to my heart's delight,*
> *sampling every blossom.*
>
> *But in the garden hides a flower of death,*
> *Whose sap is poison, and its thorns sharp*
> *as knives.*
> *Into my life came the Lady Wisteria*
> *Whose charms lured me to my downfall.*
>
> *We loved each other with a passion as*
> *hot and bountiful as summer*
> *Until anger and hatred poisoned our*
> *paradise.*
> *I bruised the soft petals of her skin, I*
> *crushed the fragile stem of her body, I*
> *drew the sap of her blood,*
> *Until my Wisteria lay dead before me.*
>
> *Now love is an empty wasteland,*
> *Where harsh winds blow over weeds,*
> *rocks, and bones.*
> *My life is a road to the execution ground,*
> *Which I walk in hopeless misery toward*
> *my death."*

Hands upturned, body slumped, and his expression tragic, Fujio let his last note fade in the silence. Then a thunder of cheers, applause, and sobbing burst from the women. Fujio bowed. Magistrate Aoki looked irritated by the spectacle.

"I pronounce you guilty of murder and sentence you to death by decapitation," he said.

As the guards escorted Fujio out of the room, the women followed him in a wailing, sobbing procession.

Hirata dreaded telling Sano that their last two suspects would be dead before they could resume the investigation.

27

"Line up the soldiers, Masahiro-*chan*," said Reiko.

Squatting on the nursery floor, the little boy carefully positioned his toy horsemen, archers, and swordsmen as Reiko and his old nurse O-sugi watched.

"That's very good." Reiko smiled at her son, but her mind was on Sano. Ever since he'd left for the palace, she'd waited in fearful suspense for him to return from his meeting with the shogun. She longed to know what was happening.

A loud crash from outside startled her and Masahiro and O-sugi. It sounded as if someone had broken down the garden gate. Then Reiko heard muttering and stomping. Puzzled, she rose, opened the door, stepped onto the veranda, and saw Sano in the garden. Head down, fists clenched, he stalked around trees. His feet trampled flowerbeds; his gait was unsteady.

"I can't stand it," he muttered. Breath puffed from him in

white vapor clouds that rapidly formed and dispersed in the cold, sunlit air. "I can't stand it anymore!"

Alarmed by his strange behavior, Reiko hurried across the garden to Sano. "What's happened?" she cried.

Sano whirled toward her, his eyes wild and face contorted by fierce emotion. "Lady Yanagisawa brought the pillow book too late." He continued prowling the garden while Reiko ran after him. "The shogun had already read it. He now suspects me of murdering Lord Mitsuyoshi!"

"Oh, no." Reiko stopped, and her hand clasped her throat as horror and comprehension flooded her. She'd never seen Sano this upset because nothing this bad had ever happened before.

"That despicable, scheming, foul Hoshina got hold of the book. He made sure His Excellency saw it." As Sano poured out a disjointed account of the meeting, his arms lashed out at bushes that got in his way. Reiko realized that he wasn't just upset, but furious. "Hoshina branded me a traitor! I barely managed to convince the shogun to give me a chance to prove I'm innocent!"

Reiko caught up with Sano and reached for his arm. "Everything will be all right," she said, trying to soothe him despite her own terror.

But Sano careened backward across the grass, shouting, "For four years I've done everything the shogun has asked of me. I've shed my blood for honor!" Sano halted and tore open his garments to reveal the scars on his torso. "I know His Excellency owes me nothing in return, and I wish for nothing except for him to see me as the loyal retainer that I am!"

Reiko noticed O-sugi and Masahiro standing on the veranda, gaping as Sano raved. "Go back inside," she called to them, then urged Sano, "Please calm yourself. Come in the house before you freeze."

He appeared not to hear her. "You'd think that once— just once—His Excellency could have faith in me and disregard the slander of my enemies," Sano said, addressing the world at large. "But no—he was quick to believe everything Hoshina said against me. He was ready to condemn me on the spot, without even hearing my side of the story!" Sano gave a bitter laugh. "The only thing that saved me is that I've been in these situations enough times to know how to talk my way out of them."

Although the shogun's frequent injustices toward Sano pained her, Reiko had never heard him complain. The Black Lotus case had taxed his endurance, and this outrage had finally shattered it. Frightened for her husband, and frightened of him, Reiko crept toward Sano.

"You'll get out of this one, too," she said. "The shogun will trust you again."

"Oh, no. He won't." Eyes dark with anger, Sano backed away from her. "Because I'm finished. I've had enough violent death, enough dirty politics, enough of trying to please a master who always threatens to kill me." He pumped his fists at his sides and threw back his head. *"I can't stand any more!"*

Reiko gasped. "What will you do?" she said, and heard her voice quaver with fear. If Sano renounced his servitude to the shogun, he would lose his livelihood and home as well as his honor. Her cold hands pressed her cheeks. "Where will we go?"

"I don't know." Sano resumed his blind, furious strides around the garden. "I don't care, as long as it's far from Edo Castle and everyone here!"

"But you can't just give up everything," Reiko said, following him in panic. "Please think about Masahiro's future." Sano knew the hardship of growing up the son of a *rōnin*. Surely he wouldn't want the same for Masahiro.

"I am thinking of it! I won't have my son trapped in the same impossible circumstances as I!"

A branch of an azalea bush snagged his sleeve. With a cry of rage, Sano drew his sword and began hacking viciously at the bush. Branches and twigs flew at every touch of his blade, while he shouted curses. Reiko shrank away

from him in stark, wide-eyed terror. This wasn't her husband;
it was a demon who'd possessed him.

Suddenly Sano halted. With an anguished groan, he flung
away his weapon. He sagged to his knees before the mutilated bush, his temper spent. Shudders convulsed him.
Reiko's terror dissolved. She went to Sano and put her arms
around him.

Inside his private chamber, Sano sat wrapped in a quilt,
drinking a hot herbal infusion that Reiko had given him to
restore his spirits, while she knelt watching anxiously.

"I'm sorry," he said.

And he was sorry—for saying deplorable things; for suc-
cumbing to emotion and displaying weakness; for destroying
the bush in a fit of undignified temper; for scaring Reiko. He
hadn't realized how much bad will had built up inside him.
Releasing it had given him an exhilarating sense of freedom;
but now, although he felt more peaceful than he had in ages,
he was deeply ashamed. And nothing had changed. The shogun still suspected him of murdering Lord Mitsuyoshi; Police
Commissioner Hoshina was still determined to incriminate
him. If he wanted to survive, Sano mustn't lose his self-
control again.

"Do you really mean to give up your post?" Reiko asked,
her manner still troubled.

"No." Sano's moment of rebellion had passed. He had
nowhere to go, and he couldn't sacrifice his honor or his
family's future. Nor could he sacrifice the vocation that was
his path along the Way of the Warrior, the strict code of
duty, obedience, and courage by which samurai lived.

"Then what will you do?" Reiko said.

"I'll find the real killer, prove my innocence, and regain
the shogun's trust." Determination and a desire for justice
rekindled in Sano. "It will be hard, because all the clues have
so far led nowhere, but there's still hope."

He and Reiko looked up as Hirata appeared in the doorway. "*Sumimasen*—excuse me, but there's bad news." Vis-

ibly distraught, Hirata said, "Magistrate Aoki just convicted Fujio of murdering Lady Wisteria, and Momoko as an accomplice. They've been taken to the execution ground."

Reiko murmured in dismay. Sano had anticipated Fujio's conviction when he'd heard Magistrate Aoki had convened the trial, but Momoko's took him by surprise.

"Come in. Sit down and explain," Sano said to Hirata.

Hirata complied, and Sano marveled that the magistrate had based the verdict on a story he'd invented and couldn't prove. After Hirata had finished, Sano said, "This seems to be the day for bad news," then told Hirata what had happened to him.

"All three of our suspects are gone." Hirata's face reflected his horror. "That leaves you as the only target for the shogun's wrath."

Sano perceived cosmic forces shifting and heard the approaching thunder of doom as the onus settled upon him.

Reiko said, "Maybe Fujio, Momoko, or Treasury Minister Nitta did murder Lord Mitsuyoshi. They're still good suspects and worth investigating even if they're no longer alive."

"We can still look for proof of their guilt," Hirata said, following up her attempt to look on the bright side.

"And hope that it exists," Sano said, "because I'm afraid that if we can't find a witness or some solid evidence that points to someone other than me, the only thing that will convince the shogun I'm innocent is the killer's confession. Which would be difficult to get from a dead person."

His companions nodded in glum agreement. Then Hirata spoke hesitantly: "Police Commissioner Hoshina isn't above falsifying evidence against you. That second pillow book stank of him. He's sure to invent more 'proof' that you're a traitor."

Sano pursed his mouth, aware that Hirata meant they should follow Hoshina's example and fabricate evidence against Fujio, Momoko, or the treasury minister to save Sano.

Understanding flashed in Reiko's eyes. "False incrimination is less harmful to a dead person than to a live one," she said with cautious hope.

That Hirata and Reiko would even consider such dishonesty meant they were at a loss for what else to do. "It's already occurred to me," Sano admitted. "But I'm not desperate enough to frame someone who might be innocent, whether the person is alive or dead. Especially since there's a whole area of inquiry that we haven't yet explored."

"What's left?" Reiko said, puzzled.

"Lord Mitsuyoshi himself," Sano said.

Hirata frowned. "The shogun forbade you to investigate his background."

"And I would hate to disobey." At the very thought of defying his lord, Sano tasted nauseating disgrace. "But Mitsuyoshi represents a direct connection to the killer. Investigating him and his associates should produce new clues. And what are the alternatives?

"We can keep on investigating Fujio, Momoko, and Nitta, and maybe find new evidence on territory we've already covered. We can hope for new suspects to emerge, and Wisteria's lover from Hokkaido to turn up, or Police Commissioner Hoshina to drop dead." Sano watched Reiko and Hirata shake their heads, doubting the likelihood of these events. "We can pray for a miracle."

"Investigating Lord Mitsuyoshi does seem the most promising course of action," Reiko said.

"The shogun will punish you for insubordination," Hirata reminded Sano.

"I'll risk that because he'll put me to death unless I prove my innocence," Sano said.

"Maybe he'll forgive you when he realizes you're not a traitor," Hirata suggested hopefully.

The odds against Sano outweighed those in his favor. He said, "Maybe we can solve the case without the shogun finding out I've disobeyed him—and before Hoshina or our other enemies can cause us any more trouble."

. . .

Lady Yanagisawa stood alone in her chamber, waiting for the only guest she'd ever invited to visit her.

She wrung her cold, perspiring hands and breathed deeply to loosen the knot of anxiety in her stomach. She dreaded receiving a virtual stranger, and the thought of anyone breaching the sanctuary of her room. But the visit must take place here, in the privacy she needed.

Her chief attendant appeared in the doorway. "There's a girl here to see you."

Lady Yanagisawa's heart lurched as she fought the urge to run and hide. "Bring her here," she said.

Determination fostered courage. She'd already taken a step against Reiko, but the consequences were too uncertain. If Lady Yanagisawa expected to sway the balance of fortune in her favor, she must persevere, despite her regret over her malice toward her friend.

Reiko's nursemaid O-hana entered the room. She wore a fashionable red kimono printed with a design of snow on black tree branches. Avid curiosity shone through her modest demeanor, belied her hesitant step.

"Welcome," Lady Yanagisawa murmured. She clasped her trembling hands under her sleeves, intimidated by O-hana's bold, pretty face.

O-hana knelt and bowed. "It's a privilege for this insignificant person to be summoned to your presence, Honorable Lady." Her voice brimmed with eagerness to ingratiate herself with her hostess. "A million thanks for inviting me."

Lady Yanagisawa had recognized O-hana as a good prospective accomplice the moment she'd laid eyes on the girl at Reiko's house; yet she needed another chance to judge O-hana's character. Kneeling opposite her guest, Lady Yanagisawa forced herself to look at O-hana. The girl's eyes sparkled with a verve and cunning that repelled, yet gratified Lady Yanagisawa.

"May I offer you some refreshment?" Lady Yanagisawa asked.

While they waited for a servant to bring tea and food, O-hana said, "Your chamber is nicer than Lady Reiko's."

Her sharp gaze took in the gilded murals, the shelf of antique porcelain ware, the lacquer tables, cabinets, and chests inlaid with gold and mother-of-pearl. "And this estate is much bigger than the *sōsakan-sama*'s."

She liked expensive things and aspired to a higher station than her job as a nursemaid, Lady Yanagisawa noted with satisfaction. Whatever loyalty O-hana had to her mistress would likely matter less to her than the chance for a connection with someone who could give her things that Reiko couldn't.

"Please enjoy my home during your time here," Lady Yanagisawa said, her self-confidence rising.

"You're so kind. Many thanks." Smiling vividly, O-hana said, "When I got your message, I couldn't imagine what you could want with me."

It wasn't her place to turn the conversation toward the reason for the invitation. O-hana was a little too forward for her own good, but that suited Lady Yanagisawa. Her aims would benefit from the girl's bold initiative.

"We shall discuss that soon enough," Lady Yanagisawa said.

The refreshments arrived. Too tense to eat, Lady Yanagisawa watched O-hana consume trout roe served in an orange rind, sashimi, shrimp stuffed with quail eggs, roasted gingko nuts, and sweet cakes. The nursemaid ate very fast, as if the food might be snatched from her before she got enough. Lady Yanagisawa liked O-hana's insecurity as well as her greed.

"That was delicious," O-hana said, licking her lips. "How I regret that I, a poor nursemaid, am not in a position to give you something in return."

Lady Yanagisawa smiled. Her shyness ebbed as she felt herself gaining mastery over the girl. "You could tell me about yourself," she said.

O-hana's eyebrows rose in surprise that a lady of high rank should care to know about a servant, but she gladly complied. "My father is a clerk at the Hinokiya Drapery Store. One of the *sōsakan-sama*'s soldiers is a customer. He befriended my father and arranged for me to be a nurse to Masahiro-*chan*. I didn't really want to be a servant because I'd rather get married. But the work isn't too hard, and I love Edo Castle. Here I get to meet better kinds of men than I can meet at home. I'm hoping I'll find a husband who can give me a nice house and pretty clothes and I won't have to earn my own living anymore."

And if she snared a Tokugawa samurai retainer, she would move far up the social scale. Lady Yanagisawa was glad to find that O-hana wanted something so ordinary and easily granted. "I can arrange that," Lady Yanagisawa said.

"What?" O-hana said, startled.

"A good match for you, with a Tokugawa samurai." Lady Yanagisawa's money and her husband's position would be enough to entice someone to marry a pretty commoner.

O-hana looked amazed by her good fortune, yet puzzled. "You would do that for me?" She touched her chest. Then suspicion sharpened her eyes: She wasn't a fool; she knew favors didn't come free. "Why?"

"Because there's something I want you to do for me," Lady Yanagisawa said. Her heart began to pound with her urgent need to engage O-hana's cooperation and her fear that she would fail.

"What is it?" Though her voice was cautious, O-hana leaned forward, as if to jump at her heart's desire.

"First I want you to tell me everything Lady Reiko does. Second . . . I can't tell you just yet," Lady Yanagisawa said.

"You want me to do something to Lady Reiko?" O-hana wilted; her face took on a queasy expression. "I wouldn't want to hurt her." The girl was ambitious, but not evil, Lady Yanagisawa realized. "And I don't want to get in trouble."

She had an instinct for self-preservation that was stronger than any affection she felt for Reiko. This discovery heartened Lady Yanagisawa. She understood that O-hana might be persuaded if she knew she would escape blame.

"I promise you won't have to lay a hand on Lady Reiko, and you won't get in trouble," Lady Yanagisawa said. "Let us strike a bargain. In the near future I shall give you instructions about what to do. You shall follow them. Afterward, I shall arrange your marriage to a rich, handsome Tokugawa samurai, and you shall want for nothing."

O-hana hesitated, obviously weighing the reward against the unknown dangers. At last she shook her head in regret. "I can't decide until I know what you want of me."

Dismay spread cold tendrils through Lady Yanagisawa, but she had planned for the possibility that O-hana would balk. She said, "Do you see that green box on the shelf of porcelain ware?" O-hana looked, then nodded. "Go see what's inside."

O-hana rose, walked to the shelf, and removed the lid from the little box. She took out a square packet of red paper. Her lips parted as she felt the heavy gold coins in the packet.

"I offer this gift as a token of my good faith," Lady Yanagisawa said. "Agree to my proposition, and it's yours."

O-hana stood immobile, the packet resting on her open palm. She stared at it as if trying to discern whether she held her dearest dream or a poisonous snake that would bite her. Lady Yanagisawa watched, her breath caught by anxiety. What if O-hana refused? Would she tell Reiko about the proposition? If so, what would happen, and how could Lady Yanagisawa achieve her aim without O-hana?

Guile and avarice, distrust and fear played across the girl's features like wind shifting sand. "I . . . need to think," she said.

"Then think about how my husband is the most powerful man in Japan," Lady Yanagisawa said, her quiet, flat voice disguising her emotions. "People who offend him or his kin pay dearly. Many are assassinated or executed. Some disappear and are never seen again. No one knows what becomes of them. But I could arrange for you to find out."

The nursemaid lifted her gaze to Lady Yanagisawa. Her eyes glittered with terror and need. Then a sigh of capitulation deflated her. Nodding, she slowly closed her fingers over the packet of coins.

Lady Yanagisawa experienced such an overwhelming sense of triumph that she nearly swooned. She also quaked with sudden apprehension because she'd taken her second step in her campaign against Reiko, and victory would cost her Reiko's friendship. The loss encroached upon her mind like a cloud bringing darkness and desolation.

But she addressed her new accomplice with calm authority: "Go now. I will send someone to hear your reports on Lady Reiko's doings. And you will receive my instructions soon."

28

Lord Mitsuyoshi's family lived in a special enclave of Edo Castle, reserved for important Tokugawa clan members. Here, Sano and two detectives strode along flagstone lanes through landscaped forest that separated mansions surrounded by gardens and stone walls. The enclave, deserted except for sentries in gatehouses, seemed remote from the city's turbulent life. Gray clouds spread rapidly across the sky, but Sano breathed hope from the fresh, pine-scented air. Perhaps the solution to his problems awaited him inside the mansion belonging to Lord Matsudaira, father of Mitsuyoshi.

After introducing himself to the gate sentries, he said, "Please tell Lord Matsudaira that I must speak with him."

The sentries conveyed his request, and so quickly obtained permission for Sano to enter that he dared believe Lord Matsudaira hadn't yet heard what had happened to him or become prejudiced against him. An attendant escorted him and his men into an audience chamber, where they found guards stationed along the walls and Lord Matsudaira standing on the dais.

"Why have you come here?" Lord Matsudaira demanded. He had the shogun's aristocratic features, but set in a broader, more intelligent face; his robust physique wore black ceremonial robes. Hands balled on his hips, surrounded by his troops like a general in a military encampment, he glared at Sano, who realized with dismay that his host already knew he'd been branded the murderer of Mitsuyoshi.

Bowing quickly, Sano said, "Before I explain, please allow me to offer you my condolences for the loss of your son."

Lord Matsudaira dropped his hands and tilted his head, staring as though he couldn't believe what he'd heard. "I'll not accept false sympathy from the man who killed him." His voice was harsh with indignation.

"Please understand that you've been misinformed," Sano said, as his men clustered defensively around him. "I did not kill Mitsuyoshi-*san*."

"So you say," Lord Matsudaira retorted. "The word around the castle is that you did. Do you think I don't know you've been accused by the shogun?" Disgust and hatred twisted his face as he took a step toward Sano. "I also know about the book that describes your plot against my son and His Excellency. Police Commissioner Hoshina told me this morning."

Hoshina had been quick to spread the news, turn public opinion against him, and prevent him from getting Mitsuyoshi's family to aid his investigation, Sano thought. "The book is a fraud," he said. "The accusation was initiated by Hoshina. It's no secret that he's out for my blood."

Lord Matsudaira waved his hand in a gesture that dismissed Sano's explanation as a poor excuse. "The shogun, chamberlain, elders, and police commissioner all believe you're a killer and traitor. That's proof enough for me."

"The shogun hasn't yet decided I'm guilty, in spite of the book and Hoshina's slander," Sano said. "His Excellency has allowed me to continue investigating the crime and prove my innocence."

"Your clever tongue has saved you from execution," Lord Matsudaira said disdainfully. "But I'll use all my influence and power to ensure that you die." Moving to the edge of the dais, he raised his left fist at Sano and rested his right on the hilt of his sword. Then a sob choked him. His belligerent posture crumpled; he averted his face.

Sano thought of Lord Matsudaira's reputation as a kind master to the citizens on the Tokugawa lands he managed, and perceived that he genuinely mourned Mitsuyoshi, not just the loss of political advantage he'd enjoyed as father to the shogun's heir. Sano pitied this grieving, misguided man.

"It would be better to use your power and influence to discover the truth about your son's death," he said. "I've come to enlist your help in exposing the real killer."

Lord Matsudaira's head snapped around; fury glittered through his tears. "You've come to stage a show of innocence and gloat over the misery you've caused this clan! I'll not help you save yourself." He leapt off the dais, advanced on Sano until they were a mere step apart, then thrust his face so close that Sano could see the red veins in his blazing eyes. "The only reason I let you in was so I can tell you in person that you, who have destroyed my son and betrayed our lord, are the most disgraceful creature on this earth!"

The insult struck Sano like blows to his spirit, and he retreated backward even as he said, "Please hear me out. In most murder cases, the victim was killed by someone close to him. Things he did, or trouble in his relations with people, can have led to the crime, and—"

"You would blame my son for his own murder?" Lord Matsudaira interrupted in outrage. "You're an even worse villain than the courtesan's pillow book portrays you. I'm ashamed that I ever thought you were an honorable samurai!"

"I'm not blaming Lord Mitsuyoshi," Sano hastened to say. "The fault belongs entirely to his killer. All I meant was that the key to solving a murder case usually lies in the victim's background."

Lord Matsudaira shook his head, scorning Sano.

"Your son must have had an enemy," Sano persisted. "You knew him all his life, and you must know what his activities were, whom he associated with, the places he frequented." Sano extended a hand and infused his voice with all the persuasiveness in him. "Please help me identify the enemy who killed him."

"My son was a harmless, respectable young man, and liked by everyone around him. He had no enemies, and he didn't die because of anything that happened in his personal life."

It had occurred to Sano that Lord Matsudaira might not be the best source of facts about Mitsuyoshi, whose reputation for debauchery suggested he'd had plenty to hide from his father. "Perhaps other family members were more familiar with your son's business than yourself," Sano said. "Perhaps they would be more willing to talk to me." Though he saw little chance that Lord Matsudaira would allow him to interview anyone else here, he had to ask.

Lord Matsudaira huffed in shock at this new affront. "My wife is ill from grief. I'll not let you bother her with questions or insinuations about our son."

"Then may I speak with Mitsuyoshi's brothers?" Sano said. "Or his personal retainers?"

Just then, Sano noticed one of the guards watching him with closer attention than the others. The man, perhaps thirty-five years old, had the powerful body of a fighter and the sensitive face of a scholar. His gaze met Sano's, then veered away. Sano recognized the guard as one of Mitsuyoshi's men whom he'd seen in Yoshiwara after the murder.

"This murder was strictly political, as you well know," Lord Matsudaira said. "My son fell victim to your quest for power. You murdered him so your son could take his place as the shogun's heir. He was an incidental casualty of your attack on the Tokugawa regime. Now you seek a scapegoat to frame for your crime, so you can escape treason charges."

"I'm neither a murderer nor traitor," Sano denied vehemently. "I'm innocent, and I'll prove it."

Lord Matsudaira jabbed his finger into Sano's chest. "Mitsuyoshi's brothers and retainers know what you are, and if you approach them, they'll kill you to avenge his death. Consider it a favor from me that I deny you permission to speak to them. I wouldn't willingly trespass on His Excellency's right to determine your fate, but if you come here again or go near any members of my household—" He drew his sword, brandished it at Sano, and shouted, "I'll kill you myself and save the executioner the trouble!"

The detectives leapt between Sano and Lord Matsudaira's sword; the guards drew their weapons, anticipating a battle. "Even as you accuse me and threaten me, the real killer is out there somewhere," Sano said. "If you won't cooperate with my investigation and you join my enemies in condemning me, you'll deny your son the justice he deserves. The murderer will walk free."

Fixing a long, hostile look on Sano, Lord Matsudaira said, "He already has." Then he addressed the guards: "Escort the *sōsakan-sama* off the premises before I personally deliver him to justice."

As soon as Sano and Hirata had left her to begin their inquiries into Lord Mitsuyoshi's background, Reiko had gone to the palace to begin hers. She'd hoped to coax her cousin Eri and friends among the shogun's concubines and their attendants into telling her what they knew about Lord Mitsuyoshi. But the chief female palace official said everyone was too busy to talk. Her cold manner told Reiko the unhappy truth: The women had heard that Sano was on the brink of ruin, and they all had withdrawn their friendship from his wife because they didn't want her troubles to infect them. Visits to friends and relatives in the official quarter ended the same way, and Reiko went home feeling like a pariah.

As she sat in her parlor, terrified that she'd lost her power to help Sano, one of Sano's detectives appeared at the door. He said, "I have information that the *sōsakan-sama* told me to report to you if he wasn't available. I've found the bath-house where Lady Wisteria's friend Yuya works." He gave a location in Nihonbashi. "I searched the place this morning, and there was no sign of Wisteria. Everyone denies knowing anything about her—but I think Yuya was lying."

Reiko was thrilled, because her visit to the courtesan's family had produced a possible lead. Perhaps if she talked to Yuya, she could get the truth. "Please summon an escort to take me to the bathhouse at once," she said.

The detective went off to obey. Reiko hurried to her chamber to dress for the trip. She'd just strapped her dagger under her sleeve, when the nursemaid O-hana sidled into the room.

"You're very busy lately, Honorable Mistress," O-hana said.

Reiko frowned at the intrusion. She suspected that O-hana had been eavesdropping. "Yes, I am," Reiko said in a tone that discouraged conversation. She noted that O-hana seemed nervous and her eyes were brighter than usual.

O-hana ignored the hint that she should go. "Are you go-ing out again?" she said eagerly.

"Yes." Reiko's dislike of the girl increased, even though O-hana had done her a service by introducing her to Wis-teria's family. Her senses stirred alert to a new malevolence about O-hana. She inwardly rebuked herself for feelings based on fancy, not reason. How could she break the spell of the Black Lotus, stop imagining threats that didn't exist, and concentrate on the ones that did?

"I heard that the *sōsakan-sama* has been accused of mur-der and treason." O-hana edged closer to Reiko. "How aw-ful!"

"Indeed," Reiko said flatly. O-hana had overstepped the bounds of courtesy by mentioning Sano's problems, and Reiko resented O-hana's obvious hunger for sordid details.

"I'm so sorry. You must be very worried about what's happened." O-hana knelt cautiously, like a cat settling down in a place where it feels insecure. "I hope I haven't upset you more by speaking of it."

Instead of heeding her wish to order the girl back to work, Reiko forced a smile and said, "It's all right." O-hana was only offering sympathy as best she knew how. Personal problems were no excuse for ill temper toward an innocent servant.

"You and the *sōsakan-sama* have been good to me, and I'd hate for anything bad to happen to you," O-hana said. An odd, furtive note echoed in her voice, almost as if she felt the opposite of what she said. After a pause, she blurted, "I wish I could make all these troubles disappear."

Reiko fought her suspicion, because there was no reason to think O-hana meant her harm. "Thank you," Reiko said more warmly. "I'm sorry if I seemed harsh. I am a little worried."

O-hana blushed, hunching in inexplicable shame. "I don't deserve your apology," she mumbled.

But there definitely was something off about O-hana that Reiko couldn't attribute to her own overactive imagination. "What's the matter?" she said.

"Nothing!" The girl sat up straight, as if jabbed in the back. "It's kind of you to ask, but I'm fine." She gave Reiko a too-bright smile. "It's your situation that concerns me. What are you going to do?"

Unconvinced, Reiko eyed her closely. "I'll try to discover who killed Lord Mitsuyoshi and prove my husband's innocence."

"Maybe I can help," O-hana said. "Shall I go with you?"

Her readiness to intrude again aroused new suspicion in Reiko. "You can help me by staying here and attending to your duties," Reiko said.

"Yes, Honorable Mistress."

A look of pique and disappointment flitted across O-hana's face, but she bowed meekly, rose, and sidled away. Reiko hurried outside to her waiting palanquin.

Sano and his detectives walked down the passage leading away from the Tokugawa family enclave. Through the gun holes and arrow slits in the enclosed corridors that topped the high walls, Sano heard the guards conversing while they waited to shoot anyone who invaded the castle. He kept his eyes focused straight ahead and his face expressionless, concealing his fear as he passed beneath watchtowers occupied by more guards. There was no security here for a man accused of treason. Sano felt like an enemy soldier trapped in the castle, because the might of the Tokugawa would turn on him unless he somehow obtained the information he'd failed to get from Lord Matsudaira and cleared his name.

"*Sōsakan-sama*!" Rapid footsteps behind Sano accompanied the call. "May I please speak with you?"

Sano turned and saw, running down the passage toward him, the guard who'd watched him so intently at the Matsudaira estate. He halted, glad that someone from the household was willing to talk to him.

"Yes," Sano said. The guard lurched to a stop before him, panting from exertion, and bowed. "Go ahead."

The guard looked around, his sensitive face taut with nervousness. He mumbled, "In private, if we may?"

"As you wish." Sano signaled his men to move ahead, while he walked with the guard.

"Many thanks." Though the guard spoke with breathless relief, he dawdled, his shoulders hunched and his gaze furtive.

Sano studied the man while allowing him time to compose himself. He had a frown that wrinkled the skin of his upper eyelids, and a delicate mouth that lent him a vulnerable air despite his muscular heft.

"What's your name?" Sano said.

"Wada," the guard said, as if making a guilty admission.

"Don't be afraid, Wada-*san*. I appreciate your coming to me," Sano said.

They traveled some twenty paces before Wada said in an almost inaudible voice, "Family reputation is very important to my master. He loved his son and wants to preserve only the good memories of him."

"But someone who cares less about appearances might

reveal the truth about Lord Mitsuyoshi?" Sano suggested.

Wada hesitated, his gaze fixed on the ground as they walked. "My master has forbidden his family, retainers, and servants to talk to you. I don't want to disobey him."

And he certainly didn't want to be punished, Sano thought. Was the man fishing for a bribe? Sano scrutinized Wada's profile, but saw no avarice, only the worry of a man torn between loyalty and the desire to speak his mind. "Your ultimate duty is to the shogun," Sano said. "His Excellency has ordered me to investigate Lord Mitsuyoshi's murder, and you must cooperate by telling me everything you know that might be relevant."

Wada's frown relaxed, but he still looked perturbed. "My family has served the Matsudaira for five generations," he said. "I was part of Mitsuyoshi-*san*'s retinue since the day he was born and looked after him all his life. He was as dear to me as a younger brother. I don't want to lose my post, but I couldn't bear it if the wrong man was punished for his murder and his killer went free because I kept silent."

"I'll do everything in my power to avenge Mitsuyoshi-*san*'s death," Sano promised.

"Well . . ." Although Wada seemed reassured, hesitation inserted uneasy pauses between his words. "When Mitsuyoshi-*san* was very young, the clan's fortune teller predicted that he would someday rule Japan. From that moment his life was a preparation for becoming shogun. His father hired teachers to make Mitsuyoshi-*san* study books and practice martial arts all day long, and priests to discipline his spirit. Eventually he was introduced to the shogun, who took a liking to him. It looked as if the prophecy would come true. So much was expected of him because he was going to inherit the regime . . ."

"That he rebelled?" Sano said.

Nodding, the guard continued with reluctance: "He was a strong-willed boy. He craved adventure. When he was sixteen, he got tired of constant discipline and protection. He ordered me to help him sneak out of the castle. We would roam the town while his father thought he was studying.

Mitsuyoshi-*san* loved the entertainment districts. He had good looks, charm, and money, and he made friends at the teahouses and gambling dens. Soon he discovered Yoshiwara, and the trouble started.

"One night when the shogun wanted his company, he was nowhere to be found. Lord Matsudaira learned he'd been visiting a courtesan. When Mitsuyoshi-*san* came home, they had a terrible argument. His father was furious that he'd disappointed the shogun and risked falling out of favor. Mitsuyoshi-*san* begged a little freedom in exchange for sacrificing himself to the clan's ambitions. They both wanted him to be the next shogun, but Mitsuyoshi-*san* was the one who paid the price."

Apparently, Mitsuyoshi had been the shogun's sexual object, and disliked the role forced on him. "What happened then?" Sano said.

"The arguments continued," said Wada. "Lord Matsudaira ordered Mitsuyoshi-*san* to dedicate himself to pleasing the shogun. Mitsuyoshi-*san* pursued his own enjoyment, and the shogun began to complain that he was never available when he was wanted. Eventually his father cut off his allowance so he couldn't afford his habits.

"Mitsuyoshi-*san* began paying closer attention to the shogun because he didn't want to lose his chance at the succession," Wada said, "but we still went out together, to teahouses and brothels that often served him without payment because he was a Tokugawa samurai and the shogun's favorite. But there was one place he ran into trouble. It's a gambling den in Nihonbashi. The patrons are hoodlums and gangsters."

Sano experienced the internal stir that signaled the advent of an important clue. "Did he lose money to them?"

Grimness hardened Wada's features as he nodded. "He should never have gotten involved with them, but he loved the thrill of Edo's underside. He should never have put himself in their debt because they're dangerous. The owner of the place is a wild, tough *rōnin* who fears no one, not even the Tokugawa. One night while Mitsuyoshi-*san* and I were in town, he cornered us and demanded that Mitsuyoshi-*san* pay him and his friends their money. When Mitsuyoshi-*san* said he couldn't, the *rōnin* threatened to kill him unless he paid."

Here, at last, was a possible suspect other than the three already executed. Elation flared in Sano. "When was the threat made?"

"About two months ago." Wada pondered for a moment. "But even before Mitsuyoshi-*san* owed money, the *rōnin* hated him. They had some sort of feud."

"Did Mitsuyoshi-*san* pay what he owed?" Sano said as his excitement increased.

"Not to my knowledge." After another pause, Wada said, "Even though Treasury Minister Nitta was convicted of the murder and now you've been accused of it, I can't help wondering if the *rōnin* was involved in Mitsuyoshi-*san*'s death."

Nor could Sano. But there was still the matter of determining that the *rōnin* could have killed Mitsuyoshi.

"I didn't come forward earlier and tell you or the police about the *rōnin*," Wada said, "because I knew my master wouldn't want his son's reputation ruined. And later, when the treasury minister was convicted, I thought the killer had been caught and I needn't speak." He hung his head. "I'm sorry."

Sano couldn't be angry at the guard for withholding information because he understood the code of loyalty that bound them both. He also understood the agonizing guilt Wada suffered because he'd violated that code for the sake of the truth.

"I want to make up for whatever trouble I've caused, by telling you everything I know, including one last thing," Wada said earnestly. "The *rōnin* was in Yoshiwara that night. When I went with Mitsuyoshi-*san* to the *ageya* for his appointment with Lady Wisteria, I saw the *rōnin* in the crowd outside."

Sano inhaled the fresh, invigorating atmosphere of joyous possibility; his heart soared because he now had a new suspect and a whole new line of inquiry.

"Who is the *rōnin*, and where can I find him?" Sano said, wanting to fall on his knees and thank the gods for this new chance to prove he wasn't a murderer or traitor.

"I can take you to the gambling den now, if you like," Wada said, "but I don't know the *rōnin*'s proper name. Everyone calls him Lightning."

29

The bathhouse where Yuya worked was located near a canal that ran through a slum in the Nihonbashi merchant district. Reiko peered out the window of her palanquin at ramshackle buildings where children flocked and screamed on balconies and old people huddled in doorways. Crowds of drab women separated to let the palanquin and Reiko's mounted guards pass through a produce market. Bonfires of reeking garbage smoldered. The canal, a muddy stream that flowed sluggishly between stone embankments, teemed with houseboats. Beyond lay more ugly slums, blurred by smoke and sleety drizzle. Reiko smelled the powerful fishy stench of the canal and spied a roving gang of hoodlums carrying iron clubs. Stifling a shiver, she leaned out the window.

"Stop around the corner from the bathhouse," Reiko ordered her escorts.

They obeyed. The procession halted, and the bearers set down the palanquin. Reiko pulled the hood of her cloak over her head and stepped out into the drizzle, hesitant to venture into such hostile territory. But if she wanted information that might save Sano, she must take a risk. The dagger strapped to her arm under her sleeve gave her confidence.

"Follow me at a distance," she said to her guard captain. "Wait for me down the street from the bathhouse." She thought Yuya might be more willing to talk if not intimidated by soldiers. "While I go inside, count quickly to five hundred. If I'm not out by then, come in and get me."

The captain bowed and nodded. Reiko set off alone, past archways that led to mazes of dank alleys in which buildings constructed of weathered planks and peeling plaster resounded with harsh babble from the inhabitants. Rancid cooking odors mingled. None of the people Reiko passed appeared to notice her, but she felt their covert scrutiny.

She entered a gate into a street of houses with barred windows and recessed doorways. A tattered blue cloth banner above one bore a white character for hot water. Steam billowed from the roof and condensed on the tiles; moisture dripped from the eaves. Surly-looking men loitered outside the bathhouse. Reiko knocked on the door. Presently it opened, and a young woman appeared. She was barefoot, and wore a flowered robe that she held closed around her voluptuous body; her hair was piled untidily on her head.

"This bathhouse is for men only," she said with a curious look at Reiko.

"I don't want a bath. I'm looking for Yuya," said Reiko.

The woman's expression turned suspicious. "I'm Yuya." She had a round face with full cheeks, a pointed chin, and a pouting mouth painted scarlet. Her skin had the moist, starchy color and texture of stale tofu. Her eyes, hard beneath puffy lids, cast a wary glance at Reiko. "Who are you?"

"My name is Reiko."

"What do you want?"

"To talk to you," Reiko said.

Yuya's gaze moved over Reiko and turned hostile. "No," she said, and started to close the door.

"I'll pay you," Reiko said quickly. She reached into her

sleeve and drew out the paper packet she'd hidden there. She unwrapped the packet, revealing silver coins. Yuya stared at them with hungry yearning. She grabbed for the coins, but Reiko held them out of her grasp.

"After we talk," Reiko said.

The woman's red mouth twisted; she said grudgingly, "Come inside."

As she and Yuya entered the bathhouse, Reiko glanced at her guard standing by the neighborhood gate. Places like this harbored danger, and she was uneasy. Inside, a dim passage smelled of urine. A doorway framed a view of a tattooed hoodlum seated at a counter and a big sunken tub. Naked couples fondled in the steamy water. The men moaned and grimaced; the women were stoically quiet. Grunts and thumps emanating from partitioned rooms indicated the presence of more amorous couples. While Reiko tried to hide her shock, Yuya sneered at her.

"You've never been to a public bath before, have you?" she said, then nodded sagely. "Not one where the girls do more for the customers than wash their backs."

Reiko realized that the bathhouse was an illegal brothel, and Yuya a prostitute. Cringing in shame, she followed Yuya into a bedchamber. They sat, and Yuya filled a tobacco pipe and lit it with a hot coal from the brazier while Reiko avoided looking at the stained futon.

"Well?" Yuya said, tossing her head and puffing smoke.

Reiko cut straight to the point: "You knew Lady Wisteria, didn't you?"

"Oh, yes, I did." A distasteful smile curved Yuya's lips.

"When did you last see her?" Reiko said.

"Maybe three years ago? She came here, to this place."

That was long before Lord Mitsuyoshi's murder, but Reiko wanted any information she could get. "How did Wisteria happen to come here?"

"People said the man who freed her from Yoshiwara had given her money to live on, but she was a big spender. She wanted to live like she did when she was a courtesan. She rented a mansion, bought expensive furniture and kimonos, threw parties. The money disappeared in no time. Wisteria borrowed more and got deep in debt. Finally, she had to sell her things, move out of her house, and run away from the moneylenders who were hounding her to repay them."

This was quite a different scenario than the second pillow book described, thought Reiko, and Yuya had less reason to lie than did the person who'd written the book to slander Sano.

"Wisteria ended up at the bathhouse, like lots of women who fall on hard times." Yuya chuckled at Wisteria's misfortune. "When she came here, she acted like an empress, always talking down to the rest of us, expecting us to wait on her. She thought she was better than everyone else here."

"Because she'd been a *tayu*?" asked Reiko.

"Well, that was part of it," Yuya said, "but as far as I'm concerned, a whore is a whore, no matter what her price." She dumped ashes from her pipe into the brazier. "Wisteria was the mistress of the man who owns this place. They'd known each other since we were young girls. The master was her lover then, and he was still mad for her. She lived here, but she didn't have to serve the customers like the rest of his women do."

Resentment inflected Yuya's voice. "Our work put rice in her mouth. And whenever we did anything that offended Wisteria, she told the master, and he beat us."

The more Reiko learned about Wisteria, the less admirable the courtesan seemed. Had her bad nature led to her death? Yet the incidents Yuya described had occurred long ago, and might have no bearing on Lord Mitsuyoshi's murder.

"We girls were all delighted when Wisteria got sent back to the pleasure quarter," Yuya said with a vindictive smile.

"How did Wisteria end up back in Yoshiwara?" Reiko said, still eager to hear the rest of the story. Perhaps she could present Yuya to the shogun as a witness whose account of Wisteria's life would discredit the pillow book, and thereby clear Sano's name.

"The master introduced Wisteria to merchants he knew. She bedded them, and they gave her money. But Wisteria got greedy. One night, a wealthy wine dealer took her home with him, and after he fell asleep, she stole a cash box full of gold coins and sneaked out. The next day he discovered that she was gone and so was his gold. He reported her to the police." Yuya shrugged, leaving unspoken the end to this common tale of a female criminal sentenced to Yoshiwara.

"Was that the last you saw of Wisteria?" Reiko said. Yuya nodded, but thoughts slithered beneath the hard surface of her gaze. Reiko's heart beat faster. "You've seen her lately?"

"I didn't lay eyes on her, but she came here. I was in this room with a customer, when the night watchman let someone into the house." Yuya stirred uneasily. "It was the master and Wisteria. I recognized their voices."

"When was this?" Anticipation caught Reiko's breath.

"Three days ago," Yuya said.

Reiko experienced the heady soaring of her spirits that always accompanied successful detection. Wisteria had been here after disappearing from Yoshiwara! Reiko had picked up the first glimpse of the trail left by the courtesan.

"What is your master's name?" she said, eager to identify this man who might have been involved in Wisteria's escape, and the murder of Lord Mitsuyoshi.

Yuya started to speak; then she paused in belated caution. "Why do you want to know about him? I thought you were interested in Wisteria."

"They might be witnesses to a crime," Reiko said. "I must find out what they've seen."

"You mean you think he killed the shogun's heir." Yuya slowly laid down her tobacco pipe, as though freeing her hands for self-defense, but not wanting Reiko to notice her fear.

"Tell me everything you heard when they were here," Reiko urged.

"I didn't hear anything," Yuya said. "They went in the bathchamber. I couldn't make out what they said."

Reiko sensed a lie. "Did they talk about Lord Mitsuyoshi?"

"I don't know. I told you, I couldn't hear them. But

wait—I know who you are, I've heard about you. You're the *sōsakan-sama*'s wife." Yuya drew back from Reiko in appalled enlightenment. "You'll tell your husband what I said. He'll go after my master."

"Did they say who killed him?" Reiko persisted.

A breathy, nervous laugh escaped Yuya. She shook her head and stood, palms raised toward Reiko. "I don't want to get mixed up in this. You asked about Wisteria, and I told you. I've got nothing more to say."

"Please," Reiko said as desperation clutched her. She felt so close to discovering the truth about the crime and saving Sano, yet saw opportunity slipping away. Rising, she beseeched Yuya: "You must tell me. Where is your master now?"

"I don't know. He and Wisteria left the next morning."

"Where did they go?"

"I don't know!" Yuya backed toward the door.

Outside it, a gruff male voice called, "Yuya! Here's a customer for you."

Yuya started in fright; her puffy eyelids opened wide. "That's the manager. I have to get back to work," she told Reiko, and thrust out her hand. "Give me my money and leave."

"It's very important," Reiko pleaded with Yuya. "Lives are at stake."

She clutched Yuya by the arm. The prostitute shrieked and slapped at her, and they tussled as the manager shouted, "What's going on in there?" Men in adjacent rooms yelled curses. Afraid to start a brawl, Reiko let go of Yuya and handed over the money.

"I'll tell you this much," Yuya hissed, her eyes glittery with panic. "Lightning strikes during storms. Gangsters are dangerous when anybody crosses them. My master and Wisteria had a big fight when they were here. I heard her screaming. It sounded like he almost killed her. If he finds out I told you about him, he'll kill me!"

A thrill of excitation tingled in Reiko, for this dangerous, violent man posed an answer to Sano's problems. She said,

"Thank you for your help. If your master comes back, or you learn where he is, will you let me know? I'll pay you."

Yuya nodded too quickly, as though willing to agree to anything just to get rid of Reiko.

"Send me a message at Edo Castle," Reiko said, then hurried past the glaring tattooed attendant and out of the house.

She met her guard captain in the street, and he accompanied her back to the palanquin. Climbing in, she ordered her escorts to take her home. She must tell Sano what she'd discovered, so he could begin the search for the new murder suspect.

30

"What do you mean I can't come in?" Hirata demanded.

"The palace is off limits to the *sōsakan-sama* and everyone in his retinue," said the guard stationed at the door of the Edo Castle women's quarters. "The shogun has ordered you kept out."

Hirata stared in amazement and horror. That Sano had been barred from the palace meant the shogun thought him guilty of murder and treason, even though he'd received a chance to prove he was innocent. Tokugawa Tsunayoshi feared Sano as a threat to himself! This seemed the first stage of an inevitable downfall for Sano and everyone associated with him.

"I just stopped by to see Lady Midori," Hirata said. "Will you tell her to come out?"

The guard shut the door in Hirata's face. Hirata stood momentarily paralyzed by helpless outrage, then hurried around the building. The grounds lay vacant in the wet afternoon. Raindrops glittered on bare branches, stippled the pond, and pelted Hirata as he trudged through damp grass to the window of Midori's chamber. Taking shelter beneath the eaves, he rapped on the wooden bars that screened the window.

"Midori-*san!*" he called.

The shutters and paper pane inside the window opened. Midori appeared, her eyes huge and scared. "Hirata-*san!*" she exclaimed in a whisper.

"I'm sorry I frightened you," Hirata whispered, "but the guard won't let me in."

Midori pressed her face up against the window bars and spoke with breathless urgency: "The ladies say the *sōsakan-sama* killed Lord Mitsuyoshi so that Masahiro-*chan* can be shogun someday. They say he's a traitor, and so are you because you're his chief retainer. Tell me it's not true," she pleaded.

"Of course it's not," Hirata said, alarmed to learn how fast the news had spread around the castle. "Don't listen to the rumors. The *sōsakan-sama* has been falsely accused."

A sigh of relief gusted from Midori; her lips quivered in an eager smile. "That's what I've been telling everyone who criticizes him or you." Then her face crumpled. "But the palace officials told me I should stay away from you because you're in trouble, and I could get in trouble, too. They said that if you and the *sōsakan-sama* are condemned, I could be thrown out of the castle, or even put to death along with you." Midori's voice quavered with fear. "Things aren't that bad, are they?"

As Hirata searched for words to tell her gently and console her, his face must have revealed the awful truth. Midori whimpered, "Oh, no," and began to sob.

"I'm sorry," Hirata said. "I've brought you nothing but unhappiness." Although the idea of giving up Midori appalled him, he had to think of her welfare. He forced himself to say, "Maybe we'd better not see each other anymore. That would please our families. And you'll be safe."

"No!" Midori's protest was immediate and vehement. Her

streaming eyes filled with horror; she grasped the window bars.

She was making this so much harder that Hirata almost couldn't bear to continue. "I love you," he said brokenly. "I don't want to give you up. But I can't let you suffer because of me. We must say good-bye before my troubles destroy you."

He backed away from the window while Midori darted back and forth sideways, like a caged, frantic animal. "Don't leave me!" she cried. "If we can't marry, I'm doomed!" Her weeping rose to a hysterical pitch, and she hunched over, sobbing into her hands. "Oh no, oh no, oh no!"

The force of her reaction halted Hirata. She was even more upset than the occasion merited. "What is it?" he said.

Midori shook her head violently, still sobbing. Hirata stepped up to the window. "Tell me," he said, bewildered.

He leaned close, and after a moment Midori's answer emerged in a tiny squeak: "I'm with child." Then she dissolved into weeping again.

"Oh," Hirata said, his stomach jarred by shock. Now he understood Midori's panic. He rued the consequences of their forbidden pleasures.

"I couldn't tell you before," Midori whispered. "I was so ashamed. I was so afraid you'd be angry at me."

Hirata reached through the window bars. "I'm not angry," he said. "It's my fault. I should have controlled myself." As Midori pressed her wet, teary face against his hand, he ached for them both; yet she would suffer more than he from bearing their child out of wedlock. He feared for the child, whose prospects were dire.

"What are we going to do?" Midori wailed in desperation.

Although their circumstances had never been worse, Hirata felt an unexpected pang of hope. "We'll find a way," he said. "The child is proof that we're destined for each other."

"Are we?" Midori gazed longingly at him.

"Yes," Hirata said. "Our love is stronger than ever." It swelled his heart, renewed his confidence. The child gave him added reason to persevere. "We'll be married soon. I promise."

Doubt vied with hope in Midori's expression. "But how?"

"First I'll find evidence to clear the *sōsakan-sama*'s name," Hirata said. "Then everything else will turn out fine."

Midori nodded, calmed by his reassurances. Hirata wished he had more faith in them. Restoring his master to the shogun's good graces wouldn't automatically solve the other problems that stood in the way of his marriage to Midori.

"I have to do some more investigating now," he said. "I'll come back with good news as soon as I can."

As Hirata withdrew his hand from the window, Midori let go reluctantly, as though she feared she would never see him again.

Hirata arrived in Yoshiwara with two of Sano's detectives, when the evening's festivities were already in full sway. They interviewed the courtesans whom Lord Mitsuyoshi had tricked into believing he would marry them, but all three had been able to prove they'd been elsewhere the night Mitsuyoshi died at the Owariya. When Hirata and his companions left the brothel, the rain had ceased; wet roof tiles and streets reflected the lanterns in streaks of gold. Servants hauling trays of food from cookhouses to banquets rushed through the noisy crowds. Maids led clients to the brothels; a vendor sold rice crackers mixed with love poems. As Hirata neared the Owariya, a courtesan and her entourage promenaded up to the door. He experienced a peculiar illusion that he'd been transported backward in time, and the courtesan was Lady Wisteria, arriving for her appointment with Lord Mitsuyoshi.

The illusion grew stronger when Hirata entered the *ageya* and found a party in progress. The guests weren't the same men who'd been here when Mitsuyoshi died, and the *hokan* singing for them wasn't Fujio, but Hirata recognized the courtesans he'd interviewed the morning after the crime. A magic door to the past had opened, and his heart beat quicker with a premonition that he would discover new, important evidence tonight.

The proprietor circulated through the parlor, chatting with guests. Hirata walked over to the squat, gray-haired man.

"Greetings," the proprietor said, smiling uneasily. "How may I serve you?"

"I want to know if you or your staff have remembered anything more about the night of Lord Mitsuyoshi's death," Hirata said.

The man winced and looked around the room, obviously loath to spoil the festivities with talk of murder. "I already told you. I was busy with the guests. I didn't see or hear anything unusual. I wish I could help you, but I can't. I'm sorry."

Hirata and the detectives questioned the courtesans and servants. One after another said they didn't remember anything more. Hirata thought longingly of Midori, and their marriage seemed more impossible than ever. Then, as he pondered his next move, he felt someone watching him. He turned and saw, standing in a doorway leading to the rear of the house, a little girl dressed in a pine-leaf-patterned kimono. Their gazes met, and Hirata recognized Chidori, the *kamuro* who'd waited on Lady Wisteria. Fright blanched her face. She whirled and fled. Instinctively Hirata bolted after her.

She ran down a dim, cold hall and swerved to avoid a man rolling a wine barrel out of a storeroom. Hirata passed maids working in a kitchen as he called, "Chidori-*chan*! Stop!"

The hall ended at a closed door. Chidori tried to pull it open, but it stuck firm. She stood with her back pressed against the door and helplessly faced Hirata, her eyes and mouth round with terror.

"Don't be afraid." Hirata halted several paces from her and lifted his hands in a calming gesture. Loud music and laughter rang out from the party. "I won't hurt you."

Chidori must have gleaned reassurance from his manner, because her frozen stance relaxed.

"Why did you run?" Hirata said.

"I—I heard you asking questions," she whispered.

An internal stimulus alerted Hirata that here was a witness with information he needed. "Do you know something about Lord Mitsuyoshi's murder that you haven't told us?"

The *kamuro* looked away, biting her lips. "I didn't mean for anyone to get hurt!"

"I know you didn't," Hirata said, but he regarded her with consternation. Had *she* stabbed Lord Mitsuyoshi? Was this what she'd concealed, and the reason she'd run away just now? Her little teeth were stained with lip rouge, and tears slid down the white makeup on her thin cheeks. She was just a child.

"He told me that unless I did what he said, he would hurt me," Chidori wailed.

"Who are you talking about?" Hirata said, puzzled.

A word escaped Chidori in a rush of breath: "Lightning."

"Who is Lightning?" As he asked, Hirata's pulse raced. This was a name that hadn't yet arisen in connection with the murder. Chidori had implicated a potential new suspect who had so far evaded detection. Hirata crouched before the *kamuro*, placing his hands on her shoulders. The bones felt fragile as a bird's. "Tell me," he urged.

Chidori shook her head so hard that her limp hair flopped. "I can't. He made me promise not to tell. I'm afraid of him."

"Don't worry. I'll protect you," Hirata said.

She looked around to make sure nobody else was near, then mumbled, "He's Lady Wisteria's lover."

"You mean one of her clients?"

"No. He never had appointments. He never paid for her. The master didn't know about him and Wisteria. Nobody did, except me." Now Chidori spoke eagerly, as if relieved to confess. "They made me help them meet in secret."

Hirata rose upright as surprise struck him. "Is this man from Hokkaido?"

"I don't know where he's from."

Still, Hirata thought he'd at last picked up the trail of the secret lover described in the first pillow book, which must be the genuine one. Whether the man came from Hokkaido didn't matter—Wisteria could have altered details about him to disguise his identity.

"Tell me how you helped Lightning and Wisteria meet," Hirata said.

"I was supposed to watch for him," Chidori said. "He would come and stand in the street in front of the house, and whenever I saw him, I would tell Lady Wisteria. That night she would put sleeping potion in her client's drink. I would go outside every so often to check her window for the signal. After her client fell asleep, she wrapped a red cloth around the lantern in her room so the light would look red. When Lightning saw it, he would go to the back door of the *ageya*. I would make sure no one was around, then let him in."

And he'd made love to Wisteria while her clients slumbered, just as she'd written in the book, Hirata thought.

"I didn't want to do it," Chidori blurted. "Courtesans aren't supposed to entertain men for free. I shouldn't have helped Lady Wisteria break the rules. My master would beat me if he ever caught me disobeying. Once I told Lady Wisteria that I wasn't going to help her anymore because I didn't want to get hurt. The next time Lightning came—"

She shuddered, and her hands clutched the front of her kimono. "I pretended I didn't see him. I didn't open the door. In the morning, when I went to the market, he chased me into an alley. He said he was going to teach me a lesson." Chidori turned her face away from Hirata, opened her kimono, and whispered, "He did this."

An ugly red scar ran down the center of the girl's bony chest to her navel. Hirata winced in sympathy. "So you knew his threat was serious. Did you let Lightning in the *ageya* the night of the murder?"

Eyes downcast in misery, the *kamuro* closed her robe and nodded. The illusion of venturing back in time recaptured Hirata. He pictured Chidori opening the door, and the blurred figure of a man slipping into the house.

"What happened when you let him in?" Hirata said.

"He said that if I told anyone he'd been there, he would

kill me. Then he went upstairs. I went back to work."

Hirata listened to the *hokan* performing a lewd song, and the party guests roaring with laughter. In his mind he saw Wisteria embrace her lover while Mitsuyoshi lay unconscious. He felt the residue of passion and violence left by the murder.

"That's all I know," said Chidori, and Hirata knew she was telling the truth. A sob burst from her. "Are you going to arrest me?"

"No," Hirata assured her. "Lightning forced you to obey him. You're not responsible for the murder."

"But if I hadn't let him in, maybe Lord Mitsuyoshi would still be alive."

That was possible, but Hirata said, "His death wasn't your fault. Whoever killed him is to blame." The murderer could be Wisteria, Treasury Minister Nitta, Fujio, or some yet unidentified person, but Hirata would bet on Lightning. A man who would cut a little girl was brutal enough to have stabbed Lord Mitsuyoshi.

"Tell me everything you know about Lightning," said Hirata. "Does he have another name?"

Chidori puckered her brow in an effort to recall. "Not that I ever heard."

"What does he look like?"

"He's not very tall. But strong." The girl spread her arms to indicate muscular bulk. Under Hirata's questioning, she revealed that Lightning carried two swords, traveled on horseback, and wore his hair in a topknot, his crown unshaved. "And his eyes are funny—they move all the time."

This description wasn't much, but Hirata deduced that Wisteria's lover was a *rōnin*. "Can you think of anything else?" he asked Chidori.

"Lightning always comes to Yoshiwara with a bunch of friends. They look as mean as him."

A minor detail from his first day on the case took on new significance for Hirata. He realized how Lightning fit into what he already knew about the crime.

Chidori regarded Hirata anxiously. "What if Lightning

comes back? What if he finds out I told on him?"

"Don't worry. He won't be back," Hirata said, determined to apprehend the man before he could do more harm.

After thanking Chidori for her help, he gathered his companions. They left the *ageya* and hurried down Nakanochō. The night sparkled with light, sizzled with the smells of cooking, resounded with gay music from teahouses. Ever more attuned to the past, Hirata followed the route that Lord Mitsuyoshi's killer must have taken out of Yoshiwara. He could almost see ghostly footsteps on the road. When he and his party reached the gate, Hirata found the same guards he'd questioned during his first inspection of the crime scene.

"I want to talk about the night Lord Mitsuyoshi died," Hirata said. "Tell me again who left Yoshiwara after curfew."

"Treasury Minister Nitta," said the lean guard.

Hirata was more interested in the others he'd disregarded while Nitta had been the focus of his inquiries. "Who else?"

"The oil merchant Kinue," said the swarthy guard.

"And the Mori gangsters," added his companion.

A flare of elation lit within Hirata. "Was one of the Mori gang a man named Lightning?"

"I don't know," the lean guard said.

"They're thieves, brawlers, and killers," the swarthy guard said. "It's best not to know them."

"The one I mean is short and muscular, with eyes that are always moving," Hirata said.

The lean guard said, "That sounds like the leader." His companion nodded.

Hirata's elation flared higher because the guards had confirmed his theory that the gangsters were the friends Chidori had said always accompanied Lightning. Now that he'd linked them to Lady Wisteria and the murder, they represented a new chance to solve the case and exonerate Sano.

"Did they say anything to indicate where they were going?" Hirata asked. The Mori had lairs scattered all over Edo. When the guards shook their heads, he said, "Tell me exactly what you saw them do."

"They came up to the gate," said the swarthy guard.

"They were moving fast, shoving their way through the crowds," said the other.

"The leader had his arm around one of the others—a boy who looked drunk."

"He was pale and stumbling over his feet, and his eyes were closed. The leader held him up and whispered to him as they came near us. But I couldn't hear what he said."

"Then he ordered us to let the gang out. When we told him it was too late, he threw some coins at us and said, 'Now open the gate.' "

"So we did. And the gangsters hurried out."

"They got on their horses. The leader helped the drunk boy into the saddle and climbed up behind him. They all rode away."

Hirata felt a victorious swell of enlightenment as he fitted a crucial missing link into the sequence of events associated with Lord Mitsuyoshi's death. He grew certain that both his luck and the investigation had taken a positive turn.

"I just remembered something," the lean guard said. "When the Mori came into Yoshiwara early in the evening, I counted nine of them. But when they left, there were ten."

"The tenth person was Lady Wisteria," Hirata said, summarizing his discoveries for Sano and Reiko. "She was Lightning's drunken boy."

Sano nodded, accepting a cup of tea that Reiko handed him. Temple bells tolled midnight as they sat together in his office; coals hissed in the brazier. "It all fits," he said. "The red cloth and the hairs by the dressing table in Wisteria's room at the *ageya*, the fact that we couldn't find any witnesses who saw her leave the quarter. She signaled Lightning to come. She cut her hair and put on male clothing to disguise herself as a boy. She walked right out of Yoshiwara with the Mori gang, and no one recognized her."

Satisfaction and fresh hope banished the despair Sano had felt last night, even though the cloud of suspicion still hovered over him. Today's discoveries were a ray of light that penetrated the nightmare he'd been living since the shogun accused him of murder and treason.

"What I learned this morning confirms that Wisteria escaped with the gangster," Reiko said, her face aglow with excitement. She described her visit to Yuya the bathhouse prostitute. "Yuya wouldn't tell me the name of the man who owns the bathhouse and brought Wisteria there, but she said, 'Lightning strikes during storms,' and mentioned gangsters. I didn't know what she meant then, but now I understand that Yuya was giving me a hint. The man must be the same lover who sneaked into Wisteria's room the night of the murder and took her away."

"Now we know Lightning was involved in Lord Mitsuyoshi's death, and one place where he and Wisteria hid." As Sano beheld Reiko and Hirata, gratitude for their perseverance and loyalty overwhelmed him. "Thank you," he said in a voice gruff with emotion.

He bowed to them, and they bowed back. After an awkward silence, Sano said, "Here's additional evidence that Lightning is the killer," and told Reiko and Hirata about his conversation with Mitsuyoshi's retainer. "According to Wada, Lightning threatened to kill Mitsuyoshi if he didn't pay his gambling debts, and they were enemies. Lightning had a motive for murder, as well as the opportunity."

"He could have killed Wisteria, too," Reiko said. "According to Yuya, they got into a terrible fight at the bathhouse. Maybe she took him to Fujio's cottage to hide, they argued again, and he beat her to death."

"The Mori are vicious beasts," Hirata said. "When I was a police officer, I saw teahouse girls they attacked, and shopkeepers murdered for resisting extortion. A woman falls in love with one of them at her own peril."

The mounting evidence that Wisteria was dead eroded Sano's hope of finding her alive. He said, "We must find Lightning. Wada has already taken me to his gambling den. He wasn't there. The place was shut down, and I spent the day trying to pick up his trail, without luck. But I can send men to watch the bathhouse in case he shows up there again. Right now he represents our best chance of solving the case."

And Sano's life might depend on capturing Lightning. "That he's been identified as a member of the Mori gang is fortunate for us," Sano said, "because we know where to start looking for him tomorrow."

31

Edo's central fish market awoke to life before dawn. When Sano arrived early the next morning, fishermen had already moored their boats at the bank of the canal that ran beneath the Nihonbashi Bridge and begun unloading their catch. Dealers, servants from daimyo estates, and restaurant owners yelled bids. Inside the cavernous building that sheltered the market, porters hauled barrels of live, squirming fish to the stalls. Vendors arranged their wares and greeted hordes of customers. Sano trod paths already slick with slime and scales. Although women busily mopped and scrubbed, a powerful miasma of rotting fish tainted the air.

Sano approached a vendor who worked for him as a spy. "Good morning, Kaoru-*san*."

"Good morning, *Sōsakan-sama*." The short, jovial man was cutting up a huge tuna, his knife moving so fast that the pink flesh appeared to slice itself. "What can I do for you today?"

"I'm looking for a man named Lightning," Sano said. "He's one of the Mori gang."

When the vendor heard the name, his knife slipped. A line of blood welled on his finger and stained the fish, but he kept slicing. "I'm sorry, I don't know any Lightning."

"Have you seen him here recently?" Sano persisted.

"No, master." Fear of the Mori apparently outweighed the vendor's need for the salary Sano paid him. "I'm sorry."

Down the aisle, Hirata was arguing with a tea-seller. "I know that everyone here pays extortion money to the Mori," Hirata said. "Don't tell me you've never heard of them!"

Sano watched in frustration as his detectives questioned other people who shook their heads and looked terrified. The market was a center of the Mori's criminal activity, and the gangsters usually infested the place like vermin, but today they'd made themselves scarce.

When Sano joined his men outside the building, Hirata said, "It's as if the Mori smelled us coming and disappeared. And they've silenced everyone with threats."

"I know another place to try," Sano said, hiding the desperation that burgeoned within him.

Only a day had passed since the shogun accused him of murder and treason, but time was speeding away. The longer Sano took to solve the case, the more chance he gave Police Commissioner Hoshina to ruin his reputation and fabricate evidence against him. And Sano had serious misgivings about focusing his investigation on Lightning. If, in spite of all the clues that indicated Lightning's guilt, someone else had killed Lord Mitsuyoshi, then Sano was wasting precious time now.

Yet he still considered Lightning his best suspect. He led his men into a labyrinth of alleys surrounding the market. Here, dilapidated buildings contained businesses that served the fish trade. Laborers crowded noodle and sushi restaurants. Shops selling nets, pails, and fishing tackle overflowed into the streets. Sano stopped outside a teahouse. He signaled Hirata and two detectives to go around to the back. Then

Sano and the other three detectives drew their swords and ducked under the blue entrance curtain.

A trio of men inside the teahouse sprang to their feet. All were shabbily dressed ruffians. The lone samurai among them bolted out a back door, while his comrades drew daggers and advanced on Sano and his men. A maid shrieked, dropped a tray of sake cups, and cowered in the corner.

"Drop your weapons, and no one will get hurt," Sano shouted.

The ruffians scowled, ready to fight, when suddenly Sano's detectives burst in through the back door. They grabbed the ruffians from behind and wrested away their daggers. Hirata followed, holding captive the samurai who'd run away. The samurai, already relieved of his weapons, struggled in Hirata's armlock.

"Well, see who we've got," Sano said. Though none of the men fit Lightning's description, the raid had paid off. "It's Captain Noguchi, former weapons master at Edo Castle. I've been looking for you."

Captain Noguchi was a rawboned man whose feral, unblinking eyes regarded Sano with hostility. "Tell your lackey to let go of me," he said.

"What's the matter, are you afraid to face your punishment for stealing weapons from the Tokugawa armory and giving them to the Black Lotus sect?" Sano said. "Did you think you could hide forever?"

Although most of the surviving Black Lotus members had been captured, some remained at large. Sano headed an ongoing effort to clean up this human scum.

"I was only following the true path of destiny." Fanaticism shone on Noguchi's face. "I'm an innocent victim of persecution by you, the evil destroyer who would wipe out all my people and condemn the world to eternal suffering!"

"Spare us the excuses." Sano noticed a mark on the skin below Noguchi's collarbone. He yanked open the man's kimono, revealing scar tissue that didn't quite obscure a tattooed Black Lotus symbol, and under it, another tattoo of a dragon.

"So you've joined the Mori," Sano said, recognizing the gang's crest. "Trust you to find another set of hoodlum friends after the Black Lotus sect disbanded. Where is Lightning?"

"I don't know." Noguchi viciously spat the words.

Sano shot out a hand, gripped the man's throat, and squeezed hard. "Has he been here?"

Noguchi squealed in pain and fright. His eyes rolled, and he jerked away from Sano, but Hirata held him in place. Although Sano disliked using violence against witnesses, he had little compunction about coercing this man who'd stolen their lord's weapons for the massacre at the Black Lotus Temple. Furthermore, Noguchi was his connection to the Mori, and Sano had neither time nor patience to waste.

"Tell me!" he demanded, digging his fingers into Noguchi's windpipe.

His face purple, Noguchi struggled in Hirata's grip and gasped for air.

"Have you seen Lightning?" Sano hated abusing his power; yet he could gladly choke the breath out of Noguchi.

Panic shone in Noguchi's gaze. His voice emerged in a croak: "All right, I'll tell you. Just please let me go!"

Sano and Hirata released him. He staggered, wheezing and coughing. "Lightning was here yesterday," he rasped. "He took all the money from the cash box. But no one around here has seen him since. I swear that's the truth!"

The letter came to Reiko soon after Sano went out to search for Lightning. She opened the bamboo scroll case that a castle messenger had delivered to the estate. The message inside was scrawled on cheap paper. Reiko read:

> I've found Wisteria. If you want to see her, go to
> the noodle stand around the corner from the bath-
> house, tell someone there to fetch me, and I'll take
> you to where she is. Don't wait too long, or she'll

be gone. And bring the money you promised me.
    Yuya

Reiko was thrilled at this sign that Yuya wanted to help her and that Wisteria was alive after all, but suspicion tempered her hope of obtaining news that would benefit Sano. Yesterday, Yuya had seemed so averse to cooperating further that Reiko wondered at the motive behind the message. What had changed Yuya's mind? Reiko paced swiftly around her chamber, holding the letter, as she debated what to do.

She feared walking into a trap, despite the lack of apparent reason for Yuya to hurt her. Reiko recognized this as a situation where instinct must yield to need, and decided to follow Yuya's instructions rather than miss any opportunity to gain valuable facts. She had doubts about meeting Wisteria, and she hesitated to go on her own, but she had no time to consult Sano; she didn't even know where he was, and she couldn't dally while a chance to save him slipped away.

Reiko called a servant to bring two of Sano's best detectives to her. Fortunately, they hadn't yet joined the hunt for Lightning. When Detectives Marume and Fukida came to her, she showed them the message, then said, "Please organize a party of troops and take me to Yuya."

As the detectives and soldiers escorted her palanquin out of the courtyard, Reiko glimpsed O-hana watching her somberly from the door. Her procession traveled fast through town, and soon Reiko alighted in a neighborhood of slum dwellings that tilted crookedly. A wind with a keen, icy edge blew debris down the street, rattled the buildings, and rippled puddles of sewage. While her entourage waited outside, Reiko entered the noodle stand, a narrow cubbyhole beside a grocer's shop. There, a slatternly woman stirred boiling pots on a hearth. Children squabbled in a room behind the kitchen.

"I want to see Yuya," said Reiko.

The woman nodded, then sent one of the children to the bathhouse. Reiko waited nervously. Soon Yuya slipped into the room. She wore a drab, threadbare cloak and an air of furtive excitement.

"Where is Lady Wisteria?" Reiko said at once.

Yuya responded with pouting lips and a martyred expression. "Buy me something to eat first," she said, kneeling on the floor. "I missed my meal because of you."

Impatience nettled Reiko, but she ordered a bowl of noodles in miso broth. They sat together while Yuya ate with maddening slowness.

"Last night, I woke up when someone tapped on my window and called my name," Yuya said. "I looked outside and saw Wisteria in the alley. She was crying. I said, 'What are you doing here?' She said she needed my help and she didn't have anyone else to turn to. Her face was all bruised and bloody."

Grimacing, Yuya sucked up noodles. Reiko stifled the urge to hurry her. "Wisteria told me that she'd had a big fight with Lightning—the man who owns the bathhouse," Yuya said. "He hurt her so bad, she was afraid for her life. She waited until he went out, then she ran away. She'd stolen some of his money, but she didn't know where to go. She said she'd pay me if I would find her a place to stay. She begged so hard that I took her to an inn where she would be safe. She's still there."

"Can we go to her now?" Reiko said anxiously.

Yuya gave Reiko a sour look and held up her half-full bowl. "Wisteria says she's tired of hiding. She wants to turn herself in and tell what she knows about the murder."

"What does she know?" Reiko's heart lurched; she leaned toward Yuya.

The prostitute smirked at her eagerness. "Wisteria saw Lightning kill Lord Mitsuyoshi. Afterward, Lightning took her out of Yoshiwara. She didn't want to go with him, but he told her that unless she did, he would kill her."

Reiko felt a rush of exultation, stanched by skepticism. While investigations often turned upon a stroke of luck, this news that would exonerate Sano seemed too good to be true.

"Wisteria hasn't gone to the police because she's afraid

she'll get in trouble," Yuya continued, apparently unaware of Reiko's doubt. "Whatever she says, people might think she's lying to protect herself. With Lightning gone, everyone would just as soon blame her."

The story made sense, and fabricating it would require more imagination than Reiko thought Yuya had; yet misgivings still restrained Reiko's need to believe.

"I told Wisteria that you came to see me," Yuya said. "I convinced her that if you talked with her and believed her story, you would convince your husband that she's innocent. She agreed to surrender to you if the *sōsakan-sama* will help her."

Setting down her empty bowl, Yuya raised her eyebrows at Reiko. When Reiko hesitated, Yuya added, "Lightning will be looking for Wisteria, and if he gets to her before you do, he'll kill her."

Reiko decided she had less to lose than to gain by taking Yuya at her word. If the story was true, Reiko could deliver Wisteria to Sano today. The courtesan would be safe from Lightning and the authorities, and Sano absolved from charges of treason and murder.

"All right," Reiko said.

Yuya gave her a smug, conspiratorial smile and held out a hand. "Pay me first."

"My escorts are coming with us," Reiko said, taking a packet of money out of her sleeve.

The prostitute shrugged. "That's fine with me," she said, tucking the money inside her robes.

They left the noodle shop and climbed into the palanquin. "Go straight ahead four blocks, then turn right," Yuya said.

Reiko conveyed these directions, and subsequent ones, to her escorts. As the procession wound through the streets, anticipation and anxiety coiled tight inside her. Curiosity about meeting a woman who'd been on intimate terms with Sano vied with dread of a hoax. Yuya lounged against the cushions, yet the sharpness of her gaze belied her body's relaxed posture. Reiko alternated watching her companion and watching the scenery. Dingy neighborhoods that all looked alike made it hard for her to measure their progress.

"How much farther is it?" Reiko asked.

"We're almost there," Yuya said.

After almost an hour had passed, Reiko said with growing suspicion, "Do you really know where Wisteria is?"

"Of course I do." Yuya bristled indignantly. "You're a high-class lady, and I'm a lowly whore, but if you want Wisteria, you better be nice to me."

The palanquin turned onto the main east–west road that crossed Edo. A mounted daimyo, escorted by many troops and attendants, filled the broad avenue. Pedestrians fell to their knees and bowed, while Reiko's procession slowed behind the daimyo's rear guardsmen. An inaudible sigh issued from Yuya; her body relaxed slightly. This tiny lapse of self-control struck ominous certainty into Reiko's heart.

Yuya was taking her on an aimless ride. If they ever reached an inn, they would find no Wisteria, and Yuya would say the courtesan had run away. And Yuya was glad of a delay because she wanted the fraud to last as long as possible.

"Your story about Wisteria was a lie," Reiko said, adamant in her conviction. "This is a trick."

"No, it's not." Yuya regarded her with incredulity. "Why would I trick you?"

Suddenly Reiko's amorphous fears crystallized. Incidents that had previously seemed to have neither relationship nor significance now fell into a chilling pattern. Yuya's sudden readiness to cooperate; an uninvited friendship at an opportune time; strange behavior and a generous gesture with a hidden motive—all centered around Reiko's memory of O-hana standing inside the estate while Reiko left it. Logic drew connections across gaps where facts were absent, forming a picture of a madwoman's brilliant treachery.

"You want to lure me away from home," Reiko said, stunned. "How much did she pay you?"

"Who? I don't know what you're talking about."

But guilt quickened in Yuya's heavy-lidded eyes, and she sat up straight. Now Reiko understood that the danger she'd sensed was not here, nor to her own person; she had never been the direct target of malice. The awful truth horrified her.

Grabbing Yuya's wrist, Reiko demanded, "What is she doing while you occupy me?"

"Let go!" Yuya cried. She and Reiko struggled together, rocking the palanquin. "You're talking nonsense. Why are you attacking me? Have you gone mad?"

"Tell me," Reiko shouted, wild with panic.

Detective Marume rode up beside the palanquin. Peering through the window, he said, "What's going on in there? Lady Reiko, are you all right?"

Reiko's instincts blared a warning that no amount of reason could quell. She didn't know exactly what would happen, but she could guess the consequences. The street had cleared, and her procession speeded up, carrying her farther away from home, where she needed to be.

"Stop!" she called to Marume.

The procession halted. Yuya twisted out of Reiko's grasp, pushed open the palanquin's door, and jumped out. As she ran away down the avenue, the soldiers started chasing her.

"Never mind her," Reiko shouted. "Take me home!"

The procession laboriously turned in the direction of Edo Castle. Reiko sat desperate and frantic, her heart pounding with the fear that she was making a mistake, yet transfixed by the certainty that she was right about everything, despite the lack of any proof.

She hoped she hadn't thrown away her chance to solve the murder case and save Sano. She prayed she would arrive home in time to avert disaster.

32

"Lightning and the Mori gang are on the run," Sano said to Hirata as they rode across the Ryōgoku Bridge, which connected Edo to the suburbs east of the Sumida River.

"That would explain why they're not in any of their usual places," Hirata said.

Below the bridge's high wooden arch, ferries and barges tossed on choppy gray waves. Behind Sano and Hirata, on the eastern bank, lay a popular entertainment district known as Honjo Mukō—"Other Side"—Ryōgoku. Sano and Hirata had spent the early afternoon searching teahouses, shops, and gambling dens frequented by the Mori, but found no trace of the gangsters.

"We can't just keep roaming around, hoping to run into Lightning," said Sano. "There's not enough time, and too much area to cover."

He gazed ahead toward Edo. Windblown clouds obscured the hills and misted the entire sky. Around the castle spread the houses where a million people lived. Somewhere in the teeming city were the detectives Sano had ordered to hunt for Lightning. Sano thought of his men slowly, laboriously combing the streets. Despair filled him.

"Lightning may have already left town," Sano said.

"The detectives we sent out on the highways will watch for him at the checkpoints," Hirata said.

"He won't use the highways. Men like him travel by secret routes," Sano said. "To catch him outside Edo, we'd need an army spread across the country, searching every forest, mountain, and village. I still have allies who might lend troops for a nationwide manhunt. That may be our only option, now that we've run out of contacts and places to look."

Hirata said, "The police must have information on the Mori. There was a time when I could have counted on their help. But with Hoshina controlling them, I can't get a single tip anymore." He gave a bitter laugh. "My clan served on the force for generations, and I'm no longer welcome at headquarters."

"We'll try there anyway," Sano decided. "We've got nothing to lose."

"Many of the *doshin* have blood ties with my clan," Hirata said. "Maybe I can convince them that their obligation to help me find Lightning outweighs any loyalty that Hoshina has extorted from them."

Sano and Hirata rode to police headquarters, which was located in a walled compound in the southern corner of the Hibiya administrative district. There they dismounted in a lane outside a back gate, then entered the compound, walking rapidly along paths between the kitchens and servants' quarters, hoping to attract as little notice as possible. They arrived at the *doshin* barracks, a cluster of two-story, half-timbered structures and nearby stables, set around a courtyard.

A peremptory voice behind them called, *"Sōsakan-sama."*

Halting, Sano turned and saw Police Commissioner Hoshina striding toward him, flanked by *Yoriki* Hayashi and Yamaga. Dismay struck Sano as Hirata muttered a curse.

Hoshina wore a sardonic smile; Yamaga and Hayashi glowered. The two sides faced off in the courtyard. Sano felt his heartbeat accelerate with the surge of energy that precedes a battle.

"Have you come to turn yourself in?" Hoshina asked him.

Sano gave Hoshina a venomous look as he realized that he could forget the idea of seeking tips from the police. The officers might have been willing to help him on the sly, but not in front of their superiors, and Hoshina would stick to him like a burr until he departed the compound.

Hastily revising his strategy, Sano said, "I've come to obtain your assistance, Hoshina-*san*."

"My assistance?" Blank confusion erased Hoshina's smirk. "Why should I help you?"

"To serve our mutual interests," Sano said. Yamaga and Hayashi looked puzzled, but Sano saw comprehension gleam in Hirata's eyes.

"We have no mutual interests," Hoshina said in a tone replete with scorn. "Have you gone mad?"

"No," Sano said, "I have identified the probable murderer of Lord Mitsuyoshi."

The police commissioner's expression turned disdainful. "Spare me your lies. You're so desperate to save yourself that you're trying to frame another innocent person."

Into the hostility that thickened the atmosphere, Sano enunciated a single clear, quiet word: "Lightning."

Hoshina started; his features involuntarily tensed.

"Then you know who Lightning is," Sano confirmed.

"Of course. He's one of the Mori gang," Hoshina said, recovering his poise. "So you've chosen Lightning as your scapegoat? How convenient. But we both know he had nothing to do with the murder."

Yet Sano could discern the thoughts racing behind Hoshina's calm façade. The police commissioner was frantically trying to determine whether his investigation had missed an important suspect, or Sano was bluffing.

"We both overlooked Lightning because we were concentrating on the more obvious suspects," Sano said. "But Lightning was Lady Wisteria's lover, and he was in Yoshiwara that night."

"So were a lot of other men," Hoshina said dismissively. "That means nothing."

Sano sensed Hoshina weighing what he knew of Lightning against the facts of the murder case. Hoshina couldn't hide his discomfiture at recognizing how well a brutal, reckless gangster fit the crime.

"We have witnesses who've implicated Lightning in the murder," Sano continued. "Lady Wisteria's *kamuro* has admitted that Lightning forced her to let him into the *ageya* where Wisteria was entertaining Mitsuyoshi. Afterward, he bribed the guards to let him out the gate. They observed that he'd come into Yoshiwara with eight men, but left with nine. The extra man was Wisteria, in disguise."

"You forced those people to say what you wanted," Hoshina said. "Your story is pure, ridiculous fabrication, and I'm too busy to listen any longer."

"Busy creating more fraudulent evidence against me, I suppose," Sano mocked him. "Do you really think you should gamble that you'll win this game?"

"Don't make me laugh," Hoshina said.

But Sano could tell that the news about Lightning had shaken Hoshina's nerve. Yamaga and Hayashi stirred uneasily; Hirata hid a smile.

"The odds have changed," Sano told Hoshina. "Now you're as likely to be ruined by your scheme as I. That's the basis for the mutual interests that I mentioned, and the reason you'd better listen to what I'm going to say next."

Hoshina's stance and gaze shifted; his face acquired a look of intense concentration as he tried to decide whether to comply with Sano. He reminded Sano of a man jumping from stone to stone across a deep, turbulent river. Then he addressed his two *yoriki*: "Leave us."

They grudgingly departed. Hoshina fixed a narrow-eyed stare on Sano.

"If you convince the shogun that I'm a murderer and traitor, I'll be executed," Sano said. "But if I capture Lightning first, and he proves to be the killer, then you'll be exposed as a fraud who interfered with my attempt to avenge Lord Mitsuyoshi's death. Everyone will turn against you as fast as you turned them against me. You'll die instead.

"Now think about what you would gain from destroying me. A moment of public acclaim? The shogun's favor, which changes with the wind?" Sano infused his voice with contempt. "Are those prizes worth risking your life?"

Hoshina took an involuntary step sideways, then froze, as if he'd reached midstream and run out of stones. Sano and Hirata waited in suspense because their future depended on crushing Hoshina. Dead silence absorbed the police compound's usual noises; the world outside the courtyard ceased to exist.

"Better you should postpone our rivalry and cooperate with me," Sano said softly.

The police commissioner stared, furious; then capitulation slackened his muscles. He looked beaten and bruised, yet antipathy radiated from him like heat from doused coals. "What do you want?" he said in a dull voice.

Sano experienced a tremendous sense of relief. He'd known that Hoshina tended to yield when he felt threatened enough; but Sano hadn't been sure that he could overpower Hoshina.

"I want to make a deal," Sano said. "I'll give you credit for helping solve the murder case if you'll help me capture Lightning. He's abandoned all the usual Mori gang places in the fish market and Honjo Mukō Ryōgoku. Tell me where else he would go."

"You expect me to hand over the murderer to you, in exchange for empty words of praise?" Regarding Sano with bitter resentment, Hoshina shook his head. "I can capture Lightning myself, and reap all the glory."

"Do as I ask, and you'll live to fight another day," Sano said. "Refuse, and I'll make sure the shogun understands how you tried to climb to power over the corpses of his heir and his *sōsakan-sama*."

"So you expect me to be content with mere survival?

Well, that's not enough." Brazen greed emboldened Hoshina; his fists opened and closed. "I want more, or there's no deal, and we can both take our chances."

"What are you asking?" Sano said, ready to make a concession.

"A favor."

"What favor?"

A crafty smile flashed on Hoshina's face. "I'll decide what I want, when I want it. And you'd better deliver."

Hirata widened his eyes and rolled them at Sano, who realized how high a price a tip from Hoshina would cost him. He hated to obligate himself in advance to something he probably wouldn't want to do; yet he had little choice, with his own immediate survival at stake.

"Agreed," Sano said.

Hoshina responded with a look that promised retribution while acknowledging Sano's triumph over him. "The Mori gang rents a warehouse by the river. I've had spies watching the place because I suspect that the gang uses it to store and deal stolen goods. Lightning might have gone there."

Inside her chamber, Lady Yanagisawa knelt before Kikuko and fastened a padded silk cloak around the little girl. "There," she said. "You're all ready to go."

Her spirit was a cauldron of tumultuous emotion. This was the day she would achieve all she'd ever desired. The critical hours ahead represented a bridge between her present life of suffering and a future blessed with happiness. Lady Yanagisawa experienced a dizzy, whirling sensation, as if the winds of change buffeted her body. Strange lights and shadows flickered across her vision, like the sun's rays piercing storm clouds.

"You come, too, Mama?" Kikuko said.

"No, dearest," Lady Yanagisawa said, because she must appear innocent of what happened at the scene where her plans would culminate.

"Why not?"

"I can't," Lady Yanagisawa said. "Someday I'll explain."

Someday soon, Kikuko would be able to understand and appreciate what her mother had done for her. Now Lady Yanagisawa said, "Rumi-*san* will take you," and gestured toward the elderly maid who waited in the doorway. She placed her hands on Kikuko's shoulders and gazed into her daughter's face. "Do you remember all that I told you?"

"Remember," Kikuko said, nodding solemnly.

"Do you know what you're supposed to do?"

Kikuko nodded again. Lady Yanagisawa had labored hard to instruct the girl; they'd play-acted everything together until Kikuko performed perfectly. But she could only hope that Kikuko would follow her directions when the time came.

"Go, then," Lady Yanagisawa said. She gave Kikuko a fierce hug as the winds of destiny howled louder and stronger. Through the storm clouds whirling in Lady Yanagisawa's mind shone a vision of her husband. He smiled upon her with the tenderness she craved; he reached out his hand, beckoning her to cross the bridge she'd built to join her to him.

Lady Yanagisawa released Kikuko and rose. "Be a good girl."

Kikuko trotted off with the maid. Lady Yanagisawa stood alone. Having placed her fate in her daughter's hands, all she could do was wait.

Along the Sumida River rose a long line of warehouses, high buildings with whitewashed plaster walls. Signs bore the owners' names; the Tokugawa crest marked the *bakufu*'s rice repositories. Alleys between the buildings led to the river, where docks extended into the choppy, turbid water. On the inland side, porters and oxcarts carried goods along a boulevard that paralleled the river, and up streets through neighborhoods that clung to the gradually ascending terrain.

Sano, Hirata, and their fifty troops rode down a street bordered by shops, toward the river. They halted their mounts some distance above the boulevard.

"There's the warehouse that Hoshina mentioned," Sano said.

"The one with no activity," Hirata observed.

Its wide plank door was closed; wooden shutters covered the windows on both stories. Sano saw workers pass in and out of the other buildings, but the warehouse that Hoshina had identified as belonging to the Mori gang seemed abandoned.

"Let's hope that Lightning is hiding inside," Sano said.

Anticipation grew in him as he led his troops across the boulevard and they all dismounted outside the warehouse. He heard men shouting nearby, the thump of loads against the floors of adjacent buildings, and hammering at a distant construction site; but the Mori warehouse was silent. Sano divided the fifty detectives between himself and Hirata. The two groups filed down the alleys on each side of the building. At its rear they found another closed door, and more shuttered windows overlooking a yard that sloped toward a deserted dock. Sano assigned ten detectives to stand guard behind the building, then led his other men around to the front door.

Sano knocked loudly on the weathered planks, and waited. Nothing stirred inside the building; yet he sensed a human presence, like a warm, animate smell, beyond the door.

"Open up," he called, knocking again.

Still no response. Sano tried the door, but it was fastened securely inside. He gestured to three of his strongest detectives. "Break it down."

While Sano, Hirata, and the others stood back, the three men heaved their shoulders against the door. The crash shuddered the planks. Repeated blows strained the hinges; wood splintered with small, then large cracks. Suddenly, the air hissed behind Sano. Recognizing the sound, he ducked in alarm. He heard a *thunk*, looked down, and saw an arrow stuck in the ground near his feet.

"Watch out!" he said. "They're shooting at us."

Glancing up in the direction from which the arrow had

come, he saw that the warehouse's three second-floor windows had opened. Out of every one leaned a samurai, each armed with a bow. They fired volleys at Sano and his troops.

"Retreat! Fire back!" Sano shouted to his detectives.

They scattered, regrouping across the boulevard. The archers among them shot at the samurai in the warehouse windows, who returned fire. Pedestrians screamed in fright. An arrow struck the leg of a porter; dropping his load, he crawled away. Workers from nearby warehouses hurried to see the commotion.

"Go inside!" Sano yelled, waving at them.

More arrows flew; people took cover. In an instant, the area was deserted, except for Sano, his troops, and their opponents. He felt an arrow ricochet off his armor tunic, saw a detective take an arrow in the neck and fall, spurting blood. Yet even as the battle horrified him, he experienced a thrill of elation because he'd found the Mori gang.

"We're going in after Lightning," Sano told Hirata.

Crouching, they and a squadron of detectives zigzagged across the boulevard, swords in hand, while arrows whistled over their heads. One of the Mori gang shrieked, toppled from a window, and landed with a thud, killed by an arrow through his stomach. Men popped up through skylights and hurled rocks down on Sano and his men.

Sano flung up his free arm to shield himself, and a stone struck pain into his elbow. Looking up, he saw a Mori gangster take an arrow in the chest, skid down the roof, and plummet to the ground. A detective near Sano went down under a hail of rocks. As Sano, Hirata, and the others neared the door, a loud male voice called, "Stop right there!"

Halting, Sano looked up and saw a man framed in the window above the door. He was broad and muscular, with a face whose angles and hard planes appeared carved from stone. Coarse hair had tumbled out of his topknot, over brows slanted in a scowl. His eyes darted in speedy, unnatural flashes.

Recognition struck Sano. "Hold your fire," he called to his men. The torrent of arrows ceased. Exhilaration overwhelmed him, for here was the man he believed had killed Lord Mitsuyoshi and Wisteria, and represented his salvation.

"Lightning," he said.

"*Sōsakan-sama*," the gangster said in a harsh, mocking voice. "You've found me."

"Surrender," Sano ordered. His archers trained their bows on Lightning. "Come out."

Lightning sneered. He pulled a small human figure against him. The person had the shaved crown and topknot of a samurai, and wore a drab indigo robe; yet her delicate face belied the masculine trappings. Sano gazed dumbstruck into round, lovely eyes he'd once admired, that were now glazed with terror.

It was Lady Wisteria.

"Here's somebody you've been looking for," Lightning said to Sano. "Either you let me go, or I'll kill her."

33

Sano stared up at Lightning and Wisteria in shock as thoughts raced through his mind.

Wisteria was alive after all. She still wore the disguise in which she'd escaped from Yoshiwara with the Mori gang.

He'd located his murder suspect, but the presence of Wisteria complicated Lightning's arrest.

While Sano and his men stood immobilized, Lightning grinned malevolently. Wisteria uttered a pleading cry: "Sano-san."

Her husky voice awakened memories and sympathy in Sano. Her obvious fear of her companion stimulated his need to protect a woman in trouble. Quick action was needed to save Wisteria's life and Sano's witness to the murder of Lord Mitsuyoshi.

"Take aim," Sano ordered his troops. On either side of him, archers raised bows; arrows pointed toward Lightning. "Let Wisteria come out," he told the gangster.

Lightning's gaze shifted rapidly. He pulled Wisteria in front of him. Her eyes rolled in panic. "Tell your men to drop their bows," Lightning said.

"Do it," Sano told his men, because they couldn't shoot Lightning without the risk of hitting Wisteria.

The archers obeyed. Lightning drew his dagger and held the blade at Wisteria's throat. As she squealed and writhed, he shouted at Sano, "Move back, or she's dead!"

Every part of Sano rebelled against conceding any ground, but he stepped backward. His troops and Hirata followed suit.

"Farther. Farther," Lightning barked. When twenty paces separated them from the warehouse, he yelled, "Stop!"

Sano and his men halted. "Killing Wisteria won't do you any good," Sano told Lightning. "You won't get away."

"Oh, yes, I will." Lightning gave a reckless laugh, then turned and spoke to someone. Activity stirred beyond the other second-floor windows. Into each one stepped a gangster holding a flaming metal lantern.

"This warehouse is full of lamp oil, hay, and other things that burn," Lightning said. "Either you help me get out of town safely, or I'll set the place on fire—with me and Wisteria inside."

Disbelief stunned Sano. He heard his men murmur in surprise, and a stifled exclamation from Hirata.

"What? You don't want that to happen?" Lightning mocked them. "All right, then: I'll tell you exactly what to do. First, send your troops away."

Hirata's appalled gaze moved from the gangster to Sano. "We're not setting him free, are we?"

"We can't," Sano said, horrified by his dilemma. "If Lightning killed Lord Mitsuyoshi, then he and Wisteria are my only hope of proving beyond doubt that I'm innocent. But I can't refuse his demands and let him make good on his threats."

"Would he really burn himself to death?" Hirata said skeptically.

"He's got samurai blood. And a samurai would rather die than surrender."

Wisteria cried, "Please give him what he wants! He means everything he says!"

The wind blew with powerful gusts, and dread pierced Sano. Fire was the greatest hazard of the city. If Lightning did set the warehouse on fire, flying sparks would spread the blaze across Edo. Hundreds of buildings might burn; hundreds of people might die. And Sano would be responsible for a catastrophe that made the problem of clearing his name, saving his life, and regaining the shogun's trust seem minor.

Turning to his troops, he said in a low voice, "Get the men from behind the warehouse, and go order the citizens in the area to prepare for a fire. They should fill buckets with water and wet down their roofs and walls. Then hide someplace close by, keep watch on the warehouse, and await orders."

The men mounted their horses and hurried off to comply, leaving Sano and Hirata alone. Lightning said, "Very good, *Sōsakan-sama*," in a tone that revealed how much he enjoyed his authority. "Now your retainer will fetch me a thousand *koban*."

"I hate paying off a criminal," Hirata said.

"So do I," Sano said grimly.

Lightning continued, "After you pay me, my gang and I will leave town with Wisteria. You won't follow us, because if you do, I'll kill her before you can touch me."

"Bring the money," Sano told Hirata, "so we can bargain for Wisteria's life and the safety of the city, while we figure out how to capture Lightning." Sano called to the gangster: "You've got a deal."

"Not so fast. You come wait inside with me."

Aghast, Hirata said, "He wants to take you hostage!"

Sano was certain now that Lightning had murdered Lord Mitsuyoshi, and he had no intention of placing himself in the hands of a killer. "I'll wait out here, or you don't get the money," he called to Lightning.

Lightning's expression turned furious; he muttered a command to the other gangsters. They held wads of hay to their lanterns. As the hay ignited, they flung it outside.

Panic leapt in Sano as the wind tossed the hot, flaming

straws. "He's not bluffing. We've no choice but to play along with him." Fiery wisps caught and burned on the roofs of other warehouses.

Hirata regarded Sano with horror as they stamped on smoking hay that landed on the ground near them. "You're not thinking of going in there?"

"Have you changed your mind yet?" Lightning shouted.

The gangsters continued to throw burning hay that wafted toward the city. Faced with a choice between putting himself or countless other people in danger, Sano raised his hands in a gesture of assent. "Stop. I'll come inside."

At an order from Lightning, the gangsters ceased their activity. Sano started toward the warehouse door. Lightning commanded, "Wait. Throw down your weapons."

Sano hesitated, loath to enter unarmed, then reluctantly unfastened his swords and laid them on the ground. Hirata blocked his path to the warehouse. "I can't let you," Hirata said, his face stricken by alarm.

"If I go in, maybe I can convince Lightning to surrender. Go get the money," Sano said in a tone meant to reassure as much as compel Hirata's obedience.

As Hirata unwillingly departed, Lightning and his men closed the windows. Sano beheld the warehouse's blank façade and deserted surroundings. He felt naked and vulnerable without his weapons, and angry at being manipulated into this position. But there had been too many occasions in the past when he'd blamed himself for deaths that he thought he should have prevented. Wisteria would not be another such casualty. And the warehouse harbored the solution to the murder case.

Sano walked toward impending doom.

The guards stationed outside Sano's mansion opened the gate for Kikuko and her maid Rumi.

Kikuko skipped gaily across the courtyard toward the big house. She was happy because she liked this place. The little boy and his mother lived here. The boy was so much fun, like a baby doll who could walk and talk. And his mother was so pretty. Kikuko liked them. She was so glad to come again, she hummed a happy song.

A lady opened the door and came out on the veranda. It was the little boy's nursemaid. Kikuko didn't like her much. There was something mean about her face, even when she smiled, and she wasn't smiling now. She looked upset and sad. Mama was often sad, and that made Kikuko sad, too. But after today, they would be happy all the time. Mama had promised.

The nursemaid brought Kikuko and Rumi into the big house, and they took off their shoes and outdoor clothes. She said to Rumi, "You can wait in the parlor."

Then she took Kikuko by the hand and led her through the house. Kikuko went willingly, but she was puzzled because the house was so quiet and empty today. Where had everybody gone? Kikuko didn't ask, because the nursemaid frightened her a little, even though Mama had said she was their friend. Kikuko was glad when they went into the boy's room.

He was sitting all alone, playing with his toy animals. Kikuko was disappointed that his pretty mother wasn't there, but happy to see him.

"Hello, hello," she cried, bouncing up and down and waving.

The little boy smiled. "Kiku," he said.

They laughed together, and the nursemaid stood watching them for a moment. Then she went away. Kikuko remembered the game that Mama had told her to play, and she was happy she'd remembered. She wouldn't want to disappoint Mama and make her sad. She began to run around the room, flapping the long sleeves of her pink kimono.

"I'm a butterfly," she said to the little boy. "Catch me!"

He chased her, giggling with excitement. Kikuko swooped out of his way. Then she ran to the door that led outside. She pushed open the door and ran onto the veranda.

"Catch me!" she called.

The boy toddled after her. She hopped down the steps, and he crawled down them. The garden was a wonderful place to play, even though the day was cold and cloudy. Kikuko fluttered around trees, bushes, and rocks. The boy ran after her, yelping. She liked that there were no adults to tell them to be quiet. That made the game more fun.

A glance around the garden showed Kikuko the pond, an irregular oval of water amid leafless cherry trees. She dashed to the pond and stood at the edge. The water was murky, and dead brown lily plants floated on top. Kikuko wrinkled her nose in disgust. But she had to obey Mama.

The little boy ran toward Kikuko, arms spread, delighted because he thought he was going to catch her. Kikuko hesitated, then waded into the water. Oh, it was cold! She shivered as the first step chilled her up to her ankles. The next step plunged her knee-deep.

Turning to the little boy, Kikuko called, "Follow me!"

As Sano crossed the threshold of the warehouse, two gangsters seized his arms, yanking him into a vast, dim space that smelled of hay, manure, and smoke. Sano glimpsed crates, bundles, and ceramic urns stacked against three walls; along the other, horses occupied stalls. His captors propelled him across the stone floor, toward a plank staircase that led to an open loft built along the upper story. Lightning stood at the top of the stairs. Wisteria huddled near him. Six more gangsters crouched around the loft. They all watched Sano climb the stairs. Burning metal lanterns hung on the walls of the loft, casting strange shadows. Heat shimmered the air above charcoal braziers. Smoke drifted upward.

When Sano mounted the top step, his escorts gave him a hard shove. He stumbled onto the loft on hands and knees. He gazed up in indignation at Lightning, who towered over him.

"Behold, the proud Tokugawa soldier," Lightning said with a cruel grin. His eyes flashed in the lantern light. Rocking on his feet, clenching and unclenching his hands, he appeared consumed by nervous energy.

Sano cautiously began to rise, but Lightning kicked his

chin, knocking him down. "How brave are you without your weapons and your troops and your shogun to protect you?" Lightning jeered, then ordered, "Show me some respect!"

Goaded into outrage, Sano swallowed his urge to retaliate against this violent, impulsive man and make a bad situation worse. He knelt, bowed, and said, "I'm at your service."

Lightning smirked, apparently placated, though wariness glinted in his eyes. Sano turned to Wisteria. Her face was bruised, her naked scalp pitiful, her beauty turned haggard.

"Are you all right?" Sano asked.

Wisteria nodded, eyeing him with a strange expression of hope and dismay. While gangsters guarded Sano, Lightning prowled around the loft. "I have to get out of here," he said through gritted teeth. "When will your man bring the money?"

"As soon as he can," Sano said, disturbed by Lightning's impatience and wondering what were his chances of effecting a peaceful surrender, if the gangster was already so jittery.

"I'm sorry things turned out like this," Wisteria murmured. Creeping close to Sano, she whispered urgently, "Please don't let him take me."

"He won't," Sano promised with feigned confidence.

Lightning stalked toward them. "What are you doing?" he demanded of Wisteria. "Trying to seduce him into rescuing you?" He raised a hand to strike her.

Wisteria shrank against Sano. His arm circled her protectively. "Nobody's trying anything," he said to Lightning. "Just calm down."

But the gangster turned livid with fury, shouting, "Don't touch her! You had her once, but she's mine now. Take your filthy hands off her, or I'll cut them off!"

His rabid jealousy appalled Sano, as did the fact that Lightning knew about his past affair with Wisteria. He hastily moved away from her, aware that the odds of negotiating a surrender were even poorer than he'd thought because Lightning viewed him as a rival.

Anxious to gain control of the situation, he said, "We're all going to be here together for a while, so why don't you just sit down, and we'll talk——"

"Shut up! Don't tell me what to do!"

Now Lightning drew his sword. Sano rose and automatically reached for his own weapon, but his hand clutched empty air. Panic jolted him. Wisteria gasped in fright. Exclamations of protest came from the other gangsters.

"Stay out of this," Lightning ordered them, and advanced on Sano.

Backing away, Sano tried to reason with Lightning: "Hurt me, and you won't get your money."

But Lightning kept coming until Sano was trapped in a corner, his back pressed against the wall and the tip of Lightning's blade at his throat. Lightning jittered to a standstill; his breathing, and the twitching of his muscles, sped up beyond normal human velocity. Sano saw reckless temper in the gangster's wildly flickering gaze, and blood lust in his snarling mouth.

"Let's see whether you die like a samurai or the coward I think you are!" Lightning said.

"Kill me if you will," Sano said, gulping down terror born of the knowledge that Lightning was capable of murdering him. "But you'll never get away with it. My men will hunt you down to avenge my death."

A long beat passed. The only sounds Sano heard were his own thudding heart and his tormentor's breaths. Suspense paralyzed everyone except Lightning. Then the gangster threw back his head and laughed.

"Scared you, didn't I?" He sheathed his sword and stepped away from Sano. "I'm too smart to kill a hostage that I still need. After I get the money, I'm taking you with me to ensure me a safe trip out of Edo. But as soon as I'm far away, and you've served your purpose—then I'll kill you."

Sano's transient relief turned to dread of his death in some remote place. But maybe Lightning couldn't wait till they got that far; maybe Sano was destined to die today. He thought of Reiko and Masahiro, and his determination to prevail braced his spirit. He would live to see his family again. He would deliver Lord Mitsuyoshi's killer to justice and prove his own innocence.

If he could first prevent Lightning from exploding and killing him and Wisteria and everyone else nearby.

Lady Yanagisawa stood on the veranda, her hands resting on the railing and face lifted in the wind, scanning the sky above her home. She waited with fevered impatience for tidings that the blood sacrifice had realigned the cosmic forces.

She knew exactly how it would be. The wind would turn to glad song. The tragedy of Masahiro's death would settle upon Reiko in a dense black shroud of grief, while bliss elevated Lady Yanagisawa. Her husband would adore her. Kikuko would be freed from the curse of imbecility. The gray heavens would part, the sun shine, green leaves unfurl, and the air turn balmy as in springtime on the morn of Lady Yanagisawa's new life.

Yet as moments passed and the cold, dreary afternoon remained unchanged, misgivings infected her anticipation. She remembered the hospitality Reiko had shown her. She thought of plump, sweet Masahiro. As she imagined water closing over him and his terror as it filled his lungs, a spasm convulsed her stomach. Memories of motherhood rushed upon her. She recalled holding the infant Kikuko, admiring her tiny hands and feet; she heard her daughter's piping voice, smelled her soft, fragrant skin, savored the adoration in her eyes. If Kikuko should die, Lady Yanagisawa would die of a grief too immense to endure.

Could she inflict such a grief on a woman who'd been kind to her?

Was her scheme a path to joy, or an evil that would condemn her to be reborn into endless cycles of woe?

She glimpsed the infinite divide between what she'd done and what she wanted to happen. There was no logical reason that her actions should effect miracles, she suddenly realized. A battle between belief and indecision churned her blood. The winds inside and outside her gusted harder; swaying off balance, Lady Yanagisawa clutched the railing. Her vision of the future wavered; the sky dimmed as twilight ap-

proached. Instead of ethereal song, she heard male voices.
She saw, across the garden, a group of men walking along
a covered corridor between buildings. Her husband was in
the lead, his officials trailing. Lady Yanagisawa's heart leapt.
Perhaps the deed was done. Perhaps now her husband would
come to her.

The chamberlain turned his head in her direction. Poised
on the brink of glee, Lady Yanagisawa waited. His gaze registered her presence . . . then flitted away.

Disappointment crushed Lady Yanagisawa. The magni-
tude of her husband's indifference toward her shriveled her
spirit. The winds suddenly ceased. A vacuum enveloped her,
and her perception altered with nightmarish effect.

She saw herself as a tiny, trivial person isolated in a tiny
world apart from the big, important one that her husband
ruled. As she watched him enter a building and disappear
from view, she thought of herself manipulating events like a
child playing with toys. Could anything she did bend her
husband, or fate, to her wishes?

Reality encroached upon desire in the terrible stillness of
clear thought. What if her wishes had deluded her? What
would come of her scheme?

She would have destroyed an innocent child and made her
daughter an accomplice in murder.

Even if Reiko believed that Masahiro's death was an accident, she would never forgive Kikuko, or Lady Yanagisawa.

Lady Yanagisawa's life would go on much the same as
always, but without friendship to comfort her. She would be
more alone than ever.

Horror like a flock of black, predatory birds assailed Lady
Yanagisawa. A moan of anguish rose from the depths of her
spirit. Her doubts about the wisdom of her actions swelled,
yet so did the force of her desires. Should she risk the chance
that she'd done wrong, for her dream of fulfillment? Or must
she stop the events she'd set in motion?

Was it already too late to change her mind?

34

The atmosphere in the warehouse was noxious with foreboding. Sano had heard temple bells toll the passage of two hours since Lightning had taken him hostage. Now he knelt in the loft, near Wisteria, who sat bowed under the weight of fear, eyes downcast. Lightning paced around and around the loft, peering out the windows every few moments, muttering angrily. The eight gangsters crouched apart from each other, their faces stony. Whenever Sano had tried to speak, Lightning had ordered him to be quiet. But Sano believed that the only hope of his survival, and Wisteria's, lay in developing a rapport with Lightning.

Soon the gangster's endless prowling brought him toward Sano. Urgency compelled Sano to take a risk. "Where will we go when we leave here?" he said.

Ire flashed in Lightning's mobile gaze, but he paused near Sano and said, "I don't know."

"Do we have supplies for a journey?" Sano said.

"Quit pestering me with chatter."

"I'm sorry," Sano said, "but we must talk." Lightning gripped the hilt of his sword; Wisteria watched them with dread. Sano hurried on: "Holding me hostage won't guarantee your freedom. The police know you killed Lord Mitsuyoshi. The commissioner is my enemy. He'd gladly attack us and let me die to catch you. That puts us on the same side."

Lightning snorted in contempt, rejecting Sano's suggestion that they were comrades. Sano eyed the gangsters, wondering if they were more worried about saving their own skins than loyal to Lightning. "We should work together," Sano said to Lightning, but he glanced at the other men and pitched his voice so they would hear. "You help me, and I'll help you."

The gangsters resisted eye contact, their expressions inscrutable. Sano couldn't tell whether they'd caught his meaning that if they helped him capture Lightning, he would spare them punishment for their leader's crimes.

"No place will be safe for us. We'll be pursued wherever we go," Sano said, hoping to impress upon the gangsters that if they stayed with Lightning, their futures were bleak. "All of us will die—unless we're smart enough to take the opportunity to escape when we can."

"If you think you can scare me into turning myself in, forget it," Lightning retorted in annoyance. "I'd rather die in battle than surrender." The gangsters ignored the hint to desert. Sano's hopes plunged. Lightning said to his men, "I want a drink. Go get me some sake."

Three men descended the stairs, and Sano heard them rummaging through the warehouse's goods. Only one man returned, bearing a sake jar. Lightning didn't seem to notice; he just took the jar and drank. But Sano was jubilant to think that the other two men had fled and his plan was working.

"Surrender is your best bet," he told Lightning.

"Are you crazy?" The gangster wiped his mouth on his sleeve and stared at Sano. "The shogun will execute me for stabbing his precious heir."

Out the corner of his eye, Sano saw two more men amble downstairs. Lightning opened a window, looked outside, and said, "I wish your man would hurry up and bring the money!"

"We may be on the run for months," Sano said. "How will you be able to stand hiding much longer? Captivity can be worse than death."

"I'm not giving up." Lightning hurled away the empty jar; it shattered on the warehouse floor below. Wisteria flinched. "I'll keep my head on my neck as long as possible, and if the army finds me, I'll kill as many of them as I can before I die."

He turned to his four remaining comrades. "Go make sure nobody's trying to sneak in."

The men went, leaving Sano, Lightning, and Wisteria alone. Sano waited in suspense. The men didn't return. Lightning began to pace again. While he was at the other end of the loft with his back turned, Sano caught Wisteria's eye and signaled her to run down the stairs, before Lightning came near them again or guessed what was happening. But Wisteria frowned at him in bafflement: She didn't realize the gangsters had gone. Suddenly, from the lower story, came the clatter of horses' hooves. Dismay struck Sano as he comprehended that the gangsters had waited to escape until they were all downstairs, then fled together, noisily, on their mounts.

Lightning froze. "Hey, what's going on?" He rushed to the edge of the loft and gawked at the empty warehouse. Sano heard the horses galloping away. "Those cowards have deserted me!"

He turned, and Sano watched spasms of panic ripple his features. "My chances of surviving are almost none because I'm all alone!" he shouted, and stalked over to Wisteria. "This is all your fault!"

Like many bullies, he derived his strength from his confederates, and shifted responsibility for his troubles, Sano observed. Wisteria stood and faced Lightning. "It isn't my fault," she said, boldly defiant now that he was weakened.

"If you hadn't killed Lord Mitsuyoshi, we would be safe now."

The gangster jerked backward with surprise that she dared stand up to him. Heaving as though ready to explode from outrage, he said, "Quit blaming everybody else for problems you cause. If you hadn't cooked up your crazy scheme, none of this would have happened."

"If you'd done as I asked, everything would have worked out fine," Wisteria retorted. "But no—you wouldn't listen. You had to stab him. And now we're paying, instead of just them!"

The conversation perplexed Sano. There was obviously more to the murder case than he'd thought. "What are you talking about?" he said.

"Go ahead. Tell him." Lightning's gaze raked Wisteria.

She eased away from the gangster and addressed Sano in a small, meek voice: "When I was young, Lightning and I fell in love. Later, I found out he was bad and tried to leave him, but he threatened to kill me if I broke off our affair. When I went to Yoshiwara, he forced me to sneak him into my room in the *ageya*. That night he came and found Lord Mitsuyoshi there. They were enemies because Lightning hated any man I bedded, and Lord Mitsuyoshi had refused to pay Lightning the money he owed. Lightning was so jealous of Mitsuyoshi, he stabbed him to death. Then he kidnapped me so I couldn't tell anyone what I'd seen."

This was the scenario that Sano had envisioned; yet the interchange between Wisteria and Lightning, and Lightning's incredulous expression, contradicted her statement. With an utterance of fury, Lightning grabbed Wisteria by the shoulders and flung her against the wall. "Liar! That's not how it was!"

He smacked her face. She screamed, her body twisting and arms flying up to protect herself. Sano considered rushing the gangster and seizing his weapons, but Lightning's reactions were so quick, and his mood so combative, that Sano was likely to end up dead if he tried to disarm Lightning. Instead Sano said, "If she's lying, then tell me what really happened."

Teeth gnashing, face livid, Lightning wavered between the impulse to violence and the need to air his side of the story. He said, "She wanted me to help her get out of Yoshiwara and get revenge."

"Revenge on whom?" Sano was more mystified than ever.

"Fujio. Her *yarite*, Momoko. Treasury Minister Nitta."

"Don't listen to him," Wisteria pleaded, her eyes big with consternation as she hugged the wall. "He's insane."

"She stole Momoko's hairpin," Lightning said. "Then she waited until she had Lord Mitsuyoshi alone, and Fujio and Nitta were in the *ageya*. That night, after the *kamuro* let me in, Wisteria said the time was right, and we should go through with her plan. I would kill Mitsuyoshi. She would cut her hair and dress in the men's clothes she'd hidden in the room, then walk out of Yoshiwara with me. Later, Momoko would be blamed for murdering Mitsuyoshi. She had other plans for Fujio and Nitta."

The murder had been Wisteria's idea? Astounded, Sano looked at her.

"You were only supposed to wound him," she berated Lightning in a ragged voice. "He wasn't supposed to die!"

Her gaze flew to Sano, and her jaw dropped because she'd thoughtlessly admitted her responsibility. Shock robbed Sano of speech. Lightning chuckled in cruel glee. "She knew Fujio and Nitta would be suspected of having something to do with the murder or her disappearance or both," the gangster said. "Nitta was stupid enough to tell her he'd stolen from the treasury. She told Fujio, so that when he was questioned by the police, he would tell on Nitta, and Nitta would be put to death. Then I would kill a woman and put the body in Fujio's house."

"Who was she?" Sano said, as he began to fit the new revelations with what he'd already known about the crime.

"Just a whore from a bathhouse," Lightning said.

Sano noticed scratches on the gangster's wrists, where the

victim had clawed them. "And Wisteria sent me the anonymous tip so I would find the body?"

Lightning nodded. "Fujio was supposed to be blamed for
murdering Wisteria. Everyone was supposed to think she was
dead and stop looking for her."

"You should have put animal blood on my clothes and
left them in the house, the way I told you," Wisteria railed
at Lightning. "But you can't resist a chance to kill." Flustered
and defensive, she turned to Sano. "No one was supposed to
get hurt except Momoko, Fujio, and Nitta. They deserved it.
Momoko made my life hell when I was a young courtesan.
Fujio and Nitta broke their promises to marry me. I had to
pay them all back."

Sano was astonished to learn that Wisteria was such a
vengeful schemer. Her beauty and charm had disguised her
true nature. He'd correctly guessed that Lightning had killed
Lord Mitsuyoshi, while never suspecting that Wisteria was
behind the crime. Now he recalled the clues that had hinted
at the truth.

"The treasury minister confessed at his trial that you
wanted him to marry you but he wouldn't," Sano said. "You
ruined your mother's clothes because she sold you to Yoshiwara. Now Momoko, Fujio, and Nitta are dead because
they hurt you." Magistrate Aoki had unwittingly aided Wisteria's scheme. "And you might have escaped the consequences, except that you chose an accomplice you couldn't
control." Her selfish depravity horrified Sano.

"Those weren't the only people she meant to hurt," Lightning said. "Do you want to know who her last target was?"

"Be quiet!" Wisteria shrilled. "You've done enough
wrong!"

Lightning jabbed a finger at Sano and grinned. "It was
you."

"Me?" Flabbergasted, Sano stared at Wisteria.

"She wrote in her pillow book that you'd plotted to mur-
der the shogun's heir so your son could rule Japan someday,"
Lightning said. "Then she sent the book to the chamberlain.
You should have seen how glad she was when we heard the

news that you'd been accused of killing Lord Mitsuyoshi."

Shock reverberated through Sano. The book he'd deemed a forgery was genuine. Police Commissioner Hoshina was guilty of nothing except using the book to his advantage. Wisteria herself had mixed lies about Sano with authentic details of their affair, then delivered her slander to Hoshina. Enlightenment removed Sano's last illusions about Wisteria. Horrified fascination propelled him a step closer toward the wicked stranger who'd been his lover.

"Why?" he said, his voice hushed and his brow creased with his effort to understand Wisteria.

Her lips trembled in a smile that begged for mercy; she looked small and harmless. But Sano likened her to a woman in a No drama, played by an actor wearing a mask with moveable parts that shift, turning her beautiful face into an ugly one and revealing her as a demon. Wisteria's mask had shifted.

"It was a mistake. Please let me explain," she said, breathlessly eager. "Four years ago, you asked me questions about a murder. I was punished because men in high places didn't want you investigating the case or anyone to help you. I was demoted to *hashi*—the bottom rank of courtesans. My private room and nice kimonos were taken away from me. I had to live in a crowded attic infested with lice, eat leftovers from other people's plates, and wear cheap clothes. I lost my rich clients. I had to serve the poorest, crudest men—three or four a night. I suffered because of you."

Sano acknowledged his culpability, yet marveled at the lengths she'd gone to retaliate.

Memory and hatred darkened Wisteria's eyes. "Then I learned that you'd risen in the world and meant to free me. I thought you would take me to Edo Castle to live with you. But you just sent someone to pay off the brothel and give me money." Her voice turned jagged with ire. "And later, you visited me and took your pleasure from me, as if it didn't matter that you'd left me to struggle on my own."

Now Sano understood why Wisteria had acted cold toward him during those visits. She'd expected more of him, and he'd disappointed her.

"She got in trouble and went back to Yoshiwara." Lightning paced around Wisteria and Sano, clearly enjoying the drama he'd provoked. "She thought you owed it to her to rescue her again. But you didn't, and she wanted to make you pay."

A spark of anger within Sano ignited as he recalled what Yuya had told Reiko. "You squandered the money I gave you," he reminded Wisteria. "You ran up debts and became a thief. I compensated you for suffering on my account. What you did afterward was your fault, not mine."

Anger blazed into outrage. Fists clenched, Sano advanced on Wisteria. "You framed me for murder and treason because you couldn't handle your freedom. You almost destroyed my whole family instead of taking responsibility for your own mistakes!" His offense against Wisteria didn't justify her attack on him. The last of his sympathy toward her vanished. "To think I risked my life to rescue you!"

"I know now that I did wrong. I'm sorry I hurt you," Wisteria said in a wheedling tone. She gave him a coy smile that faltered, exposing her terror of his wrath. "Please forgive me."

Dropping to her knees, she clutched Sano's hands against her bosom. Her attempt to propitiate him repelled Sano. He yanked his hands out of hers, just as Lightning seized her by the hair.

"You think you can blame me for everything and save your own hide," Lightning shouted. "Well, you won't get away with it. This is all your fault, and now you'll pay!"

He smote her face. He threw her to the floor and kicked her. Wisteria curled up, sobbing.

"Help!" she screamed to Sano. "He'll kill me!"

Sano was tempted to walk out and leave Wisteria to Lightning. As he thought of how she would have condemned his wife, son, and all his retainers to execution just to punish him for sins she'd magnified out of proportion, her agony gladdened him. Yet his honor deplored his own thirst for vengeance. He couldn't permit another murder, and Wisteria was still a witness he needed alive. Tokugawa law would mete out justice to her.

Now Lightning drew his sword and raised it high over Wisteria, who shrieked in terror. "Stop!" Sano ordered. He lunged, and seized the gangster's arm. Lightning wrenched free; he slashed at Sano. As Sano dodged, Wisteria crawled away toward the stairs. Lightning charged at her, sword poised to kill. Sano dashed after Lightning, when suddenly, a shout came from outside the warehouse.

"Lightning! *Sōsakan-sama!*" Hirata's voice called. "I've brought the money."

Reiko didn't wait for her palanquin to carry her to her door. As soon as it entered the official quarter, she leapt out of the vehicle, ran up the street, and burst through her gate. Heart thudding, she raced into the courtyard. She experienced cold, nauseating fear that what she sought to prevent had already come to pass. A wail rose in her throat as she dashed into the mansion.

"Masahiro-*chan!*" she called, hurrying down the corridor.

Her voice echoed through emptiness. Fright constricted her lungs. Skidding around a corner, she almost fell through a doorway. She saw, inside the room, all five housemaids and three of Masahiro's nurses asleep on the floor. Their eyes were closed; air hissed softly through their open mouths. Empty wine cups littered a table. Reiko stared with alarm as her suspicions found anchor in reality. Lady Yanagisawa must have drugged the servants so she would have the house to herself, and no witnesses to what she did. Reiko ran into the nursery.

Toys lay scattered around, but Masahiro was nowhere in view. The exterior door was open, the room bitterly cold. Stricken by terror, Reiko hastened outside to the garden.

"Masahiro-*chan!*" she called again.

The wind whipped her as she frantically searched the deserted lawn and wilted flowerbeds for her son. Then she heard childish laughter—and splashing noises. Reiko's heart lurched. She sped around the cherry trees to the pond.

Kikuko stood waist-deep in the water. She was pushing something under the surface, holding it down with both hands. Water splashed, showering her with droplets. Giggling, she pushed harder. Reiko saw little feet kicking and arms flailing. Horror stabbed her. She inhaled a deep, wheezing gasp, then screamed: "No!"

Panic launched her forward to rescue Masahiro. Suddenly a figure darted out through the pine trees on the pond's opposite bank. It was Lady Yanagisawa. Agony contorted her face almost beyond recognition. Her gray robes streamed behind her as she ran awkwardly to the pond.

"Stop, Kikuko-*chan*!" she cried.

The little girl looked up, saw her mother, and wrinkled her brow in confusion. Masahiro's struggles weakened. Reiko and Lady Yanagisawa plunged into the pond. The cold water chilled Reiko's legs and soaked her garments; mud sucked at her feet. Lady Yanagisawa seized Kikuko by the arm and hauled her away from Masahiro. Mother and daughter lost their balance and fell with a huge splash as Reiko reached Masahiro.

He lay face-down and motionless on the bottom of the pond, his pale clothes visible through the murky water. His outspread arms and legs floated limply.

"Oh, no, oh, no," Reiko moaned.

She lifted her son. Carrying his heavy, dripping weight, she staggered up on the bank. Lady Yanagisawa followed, towing Kikuko. The wet, bedraggled pair collapsed onto dry land together and watched Reiko lay Masahiro down on his back.

"Masahiro-*chan*," she cried.

His eyes were closed, his lips slack, his skin pale. Not a sound nor movement did he make. In desperation, Reiko shook Masahiro, then pushed on his stomach. A flood of water gushed from his mouth. He coughed and wriggled. His eyes blinked open and gazed up at Reiko. He started to bawl.

Reiko exclaimed in joyous relief. She gathered up Masahiro and wrapped her cloak around his cold, shivering body. "It's all right," she soothed. Belated tears streamed down her cheeks. She looked over her son's head, at the woman whose daughter had almost killed him.

Lady Yanagisawa clung to Kikuko. "I'm so sorry," she said earnestly. "I brought Kikuko to play with Masahiro. Please believe that I never imagined what would happen. Kikuko didn't know any better."

The woman's excuses couldn't deny what Reiko saw in her eyes: Lady Yanagisawa had wanted Masahiro to die. His near-drowning was no accident. She'd gotten the maids out of the way and sent Kikuko to murder him. That she seemed to have changed her mind at the last moment didn't absolve her.

"Can you ever forgive us?" Lady Yanagisawa's tone was anxious, pleading.

And all Reiko's distrust and suspicion of Lady Yanagisawa had been justified. Her instincts had proved true. Though Reiko had only begun to guess why the woman wanted to hurt Masahiro, she knew with profound certainty that Lady Yanagisawa was her foe.

"Get out," Reiko said in a voice that shook with outrage.

The sound of Hirata's voice outside froze Lightning with his sword poised to kill Wisteria. Sano halted his rush to stop the gangster. Wisteria hunched on her elbows and knees, arms shielding her head. She cautiously looked up. Sano held his breath while silence pervaded the warehouse.

"Lightning!" Hirata called again. "*Sōsakan-sama!*"

Sano watched the anger dissipate from Lightning and satisfaction dawn on him as he recollected that his primary goal was escape, and understood that the means of escape had arrived. Lightning lowered his weapon, seized Wisteria by her collar, and yanked her upright. He backed away from Sano, toward the front of the loft, dragging Wisteria.

"You come, too," he ordered Sano, then warned, "Try anything, and she's dead."

As Sano followed, his mind worked frantically to think how he might use this circumstance to capture Lightning.

"Open the window," Lightning commanded him. Sano obeyed. Fading daylight brightened the warehouse; icy wind blasted inward. Still gripping Wisteria and his sword, Lightning leaned out the window. "Hey!" he shouted.

Hirata shouted back: "Before I give you the money, I want to see the *sōsakan-sama*."

Lightning moved aside, pulling Wisteria with him. He jerked his head at Sano. "Go on."

Stepping up to the window, Sano spied Hirata standing in the street, holding a cumbersome box, his face worried. He smiled in relief when he saw Sano alive and unharmed. "I had to go all the way to Tobacco Lane to get the money," he called.

His emphatic tone suggested a hidden meaning, but Sano was baffled. He couldn't understand why Hirata would mention Tobacco Lane, a street of tobacco shops and warehouses that had no moneylenders. Then Lightning's sword poked his armor tunic, prodding him away from the window.

"Bring the money to the door and knock," Lightning shouted to Hirata. "Then go home."

"Very well," Hirata called.

Suddenly Sano remembered an investigation that had taken him and Hirata to Tobacco Lane. Enlightenment struck him. As he comprehended Hirata's intent, three loud knocks on the door echoed through the warehouse.

Lightning hesitated, clearly wondering how to get the money and control his hostages at the same time. His breath huffed and his gaze darted with accelerating rapidity. His grip on the sword and on Wisteria's collar tightened. Sano saw the gangster's quandary urging him toward more violence instead of rational action. Wisteria shut her eyes and bunched up her face, as if she anticipated a fatal lash of the blade.

"We'll all go downstairs," Sano said, thinking fast about how to help Hirata's plan succeed. "You can hold onto Wisteria, while I bring in the money."

After an instant of deliberation, Lightning said, "All right. You go first."

Sano descended; Lightning and Wisteria followed several steps behind him. They all crossed the warehouse. Sano unbarred and slowly opened the door, while his companions waited in the shadows. His pulse raced; expectation thrummed along his nerves. The wooden chest sat outside the door. Sano bent to lift the chest. Then came a scrambling noise on the roof.

"What's that?" Lightning exclaimed. Panic edged his voice.

Turning, Sano saw the gangster spin in a circle, his gaze on the ceiling, as he clutched Wisteria against him. The skylights opened, raised by Sano's troops, who'd climbed onto the warehouse. In dropped several dark objects the size and shape of turnips. Each had a short, flaming tail. As they fell, Lightning cried out and ducked. The objects plopped to the floor around him. Sano lunged for Wisteria. He caught hold of her hand, just as the bombs exploded with multiple thudding noises.

Dense, yellowish smoke billowed, clouding the air. Lightning emitted an enraged, terrified yowl. Wisteria shrieked. Sano tugged her toward the doorway, a rectangle of brightness that was barely visible through the smoke. But a hard yank from the opposite direction tore her hand out of his. Sulfurous fumes stung Sano's eyes, obscured his vision. Though he heard Hirata calling him and Lightning and Wisteria coughing, he could see nothing but smoke. He wished he'd managed to remove Wisteria from the building and let the smoke flush out Lightning. His lungs constricted, and coughs wracked him; yet he couldn't go and leave Wisteria in here with the gangster.

"Help!" she screamed, retching.

Covering his nose and mouth with his sleeve, Sano groped blindly toward the sound of her. Light from the lanterns filtered through the smoke clouds. Sano's instincts blared a sudden warning. He crouched, and Lightning's blade flashed out of the smoke, over his head. More pleas for help came from Wisteria; Lightning alternated curses and wheezes. Blurred shapes flailed like ghosts in the smoke, while the blade whistled around Sano. He fell to the floor, rolled away. Wisteria loosed a scream of agony.

Loud, splintering crashes reverberated as Sano's troops hacked the window shutters open with axes. While the fresh air dispersed the smoke, Sano clambered to his feet in the center of the room. He saw Lightning lurch toward the door, choking and gagging, just as his detectives charged through it, their swords drawn. Lightning staggered into their midst, wildly swinging his blade in a desperate bid to escape or die trying. Sano launched himself at the gangster. He tackled Lightning around the knees. Lightning crashed to the floor. Sano's men fell upon him and wrested his sword away. He struggled like a captured beast, uttering incoherent protests.

"Are you all right?" Hirata asked Sano.

Nodding, Sano panted from exertion and coughed up phlegm as he stood. "Where's Wisteria?" he said.

Then he heard a moan, and saw her. She lay on her side, torso raised on her elbows, inching toward the door. Pain wrenched her features. Her legs were soaked with blood, injured by Lightning. Now pity overrode Sano's ill will against Wisteria. He and Hirata walked over to her. When she saw them, she strained her body and groaned with a last, futile heave toward freedom. Then she collapsed, weeping in defeat.

35

"Hirata-*san*!" Midori ran out on the veranda of the Edo Castle women's quarters as he hurried up the path toward her. In her red silk kimono, she was a warm spot of color in the chill, cloudy afternoon and drab garden. "What has happened?"

"Lightning has been convicted of murdering Lord Mitsuyoshi and beating the prostitute to death," Hirata said, glad to bring her good news at last. Two days had passed since the capture of the gangster, and Hirata had just witnessed the trial at Magistrate Ueda's court. "Wisteria has been convicted as an accomplice to murder and treason."

He joined Midori on the veranda, and as he described the events that had led to the trial, Midori regarded him with wide-eyed awe. "What will become of Wisteria and Lightning?" she said.

"They're on their way to the execution ground," Hirata said. "Their severed heads will be displayed by the Nihonbashi Bridge as a warning to other would-be criminals." To-kugawa law had meted out harsh justice for the couple's serious crimes.

"Are you safe now?" Midori asked anxiously.

"Yes. The *sōsakan-sama* has been exonerated. He and I have met with the shogun. His Excellency apologized for doubting Sano-*san* and welcomed him back into favor." Overwhelmed by relief, Hirata said, "The threat to everyone in his retinue has passed."

"I'm so happy for you!" Midori smiled, her eyes shining. "And your smoke bomb was such a clever idea."

Hirata had used a tactic once used against him and Sano in Tobacco Lane. He was proud of his quick thinking, and glad Sano had taken his cue to get Lightning downstairs for capture. Then Midori's face fell; she sighed in desolation.

"But we're no closer to marriage," she mourned.

"Oh, yes we are," Hirata said, because the revelations in the murder case had unexpectedly produced a solution to their problems. "Come on. We're going into town. I'll explain on the way."

Soon, Hirata and a squadron of detectives were seated in a teahouse in Nihonbashi. Lord Niu entered with his guards and his chief retainer, Okita.

"Greetings," Hirata said, bowing to Lord Niu. "Thank you for coming."

"Your invitation said you were ready to discuss a surrender." Lord Niu regarded Hirata with contempt. "Does this mean you've come to your senses?"

"Indeed it does," Hirata said politely.

Lord Niu and his men sat. Hirata beckoned a maid, who poured cups of sake for everyone.

"It's high time you realized that your campaign against me is futile," Lord Niu said.

"Your clan is far more powerful than mine," Hirata said, feigning meekness. "And you're too clever for me to conquer by treachery."

Gloating satisfaction swelled the daimyo's countenance. "How right you are."

"It was especially clever of you to write those pages about Lady Wisteria and her lover from Hokkaido, then hire the following horse to sell them to me as the missing pillow book," Hirata said.

He and Sano had tracked the one remaining loose end in the investigation to Lord Niu. After Lady Wisteria had admitted her authorship of the book that had almost framed Sano for Lord Mitsuyoshi's murder, Sano and Hirata had recognized the other book as a forgery. Hirata had recalled that the pages had been delivered straight into his hands— and not, he realized, by chance. Someone had intended for him to take possession of the forgery and pursue the false clues in it. Furthermore, Hirata knew only one person who hated him enough to lead him astray and had threatened him with ruin.

Lord Niu laughed heartily. "I had you running all over town, looking for a man who doesn't exist!"

"Then you admit you wrote the story?" Hirata wanted absolute confirmation that the daimyo had done it, so he could turn the deception to his advantage. "And you gave the pages to Gorobei, with orders to watch for a chance to pass them to me and lie about how he found them?"

"Oh, yes," Lord Niu said with a proud smile that lifted the left side of his mouth. "What a good joke on you."

"And I fell for it." Hirata hid his delight by pretending chagrin. When he'd told Midori what her father had done, she'd been horrified, but Hirata had explained what a unique opportunity Lord Niu had inadvertently given them. "I suppose you meant for me to disgrace myself and be executed."

Lord Niu nodded smugly. "My daughter couldn't marry a dead man. When I heard the *sōsakan-sama* had solved the case in spite of me, I planned other schemes to destroy you. But now that you've decided to surrender, I'll spare your life."

"No," Hirata said. "It is *I* who shall spare *your* life, and *you* who shall surrender."

Frowning in surprise and confusion, Lord Niu cocked his head. "What nonsense are you talking?"

"Midori-*san*!" Hirata called.

She emerged, hesitant and frightened, from the back room of the teahouse and edged over to Hirata. He took her hand, and she knelt beside him.

"What's going on here?" Lord Niu demanded. Furious, he surged to his feet and addressed Midori: "I told you to stay away from him. Get out!"

Hirata held tight to Midori's hand. "We're going to discuss the terms of your surrender."

"Never!"

"You've just confessed to planting a false clue in the *sōsakan-sama*'s murder investigation," Hirata said. "That was sabotage against the shogun's quest for justice for his heir."

Shock stiffened Lord Niu and blanched his crooked face: He'd obviously never thought of his scheme in this light.

"If I tell His Excellency what you did," Hirata said, "he'll confiscate your lands and strip you of your title. You'll lose your retainers, your subjects, and your wealth. Your family will live as paupers. I'll marry Midori, and you'll be powerless to stop me."

Realization, then outrage, dawned in Lord Niu's eyes. "You tricked me!" he roared.

"One good turn deserves another," Hirata said, pitying the daimyo not at all. Midori whimpered, and Hirata said, "But I would rather not destroy the father of the woman I love. And I won't—if you'll agree to a deal."

"I won't stoop to deal with the likes of you." Lord Niu trembled with indignation, his face twitching.

Hirata continued calmly: "You will go to my father, apologize for insulting him, and swear on your honor to form an alliance with our clan. Then you will give your approval to a marriage between Midori-*san* and me."

"No!" Lord Niu shouted. He clenched his fists and advanced on Hirata.

"In exchange, I'll forget your sabotage," Hirata said. "The shogun will never know about it."

"I'll kill you!"

Lord Niu reached for his sword, but his guards grabbed and restrained him. As he struggled and yelled curses, Okita said, "I advise you to accept his terms. Your daughter's hand is a small price to pay to preserve your rank and estate."

"I won't lose face by bowing down to him!"

Yet Hirata sensed the daimyo blustering, weakening. "The spirits of your ancestors will repudiate you for throwing away your heritage," he said.

The daimyo gave one last bellow, tore free of his men, then dropped to his knees. He panted with frustrated rage, broken by defeat. "Agreed," he muttered.

He and Hirata bowed to each other, then drank their sake. Hirata tasted triumph as Midori gave him a radiant, admiring smile. He saw murder in Lord Niu's eyes, and shuddered to think of life with a mad father-in-law who despised him. But come what might, he and Midori would be married, and their child born in wedlock. That was cause enough for joy.

Reiko had never imagined she would ever set foot inside the residence of Chamberlain Yanagisawa, but important business had brought her here. As guards led her and her escorts along tree-lined paths through the fortified compound, Reiko's serene face betrayed no sign of the anger seething within her.

Lady Yanagisawa received her in a private chamber hidden deep inside the estate. They knelt opposite each other, in a silence thick and turbulent with the memory of their last encounter. Lady Yanagisawa's cheeks were flushed, her features marked by distress, her hands clasped tight under her bosom; she bowed her head as though expecting punishment. As Reiko contemplated her hostess, hatred stoked her anger into a firestorm she could barely contain. She drew a deep breath, willing calmness.

"I'm sorry for being rude to you at my pond the other day," Reiko said in a stiff, formal tone. "I was upset, and I shouldn't have spoken to you the way I did. Please forgive me."

The words tasted foul in her mouth. The injustice of having to apologize to the woman who'd almost caused Masahiro to die outraged Reiko. But political considerations forced her to abase herself to Lady Yanagisawa. The chamberlain was Sano's superior, and any offense Reiko gave his wife extended to him. When Reiko had told Sano what Lady Yanagisawa had done, he'd been shocked and horrified, but he hadn't needed to tell her what she must do. Reiko understood her duty. Therefore, she had come, against her will but of her own volition, to mend the breach between her and Lady Yanagisawa.

Lady Yanagisawa lifted to Reiko a gaze filled with relief; she spoke in breathless rushes: "There's nothing to forgive. . . . You had every right to be upset. . . . It was a terrible thing that happened."

"Thank you for your understanding and generosity." That Reiko must protect Sano was all that kept her from tearing Lady Yanagisawa apart with her bare hands.

"Is Masahiro-*chan* all right?" Lady Yanagisawa asked.

Guilt lurked behind her concern, tainted her voice, wafted from her like a bad smell. Reiko could tell that Lady Yanagisawa knew she knew the truth about Masahiro's "accident." She said, "He was a little shaken, but he's fine now."

"I'm so glad. . . ." Eager to placate, Lady Yanagisawa said, "Is there anything I can do?"

Reiko wanted to demand that Lady Yanagisawa admit she'd induced Kikuko to drown Masahiro, and confess she'd befriended Reiko so she could get close enough to do harm. Instead Reiko said, "Perhaps you would answer two questions for me."

". . . Yes. If I can." Caution tempered Lady Yanagisawa's eagerness.

"Before you brought Wisteria's pillow book to me, did you know that your husband and Police Commissioner Hoshina had already read it?" Reiko asked.

Lady Yanagisawa hesitated, her face reflecting surprise, then indecision. She looked downward and nodded.

Reiko had wondered why Lady Yanagisawa had risked

angering the chamberlain by stealing the book. Why had she put herself in danger to help Sano, when her attack on Masahiro proved she'd wanted to hurt Reiko? Now Reiko understood. Lady Yanagisawa had wanted her to read the story about Sano and Wisteria, and suffer from learning that Sano had been unfaithful. She'd known that giving Reiko the book wouldn't benefit Sano because Hoshina was already preparing to use it against him. Reiko thought of the pain the book had caused her, and her antipathy toward Lady Yanagisawa burgeoned. The woman's "helpful" gesture had been a prelude to her attempt to murder Masahiro.

"And your second question?" Lady Yanagisawa said.

"Let's suppose—just for the sake of speculation—that there are two women friends, both married to high-ranking officials, both mothers of young children." Reiko chose her words carefully, watching Lady Yanagisawa. "Why would one of the women attack the other?"

The skin around Lady Yanagisawa's eyes constricted, giving her the look of a cat with its ears laid flat by alarm. A shiver twisted upward through her body. She rose, turned away from Reiko, and spoke in a muffled voice: "Perhaps she thought that by destroying her friend's good fortune, she would gain what her friend lost."

This was as close to a confession and explanation as Reiko expected from Lady Yanagisawa. Though she'd already guessed the woman's motive, hearing it shocked Reiko. She released her breath as nausea rose in her throat. Lady Yanagisawa was less evil than insane.

"But she undid what she'd done . . . and all was well," Lady Yanagisawa continued. "There would be no bad consequences for her."

"No. There wouldn't be," Reiko said.

Since Masahiro hadn't died, Lady Yanagisawa was a murderer by intention, but not by deed. No one except her and Reiko had witnessed Kikuko pushing Masahiro under the water. Sano and Reiko had afterward discovered that the nursemaid O-hana had vanished. They'd deduced that Lady Yanagisawa had bribed Yuya to lure Reiko away from home, and O-hana to drug the other servants with a sleeping potion and let Kikuko into the house, where Masahiro was alone. Sano had ordered a search for O-hana, but found no trace of her yet. The nursemaid must have fled town because she feared Reiko and Sano would punish her for her betrayal. No one except Reiko and Lady Yanagisawa knew the truth, except for Kikuko, who could not speak it.

Besides, even if Reiko did have any evidence against Lady Yanagisawa and Kikuko, she couldn't accuse them of attempted murder. Chamberlain Yanagisawa's power shielded his wife and daughter from the law. Even if they had killed Masahiro, they would have escaped punishment.

"Perhaps the woman who attacked her friend is more fortunate than she deserves," Reiko said.

She rose to go before she did or said something she would regret. She wanted to get as far away from Lady Yanagisawa as possible and never see her again.

Lady Yanagisawa turned, her eyes filled with naked pleading. She said, "We'll still be friends, won't we?"

The very idea of keeping up their acquaintance, as if nothing had happened, stunned Reiko. To let the woman into her home, to have their children play together, never to know whether Lady Yanagisawa had recovered from a temporary murderous impulse or was incurably mad, and always to live in fear, was beyond possibility. Then Reiko experienced pure horror as she understood that she couldn't refuse the wife of the shogun's second-in-command; nor should she reject Lady Yanagisawa and spur her to more attacks. Now Reiko realized that she'd acquired a most dangerous kind of enemy— one who craved her love as well as her destruction.

"Of course we'll be friends," Reiko said.

A night of freezing rain enveloped Edo Castle. Outside Sano's mansion, ice glazed the branches of the trees in the garden and formed glittering pendants on the eaves. Inside, Sano and Reiko lay in bed, covered by a thick quilt. Masahiro slept between them, breathing softly. Warmth radiated from charcoal braziers; the lantern shone like a small sun. Sano basked as the tension of the last few days departed from him and peace lulled his spirit.

"The outcome of the investigation still astounds me," Reiko said. "My friend proved to be my enemy. Your enemy provided the clue that led you to the killer. The pillow book that we decided was a forgery was the real one."

"Life is unpredictable," Sano agreed. "Things are not always what they seem at first."

"And a woman we thought was a murder victim turned out to be the person ultimately responsible for the crime, as well as the deaths of Fujio, Momoko, and the prostitute." Reiko turned to Sano, her expression concerned. "Does that disturb you?"

Unsettling memories encroached upon Sano's contentment. "While I was presenting evidence at the trial, Wisteria stared at me with terrible, bitter hatred in her eyes. I know she blamed me for her downfall. When the magistrate permitted her to speak for herself, she said, 'They drove me to it.' She never stopped believing that everything she did was justified by what other people had done to her. She went to her death without accepting responsibility for her own actions."

"Wisteria was consumed by her desire for revenge. In the end, it destroyed her." Reiko mused, "I pity her so much that I can forgive her for the trouble she caused you."

"As can I," Sano said.

They lay in silence, pondering the dangerous power of vengeance, regretting the courtesan's obsession, and sharing gratitude because fate had spared them the ruin that Wisteria had intended for Sano.

Then Sano said, "At least some good has come of this investigation. Your instincts saved Masahiro's life. You should never again lack confidence in them."

Reiko smiled, proud yet humble.

"I'm troubled that Lady Yanagisawa promises to be a continuing threat to you and Masahiro," Sano said.

"I suppose we would have acquired an enemy sooner or

later, since enemies abound in this world of ours," Reiko said with a sigh of resignation.

"By the way, I heard some interesting news," Sano said. "Magistrate Aoki has been demoted for interfering with the investigation and wrongfully condemning Fujio and Momoko. He's now a secretary to his replacement."

"So there is some justice for corrupt men like him," Reiko said, "even if it's not enough."

"And Chamberlain Yanagisawa has introduced his son to the shogun," Sano said. "It looks as though His Excellency may soon have a new heir."

Dour amusement quirked Reiko's mouth. "Trust the chamberlain to do exactly what you were accused of trying—and to get away with it." Then she brightened. "There's better news. Midori says her father and Hirata's have made peace and approved the marriage. I look forward to a wedding soon."

"I'm not looking forward to doing Police Commissioner Hoshina the favor he extorted from me," Sano said wryly.

"You'll think of a way around him when the time comes," Reiko assured Sano, then smiled. "What we can both look forward to is our next investigation."

They joined hands across their sleeping child. Icy raindrops pelted the roof while they drowsed, safe together, strong in their confident belief that they could brave whatever the future held.

*Read on for an excerpt from
Laura Joh Rowland's next book*

The Dragon King's Palace

*Available in hardcover
from St. Martin's Minotaur*

Japan, Tenwa Period, Year 2, Month 5 (June 1682)

Across dark water skimmed the boat, bound on a journey toward misadventure. Poles attached to the narrow, open wooden shell supported a red silk canopy; a round white lantern glowed from a hook above the stern. Beneath the canopy a samurai sat, plying the oars. He wore cotton summer robes, his two swords at his waist. Though his topknot was gray and his face lined with age, his muscular body and deft movements retained the vigor of youth. Opposite him, on pillows that cushioned the bottom of the boat, a woman reclined, trailing her fingers in the water. The lantern illuminated her flowing black hair and skin, radiantly white and limpid as moonbeams. An aqua kimono patterned with pastel anemones adorned her slim figure. Her lovely face wore a dreamy, contented expression.

"The night is so beautiful," she murmured.

Lake Biwa, situated northwest of the imperial capital of Miyako, spread around them, still and shimmering as a vast black mirror. On the near shore, lights from the inns and docks of port villages formed a glittering crescent; darkness and distance obscured the farther boundaries of the lake. Many other pleasure boats dotted the water, their lanterns flickering. Fireworks exploded into rosettes of green, red, and white sparks that flared against the indigo sky and reflected in the water. Cries of admiration arose from people aboard the boats. A gentle breeze cooled the sultry summer eve and carried the scent of gunpowder. But the samurai gleaned no enjoyment from the scene. A terrible anguish tortured him as he beheld his wife.

"You are even more beautiful than the night," he said.

All during their marriage he'd taken for granted that her beauty belonged only to him, and that he alone possessed her love, despite the twenty years' difference in their ages. But recently he'd learned otherwise. Betrayal had shattered his illusions. Now, as his wife smiled at him, he could almost see the shadow of another man darkening and fouling the air between them. Rage enflamed the samurai.

"What a strange look is on your face," said his wife. "Is something wrong?"

"Quite the contrary." Tonight he would redress the evil done to him. He rowed harder, away from the other boats, away from the lights on shore.

His wife stirred and her expression turned uneasy. "Dearest, we're getting too far from land," she said, removing her hand from the water that streamed past the boat. "Shouldn't we go back?"

The samurai stilled the oars. The boat drifted in the vast darkness beyond the colorful bursts of the rockets. The explosions echoed across the water, but the cries were fainter and the lights mere pinpoints. Stars glittered like cold jewels around a filigree gold moon. "We aren't going back," he said.

Sitting upright, his wife gazed at him in confusion. He spoke quietly: "I know."

"What are you talking about?" But the sudden fear in her

eyes said she understood exactly what he meant.

"I know about you and him," the samurai said, his voice harsh with grief as well as anger.

"There's nothing between us. It isn't what you think!" Breathless with her need to convince, his wife said, "I only talk to him because he's your friend."

But the man had been more than a friend to the samurai. How the double betrayal had injured his pride! Yet the worst of his anger focused on his wife, the irresistible temptress.

"You were doing more than just talking in the summer house, when you thought I was asleep," the samurai said.

She put a hand to her throat. "How—how did you find out?"

"You let him touch you and possess you," the samurai said, ignoring his wife's question. "You loved him the way you once loved me."

Always fearful of his temper, she cowered. Panic glazed her eyes, which darted as she sought a way to excuse herself. "It was only once," she faltered. "He took advantage of me. I made a mistake. He meant nothing to me." But her lies sounded shrill, desperate. Now she extended a hand to her husband. "It's you I love. I beg your forgiveness."

Her posture turned seductive; her lips curved in an enticing smile. That she thought she could pacify him so easily turned the samurai's anger to white-hot fury.

"You'll pay for betraying me!" he shouted. He lunged toward his wife and scooped her up in his arms. As she emitted a sound of bewildered surprise, he flung her overboard.

She fell sideways into the lake with a splash that drenched the boat. Her long hair and pale garments billowed around her, and she flailed her arms in a frantic attempt to keep from sinking in the deep, black water. "Please!" she cried, sobbing in terror. "I'm sorry! I repent! Save me!"

A lust for revenge prevailed over the love that the samurai still felt for his wife. He ignored her and took up the oars. She grabbed the railings of the boat, and he beat her hands with the wooden paddles until she yelped in pain and let go. He rowed away from her.

"Help!" she screamed. "I'm drowning. Help!"

Rockets boomed, louder than her cries and splashes; no one came to her rescue. While the samurai rowed farther out on the lake, he watched his wife grow smaller and her struggles weaken, heard her gasps fade. She was a water lily cut loose and dying on a pond. She deserved her misfortune. Triumph exhilarated the samurai. His wife's head sank below the surface, and diminishing ripples radiated toward the circle of light cast by his boat's lantern. Then there was silence.

The samurai let the oars rest. As the boat slowed to a stop, his triumph waned. Grief and guilt stabbed his heart. His beloved wife was gone forever, dead by his own actions. A friendship he'd cherished must end. Sobs welled from the void of despair that burgeoned within the samurai. He didn't fear punishment, because his wife's death would seem an accident, and even if anyone guessed otherwise, the law would excuse an important man of the ruling warrior class. But remorse and honor demanded atonement. And to live was unbearable.

With trembling hands, the samurai drew his short sword. Its steel blade gleamed in the lantern light and reflected his tormented face. He gathered his courage, whispered a prayer, and shut his eyes tight. Then he slashed the sword downward across his throat.

A final explosion of fireworks painted the sky with giant, sparkling colored flowers and wisps of smoke. The flotilla of pleasure craft moved toward shore, and a hush settled over Lake Biwa. The samurai's tiny lone boat drifted in the glow of its lantern until the flame burned out, then vanished into the night.

Edo, Genroku Period, Year 7, Month 5 (Tokyo, June 1694)

The great metropolis of Edo sweltered in summer. An aquamarine sky reflected in canals swollen from rains that deluged the city almost daily. The multicolored sails of pleasure craft billowed amid the ferries and barges on the Sumida River. Along the boulevards, and in temple gardens, children flew kites shaped like birds. In the Nihonbashi merchant district, the open windows, doors, and skylights of houses and shops welcomed elusive breezes; perspiring townspeople thronged marketplaces bountiful with produce. A miasma of fever rose from alleys that reeked of sewage; pungent incense smoke combated buzzing mosquitoes. Roads leading out of town were crowded with religious pilgrims marching toward distant shrines and rich folk bound for summer villas in the cooler climate of the hills. The sun blazed down upon the peaked tile roofs of Edo Castle, but trees shaded the private quarters of Lady Keisho-in, mother of the shogun Tokugawa Tsunayoshi, Japan's supreme military dictator. There, on a veranda, three ladies gathered.

"I wonder why Lady Keisho-in summoned us," said Reiko, wife of the shogun's *sōsakan-sama*—Most Honorable Investigator of Events, Situations, and People. She looked over the railing and watched her little son, Masahiro, play in the garden. He ran laughing over grasses verdant from the rains, around a pond covered by green scum, past flowerbeds and shrubs lush with blossoms.

"Whatever she wants, I hope it doesn't take long," said Midori. She was a former lady-in-waiting to Keisho-in and a close friend of Reiko. Six months ago Midori had married Sano's chief retainer. Now she clasped her hands across a belly so rotund with pregnancy that Reiko suspected Midori and Hirata had conceived the child long before their wedding. "This heat is too much for me. I can't wait to go home and lie down."

Midori's young, pretty face was bloated; her swollen legs and feet could hardly bear her weight. She tugged at the cloth bound tight around her stomach beneath her mauve kimono to keep the child small and ensure an easy delivery. "This thing didn't work. I've grown so huge, my baby must be a giant," she lamented. She waddled into a shady corner of the veranda and sat awkwardly.

Reiko pushed away strands of hair that had escaped her upswept coiffure and clung to her damp forehead. Perspiring in her sea-blue silk kimono, she wished she, too, could go home. She shared her husband Sano's work, aiding him with his inquiries into crimes, and at any moment there might arise a new case, which she wouldn't want to miss. But Lady Keisho-in had commanded Reiko's presence. She couldn't refuse the mother of her husband's lord, though her eagerness to leave stemmed from a reason more serious than a desire for exciting detective work.

The wife of Chamberlain Yanagisawa—the shogun's powerful second-in-command—stood apart from Reiko and Midori. Lady Yanagisawa was quiet, dour, some ten years older than Reiko's own age of twenty-four, and always dressed in dark, somber colors as if to avoid drawing attention to her total lack of beauty. She had a long, flat face with narrow eyes, wide nose, and broad lips, and a flat, bow-legged figure. Now she sidled over to Reiko.

"I am so thankful I was invited here and given the chance to see you," Lady Yanagisawa said in her soft, gruff voice.

Her gaze flitted over Reiko with yearning intensity. Reiko stifled the shudder of revulsion that Lady Yanagisawa always provoked. The woman was a shy recluse who seldom ventured into society, and she'd had no friends until last winter, when she and Reiko had met. Lady Yanagisawa had attached herself to Reiko with an eagerness that attested to her lonely life and craving for companionship. Since then, Lady Yanagisawa had visited Reiko, or invited her to call, almost daily; when their family responsibilities or Reiko's work for Sano precluded meetings, Lady Yanagisawa sent letters. Her devotion alarmed Reiko, as did her unwelcome confidences.

"Yesterday I watched my husband writing in his office," Lady Yanagisawa said. She'd told Reiko about how she spied on the chamberlain. "His calligraphy is so elegant. His face looked so beautiful as he bent over the page."

Ardor flushed her pale cheeks. "When he passed me in the corridor, his sleeve brushed mine . . ." Lady Yanagisawa caressed her arm, as though savoring the contact. "He looked at me for an instant. His gaze lit a fire in me . . . my heart beat fast. Then he walked on and left me alone." She exhaled with regret.

Embarrassment filled Reiko. She'd once been curious about her friend's marriage, but now she'd learned more than she liked. She knew that Chamberlain Yanagisawa, who had risen to power via an ongoing sexual affair with the shogun, preferred men to women and cared nothing for his wife. Lady Yanagisawa passionately loved him, and though he ignored her, she never gave up hope that someday he would return her love.

"Last night I watched my husband in his bedchamber with Police Commissioner Hoshina," Lady Yanagisawa said.

Hoshina, current paramour of the chamberlain, lived at his estate. "His body is so strong and masculine and beautiful." Her blush deepened; desire hushed her tone. "How I wish he would make love to me."

Reiko inwardly squirmed but couldn't evade Lady Yanagisawa's confessions. The chamberlain and Sano had a history of strife, and although they'd enjoyed a truce for almost three years, any offense against the chamberlain or his kin might provoke Yanagisawa to resume his attacks on Sano. Hence, Reiko must endure the friendship of Lady Yanagisawa, despite strong reason to end it.

Lady Yanagisawa suddenly called, "No, no, Kikuko-*chan*."

In the garden Reiko saw her friend's nine-year-old daughter, Kikuko, pulling up lilies and throwing them at Masahiro. Beautiful but feebleminded, Kikuko was the other object of her mother's devotion. A chill passed through Reiko as she watched the children gather the broken flowers. She knew how much Lady Yanagisawa envied her beauty, loving husband, and bright, normal child, and wished Reiko misfortune even while courting her affection. Last winter Lady Yanagisawa had arranged an "accident" that had involved Kikuko and almost killed Masahiro. Ever since, Reiko had never left him alone with Lady Yanagisawa or Kikuko, and she employed Sano's detectives to guard him when she was away from home. She always wore a dagger under her sleeve during visits with Lady Yanagisawa; she never ate or drank then, lest her friend try to poison her. Extra guards protected her when she slept or went out. Such vigilance was exhausting, but Reiko dared not withdraw from the woman, lest she provoke violent retaliation. Would that she could keep away from Lady Yanagisawa!

The door to the mansion opened, and out bustled Lady Keisho-in, a small, pudgy woman in her sixties, with hair dyed black, a round, wrinkled face, and teeth missing. She wore a short blue cotton dressing gown that exposed blue-veined legs. Maids followed, waving large paper fans at her to create a cooling breeze.

"Here you all are! Wonderful!" Keisho-in beamed at Reiko, Midori, and Lady Yanagisawa. They murmured polite greetings and bowed. "I've invited you here to tell you the marvelous idea I just had." She dimpled with gleeful excitement. "I am going to travel to Fuji-*san.*" Her sweeping gesture indicated the peak of Mount Fuji. Revered as a home of the Shinto gods and a gateway to the Buddhist spirit world, the famous natural shrine hovered, snowcapped and ethereal, in the sky far beyond the city. "And you shall all come with me!"

Stunned silence greeted this announcement. Reiko saw her dismay expressed on the faces of Midori and Lady Yanagisawa. Keisho-in regarded them all with a suspicious frown. "Your enthusiasm overwhelms me." Displeasure harshened her crusty voice. "Don't you want to go?"

The women rushed to speak at once, for Lady Keisho-in had great influence over the shogun, who punished anyone who displeased his mother. "Of course I do," Midori said. "Many thanks for asking me," said Reiko. Lady Yanagisawa said, "Your invitation does us an honor."

Their insincere replies faded into more silence. Reiko said, "But religious custom bans women from Fuji-*san.*"

"Oh, we needn't climb the mountain." Keisho-in waved a hand in airy dismissal. "We can stay in the foothills and bask in its magnificence."

"Maybe I shouldn't travel in my condition," Midori said timidly.

"Nonsense. The change will do you good. And we'll only be gone ten days or so. The baby will wait until you're home."

Midori's lips soundlessly formed the words, *ten days,* as Reiko watched her envision giving birth on the highway. Lady Yanagisawa gazed at Reiko. In her eyes dawned the amazement of someone who has just received an unexpected gift. Reiko perceived the woman's pleasure at the thought of constant togetherness during the trip, and her own heart sank. Then Lady Yanagisawa looked into the garden, where Kikuko and Masahiro played ball. Worry clouded her face.

"I can't leave Kikuko-*chan*," she said.

"You coddle that child too much," Lady Keisho-in said. "She must eventually learn to get along without her mama, and the sooner the better."

Lady Yanagisawa's hands gripped the veranda railing. "My husband . . ."

As Reiko guessed how much Lady Yanagisawa would miss spying on the chamberlain, Keisho-in spoke with tactless disregard for her feelings: "Your husband won't miss you."

"But we will encounter strange people and places during the trip." Lady Yanagisawa's voice trembled with fear born of her extreme shyness.

Keisho-in made an impatient, scornful sound. "The whole point of travel is to see things you can't see at home."

Midori and Lady Yanagisawa turned to Reiko, their expressions begging her to save them. Reiko didn't want to leave Masahiro; nor did she want to leave Sano and their detective work. She dreaded ten days of Lady Yanagisawa sticking to her like a leech, and the possibility that the woman would attack her. And Lady Keisho-in posed another threat. The shogun's mother had a greedy sexual appetite that she indulged with women as well as men. Once, Keisho-in had made amorous advances toward Reiko, who had barely managed to deflect them without bringing the shogun's wrath down upon herself and Sano, and lived in fear of another such experience.

Yet Reiko dared voice none of these selfish objections. Her only hope of thwarting the trip to was to appeal to Keisho-in's interests.

"I would love to accompany you," Reiko said, "but His Excellency the Shogun may need me to help my husband conduct an investigation."

Keisho-in pondered, aware that Reiko's detective skill had won the shogun's favor. "I'll tell my son to delay all important inquiries until we return," she said.

"But he may not want you to go," Reiko said, her anxiety rising. "How will he manage without your advice?"

Indecision pursed Keisho-in's mouth. Lady Yanagisawa and Midori watched in hopeful suspense.

"Won't you miss him?" Reiko said. "Won't you miss Priest Ryuko?" The priest was Keisho-in's spiritual adviser and lover.

A long moment passed while Keisho-in frowned and vacillated. At last she declared, "Yes, I'll miss my darling Ryuko-*san*, but parting will increase our fondness. And tonight I'll give my son enough advice to last awhile."

"The journey will be difficult and uncomfortable," Reiko said in desperation.

"The weather on the road will be even hotter than it is here," Midori added eagerly.

"We'll have to stay at inns full of crude, noisy people." Lady Yanagisawa shivered.

"Highway bandits may attack us," Reiko said.

Keisho-in's hand fluttered, negating the dire predictions. "We'll take plenty of guards. I appreciate your concern for me, but a religious pilgrimage to Fuji-*san* is worth the hardship."

She addressed her maids: "Go tell the palace officials to get travel passes for everyone and ready an entourage, horses, palanquins, and provisions for the journey. Hurry, because I want to leave tomorrow morning." Then she turned to Reiko, Midori, and Lady Yanagisawa. "Don't just stand there like idle fools. Come inside and help me pick out clothes to bring."

The women exchanged appalled glances at this foretaste of traveling with Lady Keisho-in. Then they breathed a silent, collective sigh of resignation.

In the cool of dawn the next morning, servants carried chests out of Sano's mansion and placed them in the courtyard. Two palanquins stood ready for Reiko and Midori, while bearers waited to carry the women in their enclosed black wooden sedan chairs to Mount Fuji. Sano and Masahiro stood with Reiko beside her palanquin.

"I wish I could call off this trip," Sano said. He hated for Reiko to go, yet his duty to the shogun extended to the entire Tokugawa clan and forbade him to thwart Lady Keisho-in's desire.

Reiko's delicate, beautiful face was strained, but she managed a smile. "Maybe it won't be as bad as we think."

Admiring her valiant attempt to make the best of a bad situation, Sano already missed his wife. They were more than just partners in investigating crimes or spouses in a marriage arranged for social, economic, and political reasons. Their work, their child, and their passionate love bound them in a spiritual union. And this trip would be their longest separation in their four years together.

Reiko crouched, put her hands on Masahiro's shoulders, and looked into his solemn face. "Do you promise to be good while I'm gone?" she said.

"Yes, Mama." Though the little boy's chin trembled, he spoke bravely, imitating the stoic samurai attitude.

Beside the other palanquin, Midori and Hirata embraced. "I'm so afraid something bad will happen and we'll never see each other again," Midori fretted.

"Don't worry. Everything will be fine," Hirata said, but his wide, youthful face was troubled because he didn't want his pregnant wife to leave.

From the barracks surrounding the mansion came two samurai detectives, leading horses laden with bulky saddlebags. Sano had ordered the men, both loyal retainers and expert fighters, to accompany and protect Reiko and Midori. He wished he and Hirata could go, but the shogun required their presence in Edo.

"Take good care of them," Sano told the detectives.

"We will, *Sōsakan-sama*." The men bowed.

Reiko said, "Lady Keisho-in, Lady Yanagisawa, and our entourage will be waiting for us outside the main castle gate. We'd better go."

Sano lifted Masahiro; they and Reiko embraced. Final farewells ensued. Then Reiko and Midori reluctantly climbed into their palanquins. The bearers shouldered the poles; servants lifted the chests. Sano hugged Masahiro close against his sore heart. As the procession moved through the gate, Reiko put her head out the window of her palanquin, looked backward, and fixed a wistful gaze on Sano and Masahiro. They waved; Sano smiled.

"Mama, be safe," Masahiro called. "Come home soon."